Aug. 22, 2011

Murder in the Mountains

Doug + Sheila,
I hope you'll enjoy reading this novel set in 2001.
Thank you for all your help — with the website

Rich Cibrano

Murder in the Mountains

Return to Kathmandu

Dominic J. Cibrario

Review of *Murder in the Mountain*
James F. Fisher, Anthropologist
Carleton College

One thing you can say about Nick Cibrario's novels is that they cut a huge swath through the territory they cover. You'd think from the titles that they would concern only Nepal. That was not true of his first three novels, nor is it true of Murder in the Mountains.

Of course there's no mistaking the powerful Nepal theme running through this novel and the others. It is the cross-cultural connections between foreigners, mostly American, and Nepalese of a variety of ethnic, religious and political stripes that give the novel its special punch. The exotic twists and turns of the plot is also captivating and entertaining fiction, informing the reader about real people (some of them, anyway) in a real place.

Nick's latest book does not start from scratch but is the fourth in a series of novels about Nepal. It brings the reader up to date on the characters that played important roles in his Garden of Kathmandu Trilogy. Thus Murder in the Mountains transforms the previous series into what now stands as a tetralogy.

The novel takes place in 2001 when the inveterate and perennial Chicago anthropologist, Carl Brecht, heads back to do research in Nepal, with his daughter, who has just graduated from high school. In a clever joining of two worlds, Cibrario has Carl attending a conference on Alternative Medicines and the Paramedic Training of Shamans. Left behind in Chicago is his wife, Barbara, presiding over the empty nest, and their son, Mark, about to leave for a summer job at Outward Bound in Colorado.

At the time of this novel a Maoist insurgency had been raging for more than ten years against King Birendra. He was the second to the last of Shah Dynasty Kings, who ruled Nepal since 1769. Birendra's son, Crown Prince Dipendra, a heavy drinking and drug-using rogue, was carrying on a clandestine affair with the beautiful Devyani, of whom his parents did not approve, giving rise to much tension between Dipendra and particularly his mother, Queen Aishwarya.

The in-law issues involved with Barbara's father, Samuel Havlett, who appears earlier in the novel in an almost comic role, is pale by comparison to the strife in the royal family of Nepal.

In Kathmandu Carl finds another link from his past visits to Nepal, namely the British woman Margaret Porter, whose five-year old son, Christopher, was murdered in an earlier novel. This time Margaret has hired shamans to liberate her son's soul.

Meanwhile, Margaret's second son, Nigel, originally kidnapped as a child by a London coven, is now a Buddhist monk connected to the royal family through Crown Prince Dipendra.

All this leads to accusations that Nigel has conspired with the Maoists to assassinate the Royal family (an event which really did happen, although with a slightly altered cast of real historical characters). There are many theories still swirling around Kathmandu about who actually assassinated the royal family.

The novel resolves this question with an accusation against Nigel and the Maoists, but the truth is finally revealed in the mountains near the monastery in the Medicine Cave after the main characters are taken hostage. But there is no royal monopoly on murders, as the abbot at Bodhnath monastery in Kathmandu and monks at Tengboche Monastery near Mt. Everest meet similarly unfortunate ends.

All this is heady stuff, and there's something for everyone: cross-cultural medicine, conspiracy theories about the royal assassination, astrologers, Maoist rebels, shamans, and even domestic tensions as they develop and dissolve within an American family in Nepal – strangers in a strange land, indeed.

As for how it all concludes? That is for readers, whose curiosity by the end has been raised to unbearable levels, to discover. But with the shrewd and skillful story-teller Cibrario at the helm, they will not be disappointed.

This book is a work of fiction. Although the setting takes place in Nepal and historical events actually occurred, the conversations of the members of the royal family, dinner guests, and other characters are products of the author's imagination. Names, characters, and places are used fictitiously. Any resemblances to persons living or dead are coincidental.

Copyright © 2011 by Dominic J. Cibrario

All rights reserved. No part of this publication may be reproduced or transmitted in any form or by any means, electronic or mechanical, including photographs, recording, or any information storage and retrieval system, without permission in writing from the publisher.

ISBN-13: 978-1456350345
ISBN-10: 145635034X

Library of Congress Control Number
201 091 9367
Createspace
An Amazon.com Company

Cover design: Kevin Flynn
Minuteman Press

Typography and Book Design: Geri Cibrario

Painting for cover: Dominic Cibrario

Dedication

I AM the Soul,

dwelling in all living beings,

O Conqueror of Sleep.

I AM the beginning, the middle

and the end of living things.

The Bhagavad Gita 10:20

Dominic J. Cibrario

The Pomelo Tree (2004)

The Harvest (2005)

The Shamans (2006)

Secrets on the Family Farm (2008)

Acknowledgments

I am very grateful to my wife, Geri, who spent countless hours reading the manuscript; she offered me helpful suggestions for improving the dialogue of the characters and enhancing the plot. I want to thank John Brosseau for his insightful comments and his patience as we read the drafts. I am grateful to Bill DeMark for his proofreading skill with meticulous attention to detail. He frequently clarified ambiguities through research and provided editorial assistance.

I can't thank Jim F. Fisher, the anthropologist, from Carleton College, enough for writing a review of the novel and a blurb on the cover. His insightful book, *Sherpas: Reflections on Change in Himalayan Nepal* with a foreword by Sir Edmund Hillary, is a primary source of information for the chapters about Namche Bazaar, Tengboche, and Solo Khumbu.

I'm indebted to Jonathan Gregson's *Massacre at the Palace* for providing details about the assassination of the royal family and identifying the family members and guests who attended the tragic dinner party.

I'm grateful to Genevieve Sesto and Briton Road Press for publishing the first edition of *The Pomelo Tree* and encouraging me to return to Nepal for updating the trilogy. I'm also indebted to Heather Bothe and Joe Schackelman for their support during our monthly writer's group meetings. I want to thank Gopal and Samira Adhikary for inviting me to their home, where family members informed me about the paramedic training of shamans taking place in Kathmandu. I'm grateful to Prasoon Adhikary for helping translate the Nepali language in this novel.

I want to thank Ganesh Narayan for his weekly lessons in Sanskrit and his wife, Usha, for introducing me to the *Shrimad Bhagavad Gita by Swami Chidbhavananda.* I'm grateful to Dustin Block, the editor of Racinepost.com for his support and Tony & Linda Somlai from the Original Root Zen Center for their mantras.

Many thanks to Joe Sjostrom, who is a retired journalist from the Chicago Tribune, for helping me edit and correct the final draft of the manuscript along with suggestions for improving the text.

NEPAL

1

On Sunday morning Carl sat at the kitchen table across from Barbara. He paused from reading the Chicago Tribune to get a glimpse of her figure; she was wearing a pink translucent nightgown. Her pixie hair style and features still reminded him of Audrey Hepburn.

"You're as beautiful as ever," said Carl, rising from the table. He kissed her on the back of the neck as she trembled. "I love you, Barbara. Let's go back to bed."

"Oh Carl, sex, that's all you ever think about. I've got to get to work. It's getting late," she gasped, noticing his crestfallen face. "I wish I didn't have to work at the museum on Sunday. I'll try to be home early tonight so we can have some time together."

"I'll miss you," he said, kissing her on the cheek. "I'll be thinking about you every minute."

"No you won't! You'll be thinking about the Maoists," she pouted, observing him pick up the newspaper again.

"The Maoists have been getting a lot of attention in Western Nepal. Their goal is to undermine the Shah Dynasty," said Carl, gazing into her brown eyes.

"I'm not surprised. There aren't many countries left that still have monarchies," added Barbara.

"The Shahs have been in power for ten generations. King Birendra has appointed his oldest son, Crown Prince Dipendra, to be at the next meeting with the Maoist leaders.

The king's trying to reach a peaceful settlement so that violence won't erupt in the capitol," said Carl.

"I'm worried about you going back to Nepal with all the political unrest there," sighed Barbara, admiring Carl's muscular physique; he reminded her of John F. Kennedy in spite of his graying hair.

"They've also massacred the local police and extorted money from the shopkeepers," continued Carl.

"Last week they entered a district school and forced the teachers and students at gun point to go into the mountains for a weekend of indoctrination," sighed Barbara, glancing at a ruby-throated hummingbird fluttering at the window.

"The Maoists are active north of Kathmandu in Nuwankot, the ancient summer palace of the royal family. It won't be long before they arrive in the capitol," said Carl, showing her that section of the paper.

"I remember visiting that old wooden palace when we went on the trek to do research on the Mother Goddess, Durga," recalled Barbara.

"You surprised me when you arrived in Nepal during the monsoon twenty-four years ago," recalled Carl. "What a trek! It rained every day. The trails were so slippery, we had to take refuge in our tent for hours."

"We were married on August 24, 1977 by Father Kent under the pomelo tree in the garden of the Kathmandu Guest House," reflected Barbara. "We stayed in Nepal for several months after Mark was born."

"I must contact Air India and make a booking for New Delhi and the connecting flight to Kathmandu," said Carl, rising from the table. He shifted over to the desk and turned on the computer.

"There'll be plenty of seats on the plane if you book now," said Barbara. "By the way how's your research coming along?"

"My research is at a standstill. I'll book the flight for two seats on May 13th. That will give me a chance to show Kathy the highlights of the city and get oriented."

"What?" asked Barbara, her voice strained. "You can't go back to Nepal before Kathy graduates from high school. After the ceremony we've got her party in the backyard."

"I completely forgot. I'll never get my research done."

"You've got too many irons in the fire," said Barbara. "You're turning into an absent minded professor."

"I've been so busy correcting term papers," said Carl, looking at the calendar. "We must leave on May 21st."

"But you didn't forget your promise to take Kathy to Nepal for her graduation present. I wish I could come along. I'll be here all alone in this old, drafty bungalow."

"Has your vacation been approved by the director of the museum?" he asked, preoccupied at the computer.

"I asked for two weeks off starting on September 10th," sighed Barbara. "So book my flight now. I'll be busy the whole summer with tours at the museum. By the time I join you in Nepal, the monsoon season will be over."

"After the convention in Kathmandu, Kathy and I will be trekking with Moksha and Muktuba, the shamans," said Carl, not paying attention to his wife's comments.

"Carl you're not listening to me," said Barbara, raising her voice. "Please repeat what I just told you."

"You said that you are coming to Nepal as soon as you get permission from your boss," he replied.

"Carl! You didn't hear a word that I just said! Why don't you ever listen to me?" shouted Barbara. "You won't even be here for our anniversary in August!" She dashed across the room and yanked the computer's cord from the socket. "You never have any time for me anymore!" she sobbed, fleeing from the kitchen through the hallway and up the stairs.

2

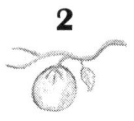

Carl was startled by his wife's reaction. He rose from the computer, hurrying after her. "Barbara, I'm sorry," he pleaded, entering the bedroom. "If I don't publish, I'll perish. I've been under a lot of stress lately."

"I…I know you're under a lot of stress, but I'm under stress too! I hate it when you leave to do research. This fall Kathy will be in college. Mark will be in graduate school, and you'll be in Nepal. I'll be here all by myself. Nobody cares about me in this family!" she screamed, sitting on the edge of the bed sobbing.

"I'll miss you Barbara. I promise to e-mail you every day," he said, sitting next to her with his arm around her shoulders, trying to comfort her.

"No you won't! You always say you'll write to me, but you don't! I hate the thought of living in this empty house all by myself, especially at night when you're gone."

"I apologize to you for not listening. Once you arrive in Nepal, it will be just like old times. I'll take you to the Royal Hotel for dinner and dancing every night," he promised.

"I'm worried about you and Kathy trekking during the monsoon season. I'm scared to death that the Maoists will kidnap you."

"The Maoist terrorists leave foreigners alone, but they always extort money from the trekkers," he said.

"I asked you to book my flight on September 10th the week after Labor Day, but you didn't listen to me. That's why I got mad," she sighed, wiping the tears. She paused to glance at the clock, and then hurried into the bathroom. She shouted from the open door, "I need to get ready for work."

While she was in the shower, Carl returned to the kitchen and plugged in the computer. He searched for the information for Barbara's flight, booked it, and printed out the confirmation.

Ten minutes later, Barbara entered, wearing a chic silk pant suit with a burnt orange blouse.

"You're beautiful in that outfit," said Carl, glancing up from the computer. "I just made a booking for you in September. I'll leave it right here on the desk."

"Be sure Kathy's back by the second week in August so she can get ready for college," insisted Barbara.

"I won't be coming back until October. Bill will be covering my classes at the university," said Carl.

"You'll be gone for months, but I'll only be with you for two weeks," sighed Barbara. "It reminds me when you left with a sabbatical from the University of Pennsylvania to do research. You were furious when my parents tried to manipulate you into marrying me by offering you a position in the family business. I wanted to go with you to Nepal, but my father, Sam, threatened to disinherit me."

"That was a long time ago," said Carl, remembering that he met a British woman, Margaret Porter, and her two unruly children on that flight. They became prominent figures as his life unfolded during his sabbatical in Nepal, causing him to delay his research for weeks.

He paused, opening his briefcase and removing a term paper, *The Buddhist Newars of the Kathmandu Valley.*

"I'll really miss you on our wedding anniversary," sighed Barbara.

"Maybe you could fly out to Colorado and spend a few days with Mark at Outward Bound," suggested Carl. "He'll be working there again this summer."

"I don't have any time off from the museum to visit Mark," she said. "He's so different from Kathy."

"That's because he was born in Nepal," said Carl, writing in the margin of the term paper with a red pen.

"Mark was born in Pokhara at Shining Hospital," said Barbara. "I remember going there from Prithivi Narayan College, where you were the department head. We were living on the campus in a small cottage with a tin roof. That rickshaw ride to the hospital was a nightmare."

"I was lucky to find a rickshaw at that time of night," said Carl. "I wandered for almost twenty minutes trying to locate a taxi, but the only person around was that rickshaw driver, wrapped in a blanket and sound asleep. I startled him when I told him my wife was going to have a baby any minute. He was very concerned about you."

"I'll never forget that bumpy ride in the rickshaw with you speaking in Nepali the whole time with the driver. It seemed to take forever before we got to the hospital," said Barbara. "I was afraid of having the baby along side of the dusty road."

"I was so worried when we finally got to the hospital because the doctor wasn't even there, only a sleepy clerk at the desk," said Carl. "He sent the gatekeeper to wake up the doctor and his wife. You were only in labor four hours. It's hard to believe that Mark's twenty-three years old and has finished his first year of graduate school."

"Mark's stubborn just like you," insisted Barbara. "He has no interest in graduation ceremonies, and he hates rituals. It's a reaction to you being an anthropologist."

"You're right about that," said Carl. "He hates going to weddings, funerals, and baptisms."

"Mark never wanted to have a graduation party from college in the backyard. He would have preferred a hamburger at McDonald's, but my father insisted that we all go to the Wellington for dinner after the ceremony," recalled Barbara, more relaxed.

"After that horrible dinner with Sam complaining about the service, we drove Mark to the airport to catch the evening flight for Colorado. He had to be at Outward Bound the next day," she added.

"Your father rented a limo so we could all say goodbye to Mark," added Carl.

"It was a nightmare. Remember how the highway was closed, and we had to go all the way to Irving Park to get to O'Hare," said Barbara. "Sam was shouting at the driver the whole time. By the time we got there, I had a splitting headache."

"Mark almost missed his flight due to the congestion at the airport. Sam thought we'd have a grand send off for him, but there wasn't enough time to park. It was just long enough for Mark to get out of the limo with his luggage and make a dash toward the gate," said Carl.

"I'm worried about my parents coming for Kathy's graduation. They'll be flying into O'Hare a week early," said Barbara, pausing. "Carl, the telephone is ringing in the hallway. Would you answer it?"

3

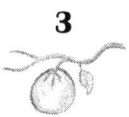

Carl answered the phone and talked for a few minutes before returning to the kitchen. He said, "It was Mark. He'll be coming home for lunch today."

"Give him my love. Mark agreed to meet Sam and Renee at the airport next Sunday," said Barbara.

"Why don't you quit your job at the museum and come back to Nepal with us?" asked Carl.

"I can't. The tours of the Pompeii Exhibit are scheduled through Labor Day. Did Mark tell you that he needs you to help him move his furniture from Evanston into our garage before he leaves for Colorado?"

"No! He's not moving again!" said Carl, distracted from correcting *The Training of Gurkha Soldiers*.

"Sam wants him to get a cheaper apartment in another building. He's agreed to pay for his tuition and rent again for the fall semester. It'll be a relief when Mark finishes graduate school and isn't dependent upon my father for financial support," sighed Barbara.

"I'm worried about Mark. He trusts Sam too much," said Carl. "I hope our flight from New Delhi to Kathmandu won't be delayed because of the monsoon."

"I'm worried about you and Kathy trekking. I remember those slippery trails with the leeches climbing up our boots. They dropped from the trees onto our necks and arms," said Barbara, shivering.

"We used to carry salt to rub on the leeches so they'd fall off. Sometimes they'd gorge themselves with our blood. And we didn't even notice they were there," said Carl, pausing to check his e-mail.

"I hated those hikes," added Barbara, circling her departure date on the calendar. "By the time I arrive in September, the monsoon will almost be over."

"Oh, look! Here is a message from Dr. Prasad. He's in charge of training the shamans at Bir Hospital," he said.

Dr. Carl Brecht,

I am pleased that you will be joining us for the convention on Alternative Medicine and Paramedic Training of Shamans at Bir Hospital in Kathmandu beginning Thursday May 24, 2001. Moksha, the Limbu Shaman, will be in attendance with his son, Muktuba. They send greetings to you and your family. I've made reservations for you and your daughter, Kathy, at the Kathmandu Guest House.

Several German anthropologists will be there to coordinate the workshops with our medical staff for the training of the shamans. All expenses will be covered by our patrons from the University of Heidelberg. Thank you for agreeing to introduce the shamans. I look forward to meeting you again.

Sincerely yours,
Dr. Rajan Prasad, Administrator,
Bir Hospital, Kathmandu, Nepal

Kathy entered the kitchen in a terrycloth robe and yawned. She removed a carton from the refrigerator and poured herself a glass of orange juice.

"Dr. Prasad sends you a greeting from Moksha and Muktuba, the Limbu Shamans," said Carl.

"Who are they?" asked his daughter, glancing over his shoulder at the message on the computer.

"They were the shamans who performed exorcisms to put Sharon Schliemann's soul to rest in the mountains north of Pokhara. She accidently fell over a cliff. Her corpse was found among the rocks along the stream. Because of her violent death, her soul was possessed by poltergeists that attacked her alcoholic husband, Paul. He was a faculty member at the university in Pokhara."

"How horrible!" said Kathy, sitting down at the table and opening the newspaper.

"The Nepalese in rural areas still believe if a person dies a violent death, his soul can't rest. If the corpse isn't cremated with the proper rituals, the soul will become possessed by evil spirits or poltergeists," said her father.

"Oh my God," said Barbara, glancing at her watch. "I'll miss my train if I don't leave now."

Carl rose from his chair in front of the computer and followed Barbara through the patio doors. He put his arms around her and kissed her on the lips. "I love you," he uttered as she pulled away from him. He kissed her a second time on the back of the neck.

"Carl, I wish you wouldn't do that," she whispered. "I get goose bumps all over."

Barbara hurried down the sidewalk and turned east toward the train station a few blocks away.

"What time will you be home?" he shouted.

"I'll call you on my cell phone," she replied, blowing him a kiss. She smiled at her barefoot husband, standing there scratching his hairy chest, wearing only his boxer shorts.

4

After returning to the house, Carl resumed his conversation with Kathy, informing her about booking their flight to Nepal. "You'll meet Moksha at the convention when we get to Kathmandu. He also performed an exorcism on Nigel Porter."

"Oh, Dad, I can hardly wait to get out of Chicago! I'm stressed out from studying for final exams," said Kathy. "Tell me more about Nigel."

"He was the eight-year-old boy, who was accused of murdering his brother, Christopher, in the pomelo tree at the Kathmandu Guest House!" said Carl, pouring himself another cup of coffee.

"The leader of the London Coven, Yorg Schmidt, was responsible for planning the grotesque murder of five-year-old Christopher and blaming Nigel. He wanted to get even with Margaret Porter for leaving the coven.

"She fled from London to Nepal with her two sons to escape from him. Margaret didn't know that Yorg had followed her to Nepal with Myrna Reynolds and members of the coven.

"Margaret had a nervous breakdown over Christopher's death. Shortly after that Nigel was kidnapped by the coven," sighed Carl. "I felt sorry for Margaret. She suffered so much over the loss of her sons."

"Whatever happened to Nigel?" asked Kathy.

"A yogi rescued him from the coven and brought him to Eastern Nepal, where Moksha performed several exorcisms on the boy. He successfully liberated Nigel's soul from numerous demons. Then the yogi took him to the Buddhist monastery in Tengboche, where he became a monk. He's been living there for the past twenty-four years.

"Margaret sent detectives to the monastery to find Nigel. She even went there herself a couple of times to find her son and bring him back to London. The abbot always had an excuse about Nigel not being at the monastery. He was either studying with the Dalai Lama at Dharmasala or learning about herbal medicine in Lhasa.

"The last time I received a letter from Margaret was about ten years ago. She wrote that Nigel was still at the monastery at Tengboche, but she never heard a word from him again. He refused to answer her e-mails."

"Nigel must be a grown man by now," said Kathy.

"He's thirty-three years old," said Carl. "It's strange that Margaret has never been able to find him."

"Maybe he doesn't want to be found," said Kathy.

"Nigel doesn't have pleasant memories about growing up in England. Margaret told me that she was constantly changing her address because she was worried the coven would find her and kidnap the children," said Carl.

"All parents worry about their children. You and mom still worry about Mark and me," said Kathy.

"That's true. Even the king and queen of Nepal worry about their children. I'll never forget going to the Taleju Temple during the animal sacrifices to the Mother Goddess. At that time the royal family arrived in a limo with their two sons and infant daughter.

"While they were worshipping in the temple, a yogi pushed his way through the crowd and pointed his finger at King Birendra and Queen Aishwarya, claiming that their five-year-old son, Crown Prince Dipendra, would someday murder his parents, his brother, Rajan, and sister, Shruti," said Carl, pacing the floor.

"You told me that a yogi predicted that after twelve generations of ruling, the Shah Dynasty would collapse," recalled Kathy, reaching for cereal from the cupboard.

"The Shah Dynasty began with Prithivi Narayan Shah conquering the Kathmandu Valley and unifying Nepal in 1763. After becoming the king, Prithivi insulted the yogi, Goraknath, who was disguised as a beggar. The king didn't know the yogi was an incarnation of Vishnu. The offended yogi cursed the royal family, predicting the Shahs would only rule for twelve generations.

"King Birendra's the tenth generation of kings. When Crown Prince Dipendra becomes king, he'll be the eleventh. That leaves only one generation left to rule before the dynasty comes to an end," concluded Carl.

"This morning's newspaper says that Queen Aishwarya is determined to arrange a marriage for Crown Prince Dipendra," said Kathy, sitting at the table.

"The problem is that the queen doesn't approve of the prince's choice for his bride," said Carl.

"The prince is old enough to make up his own mind," commented Kathy. "Here's a picture of him with his girlfriend in the newspaper.

"It says here that Prince Dipendra is dating a beautiful woman named Devyani from India. The couple was often seen at fashionable stores, restaurants, and night clubs in London. The photograph shows the crown prince giving the keys of his BMW to a valet at the entrance of Harrod's," said Kathy. "Here's another picture of Devyani coming out of the store, loaded with packages."

"Dipendra's parents want him to marry a Nepalese girl," stated Carl. "They've been trying to get him to break up with Devyani for some time now."

"That's disgusting!" asserted Kathy. "I can't understand the custom of arranged marriage. It's all about power, money, and the inheritance of property."

"You have to consider the customs and culture of the people. Dipendra will inherit the throne because he's the oldest son. Devyani also comes from a wealthy family, but she's Indian and only part Nepalese. The king and queen are fearful that an Indian bride won't be accepted by the people of Nepal.

"That article mentioned that the crown prince and Devyani are frequently seen together at the Royal Hotel in Kathmandu," added Carl.

"So what!" defended Kathy, rising from the table and setting the newspaper aside. "Is the crown prince supposed to be a prisoner in the palace?"

"Did you read about Dipendra being stopped by the police for drunken driving in Kathmandu?" asked Carl.

"No, I didn't read the whole article," said Kathy.

"The neighbors living in the vicinity of the Narayanhiti Palace were complaining that he was shooting at bats and crows in the back yard of the palace after midnight," stated Carl. "He regularly uses a machine gun.

"Those gigantic bats in the palm trees near the royal palace gave your mother the creeps. They looked like closed umbrellas hanging from the branches during the day. At night they swooped down with a three-foot wing span to feed on fruit in the royal orchard."

"Prince Dipendra's got some real problems," said Kathy, leaving the kitchen for the patio to study for her final exams.

5

Carl sat at the table and continued correcting his term papers. After two hours he had finished only ten papers. He paced the kitchen floor in his bare feet, annoyed by his slow progress.

Kathy entered the kitchen to get another glass of juice She asked, "Dad, what's wrong with you? You look like you're fed up with your students."

"This paper is plagiarized! It's not Lyle's work at all. *Mao in the Mountains* was written by Bob Rhoades, an anthropologist from the University of Georgia."

"Maybe Lyle was stressed out. That's why he copied it," concluded Kathy. "Dad, can I talk to you about something that's bothering me?"

"He must think that I'm stupid," continued Carl, not paying attention to his daughter.

"I've been accepted at Carleton College in Minnesota and Carthage in Wisconsin. They're both offering me an academic scholarship with a third of the tuition."

"I still have a stack of papers to correct, and it's already almost lunch time," complained her father.

"Dad, you're not paying attention to what I said," she stammered. "I'm in a quandary right now. I've got to make up my mind about the colleges before we leave for Nepal."

"Kathy, are you sure you want to study anthropology? There's a surplus of anthropologists these days."

"Of course I'm sure! I've always wanted to be an anthropologist ever since I was five years old," she yelled.

"I thought you enjoyed visiting Carleton in Minnesota. You were so thrilled when you met Jim Fisher, the anthropologist, who worked with Sir Edmund Hilary opening schools for Sherpas in Nepal back in the 1960's."

"I liked Carleton a lot, but it's a long way from home," said Kathy, starting to calm down. "Carthage has a new paleontology department, and I really like the campus in Kenosha along Lake Michigan."

"I would think seriously before taking a degree in paleontology. Every Tom, Dick, and Harry is majoring in it ever since the movie, *Jurassic Park*."

"You haven't been the least bit helpful. You're actually discouraging me! You've always liked Mark more than me! You just don't want women in your field," she screamed.

"I'm sorry if I hurt your feelings," said Carl stunned by her unexpected reaction.

"I've got an advanced biology test tomorrow. Then I have to study for my calculus final," she sobbed, pacing the kitchen floor. "I just found out on Friday that I was chosen to be valedictorian of my class. I've already written the first draft of my commencement speech, *The Crisis in the Himalayas*, but I haven't had a chance to rehearse it yet."

"Why, Kathy! Why didn't you tell me? What a privilege to be chosen valedictorian," said her father, giving her a hug.

"I...I'm so tired of studying," she cried, picking up her books. "I never have any time for myself. To be perfectly honest, I really want to go to Carthage College because I can take the train home on weekends."

"You'll like Carthage's campus on the lake," said Carl as his daughter left to study on the patio.

6

A half hour later Carl was working on the computer when he heard his son's voice coming from the patio. He thought Mark resembled Brad Pitt although Barbara disagreed with him.

"Hi Kathy. You're awfully tense today," said Mark.

"Leave me alone. I'm studying for my biology exam!" she snapped. "I don't want to talk right now."

"Kathy, you're taking your exams too seriously. Just relax. Don't worry. You'll get straight A's again. Congratulations! Mom told me you're the valedictorian".

"So what, I didn't get to go to prom again. Tom took my best friend Lisa because she's been taking birth control pills since her sophomore year. I'm the only senior who's still a virgin," complained Kathy.

"I've got an appointment to see the doctor on Friday to get birth control pills. But don't tell mom or dad. I'm stressed out over the commencement speech. No one has time to rehearse it with me."

"No wonder the guys don't want to date you," said Mark. "You're a nerd. Mom told me you worked on the speech instead of going to prom. If you want to practice it, I'm willing to listen to you."

"Would you? I'm almost ready to type it," she said. "It's about global warming in the Himalayas. By the way we're leaving for Nepal the day after my graduation."

"I wish I were going back to Nepal with you, but I'll be working in Colorado again with delinquent kids. I always tell them that if they share their weed with me, I won't turn them into the police."

"I hope you're kidding about that," said Carl, joining them on the patio. "Kathy and I will be attending a shaman convention in Kathmandu followed by trekking into the mountains to do further research."

"Dad took me to Nepal when I graduated from high school five years ago. We trekked for eleven days on slippery trails to Gosainkund and back to Kathmandu during the peak of the monsoon season," informed Mark. "We saw hundreds of pilgrims worshiping Shiva at the sacred lake."

"According to the legend Lord Shiva turned blue from drinking poison from the ocean to save the world from being destroyed by pollution. He quenched his thirst by stabbing his trident in the mountain near Trisuli. Then he reclined in the sacred lake at Gosaindkund," said Carl.

"You don't believe that myth?" asked Kathy. "It's certainly not scientific."

"There's always something to learn from a myth," laughed Mark.

"You sound just like dad," snapped Kathy, searching her backpack for her speech.

"There must have been a lot of pollution when that myth was written," said Carl.

"Overgrazing and deforestation are responsible for the global warming in the Himalayas," added Kathy. "There's a four mile black cloud hanging over the mountains from cow dung fires causing pollution."

"When dad and I were trekking in Nepal there weren't any Maoists stopping us on the trail," said Mark. "I understand they're active north of Kathmandu."

"Do you think we'll run into Maoists on the trail, Dad?" asked Kathy. "I'd be scared to death if they stopped us with their guns to extort money."

"You don't have to be afraid of them. They usually demand a 1000 rupees, about 15 dollars per trekker. The Maoists use the money to buy weapons to kill the police and occupy their stations in Western Nepal," said Carl.

"Then foreign trekkers are enabling the Maoists to murder the police," concluded Kathy.

"The Maoists don't see it that way," said Carl. "They want representation in the parliament. Their ultimate goal is to eliminate poverty in Nepal."

"Enough about the Maoists," insisted Kathy. "Mark, I've made up my mind to go to Carthage College instead of Carleton although they both only offered me a partial scholarship. It's a third of the total tuition."

"Why are you worrying about scholarships? Just ask Grandpa Havlett for the money. He's paying for my tuition and apartment at Northwestern University again next fall," bragged Mark.

"I won't sell my soul to the Devil! Grandpa never does anything for anybody without strings attached," snapped Kathy. "I have to study now. Please go into the kitchen if you want to talk about Sam. I don't want to hear about him. He's so annoying!"

"Call me when you're ready to rehearse your speech. I'll be in the kitchen with Dad," said Mark.

"Then come back in fifteen minutes," insisted Kathy. "I need to finish this chapter."

7

After chatting with his father for some time, Mark opened the patio door from the kitchen. He said, "Look outside. There's a strange bluebird in the maple tree."

Carl rose from his chair at the computer. "I'll be damned. The last time I saw a bird like that was after the Helembu Shaman performed an exorcism in the mountains north of Pokhara. He released a bird from its cage, which flew to the entrance of the Underworld at Fewa Lake.

"The shamans in Nepal wear headdresses and clothing with feathers since they believe the bird is a symbol of the soul. They also have images of birds painted on their drums like our Native Americans," said Carl.

"Where's mom?" interrupted Mark. "Don't tell me she's still sleeping."

"She working at the museum," said Carl, returning to his desk. "Your mother is scheduled to lead several tours of the Pompeii Exhibit today. I thought you'd bring Corrine here for lunch," said Carl.

"She's studying for finals," said Mark. "Corrine gets really hyper before exams."

"I hope you're not fighting with her again," said Carl. "It seems like you're breaking up every other week."

"Graduate school's stressful. We're both under a lot of pressure. She finally agreed to come with me to Kathy's graduation," said Mark. "I'm worried about her health because she never takes time to eat during finals."

"I like Corrine a lot, but she was pale the last time I saw her," said Carl. "I hope she's not getting sick again."

"She'll be fine, Dad. May I use your computer for a few minutes to rent the U-Haul for next Saturday? Don't forget you promised to help me move," added Mark.

"Next Saturday!" blurted Carl, closing his eyes and saying, "*Om namaha Ganeshaya,* invoking the name of the deity asking for help.

"Ganesh isn't going to you help you move Mark's furniture," insisted Kathy, entering the kitchen.

"But maybe he'll remove the obstacles from my life so that I can get these papers done by Friday," said Carl, feeling frustrated. "You guys can fix yourself something for lunch."

"I'll make the sandwiches, Kathy," said Mark, opening the refrigerator. "We've got sliced turkey, ham, and cheese. We'll rehearse your speech as soon as we're done eating."

8

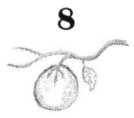

After rehearsing the speech several times on the patio, Mark and Kathy returned to the kitchen. They went right to the refrigerator to replenish their glasses with lemonade.

"Dad, do you know that Sam and Renee are flying to Chicago from Philadelphia next weekend? They're coming here to help mom with my graduation party," said Kathy.

"Barbara told me all about it," said Carl, irritated.

"No wonder mom's a basket case," uttered Kathy. "Sam hates this old house. It's never been up to his standards. I have to admit it needs a new roof and paint."

"This bungalow isn't exactly the Taj Mahal," uttered Mark. "Grandpa's going to have a fit when he sees this place. He won't let us forget that he's a millionaire with the controlling interest in Havlett Industries."

"Sam almost disinherited your mother for marrying me," said Carl, shaking his head with disgust.

"Mom stood up to Sam," asserted Kathy. "She told him to keep his millions because she was going to marry dad, even if she had to take a tug boat to Calcutta and a rickshaw to Kathmandu."

"That's ridiculous. She'd have to catch an overnight train from Calcutta and then travel all day by bus from southern Nepal to Kathmandu," said Mark, pausing. "You guys are prejudiced because Grandpa has money."

"Mom told me that Sam was the Pharoah, who imprisoned her in his tomb, filled with treasure. She was going to put an asp to her breast like Cleopatra if he wouldn't let her marry Dad."

"Barbara always has a flare for the dramatic," asserted Carl, pacing the worn linoleum.

"Mark, you're blind. Sam's controlling you just like he did mom," asserted Kathy.

Carl interrupted, "After Mark was born, your mother got sick in Nepal. We decided to move back to Philadelphia, and I returned to the University of Pennsylvania.

"Sam was furious with us. He wanted us to move to the suburbs and live in a mansion next to him, so he could be close to his grandson.

"Your grandfather was driving your mother crazy. It was her idea that we move to Chicago to escape from him. I was fortunate to get a job teaching anthropology at the University of Chicago. We didn't want to live downtown so we bought this house," said Carl.

"Grandpa told me that when I finish my PhD in microbiology, he would have a job waiting for me at Havlett Industries in his laboratory."

"Mark, you sold your soul to the Devil to get a free college education," remarked Kathy.

"Grandpa doesn't own me! I don't see anything wrong with taking his money to pay for my education. He's always been good to me.

"Dad, you should let Grandpa fix this place up before Kathy's graduation. He'd get the job done within a week. That's why he's coming here early," informed Mark.

"No!" shouted Carl, pounding his fist on the kitchen table. "*Cupiditas pecuniae radix malorum est*, the desire for money is the root of all evil! I don't want Sam remodeling our house! Your mother and I are perfectly happy living in this dilapidated bungalow!"

"Dad, I haven't seen you so angry in years. Are you going to take Kathy to the Sherpa settlement near Goasainkund?" asked Mark, changing the subject. "Remember how we stayed overnight in sleeping bags on the porch of the Cini Lama's son in Helembu?"

"Of course I remember. Helembu is where the Itinerant Shaman lives," blurted Carl, pacing the floor. "He performed exorcisms on a possessed man north of Pokhara at Kanjang."

"When I saw him five years ago, he was built like Hercules in spite of his grey hair," stated Mark.

"The Helembu Shaman has a lot of influence on the Sherpas. They come for miles to consult with him. He's planning to attend our shaman convention in Kathmandu," mentioned Carl, calming down.

"Mom told me that Sam and Renee will be flying into O'Hare next Sunday at 8:00 am," announced Kathy.

"That's Mother's Day," said Carl, his voice tense. "Mom has to work the whole day at the museum. Mark, you agreed to meet your grandparents at the airport when they arrive, and I want Kathy to go with you."

"I can't. Corrine and I are leaving for the Wisconsin Dells after our exams," said Mark.

"Sam will be furious if his only grandson isn't there to meet him. He'll have a stroke at the airport, and it will be your fault," insisted Kathy.

"I'll leave a message on his cell phone that Corrine's grandmother is dying, and we'll be out of town to attend the funeral," insisted Mark.

"That's a lie," blurted Kathy. "Why not tell Sam the truth! After all he's paying for your education."

"I don't want to upset him. Sam's already got high blood pressure, and he's taking heart medication," said Mark, scratching his head.

"Look, Mark. I'm going out of my way to help you move next Saturday," asserted Carl. "You could be decent enough to pick up Sam and Renee at the airport and take them out to lunch. It would liberate me to continue my research on the paramedic training of shamans."

"Of course, Dad," said Mark. "Just calm down. I'll call Corrine and cancel our plans. I'll meet them at O'Hare with Kathy, and we'll take them out to lunch."

"I know Grandpa's going to be mad if mom isn't there to greet him. He doesn't like dad at all," said Kathy, shaking her head.

"Sam hates you, Dad," said Mark. "He never speaks to you unless it's absolutely necessary."

"After lunch you can take Sam and Renee to see the Pompeii Exhibit at the museum," sighed Carl, his voice back to normal. "That way Mom can spend some time with her parents on Mother's Day."

"No, Dad. That's your job," insisted Kathy. "I'm spending the afternoon at Six Flags, the amusement park, with my friend, Heather."

"Corrine always gets claustrophobia in the museums," said Mark. "I don't want her ending up in the ER."

"It looks like I will have to take Sam and Renee to the museum," agreed Carl, pausing. "I must get Barbara something for Mother's Day. I thought about buying her an orchid coursage to wear at the museum like I did last year."

"You should get her a dozen red roses before Saturday," advised Kathy. "If you wait until the last minute, they won't have much of a selection, only wilted daisies."

9

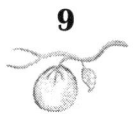

Leaving to work on the patio, Carl could hear his son and daughter arguing in the kitchen. Ignoring them, he spent the day correcting papers, pausing to say goodbye to Mark as he departed to catch the train for Evanston to meet Corrine.

When Barbara returned from the museum, Carl stood up and stretched, scratching his chest. "I'm so glad you're home early."

"You're still correcting those exams," said Barbara, hurrying toward him. Carl removed his glasses and gave her a hug.

"I missed you," he said, rising from the picnic table on the patio and kissing her on the lips.

"You haven't shaved," she sighed. "Carl, you're still in your shorts and barefoot. Let's go inside and get something cool to drink."

Carl followed Barbara into the kitchen, where she poured them each a glass of lemonade. Kathy was gone, although her biology text was open on the table.

Once again he put his arms around Barbara and kissed her on the back of the neck. She trembled, turning around to receive his kiss.

"How was work today?" he asked, noticing that she was fatigued from the heat.

"The museum was packed with noisy students taking notes, and teachers trying to keep discipline while I led them through the Pompeii Exhibit," said Barbara, opening a can of the tomato soup and pouring it into a saucepan. She snapped on the gas burner, placing a skillet on the stove as she prepared grilled cheese sandwiches.

"I want to see the exhibit before I leave for Nepal," said Carl. "It must have been expensive to bring the art all the way from the National Archeological Museum in Naples."

"It cost a small fortune," she said. "I have to work on Mother's Day again to make up for all the times I arrived late. I hate being late for work, but I can't help it when the trains aren't running on time because the tracks are being repaired. I wish Mussolini could be resurrected from his grave only to get them to run on time. Then he can go right back to the cemetery."

Carl told her that Mark and Kathy agreed to meet her parents at the airport and take them out to lunch. He also mentioned that he got angry because Sam was coming early intending to remodel the house."

"You have to admit, Carl, we've been so busy working that we haven't had time to take care of this place. Every room needs a coat of paint."

"I'll take care of everything when I get back from Nepal," promised Carl.

"No you won't. You'll be busy getting your research ready for publication," said Barbara, stirring the soup on the stove. "Sam will be mad at me because I have to work on Mother's Day. Renee told me he flares up over the slightest thing these days."

"I'm starving," said Carl, helping his wife place the bowls of soup and cheese sandwiches on the table.

"I'm sure Sam and Renee will want to see the Pompeii Exhibit next Sunday afternoon. I could squeeze them into the last tour of the day at 4:00 o'clock," added Barbara.

"I'm planning on bringing them to the museum," suggested Carl, mentioning again that Mark and Kathy agreed to meet her parents at the airport and take them out to lunch at the Wellington.

"Carl, they won't go with you in the Honda," said Barbara. "Sam will rent a limo and insist you go with them. After the tour he'll want us to have dinner with them at the Wyndham in Itasca."

"That exclusive dining room will be crowded because of Mother's Day," said Carl. "I'd rather not go there."

"I'll make Sam a tuna casserole and a pineapple upside down cake for dessert. We can have dinner on our patio."

"We can't bring your parents here," asserted Carl, trying to control his temper. "This house is a mess."

"You're right about that. I'm sure Sam won't approve of Kathy's party in the backyard either. He'll just have to accept us for who we are," replied Barbara.

"He's never done that before. Why should he start now?" asked Carl. "This grilled cheese is really good."

"Carl, I'm so mad. I could just scream!" shouted Barbara, rising from the table. "I wish they weren't coming here a week early I really don't want to take them on the tour of the museum either."

"Then put your foot down and say no!" shouted Carl. "Sam has never forgiven me for marrying you."

"Sam and Renee will want to see the Pompeii Exhibit because their home in Philadelphia has a garden designed after the House of the Golden Cupid," said Barbara. "Remember?"

"How can I forget?" said Carl, recalling that memorable dinner when Sam tried to manipulate him into marrying Barbara and working for Havlett Industries."

"I have a headache just thinking about them."

"There's Tylenol in the cabinet over the sink," said Carl.

10

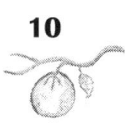

While rinsing the dishes, Barbara informed Carl that she was worried about him going back to Kathmandu.

"You told me a clerk was blamed for tying the rope on the branch of the pomelo tree, where Christopher was murdered. The clerk was arrested and committed suicide in jail," said Barbara, realizing the truth surpassed the worst nightmare that anyone could image.

"The clerk didn't do it. Yorg Schmidt, the leader of the London coven, tied the rope to the tree and enticed Nigel into murdering five-year-old Christopher," said Carl.

"I was in the garden when Margaret collapsed after seeing Christopher hanging by the neck from a rope. She was terrified when her eight-year-old son, Nigel, handed her a red rose and said, 'I didn't do it, Mummy.'"

"When I first arrived in Nepal, I was shocked when you told me about the murder in the garden, and Nigel being kidnapped a few weeks later," said Barbara.

Carl informed her that when Nigel was born, Margaret offered him to the coven during a special ceremony dedicated to Ravana, the Demon King. Margaret realized she had made a mistake and fled from London with her children, but Yorg followed her to Nepal.

"Margaret believed Nigel was possessed by demons, hoping a shaman could perform an exorcism to liberate his soul from demonic possession," said Carl.

"I promised Margaret while she was recovering from a nervous breakdown in the hospital in Kathmandu that I would try to find Nigel. When I arrived in Pokhara, Yorg took me hostage and brought me by boat to Dr. Bhinna Atma's cottage, intending to sacrifice me to Ravana. Nigel was present at the cottage witnessing the immoral activities of the coven.

"Yorg was insane from taking drugs. In fact the entire coven was high on drugs when a whirlwind caused the cottage to collapse. Yorg and his wife, Myrna, were both killed, but the other members of the coven escaped."

"You told me a yogi pulled Nigel out of the cottage before the roof collapsed," recalled Barbara.

"I managed to escape with my hands tied," said Carl. "I saw the yogi take Nigel to a boat. As they departed, I heard him say that they would travel to eastern Nepal to find Moksha, the Limbu Shaman to perform an exorcism on the boy to free his soul from the demons."

"I remember how stressed you were after being kidnapped by the coven when I came to Kathmandu. We sat under the pomelo tree, talking for hours," said Barbara.

Carl kissed Barbara. "I love you now even more than I did when you came to Nepal twenty-four-years ago."

After taking her by the hand, he led her from the kitchen to their bedroom. While he showered and shaved, Barbara undressed, slipping into her translucent pink night gown. A few minutes later Carl entered the room naked and slid under the covers next to her in bed.

"I've missed you so much the entire day," he said, kissing her tenderly on the lips.

Barbara whispered, "I've missed you too. You're hairy like a Yeti. Your heart is beating so loudly, I'm afraid it's going to burst."

11

On Monday morning Carl walked to the Metra commuter railroad station in Arlington Heights and boarded the train for downtown. Upon arriving at the university, he went directly to his office to work. He kept up this routine the entire week.

Before the students arrived on Friday, Carl posted the grades outside his classroom on the bulletin board. He entered the room to work on his research but was interrupted.

"Dr. Brecht, could I speak to you for a few minutes?" asked an attractive woman in her late twenties, standing in the doorway.

"Of course, Cindy, please come in and sit down. What can I do for you?" asked Carl, removing his glasses.

"I've come here early to check on my grade," she said.

"You wrote a perfect exam. I really liked your essay about the suppression of the monarchy during the Rana aristocracy in Nepal," said Carl.

"Oh, thank you Dr. Brecht," I'm so relieved. I was worried about my grade," said Cindy Sanders.

"You also got an A on your term paper, *Ayurvedic Medicine during the Reign of King Pratap Malla.* I wish you were presenting it at our shaman convention in Kathmandu. Most of the shamans already use herbal medicines for treating diseases. Would you read the highlighted passages to the class today?" requested Carl.

"Of course," she agreed, leafing through the paper while the students entered the room.

After Carl distributed the papers, he cleared his throat waiting for them to settle down.

"Congratulations on doing such a good job on your final exams and research. Some of you will return for the fall semester. Dr. Richard Nelson will be covering my classes until I come back in October. I'll be doing research in Nepal on *Alternative Medicine and the Paramedic Training of Shamans.*"

"During this semester I didn't have time to give a lecture about Ayurvedic Medicine. However, Cindy wrote a paper on this topic. She agreed to share some information with you this morning."

Cindy rose from her seat and went to the podium. She informed them *Ayurevedic* means the science of life, involving three humours in the body responsible for diseases when they are imbalanced. The humours are wind, bile, and phlegm.

"According to the physician of the Dalai Lama, a person's spiritual health has an affect upon his physical health. He claimed three vices influenced the humours in the body. They were delusion, attachment, and hatred.

"The role of the medical practitioner is to diagnose the spiritual maladies first and then begin treating the physical manifestations of the disease with herbal medicines.

"For example if a person has bronchitis (phlegm), the doctor will encourage a moral inventory to uncover the spiritual malady prior to giving the medicine," she said.

Cindy mentioned that medicinal herbs were found in the Hindu epic, *The Ramayana*. When Rama was wounded in battle against Ravana and his demons, Hanuman, the monkey god, travelled to the Himalayas in search of the healing herb, *Sanjibani buti*. Upon finding the herb, he applied it to Rama's wound for healing.

"Tell us, Cindy, about the future of herbal medicine," said Carl, checking his watch.

"Of course," said Cindy, leafing through her paper. "Deforestation in the Himalayas has devastated medicinal herbs growing in the mountains."

"Numerous doctors and herbal specialists have been forced to give up their practices. Others have lost their homes and businesses due to the mountains collapsing."

Cindy concluded her talk by giving the names of specific herbs that were used by shamans and practitioners to treat pneumonia, urinary tract infections, skin diseases, burns, and abrasions.

"Thank you for your summary of herbal medicine. You've been a wonderful class. I'm looking forward to seeing some of you when I return in October. Have a great summer," said Carl, shaking hands with his students as they departed.

A few students lingered in the classroom, not wanting to leave. They invited Carl to join them for coffee at the student union. After chatting with them for an hour, he returned to his office to continue with his research.

12

Late in the afternoon on Friday, Carl left the university and took the train back to Arlington Heights. Upon arrival at his home, he telephoned Mark, informing him that he'd bring the U-Haul on Saturday morning. After checking his e-mail, he continued with his research.

A few hours later Barbara burst into the kitchen from the patio. Her hair was disheveled and makeup faded.

"I'm just exhausted. Thank God it's Friday! The train was packed with people. I had to stand all the way home."

"Friday evening's the worst time to travel on the Metra," agreed Carl, pouring his wife a glass of lemonade. "How did your day go?"

Barbara sat across from Carl at the kitchen table. She was stressed over the crowded tours of the Pompeii Exhibit at the museum, especially people complaining about the air conditioning not working.

Once she was calmed down Carl mentioned that he found source material about shamans receiving paramedic training in Nepal in 1981, and how the interest had grown in alternative medicine at the universities in Germany.

"In a couple of weeks, I'll be here totally alone. Mark will be in Colorado, and Kathy will be with you in Nepal. I won't see you until after Labor Day," sighed Barbara.

"I thought you reconciled that conflict," said Carl, noticing her depression. "It's the empty nest syndrome. A lot of people go through an adjustment once the last child leaves home."

"I'm feeling abandoned even though you haven't left yet," sobbed Barbara. "I'm a basket case! I need to see a shrink!"

"You're going through hormonal changes," said Carl.

"I feel like I'm on a roller coaster," cried Barbara. "I should be grateful that I have my job at the museum. If a nuclear war breaks out, I can take the survivors on a tour of the ruins of Chicago."

"You're practicing *Karma Yoga*, the yoga of action," said Carl. "It's the essence of *The Bhagavad Gita.*"

"I'm going to take up meditation while you're gone. They're offering courses in yoga at Oakton College."

"That's great. It'll help you relax after a busy day at the museum," said Carl.

"I'll shave my head, cover my body with ashes, and wander naked through the neighborhood with a begging bowl. I'm going to tell everyone to renounce their worldly possessions and join my ashram," laughed Barbara.

"Yogis wander naked in Kathmandu during the spring festival called *Shiva Ratri*, the Night of Shiva, but not in Arlington Heights! You'll end up in jail," smiled Carl.

"I was ready for the psyche ward when you went back to Nepal without me 1976. Sometimes I wish we were still living in Pokhara on the campus.

"I loved the view of Macchapuchare, the Fish Tail Mountain, from our porch there," reflected Barbara. "We had papayas, mangoes, and a pomelo tree in our backyard. While you were teaching, I stayed home with Mark. He was such a good baby.

"Then one day the snake appeared in our Garden of Eden. I came down with amoebic dysentery and then hepatitis. I thought I was going to die. I really didn't want to go back to the states," she added, "but we didn't have a choice. Our life has never been the same since we came back here."

"I was worried about Mark getting infected," said Carl.

"It was such a relief when we finally returned to Philadelphia, but my parents came daily to check up on me and the baby. Sam always found fault with our small apartment on Chestnut Street near the campus until I couldn't stand it anymore.

"I'll never regret our decision to leave and come to Chicago. I'm worried to death about you and Kathy going back to Nepal because of the Maoists," said Barbara. "A revolution is pending there. And you and Kathy will be caught right in the middle."

"Did you hear from Mark, today?" asked Carl, changing the subject. "I'm going to help him move tomorrow."

"Mark called me during my lunch break. He told me that he's not going for the PhD in microbiology. Once he gets his master's degree, he wants to move to Colorado Springs with Corrine," said Barbara.

"Mark promised to work in Sam's laboratory to repay him for his college debts," said Carl, raising his eye brows.

"He's angry with Sam. Mark decided to take out a loan, rather than accept more money from him for his education. He's through with Sam and his threats," said Barbara.

"Did Mark tell Sam about his future plans?" asked Carl.

"Not yet," said Barbara. "He's waiting for him to calm down. If Sam finds out that Mark won't be working for him, he'll be like Mount Vesuvius erupting."

"I'll tell him not to mention a word to Sam about his plans until after Kathy's party," said Carl. "I've agreed to pick up the U-Haul and meet Mark early tomorrow morning at his apartment."

13

On Saturday morning Carl drove to Busse Road and picked up the U-Haul that his son had rented. When he arrived at the apartment building in Evanston, he rang the bell, but Mark did not answer although it was 9:00 o'clock.

Finally, his son opened the door yawning and scratching his chest. He stood there in his boxer shorts. "Dad, I'm sorry. I didn't hear you ringing the doorbell."

"Mark, you've got a terrible hangover. Your eyes are bloodshot," said Carl, shaking his head.

"I only had a few beers because I was the designated driver, but the bar was filled with smoke. Al and Jim got plastered. Corrine was upset with them and left. She took a taxi back to her apartment."

"I don't blame her. Those pals of yours are crude when they're drunk," said his father.

"Corrine and I were dancing when Al stumbled onto the dance floor. He pulled her away from me and wrapped his arms around Corrine like an octopus. I almost got into a fist fight with him."

Carl followed his son into the building. They entered the elevator, exiting on the third floor. As they walked down the corridor to his apartment, Mark told him about Jim's belligerent behavior.

"I feel sorry for Corrine. Those friends of yours spoiled your evening together," he said.

Upon entering the apartment Carl noticed dozens of cardboard boxes on the living room floor. The kitchen had more containers stacked near the stove with the oven door open and refrigerator disconnected.

"How did you do on your final exams, Mark?" asked Carl, concerned about his grades.

"I'm pissed off with Dr. Henrickson for giving me a B+ in microbiology. I slaved in the laboratory every evening doing research on antibiotic resistance bacteria," he said, putting on a wrinkled shirt, jeans, and shoes.

After listening to Mark complaining about his grades, Carl said, "Let's get busy we've got work to do."

A few minutes later, they were carrying the mattress to the elevator. After waiting for five minutes, they decided to struggle with it down three flights of stairs, blocked by students carrying sofas, chairs, and furniture.

By the time they got outside the entire street was crowded with vans and rental trucks. Students rushed past them with framed pictures, lamps, and nightstands, leaving the cardboard boxes for their parents.

"I thought Sam had hired movers for you," said Carl, nearly out of breath.

"I'm mad at Sam for being such a control freak. He agreed to hire movers and then backed down," said Mark, sliding the mattress onto the truck.

"That's strange, Sam's always been willing to help you out financially," said Carl.

"My lease expires tomorrow. Grandpa promised to pay my rent for the whole summer so I wouldn't have to move. Then he changed his mind because I didn't return his telephone calls fast enough. I was busy every night in the lab, tutoring, or studying at the library. When I finally reached him, he was mad as a hornet.

"I can't afford the rent for this apartment for the summer, and I didn't want to leave the leather furniture. Sam wants me to find a cheaper place for the fall."

Both father and son returned to the apartment. This time there was a line waiting at the elevator. The stairs were clogged with students complaining about the delay.

The second trip involved moving the leather sofa. Carl and Mark struggled, blocking the stairs with everyone behind them moaning.

"I'm fed up with Sam," said Mark. "I've got to tell him the truth. I've decided not to continue for the PhD in microbiology. I've already filled out the papers for a loan for this fall, but my chances of getting it are slim."

After putting the sofa into the truck, they carried the boxes down the crowded stairs. When everything was loaded, Mark entered the front seat on the passenger side, slamming the door. His father started the truck, inching his way along the crowded street before heading back to Arlington Heights.

"Dad, you and Mom were right. I'm a marionette, and Sam's been pulling my strings!"

"We tried to warn you about Sam," said Carl.

"He never said a harsh word to me until this year. He was always kind. Over the past couple of months he's turned into a Dr. Jekyl and Mr. Hyde. Sam stopped my monthly allowance cold turkey. He told me I had to get a part time job. I agreed with him and began tutoring.

"Earlier in the week, Sam called me. He wanted me to quit my summer job at Outward Bound and move to Philadelphia and live with him and Renee. He insisted I work in his laboratory at Havlett Industries because a technician was fired for showing up drunk.

"Sam really got mad when I told him that I won't quit my summer job because I like working with delinquent kids. That's when he threatened to stop paying my tuition and housing for next year."

"I'm proud of you for not quitting your summer job," said Carl, turning from Golf onto Arlington Heights Road.

"I'll have to pay Sam back the money he spent on my education. I've made up my mind I won't work for him after I graduate with a master's degree. I don't want to be his slave. My problem is I won't make enough money to pay for my room and board this fall," added Mark.

"Sam's been telephoning me every day this week, demanding an answer about working for him. I haven't phoned him back. I really don't want to be around him at Kathy's graduation," said Mark.

"Corrine's parents won't be coming to the party to meet you and Mom. They belong to the Assembly of God or the Seven Day Adventists. I don't remember which one.

"Corrine doesn't drink and she doesn't smoke. She became a vegetarian after studying Buddhism. Her parents were horrified. They believe she's being influenced by a pagan religion," said Mark.

"There are good people in every religion," said Carl.

"I know, one of the boys at Outward Bound last summer confided in me that he had been molested by his parish priest in Boston. When Bob told his parents about the incident, they didn't believe him.

"He wanted to change schools, but his parents refused to transfer him. Bob purposely got into trouble with the nuns, so they expelled him. That was the only way he could escape from the abusive pastor who stalked him."

"Mark, I think it's great that you're helping those delinquent kids" said Carl. "We're almost home."

"I really liked working at Outward Bound last summer. Most of the boys talked about their problems when they were away from their families. Several of them were admitted to psyche wards for attempted suicides because they were addicted to drugs and alcohol. They start with marijuana and end up on cocaine. A few of them got into oxycodin, meth, or heroin."

"Are you sure you want to be a microbiologist? You'd be a great clinical therapist," said Carl.

"Of course I want to be a microbiologist, but I like my summer job," said Mark. "All the teenagers at camp have abandonment issues. Some belong to gangs; others get in trouble with the police. Only a few are conscientious about their grades and do well in spite of using drugs.

"I always tell them not to give up when the going gets rough. They've got to face life squarely and stop running away," said Mark.

"That's good advice," said Carl, pulling the truck into the driveway.

"Dad, I plan to return to Northwestern University to finish my master's degree even if I have to go into debt. I can't run away from Sam. I must tell him the truth, but I don't want him to ruin Kathy's graduation or party."

14

On Sunday morning Carl got up early to prepare breakfast for his wife. He stood barefoot in front of the stove, wearing only his shorts when Barbara entered the kitchen. She wore a white blouse and blue skirt.

"You're gorgeous," said Carl, turning over the omelet. "You look like you're going sailing in that outfit."

"Roses, they're so beautiful," smiled Barbara, caressing the petals in a crystal vase. She reached for the envelope, removed the card, and admired the picture of a doe with twin fawns and a stag in the distant meadow.

Sitting down at the table, she sipped her orange juice and read the message inside the card.

Barbara,
We'll have a lot to talk about when we meet in September. I will be waiting for you on the stone bench in the garden at the Kathmandu Guest House. Thank you for being such a wonderful wife and mother. Happy Mother's Day!
With love, Carl

"What a pleasant surprise!" she exclaimed, rising to give him a hug. She placed her head on his hairy chest. "I can hear your heart beating."

"Barbara, I wish you didn't have to go to work this morning," he uttered, kissing her tenderly on the lips.

"Oh Carl! We never have enough time to be together. When I get to Kathmandu, we're going to sit in the garden and watch the pomelos ripen. We'll stay in bed until noon every day," she promised, sitting down to eat her cheese omelet across from him.

They reminisced about going to the Hindu Temple, Pashupati Nath, where they stood on the bridge watching the cremations along the river bank. Suddenly, several naked yogis covered with ashes rushed toward them with their hands outstretched, begging for money.

"Those yogis scared me half to death," said Barbara.

Carl laughed over the incident, pouring them each another cup of coffee.

"I remember the Shiva temple, where the priest poured milk over the lingam, representing the union of Shiva and Parvati. He rinsed the stone image with a pot of water," said Barbara.

"The Shiva lingam has its origins in sexuality and fertility, but it also symbolizes the mystical union of the Creator with his creation," said Carl.

"I know what you have on your mind," teased Barbara. "I remember browsing in the gift shops and bookstores in Tamel after staying in bed with you most of the day. Oh my God! It's late. I must get going, or I'll miss the train."

"I've got to wake up Kathy. She agreed to meet Sam and Renee at the airport at 8:30. Mark should be here any minute. I hope he's not late."

"Call me later. Let me know when I can expect you and my parents at the museum," said Barbara, kissing him on the cheek. She snatched her purse and hurried out the back door down the sidewalk toward the train station.

15

Carl was about to go upstairs to wake up his daughter when the phone rang in the hallway. He picked up the receiver, recognizing Mark's voice.

"Dad, I took Corrine to the emergency room here in Evanston. The doctor said her electrolytes are low, so he connected her to an IV. I'm going to stay with her while they run some blood tests. I'm sorry I can't come to the airport to meet Sam and Renee."

"I'm disappointed, but I hope Corrine's all right. Give her my love," said Carl. "Call me later and let me know how's she's doing. I've got to go now."

Carl bolted up the stairs and knocked on Kathy's door. When she didn't answer, he entered her room, surprised that she was gone. He hurried to his bedroom down the hall where he shaved, showered, and dressed.

A short time later he was driving down Arlington Heights Road toward O'Hare. When he stopped at a red light, he called his wife on his cell phone.

"Barbara, where in the hell's Kathy?" he asked, feeling frustrated that his children weren't available to meet their grandparents.

"I forgot to tell you that she stayed overnight at Heather's house. They're going to Six Flags Great America to unwind from taking exams," informed Barbara.

"Kathy and Mark promised to come with me to the airport. Now, I have to pick up Sam and Renee and take them out to lunch by myself. Sam hates me. He won't even speak to me!"

"I'm sorry about that. Carl, be sure to bring them to the museum this afternoon after they get settled at their hotel. I'll talk to you later," said Barbara. "I've got another call. It's from Sam!"

Upon arriving at the airport, Carl approached the multiple exits of United Airlines. He crawled along in the Honda searching for Barbara's parents. Finally, he saw them, standing behind a mountain of luggage. After parking his car behind a taxi, he hurried toward them.

Sam was wearing a Hawaiian shirt and pacing in front of the suitcases, puffing on a cigar. Renee's face was hidden behind sunglasses and a broad-brimmed hat.

Carl greeted Renee giving her a hug although Sam turned away from him as if he didn't exist.

"Sam's mad as a hornet because nobody was here to meet us. He's been screaming at Barbara on his cell phone for ten minutes because our flight arrived early. We've been waiting here for almost an hour after retrieving our luggage," stammered Renee.

"Where the hell have you been? It's after 9:00 o'clock," bellowed Sam, his cigar bobbing from his mouth like Edward G. Robinson in a gangster movie.

"I'm sorry I'm late. I didn't expect to be delayed by so much traffic," apologized Carl, offering him his hand.

Sam lowered his head, refusing to shake Carl's hand. "Why isn't Barbara here?"

"She's working at the museum," informed Carl, annoyed by the cigar smoke.

"It's Mother's Day! She was supposed to meet us here! It's obvious you're not earning enough at the university to support her," he shouted, flushed with rage.

"Barbara likes being a tour guide," insisted Carl, ignoring the criticism.

"Where's my grandson?" asked Sam. "Mark promised to be here."

"He had to take his girlfriend, Corrine, to the hospital this morning," informed Carl, irritated by his attitude.

"What's she doing in the hospital? If she's having an abortion, I'm not paying for it," uttered Sam. "I've never liked her. She's pale and skinny because she's a vegetarian. Corrine needs to put some meat on her bones."

"I'll take you to Yanni's for lunch although we might have a long wait before we're seated," said Carl.

"I'll never go back to that restaurant," blurted Sam. "The service was terrible, beside I hate Greek cuisine."

"I loved their grilled Salmon," said Renee. "Yanni's has ambience with Greek statues, a fountain, and orchids everywhere."

"Where's Kathy? She promised to be here," blurted Sam, crushing his cigar with his shoe on the sidewalk.

"Kathy's stressed out from finals," said Carl. "She's spending the day at the amusement park with a friend."

"You certainly didn't raise your children to respect their grandparents," accused Sam.

"We expected Barbara to be here with you Carl," said Renee. "It's too bad she has to work on Mother's Day."

A security guard interrupted them by speaking to Carl. "Sir, you've had your car parked here for ten minutes. You must load the luggage and move on."

"Of course," said Carl, reaching for their suitcases.

"Our luggage won't fit in your car," said Renee. "Sam rented a limo to take us to our hotel in Itasca."

"Here comes the driver," said Sam, flagging down the limousine. "It's about time Charles got here."

Sam supervised the driver while he loaded their Moroccan luggage and his golf clubs into the trunk.

"The breakfast on that flight was terrible," snapped Sam, whining about the ham and eggs and the bloody marys. "After we get a decent lunch at the Wyndham, I'm playing 18 holes of golf."

"I'll let Barbara know you're on the way to the hotel," said Carl, removing his cell phone from his coat pocket and dialing her number.

"Give me that goddamn phone," blurted Sam, rushing toward Carl and yanking it from his hand..

"You have no respect for your mother or me!" he shouted into the phone. "You should've taken the day off!"

Barbara informed her father that she couldn't talk because she was in the middle of a tour of the Pompeii Exhibit. She advised them to be at the museum at 4:00 o'clock for the last tour of the day, suggesting they go out to dinner afterwards.

Sam tossed the phone back to Carl, and entered the limousine, slamming the door.

Renee rolled down the window and, waved to Carl. "We'll meet you at the museum this afternoon."

Carl stood there bewildered by Sam's rude behavior. He telephoned Barbara, leaving her a message that he would take the afternoon train to meet her parents rather than drive to the museum in the heavy traffic.

16

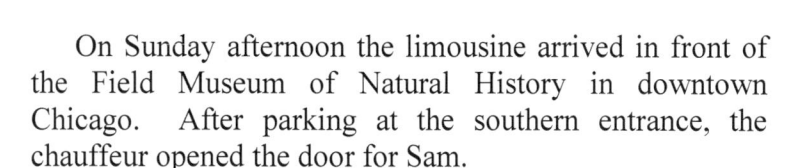

On Sunday afternoon the limousine arrived in front of the Field Museum of Natural History in downtown Chicago. After parking at the southern entrance, the chauffeur opened the door for Sam.

"Charles, you must be back here by 5:00 o'clock, or you're going to be in serious trouble," announced Sam, noticing a policeman blowing his whistle at pedestrians crossing the street.

"Yes sir!" agreed the driver, helping Renee out of the backseat. She was amazed by the crowd of senior citizens and families with children leaving the museum.

"Hurry up, Sam, or we're going to be late for the last tour," insisted Renee, high heeling up the cement steps.

"I'm coming," he uttered, gasping for breath from climbing the stairs. He paused to wipe the perspiration from his forehead with a handkerchief.

Carl was waiting at the entrance. He hurried toward them with their tickets. "I'm so glad you arrived early. Sam, do you need help?"

Renee turned around, rushing down the stairs, her eyes wide with alarm. "Sam, what's wrong with you?"

"I feel so dizzy," he uttered, clinging to the railing. "Do you have my meds in your purse?"

"I thought you took them before we had lunch," she gasped, searching her handbag.

"I forgot to take them," moaned Sam. "I need my meds, Renee! I feel like I'm having a stroke."

"What can I do to help?" asked Carl, his brow furrowed.

"You can get me a glass of water. I'll be all right in a few minutes," uttered Sam, sweating profusely.

Carl hurried back into the museum where he explained the situation to the security guard.

Renee searched her purse for the medications. She removed a bottle of hand lotion, her sunglasses, and a novel, putting them on the cement steps.

"For Christ's sake, Renee," bellowed Sam. "You've got everything but the kitchensink in that goddamn purse except my meds."

"Here they are!" she yelled, shaking a plastic container with multiple compartments and labels: heart, cholesterol, blood pressure, diabetes, and asthma. Renee removed the pills, handing them to Sam.

A few moments later Carl returned with a bottle of water, offering it to Sam, who sat on the steps with his hands covering his flushed face

"This water tastes like piss," uttered Sam, swallowing down the pills one at a time. After taking his medications, he took a deep breath.

"Barbara will be disappointed if we're late for the tour," insisted Renee, putting her hair brush, compact, and wallet back into her purse.

Carl contacted his wife on his cell phone, finding out the tour was running ten minutes late. He informed her parents they still had time to meet Barbara for the last tour of the day.

"A person could die here on the steps before any one from my family would help me out," complained Sam. "Mark's ungrateful! He's forgotten that I'm paying for his education. He still hasn't given me an answer about working in my lab this summer!"

Carl restrained himself from telling Sam that Mark decided not to accept any more of his money.

"Sam, you've got to settle down or you're going to end up in the hospital. Mark was busy studying for his finals. He wanted to meet us at the airport, but he couldn't make it because Corrine was in the hospital," stated Renee.

"I don't buy that story about her being sick. Barbara told me that Mark and Corrine were planning to go to the Wisconsin Dells, and they wouldn't be back until Kathy's graduation. Mark's a goddamn liar!"

"Let's not worry about that right now," insisted Renee. "Barbara's waiting to take us on the tour. I'll help you up the stairs."

"Leave me alone. I'm fine!" he snapped, seizing the handrail and struggling up the stairs.

"Those medications work awfully fast," uttered Renee sighing with relief. "I shouldn't have worn these high heels. My feet are killing me."

Once they were inside the museum, Carl handed them maps. "We've got a short walk to the exhibit. If you need wheelchairs, they're kept behind the information desk."

"Hell no, I don't need a wheel chair! I'm perfectly fine," shouted Sam, pausing to gaze at the brontosaurus in the distance and the towering bull elephants from Africa.

17

Carl handed the tickets to the guard at the entrance and led the way to the Pompeii Exhibit. It was 4:10 when they arrived at Barbara's station. About thirty people had gathered, ready to enter the exhibit.

"Mom, Dad. I'm so happy to see you," said Barbara, hugging them. "How was your flight from Philadelphia?"

"It was terrible," bellowed Sam, noticing that all heads were turned toward him. "We had first class tickets, but the stewardess treated us like peons."

"That's too bad," sighed Barbara, handing her parents a name tag. "Please come to the head of the line."

Barbara introduced herself to the tourists, her voice amplified by the microphone attached to her collar. She then acknowledged her parents. Sam was especially pleased by the unexpected attention.

"The artwork in today's exhibit was transported from the National Archeological Museum of Naples. Most of the pieces were excavated from the ruins of Pompeii and Herculaneum," said Barbara.

"It's hotter than hell in this suffocating museum," interrupted Sam, wiping perspiration from his forehead.

"Please bear with me in spite of the heat. The air conditioning in this part of the museum is being repaired," said Barbara. "Imagine we are in Italy at our villas overlooking the Mediterranean in August 79AD. Suddenly without warning Mount Vesuvius erupts, covering

Herculaneum with molten lava and smothering Pompeii with ash. Visualize yourself fleeing from your homes, leaving behind your precious art treasures," said Barbara.

"I'm tired and my feet hurt," complained Renee, following the tourists into a cavernous room.

"Here's a Roman copy of *Athena*, the goddess of wisdom and war," said Barbara, pausing as the crowd gathered around the statue. "Pericles dedicated this sculpture to the Greeks during the plague of 430 BC."

"It feels like I'm coming down with the plague from the heat in here," announced Sam.

"Ouch! That hurt!" shrieked Renee, crouching down.

"What's the matter, Mother?" asked Barbara, embarrassed by the behavior of her parents.

"Sam just stepped on my foot. I shouldn't have worn these heels!" she exclaimed, removing her shoes and stuffing them into her purse.

"I'll be damned. If it's not *Hercules*," blurted Sam, his mouth gaping at the huge nude figure dominating the center of the room.

"Hercules has just stolen the apples of Hesperides and is holding them in his hands. In spite of his muscular body, he's weary from his labors. This statue, made in the third century, was found by archeologists excavating the Baths of Caracalla in Rome," informed Barbara.

"Sam and I saw the opera, *Aida*, performed there. They brought elephants, camels, and chariots right onto the stage," added Renee. "It was wonderful!"

"The enormous ruins of the baths are the background for summer opera in Rome," added Barbara. "Please follow me into the next room."

"Why that's the *Farnese Bull*!" announced Sam. "It's the largest statue from antiquity. I'm amazed that they were able to ship it here!"

"The bull dominates this group of statues," said Barbara. "That poor woman tied to his horns was captured by the nude men. They're about to sacrifice her and the bull to Dionysius, the god of wine and theater," said Barbara. "Next are paintings of *Hermes at Rest*, and the *Drunken Selinus.*"

As the tourists crowded around Barbara, they became impatient with Sam, who lectured them about the *Bust of Homer,* the Greek author of *The Iliad* and *Odyssey.*

Everyone was annoyed with him for interrupting Barbara again while she was telling them about the bronze statue of *Caesar Augus*tus

Sam led the way to the *Artemis of Ephesus*. He was about to explain to the tourists about the cult of the nature goddess when a security guard arrived and spoke to him.

"Several people from this group have complained about you taking over the tour. They are annoyed because of your interruptions!" said the guard.

"What are you saying?" questioned Sam, flushed with anger. "This place is hotter than Hades!"

"I'm saying that if you don't stop interrupting the docent, you're going to be escorted out of the museum," insisted the security guard.

"What do you mean? Don't you know who I am? I'm Samuel Havlett from Philadelphia!" he shouted.

Barbara called the guard aside telling him that her father was taking several medications and probably reacting to the heat. Renee intervened so Barbara could continue her tour. She removed Sam's pills from her purse and shook the plastic container at him.

"If you don't calm down, you'll have a heart attack."

"Shut up, Renee!" blurted her husband. "I can't hear what Barbara's saying."

"Notice the four layers of papaya shaped breasts on *Artemis*, the goddess of the moon. Here she's depicted as the nurturing mother," said Barbara, moving forward.

"This mosaic was found in Cicero's villa in Pompeii. It is composed of a group of strolling musicians. And here is another mosaic, *Portrait of a Woman*. The elegant maiden is wearing a tunic with gold earrings and a necklace."

Carl followed the crowd into the next room. He whispered to Barbara. "You're more beautiful than the woman in that portrait."

"I love you Carl," she murmured, turning to the tourists. "Here we have a reconstruction of the living room in a Roman Villa known as the Atrium. It was used by the family to receive guests. Notice the square opening in the ceiling, the *compluvium*, used not only for ventilation and light, but to allow the rainwater to fill the marble pool, the *impluvium*."

"It's so stuffy in here," uttered Sam. "If I don't get some air soon, I'm going to pass out!"

He staggered toward a Roman sofa and sat down while Renee joined him, complaining about her feet. A security guard arrived to reprimand them for sitting on the furniture in the exhibit.

Barbara intervened, informing the guard that her father needed to rest due to a heart problem.

"Should I call an ambulance?" he asked, noticing that Sam was breathing heavily.

"I'm all right!" stammered Sam, rising from the sofa. He stumbled, almost falling. Carl grabbed him by the arm, leading him back to the sofa.

"I'm awfully dizzy. I need a wheelchair," requested Sam from the guard.

"Get me one too," insisted Renee. "I can hardly walk. Carl, we'll meet you and Barbara at the entrance after she finishes the tour."

Barbara glanced at the security guard, who was talking on his cell phone. She felt relieved when two attendants arrived with wheelchairs to take her parents to the cafeteria for a cold drink.

She said, "Let's culminate the tour by watching a fifteen minute video, *Pompeii: Stories from the Eruption*. Please follow me into the theater."

18

After watching the film about the eruption of Mount Vesuvius, the tourists departed from the theater, thanking Barbara. A few senior citizens lingered to enquire about the health of her missing parents.

A few minutes later they headed toward the entrance to meet Sam and Renee, but there was no sign of them. Carl checked the cafeteria while Barbara paced nervously in front of the vacant information desk.

"Let's go outside to check with the security guard," insisted Barbara, her brow furrowed from anxiety.

Upon leaving the building, they approached the guard at the bottom of the stairs. He told them that when the ambulance arrived, her father demanded that the driver take him to the Alexian Brothers Hospital in Elk Grove Village while her mother followed in the limousine.

"Samuel Havlett requested that you contact his grandchildren, Mark and Kathy, so that he could say goodbye to them. He believes he won't survive the night due to his severe chest pains," informed the guard.

"How long ago did all of this happen?" asked Carl, worried about Sam.

"It must have been around 5:00 0'clock when the ambulance came here. The driver wanted to take him to Northwestern Memorial Hospital, but your father refused to go there."

"Sam's condition could really be serious this time," said Barbara, clutching her purse.

After trying to reach Mark and Kathy on their cell phones without success, Carl and Barbara took a taxi to Wabash and then the Blue Line to Rosemont.

Upon leaving the train station, they caught another taxi to the emergency room of the hospital. The nurse on duty told them that Sam was being monitored by several physicians and that his wife, Renee, was in the waiting room over there.

"Mother," gasped Barbara. "How's Sam doing? The security guard at the museum told us he might not live."

Renee was sprawled out on the sofa reading a novel with her stocking feet propped up on the lounge table and high heels on the floor.

"I shouldn't have worn these shoes," she sighed. "My feet are swollen."

"How's Sam doing?" repeated Barbara, pacing the floor.

"There's nothing wrong with Sam that humility won't cure, but he's too stubborn to admit that he's got a problem. After all Sam's the president of Havlett Industries and has the controlling stock."

"May we see him in the emergency room?" asked Carl, trying to reassure Barbara.

"He's not in there," informed Renee. "He's having a CAT scan now but won't have an MRI until tomorrow morning. They couldn't find anything wrong with his EKG except his heart palpitations. He still needs to have x-rays."

"How awful! I feel so sorry for Sam," said Barbara.

"Don't waste your time worrying about him. He doesn't care about anybody but himself," she said rising from the sofa. She slipped her novel into her handbag and picked up her high heels.

"I'm going to the hotel to watch TV. Then I'm taking a hot bath before dinner. If you want to join me in the dining room, I'd be happy to treat. Why don't you ride along in the limo? Charles can give you a ride home after we eat."

"What about Sam?" asked Barbara. "I feel guilty about leaving him here all night by himself."

"He'll be fine! We go through this routine at least three times a year. Sam suffers from psychosomatic illnesses. He keeps changing doctors whenever he finds out there's nothing wrong with him except his ego."

"But he's taking several medications," said Carl.

"When his doctor refuses to refill his prescriptions, Sam simply finds another doctor. He never tells them how much he drinks and smokes these days," informed Renee.

"I want to check with the nurse in the emergency room before leaving," said Barbara. "I'll be right back."

"Renee, we're both exhausted. We'll skip dinner tonight. Maybe your driver can take us back to our house," requested Carl.

"I'm sorry about the stress Sam's put you through. I didn't want to come here a week early, but he threatened to divorce me if I didn't come with him. Sam's an expert at making threats and holding grudges. He's enraged with Mark for not returning his phone calls."

"Mark's also upset. He doesn't want to work for Sam this summer," commented Carl.

"Oh, that's why Sam's had a knot in his underwear all week," said Renee. "Here comes Barbara."

"You're right, Renee. The doctors haven't finished diagnosing Sam's condition. They want to keep him overnight. They said he's got high blood pressure and a heart murmur."

"What's new? He's had those problems for several years now. Let's get out of this place. I hate the antiseptic smell of hospitals," said Renee.

Carl and Barbara followed her from the waiting room to the parking lot, where the chauffeur stood beside the limousine, holding the door open for them.

"They're keeping Sam overnight for tests and may discharge him tomorrow afternoon," sighed Barbara.

"I see you're reading Steinbeck's *Grapes of Wrath*," said Carl. "It's all about the Great Depression."

"I've been telling Sam for years that our economy's out of whack. I believe we're heading for a bust," commented Renee, shaking her head.

"Carl's been saying the same thing ever since we came back to the states," said Barbara.

"I can't believe the construction going on in the suburbs. Every year expensive homes, shopping centers, and malls are springing up all over. This wild consumerism can't go on forever," asserted Carl.

"Sam's been outsourcing to India for years. He's also doing business with China. His Chinese chemists do meticulous research and are willing to work overtime without extra pay."

19

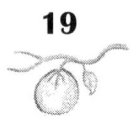

On Monday morning, Carl telephoned Sam's room at the hospital to enquire about his health. He was worried that his father-in-law would be angry and hostile.

"Sam, how are you feeling?" asked Carl, expecting him to slam down the phone.

"I'm not very well," murmured Sam in a hoarse voice. A nurse is taking my blood pressure right now."

"I hope you'll feel better soon," said Carl. "When are you going to be discharged?"

"I don't want to talk now, and I certainly don't want any visitors," he murmured, hanging up the phone.

Carl was disturbed by his response, wondering if Sam really had serious medical problems.

Turning on the computer, he continued with his research. He discovered that the Nepalese Health Ministry had already provided many shamans with training about modern medical practices.

Traditionally the shaman, *dhami-jhankri*, healed his clients by contacting a god or goddess, who assisted him in the performance of an exorcism to rid the sick person of an evil spirit, demon, or witch's spell.

Carl's research was interrupted by a call from Mark, informing him that Corrine had returned to her apartment in Evanston after being discharged from the hospital.

"Grandpa called me several times from the museum yesterday. When I called him back, he refused to answer his phone," explained Mark. "I'm going to call Renee and ask her about what's going on with Sam."

"Let me know what you find out after you talk with her," said Carl, returning to the article.

In 1980 Dr. Badri Raj Pandey had trained over 1,000 shamans in Nepal under the *Family Planning and Maternal Health Project* sponsored by the Nepalese government. The shamans had received specific medical training during their workshops in Kathmandu.

Not only were they equipped to deal with their patients' spiritual and psychological maladies, but they learned to identify and treat diseases such as diarrhea, pneumonia, skin disorders, tuberculosis, and urinary tract infections. The shamans were also given a supply of electrolyte solutions, antibiotics, salves, and birth control pills to distribute to the villagers in the mountains.

Carl was interrupted again by his cell phone ringing.

"Dad, I talked to Renee. She told me Sam was very angry because Kathy and I weren't at the airport to meet him. She also reassured me that he'll be discharged tomorrow since most of his tests are negative although he has high blood pressure and an irregular heartbeat."

"I'm surprised that Renee's so calm about Sam's tests. She won't allow herself to get stressed out," said Carl.

"I've gotta go now, Dad. I need to help Corrine with the laundry and get some groceries."

Carl continued reading the article about the shamans not charging large fees for their services unlike most doctors trained in the west. Shamans with paramedic training were willing to visit patients at their homes even if it meant walking a whole day to get there. They often accepted payment with fruit, vegetables, eggs, or poultry.

Carl answered his cell phone, ringing again on his desk.

"Dad, this is Kathy. Mom called me yesterday at Six Flags and left me a message. I didn't bother to check my phone until this morning because I was staying overnight at Heather's house. During my lunch break, I took a taxi from school to visit Sam in the hospital."

"How's he doing?" asked Carl.

"I just left his room," cried Kathy. "He told me that he might not be able come to my graduation next Sunday. He didn't think his heart could take the strain from all the excitement. The doctors have diagnosed him with a severe heart murmur that was beyond repair.

"He doesn't believe that anybody cares whether he lives or dies. Sam made me feel guilty for not meeting him at the airport. I'm so upset. I can't study for my finals."

"Sam's just trying to manipulate you to get attention," said Carl. "Renee said he's been hospitalized three times this year because he takes too many medications."

"What?" asked Kathy. "But Grandpa looked so pale. He told me that if he died at the hospital, he wanted a military burial at the cemetery in Arlington, Virginia because he was a Korean War Veteran."

"Sam deserves an academy award for his dramatic performances like Burl Ives playing Big Daddy in *Cat on a Hot Tin Roof*."

"You mean Sam's just putting on an act because he wants sympathy?" asked Kathy. "That's disgusting. I've got to study now. I'll talk to you later."

After saying goodbye to his daughter, Carl finished the article about the shamans, who usually gathered the entire community around the sick person while reciting mantras and prayers at the healing ceremony. He paused to think about Sam all alone in the hospital, alienated from everyone in the family, even his only grandson, Mark.

20

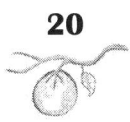

When Barbara returned that evening, she was stressed. Her brow was wrinkled as she paced in the kitchen before collapsing into a chair. She put her hands over her face and sobbed.

"The evening train was packed. I had to stand most of the way. I made the mistake of having Renee's chauffeur, Charles, meet me at the train station in Rosemont and take me to the hospital to see Sam.

"When I walked into his room, Sam could hardly talk. His voice quivered the whole time," continued Barbara. "He sounds like he's dying. Sam begged me to contact a local funeral home and make arrangements for his burial. I felt just awful."

"Sam told Kathy that he wanted a military burial at the cemetery in Arlington, Virginia," said Carl.

"You're kidding," said Barbara, suddenly becoming angry. "What kind of a game is he playing!"

"Renee said the doctors couldn't find anything wrong with him except for his high blood pressure and heart palpitations. They wanted to release him tomorrow, but Sam won't budge. He's staying for more tests," said Carl.

"What?" asked Barbara. "I swear Sam was white as a ghost when I left him."

"As long as he has unlimited insurance, the hospital will accommodate him and continue to run more tests," added

Carl. "I wish we had a local shaman available to perform an exorcism on him!"

Throughout the rest of the week Carl tried to reach Sam at the hospital. His phone rang and rang, but he never answered.

Carl concluded that Sam was getting better although he was making everyone in the family crazy by staying in the hospital a whole week for tests. Kathy came home every night in tears after seeing him. Mark was disgusted with Sam, who refused to talk to him, and Barbara was a nervous wreck after stopping for evening visits.

On Friday Renee called to inform Carl that Sam had been discharged. He was sitting under an umbrella at the swimming pool of the hotel drinking lemonade. Instead of relaxing as the doctors advised him, Sam was phoning his executives and micro-managing every detail of their jobs at Havlett Industries.

Later in the evening when Mark arrived with Corrine to have drinks with him at the pool, Sam once again tried pressuring his grandson to quit Outward Bound and spend the summer working at his laboratory. Mark controlled his temper and avoided giving him a direct answer.

Sam was pacing in front of the pool when Barbara arrived, angry. Renee suggested that they all go out to Yanni's for dinner, but Sam refused go with them. They left him at the pool, flushed with rage and screaming at his lawyer on the telephone, threatening to divorce Renee and disinherit the other family members.

21

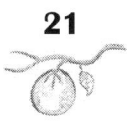

On Saturday morning Renee arrived at the bungalow. Charles parked the limousine in front of the house and opened the door for her. She stepped out of the vehicle, wearing a pink blouse and black slacks with sneakers.

"I'm here to help Barbara prepare food for the party," she shouted, hurrying up the sidewalk.

"How's Sam doing?" called Kathy, turning off the lawn mower. She rushed over to her grandmother and gave her a kiss on the cheek.

"Don't worry about Sam! We just dropped him off at the Arlington Heights Race Track. He's planning to spend the day at the races."

"What?" gasped Kathy. "When I talked to Grandpa, he was making plans for his funeral."

"Sam's been dying for years. Now that he's made his funeral arrangements and changed his will again, he'll be chatting with the jockeys, memorizing the names of the horses, and placing his bets," said Renee, going up the steps to the porch.

"Mother, I'm so glad you came to help me," said Barbara, opening the screen door.

"I love your wicker furniture," said Renee. "When I grew up, we sat on the front porch at my grandmother's house in Virginia for hours just talking and enjoying the countryside. She had a swing like yours that could seat

65

three people. It's too bad no one has time to relax these days. Everybody's too busy making money."

The two women strolled though the hallway into the kitchen and sat down at the table, exchanging recipes and chatting over coffee before making the dough for the homemade pies.

They glanced out the window at Carl working in the back yard. He was handing lights to Mark, who stood on a ladder attaching them to the maple tree

"Dad, I tried to talk to Sam yesterday about not taking any more money for my education, but he exploded and refused to join us at Yannis," said Mark.

"During dinner Renee told us that Sam's company is under a government contract doing research on germ warfare. She said Havlett Industries was supplying lethal chemicals to Saddam Hussein in Iraq, which he used against the Iranians and his own people, the Kurds."

"I'll be damned!" said Carl. "I thought his laboratories were doing genetic research on plants."

"When I agreed to work for him as a biochemist, Sam's company was trying to improve the strains of rice and wheat to feed hungry people in third world countries," said Mark, coming down from the ladder.

"Aren't you guys finished putting up the lights yet?" interrupted Kathy, turning off the lawnmower. "I still have the grass to cut and the bushes to trim."

Carl moved the ladder for his son. They continued stringing lanterns from the maple tree to the garage.

"Iraq has been at war with Iran for several years. Our government is notorious for supporting dictators, and Havlett Industries is right in the thick of it," said Carl.

"I'm more worried about you travelling to Nepal. I understand the Maoists have been creating some real problems there," said Mark.

"Ever since King Birendra made Nepal a constitutional monarchy, the parliament can't get much accomplished. There's constant quarreling among the elected tribal leaders," said Carl.

"Mom's worried that the Maoists might overthrow the monarchy while we are there," added Kathy, resting in the shade of the tree for a few minutes.

"Don't be ridiculous Kathy! The Narayanhiti Palace in Kathmandu has better security than the White House," reassured Mark.

"But, there was a prediction by a yogi made centuries ago when Pritivi Narayan Shah was the first king of the Shah dynasty," replied Carl.

"He was eating curds when a yogi begged him for food. The king was annoyed by the appearance of the unkempt beggar and insulted him.

"The enraged yogi revealed himself as an incarnation of Vishnu, *Goraknath*. He cursed the king, informing him that the Shah dynasty would end after twelve generations," reiterated Carl.

"There are only two generations left. If something happens to Birendra, his son, Prince Dipendra, will become the king," said Mark. "That leaves only one generation left to rule the country."

"When I was in Kathmandu in 1976 a yogi was arrested at the Taleju Temple. He predicted that five-year-old Prince Dipendra would someday murder his parents," replied Carl.

"This is the 21st century. I can't understand how you guys can believe such nonsense," said Kathy, starting the lawn mower to finish the backyard.

Carl and Mark worked diligently propping up the rented tent, which could seat 50 people. Afterwards they set up card tables and chairs.

Barbara opened the patio door and shouted, "Carl, put the coffee urn in the tent. You'll need an extension cord from the garage."

She returned to the kitchen where Renee was removing a lemon meringue pie from the oven. She placed it beside the apple, rhubarb, and cherry pies on the table.

"I can help with the vegetables," said Renee, arranging them on silver trays.

"The grilled chicken, roasted potatoes, and flat Italian beans are being catered by Valli's on Golf Road," said Barbara, inviting her mother to stay for dinner.

"I can't stay. Sam already made reservations at Shaw's Crab House in Schaumburg. I've got to go now," said Renee, removing her apron. "I want Charles to take me shopping at Woodfield Mall this afternoon before we go to dinner."

Barbara walked her mother to the front door and followed her down the sidewalk where the limousine was parked.

"Commencement begins at the high school at 2:00 pm tomorrow. Meet us at the entrance by 1:30. Kathy has to be there early to get her cap and gown."

"I'll be back here early tomorrow morning. I'll tell Sam to be there on time. I've got the address of the school here in my purse somewhere. He's planning to play 18 holes of golf before the graduation," said Renee, waving as she hurried down the sidewalk.

Barbara waited for the limousine to depart before returning to the kitchen.

22

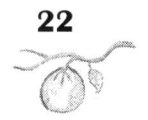

On Sunday everyone got up early to do last minute chores. Barbara was busy in the kitchen putting the hams in the oven and adding the final touches to the potato salad. Carl entered the kitchen yawning and scratching his chest, wearing only his boxer shorts.

"There's that strange bird landing again in our maple tree," announced Barbara. "It gives me the creeps."

"Sharon Schliemann had a dream about a bluebird before she fell from the mountain. She panicked believing a water buffalo was attacking her on the trail.

"It happened during the eighth day of the Hindu Festival, *Dasain*, when thousands of water buffaloes are sacrificed to the Mother Goddess," he said.

"Carl! That bluebird's attacking our hummingbird!" screamed Barbara, rushing out of the kitchen and waving her hands at the predator, swooping down with sharp claws and pecking its prey.

"Stop that!" screamed Barbara, watching the bluebird fly into the maple tree. She sobbed as she picked up the lifeless humming bird.

"Nature can be cruel," murmured Carl, attempting to console her.

"Now what's that noise? It's the doorbell," she cried, handing the dead bird to Carl to bury in the backyard before rushing into the house.

When Carl returned to the kitchen he was surprised Renee was standing there, wearing an ebony sheath dress, accentuated by a diamond necklace. She was helping Barbara insert grapes into the Jell-O molds while Kathy was placing soda, beer, and water bottles into a cooler.

"How's Sam doing this morning?" asked Carl, standing beside them in his shorts.

"He's golfing, but he promised to meet us at the high school later," said Renee, glancing at his hairy chest, legs, and barefeet.

"Excuse me. I'm going to buy more ice for the coolers at the filling station," said Carl, reaching for his wallet and keys on the desk.

A half hour later, he returned through the front door carrying bags of ice. Carl noticed Barbara gliding down the stairs in her toeless sandals. She wore a peach dress with a pearl necklace.

"You're gorgeous," he blurted, enchanted by the scent of her perfume.

"Don't tell me you went to the store in your shorts?" asked Barbara, giving him a kiss on the cheek. She winced at the stubble of his beard. "You're hairy like King Kong. You need to shave."

"Carl set down the bags of ice and scratched his chest like an ape. He grunted before departing for the kitchen.

"Here comes Kathy," said Renee, entering into the hall. "Don't you just love her lavender gown? Where did you get that golden locket?"

"It's a graduation present from Mom and Dad," she said, high heeling down the steps.

70

Carl returned and darted up the stairs, startled by his son buttoning his shirt. "Why Mark? I thought you were spending the night with Corrine at her place in Evanston."

"I got back at 5:30 this morning. I wanted to help you guys with the party, but I fell back to sleep."

Fifteen minutes later Carl came down the stairs, wearing a white shirt, and black slacks. His family was waiting for him on the porch.

"It looks like rain," he said glancing up at the sky where gray clouds were gathering. "I'll get the umbrellas."

"We'll meet you at the limo," said Renee, leading the way down the sidewalk.

A few minutes later Carl entered the limousine with the umbrellas and sat down next to Mark.

"What about Corrine?" asked Renee. "I hope she's recovered from her illness."

"She agreed to meet us at the high school," said Mark,

As they drove along, Kathy asked, "Would you guys mind if I rehearse my speech? I'm nervous about giving it in the field house."

Everyone was silent as they continued toward the high school, listening to her speech about global warming.

23

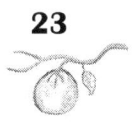

Upon their arrival at the high school, everyone departed from the limousine. They glanced up at the sun receding behind the clouds.

"It's going to rain," announced Carl. "Those clouds look like a herd of elephants in the jungle."

"Do you remember the movie, *Elephant Walk*? It took place in Ceylon," said Barbara. "The elephants actually entered the mansion and terrified Elizabeth Taylor."

"I'm going to get my cap and gown. I don't want to be late for our class picture. I'll look for you in the eighth row on the right side of the field house," said Kathy, hurrying toward the entrance.

"There's Corrine coming out of that taxi. Isn't she beautiful in that yellow dress? I'll see you guys later," said Mark, excusing himself.

"Wait a minute," shouted Barbara, reaching into her purse. "Mark, here are your tickets."

"Sam should be arriving any minute," said Renee, checking her watch. "Carl, I understand you're leaving tomorrow on the evening flight to do research on shamanism. What is a shaman? Aren't they witchdoctors?"

"You're on the right track," said Carl, explaining that the shaman is a faith healer who goes into a trance, after being possessed by a god or goddess. They help him to diagnose illnesses and exorcise evil spirits.

"There's also a psychological component involved in healing," added Barbara. "The sick person must trust the shaman's ability to cure him."

"I'd be scared to death to even go near a shaman," shuddered Renee. "Did you know anyone who was possessed by evil spirits, Carl?"

Carl informed her that he saw Nigel Porter at the Taleju Temple in Kathmandu holding the severed head of a goat during the animal sacrifices. The eight-year-old boy was dancing in a pool of blood.

After the death of his brother, Nigel was taken to St. Xavier's School where Father Kent was his guardian. During a fit of rage, the boy tore up his bedroom before he was sedated by a doctor. At that time the priest claimed Nigel had the classical symptoms of a demonic possession.

"I feel sorry for that poor child," said Renee, glancing at her watch. "I hope Sam won't be late."

"His mother, Margaret Porter, believed Nigel was possessed by demons. She brought him to Nepal with the intention of having a shaman perform an exorcism on him.

"A yogi rescued him from the coven and brought him to the Limbu Shaman, who expelled the demons from him. For the past twenty-four years Nigel has been living as a Buddhist monk in a monastery."

"What a story," sighed Renee. "Look! There's Sam coming out of that taxi!"

Sam hurried toward them carrying his golf clubs. He was wearing a baseball cap, white slacks, and golf shoes.

"Sam! Sam! We're over here!" shouted Renee, rushing toward her husband with Barbara and Carl following. "What are you doing with those clubs?"

"The insane clerk at the country club promised to have a limo waiting for me, but the driver never showed up. I didn't have time to change. I had to take a cab," blurted Sam, flushed.

"We better go right to the field house" suggested Carl, leading the way down the crowded sidewalk.

"I never had time to even take a shower. That stupid taxi driver didn't know where he was going. It took him a whole hour to get here," he bellowed.

All heads turned toward Sam dressed for golf with his clubs. The parents, children, and relatives of the graduates hurried past him, amused by his outfit.

At the entrance, a faculty member stopped Sam, telling him he couldn't bring his clubs into the field house. However, he allowed Barbara and Renee to enter.

Sam held up the line shouting so that he got the attention of the physical education teacher, who was helping the crowd locate their seats.

Carl explained Sam's predicament to the teacher, who led them down the hallway to his office, where he locked up the clubs. He agreed to meet them there after the ceremony to retrieve them.

24

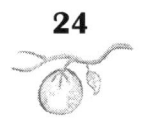

Carl and Sam entered the noisy field house where the guests were being seated in folding chairs. They finally located Barbara and Renee in the eighth row, where they were chatting with Mark and Corrine.

"I'll be damned! At last I get to say a few words to the prodigal son," blurted Sam, insisting that Renee trade seats with him so he could sit next to Mark.

"I'm not budging, Sam," said Renee, defying him.

"You don't expect me to sit next this imposter," asserted Sam, scowling at Carl. "He claims to be an anthropologist, but he's really my golf caddy."

"Sam! That's rude of you!" gasped Renee, yielding to his request to trade seats to keep the peace.

Carl ignored Sam's lame attempt to humiliate him. Sam plopped down next to Mark, trying to persuade his grandson to accept his job offer at Havlett Industries.

Mark squirmed, embarrassed by his grandfather's booming voice. He felt trapped until Corrine rose from her chair, insisting she needed to use the restroom. She and Mark excused themselves, leaving Sam bewildered.

"What's wrong with them?" he asked, annoyed.

"Nothing, but there's something wrong with you," snapped Renee. "I wish you'd take off that ugly golf cap. It's wet with perspiration!"

"I can't stand that skinny bitch," said Sam. "Corrine controls Mark like a goddamn puppy on a leash."

"Sam, there are children sitting behind us," asserted Barbara, frowning because of his vulgar language.

"I'm sure they've heard worse on their playground," uttered Sam, glancing at the agitated parents.

"If we use naughty words, our Mommy gets mad at us," said the little boy.

"She tells our daddy, and he won't let us watch TV," added his older sister.

Sam was about to call them rude little bastards, but he was interrupted by the principal, who was speaking into the microphone.

"Good afternoon parents and guests. Welcome to Rolling Meadows Graduating Class of 2001," he said, requesting everyone to stand while the color guard entered with the flags.

The faculty came down the aisle, followed by 510 graduates in their purple caps and gowns. They filed into the rows in front of the stage as the band played *Pomp and Circumstance*. The principal led the students and guests while they recited the Pledge of Alliance.

During the singing of the *National Anthem* the crowd murmured, alarmed by the thunder and the hail pelting the roof of the field house while the lights flickered.

The principal returned to the microphone and pointed out the exits in case of an emergency. He then welcomed the choir, who sang *Goodbye, Old Friend*. After a round of applause, he introduced the commencement speaker, Michael Brown PhD, from Harvard University.

"Good afternoon parents, relatives, and friends of the graduates. I am privileged to be able to speak to you today about Howard Gardner, a professor of Cognition and Education at Harvard Graduate School of Education. He is known for his theory of *Multiple Intelligences*, which is my topic for today.

"Gardener is a pioneer in this field. His thesis is that human beings learn and process information in different ways. Therefore, he challenges our current system of measuring intelligence by limited IQ tests. He simply states that each individual reveals levels of different intelligences based upon his life experiences and training.

"In 1999 Gardener listed eight intelligences grounded in biological research of the brain. They include: linguistic, logic-mathematical, musical, spatial, bodily-kinesthetic, naturalist, interpersonal & intrapersonal He is currently working on a ninth, existential intelligence."

The audience was mesmerized by Brown's speech. He gave examples of how current graduates were unable to think creatively outside the box in spite of their ability to write papers and pass exams since the focus was on linguistic intelligence at the expense of the others.

Brown pointed out that the crisis was that numerous students with advanced degrees were unable to solve problems through logic and reasoning because of ignorance of the multiple intelligences model. He encouraged the students of the future, to rebel against stagnant institutions which foster mediocrity and preservation of the status quo.

He claimed the United States was falling behind other nations especially China and India because of the lack of emphasis on logic-mathematical, naturalist, and spacial intelligences. As a result of this deficiency the U.S has been importing doctors, scientists, and engineers from other countries to fill the gap rather than training our students in these professions.

Michael Brown insisted there was a general suppression of accurate research on global warming and alternative energy sources due to the oil companies and the automobile industries controlling the Federal Government by lobbying and earmarks.

"I predict that oil dependency will lead to a war in the Middle East, and there will be an international economic crisis equivalent to the Great Depression. Thank you for your attentiveness. You've been a great audience," concluded Michael Brown.

The graduates gave the speaker a standing ovation while most of the parents and guests were bewildered by his attack on the status quo.

"That speaker's a communist," blurted Sam, refusing to stand up or clap. "He should be arrested and thrown into jail for undermining the foundations of our society. He wants our young people to rebel and destroy our democracy. That fool doesn't know that the United States is the most powerful nation in the world!"

"Sam, calm down," insisted Renee. "You're going to have a stroke."

"That asshole is out to ruin this country. He has no right calling our institutions stagnant! I've worked hard to make Havlett Industries a Fortune 500 Company!"

"Daddy, that man's using dirty words again!" blurted the little girl.

The girl's father rose from his chair threatening to call the police if Sam didn't control himself.

"Go ahead arrest me. Put me in handcuffs. Take me to jail because I'm defending our country," uttered Sam, his face flushed and fists clenched.

25

The principal returned to the podium. "Ladies and Gentlemen, may I have your attention please. I now want to introduce the valedictorian of 2001's graduating class, Kathleen Marie Brecht. I'm proud to announce that Ms. Brecht has received a four year full tuition scholarship to Carthage College in Wisconsin, where she intends to major in paleontology."

"That's my granddaughter. If it weren't for me, she wouldn't be on that stage today!" blurted Sam, waiting for the applauding to stop.

"Oh my God! Kathy got a full scholarship! I can't believe it!" exclaimed Barbara.

"What a surprise!" added Carl. "I thought she was only getting a partial scholarship."

Kathy crossed the stage, her black hair cascading over her shoulders. She stepped in front of the microphone.

"I am very grateful for the privilege of speaking to the Class of 2001, and their guests present in the field house today. I want to thank the faculty for their support over the past four years at Rolling Meadows. Most of all I want to thank my parents and family in the eighth row. Will you please stand up!"said Kathy, commenting that she was stunned by the news of the four year scholarship.

Everyone applauded and then the audience burst into laughter as Sam waved his yellow golf cap in the air.

"I forgot to mention that my grandfather, Samuel Havlett, arrived from the golf course this morning, carrying his golf clubs. You may have heard him shouting in the hallway because he wasn't allowed to bring them into the field house."

Once again the audience burst into laughter.

"My talk today is entitled, *The Crisis in the Nepal Himalayas.* As you know Nepal is the home of Mt. Everest, the highest peak in the world. Sir Edmund Hilary from New Zealand and Tensing Sherpa were the first to climb Everest in 1953. Hillary was recently featured in *Newsweek* commenting about the severe problem of debris left behind by trekkers in the mountains, which is polluting the streams and contaminating the drinking water.

"Most of you are aware that the United States is responsible for the greatest amount of carbon monoxide emission in the world today. China is the second largest polluter while India ranks third. Unfortunately, the Himalayan Kingdom of Nepal is sandwiched between these two polluting giants.

"The glaciers in the Himalayas are gradually melting due to industrial pollution from factories bordering this country. For several years now climatologists have observed a four mile black cloud, hovering over the Himalayas. This cloud is the direct result of smoke drifting into the Himalayas from cow dung fires, used by millions of villagers for cooking in the rural areas of Nepal, India, and China. The effect is the melting of the glaciers, which serve as natural dams.

"At a lower altitude there is extensive deforestation and overgrazing by sheep, goats, buffalo, cattle, and yaks. The annual burning of the mountains by the dozens of villagers contributes to the destruction of the vegetation and leads to soil erosion.

"The worst devastation takes place during the annual monsoon season when the mountains collapse, since the glaciers no longer hold back the water due to melting. The result is that thousands of people are left homeless due to flooding throughout South Asia.

"The jungles and forests, which were once a natural barrier, absorbing the silt from the annual erosion of the foothills, are gradually being destroyed by farmers. This includes the destruction of habitats of rhinoceros, elephants, tigers, and crocodiles.

"If the glaciers continue to melt at the current rate, climatologists predict that the bread basket in the plains of Nepal, India, Pakistan, and Bangladesh will be ruined by silting and flooding within the next ten years, resulting in famine and starvation."

Kathy culminated her speech by recommending that the universities of the world provide scholarships for engineers, forest rangers, and conservationists to confront the problem of the global warming at the grass roots level in the Himalayas.

The audience gave her a standing ovation. Kathy stood at the podium, grateful for their response.

The principal congratulated Kathy before announcing the names of the graduates. After an hour of handing out the diplomas, the ceremony came to an end with the graduates shouting, cheering, and throwing their caps toward the ceiling. Within a few minutes everyone was leaving the field house.

"Charles will be waiting for us at the limo," informed Renee, following the crowd past the cafeteria.

"Wait a minute! I forgot to get my golf clubs," announced Sam. "I'll be right back."

26

As the families and guests left the high school, the cloudburst had subsided, leaving the grass wet and puddles glistening. Charles held the door to the limousine while Renee entered followed by the others.

"Where's Grandpa? He should've been back by now?" said Kathy glancing at her watch.

"I'll go find him," said Mark, dashing toward the building. After fifteen minutes, he returned with Sam and carrying his golf clubs.

"I couldn't find that asshole gym teacher, who locked up my clubs. I had to search high and low for a custodian. If Mark hadn't helped me, I'd still be searching for someone to unlock the door," shouted Sam, observing his grandson put the clubs into the trunk.

"Enough of your ranting and raving," asserted Renee. "We don't want to hear any more about it."

Sam ignored his wife's remark and continued with a litany of criticisms about Michael Brown's speech, all the way back to the bungalow.

When the driver parked the limousine in front of the house, everyone was eager to escape from Sam. Carl was the first to leave, going directly to the porch where his parents were sitting on the swing.

"Sorry we missed Kathy's graduation. There was a gruesome accident on I-94 near the Waukegan exit that slowed us down," said John Brecht.

"We saw a drunken driver behind the wheel of a yellow convertible, weaving in and out of traffic. It was horrifying to watch a semi-truck smash into the convertible and crush the driver and his girl friend to death! The stunned semi-driver pulled over and stumbled out of the cab," said Emily Brecht, wiping her tears with a handkerchief.

"We were delayed near the accident for two hours. I told the police about everything that we saw. He wrote down every word," sighed John.

"I'm so happy you're here. I've been worried about you. How terrible to witness such an accident! I know if you don't keep up with the traffic in Illinois, you're liable to be run off the road," said Barbara, hugging her in-laws.

"Hello, Emily," bellowed Sam, struggling up the steps to the porch. "How've ya been, John? You haven't aged a bit since Mark's graduation five years ago."

"I just love your coral and turquoise necklace, Emily," said Renee, giving her a hug.

"Barbara gave it to me years ago when she came back from Nepal with hepatitis. Mark was just a baby at the time," said Emily.

"They shouldn't have left Philadelphia," insisted Sam. "Barbara could be living in a mansion instead of this dilapidated shack that ought to be bulldozed. It needs paint and a new roof!"

"You should have heard Kathy's speech," interrupted Renee, changing the subject." It was about global warming in the Himalayas."

"It's too bad we missed it," sighed Emily, giving Kathy a hug and congratulating her.

Barbara gathered the women to help her, leading the procession to the kitchen. After greeting his grandparents, Mark left with Carl to set up more chairs in the backyard.

Sam turned to the only person left on the porch. "John, do you people have TV in Wisconsin?"

"Of course we have TV. We have a satellite dish on our family farm," said John.

"How nice," said Sam. "You must have cows and sheep grazing in your front yard."

"We don't have cows anymore. We rent the land. We tore down the farm house and built ourselves a brick ranch style house. By the way Barbara informed us that you had been hospitalized and were given several tests this week."

"I wouldn't pay attention to Barbara. She dramatizes everything like Renee," said Sam, pacing on the porch.

"I was really worried about Barbara and Carl when they were living in Nepal with all those tropical diseases, especially when she came back with Mark," said John, lighting his pipe. "That was a long time ago."

"I wanted to buy them a house down the block from ours in Philadelphia," said Sam. "They should've never moved here. Carl would've made a fortune working for Havlett Industries."

"Gosh, Sam, you're old enough to know that you can't lead someone else's life for them," insisted John Brecht.

"What do you mean by that?" questioned Sam, flushing with anger. "Just look at this place! I could hire in a crew and get the house fixed up within a week."

"But, Sam, it's not your place to interfere. Carl and Barbara don't want it to be fixed. They like it the way it is. The world would be a better place if we all minded our own business."

"You're naïve, John. You don't understand how the system works. If I had minded my own business, I wouldn't have the controlling interest in Havlett Industries and be the president of the company," he said.

"But you're obviously not happy. What good is it to have everything you want and yet be miserable all of the time?" asked John, holding his pipe.

"Ahh...I'm perfectly happy with my life. I can travel anywhere in the world at any time I want to go," asserted Sam, pacing like a caged lion.

Kathy opened the screen door and came out on the porch. "Mom said to come to the backyard for a glass of lemonade before the guests arrive."

"Here's the band!" announced John, rising from the swing on the porch to watch them park their van.

"I'll show them where they can set up their equipment," said Kathy, going down the steps.

"What the hell's going on here?" asked Sam, following Kathy. "Just look at those guys! They're wearing loose fitting jeans with sandals."

"Their clothes aren't too much different from yours, Sam," laughed John. "You must have been playing golf."

"I...I didn't have time to change," muttered Sam.

Curly introduce himself to Kathy, removing a cello from the van. "I want you guys to meet our drummer, Phil, and our guitar player, Ed. The bald headed guy is Ray. He plays the keyboard."

"Could you gentlemen help us carry the speakers to the back yard? We want to get set up before the guests arrive," requested Curly.

"It's so goddamn humid here after the rain," said Sam. "I hope my golf clubs are safe. They're locked up in the limo. I'm worried that someone might steal them in this slum neighborhood. You must have a lot of trouble with gangs in this part of town."

"Grandpa," reassured Kathy. "We don't have any gangs in Arlington Heights."

"I should go back to the hotel and change my clothes," uttered Sam, looking for an excuse to leave the party.

"Hey man. You look just fine," replied Ed, handing him a speaker. "You're cool in those white golf shoes and that yellow cap."

"*We all live in a yellow submarine, a yellow submarine, a yellow submarine*," laughed Phil. "I love the Beatles."

"I'll carry that speaker to the backyard," said Sam. "My mouth's dry from taking those goddamn meds. I could use a glass of lemonade."

"You're really cool like an ice cube melting on a hot summer day," remarked Curly. "Is that your limo parked over there? I'll bet you're a millionaire."

"Sam's the president of Havlett Industries," said Kathy. He's my grandpa from Philadelphia, and here's my other grandpa from Wisconsin."

"Wow! They've got a lot of Menominee Indians living at the Wisconsin Dells. I've always wanted to go there and smoke their peace pipe," said Phil.

"Come on you guys! We've got to get this equipment set up," shouted Curly. "The guests will be here and we won't be ready."

27

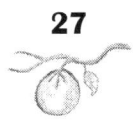

Mark and Corrine came to the front of the house to greet the guests and direct them to the backyard, where the band was playing *Blue Moon*.

Kathy, Carl, and Barbara stood at the entrance of the tent welcoming everyone. They shook hands with the guests and offered them drinks and refreshments.

"I'm so pleased that you'll be studying in Kenosha, Kathy," said her grandfather. "You can come and stay the weekends with us on the farm.

"We missed your father when he went to the University of Pennsylvania to study anthropology," recalled her grandfather. "That was a long time ago."

Kathy informed them a paleontologist was teaching at Carthage College and took his students annually on dinosaur digs in Montana.

"That's exciting," said her grandmother.. You and Mark have grown up so fast."

"I remember being scared to death when your cows chased me in the pasture. I must have been about seven at the time. I loved feeding the chickens and the pigs," said Kathy, smiling at her grandparents.

"Now that you're grown up we hardly ever see you anymore," sighed John. "Who are those guys stumbling towards us. They look like they've been drinking."

"They're graduates from my class, but I never hang out with them because I don't do drugs," said Kathy.

"When I was a child during the Roaring Twenties, people were smoking marijuana and drinking bathtub gin. Then came the Great Depression," added Emily.

"How ya doing, Kat?" uttered a dazed young man stumbling toward them with bloodshot eyes. "Ya got any booze around here?"

"Bret! You don't need any more alcohol. You're already stoned," said Kathy. "I thought your parents were having a party for you at the Wellington."

"They didn't even come to my graduation," he said, frowning. "They went to Paris to buy clothes for my mom's boutique."

"Bret, you're lucky. Your parents bought you a sports car for your graduation," added Brenda. "That goes to show that you they really do love you."

"Shut the fuck up, Brenda. If they cared about me they would've come to my graduation," he said.

"I never see my dad. He lives in California. My mom's got a new boyfriend with two little kids," said Jeff. "They came to the ceremony. Afterwards we had punch and cookies in the cafeteria. That was my party."

"Jeff's mom is real nice. She invited us to spend the afternoon with them at the Brookfield Zoo," giggled Brenda, her eyes bloodshot from smoking hashish. "We decided to come here and hang out with you guys."

"Brenda's dad was at the graduation," said Jeff. "He's a surgeon at Northwest Hospital."

"My dad came to the ceremony, but he had to leave for an emergency at the hospital. I'd rather be living with my mother in New York, but you can't have everything," giggled Brenda.

"You got anything to drink around here?" asked Bret, lighting a Marlboro.

"I'll have one of those," said Jeff, reaching for the pack of cigarettes. "I left mine in your new Mercedes."

"You guys can't drink here because you're not twenty-one. You're already high as kites, but there's plenty of food in the tent," said Kathy.

"We can steal a couple of beers when no one's looking," whispered Brenda, pausing to listen to the band playing Elvis' *You Ain't Nothing But A Hound Dog*.

"Where's the fuckin' food?" asked Bret, glancing around the yard. "I got the munchies."

"This way, Bret," said Brenda, leading the way into the tent. "It's really dark in here."

"I'm worried about them," said Kathy turning toward her alarmed grandparents. "They crashed my party high on drugs. I wish they would leave."

"How are you doing, Grandma?" asked Mark, coming toward them, holding Corrine's hand. "I put up a sign informing the guests to come to the backyard."

"Good idea," said Kathy, excusing herself. "I'm going to check on those guys, who just went into the tent. They're awfully loud. Bret's probably smuggling beers from the cooler behind Dad's back."

"Kathy, don't make such a big deal out of it," advised Mark. "Let them have a few beers. Nobody really cares."

"I don't want to be responsible for them getting into an accident when they leave," she uttered, heading into the tent to tell her father to keep an eye on them.

28

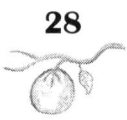

"It's such a pleasure to meet you, Corrine," said John Brecht. "Barbara's told us so much about you. I understand you want to be a social worker."

"I'm doing research on *Alcoholism and Drug Abuse Among the Pueblos* for my thesis," said Corrine. "I'm planning to interview the chief in Taos this summer."

"We visited the Pueblos in New Mexico. Their ancestors were the Anasazi Indians," said Emily Brecht.

"I understand you have a cottage in the Wisconsin Dells," said John Brecht.

"My parents have a summer place on Lake Delton, but they want to buy a house in Colorado," said Corrine.

All heads turned toward the noise coming from the patio as Sam charged across the lawn."

"Mark! Mark! There you are!" Sam shouted, carrying a manila folder. "I've been looking all over for you!"

"Grandpa, sorry I haven't had a chance to talk to you," said Mark, noticing that Sam totally ignored Corrine.

"I brought a contract with me," he insisted, opening the folder. "Just sign here on the dotted line.

Mark glanced over the contract offering him a position as biochemist for the summer at Havlett Industries.

"You mean I'd earn $60,000 for three months of work?" commented Mark.

"That's right!" smiled Sam. "You only have to work weekdays. There's extra pay for overtime and an increase in salary every year."

"When I get my PhD, the starting salary is $150,000 with a $10,000 bonus each year until my six year contract expires," said Mark, amazed by the amount of money.

"That's quite a contract," stated John Brecht "You've got a bright future ahead of you, Mark."

"Don't forget to read about the stipend to finish graduate school," beamed Sam.

"Let me read it," insisted Corrine, peering over Mark's shoulder. "The contract at the university includes tuition, rent, and a $2000 living stipend per month."

"Sam, what kind of research do you do at Havlett Industries?" asked Emily Brecht.

"We used to do genetic engineering to improve the wheat and rice crops of South Asia," said Sam.

"What do you do now in your lab?" asked John Brecht, shifting from one foot to the other.

"I can't disclose that information to the public. We're manufacturing generic brands of pharmaceuticals to keep the cost down for retired people," said Sam.

"Sam's got several contracts to do research from the Federal Government," informed Renee. "Our government's worried that Iraq and Iran might attempt to destroy our crops through germ warfare."

"What kind of research would I be doing in your lab this summer?" asked Mark.

"You'll be developing microbe-resistant crops in case of germ warfare," informed Sam. "You'll also be protecting the Heartland from being attacked by our enemies."

"Wow! Grandpa! Why didn't you tell me this before?" asked Mark, impressed by the offer.

"Mark, you've been too busy taking final exams and nursing your sick girlfriend back to health to be bothered with an old fogey like me," laughed Sam.

"But Mark, you made a decision to continue graduate school without your grandfather's money," said Corrine.

"That's ridiculous!" shouted Sam.

"I'm not Mark's sick girl friend! He asked me to marry him on Friday night. I agreed to accept his proposal, but not until we finish our studies," insisted Corrine.

"Congratulations!" said John Brecht.

Sam was flushed with rage, not knowing what to say. He clenched his fists, listening to everyone congratulating the couple.

"Let me see your diamond. It's gorgeous," said Emily.

"What's all the commotion about?" asked Barbara, arriving with Carl.

"Mark and Corrine are engaged to be married," announced John Brecht.

"Married? Well I'll be darned," said Carl. "Mark, you never said a word about your engagement when we were moving your furniture."

"Congratulations to you both!" boomed Sam wiping the perspiration on his forehead with a handkerchief. "I...I can't understand why you didn't come to the hospital and tell me about your engagement."

"Grandpa, I left you a dozen messages on your cell phone. You never returned my phone calls."

"Mark, I...I'm still not well," he uttered, stumbling. "I feel dizzy. I need to sit down."

"There's nothing wrong with Sam. I talked to his doctor yesterday. The only thing he has to watch is his blood pressure and his heart murmur. They are being controlled with medications," said Renee.

"I think I'm having a reaction to the light," said Sam, squinting at the feeble sun appearing from behind clouds.

"Sam, here's a chair," said Carl, placing it behind him.

"I need to sit down for a few minutes. Get me a glass of water. I have to take my meds," said Sam.

"I hope you have them with you this time," said Renee.

"I've got them here in my pants pocket," he sighed, extracting two plastic bottles. "It says here on the label to avoid direct sunlight or dizziness may occur. I feel like I'm having a stroke," said Sam.

"Do you think we ought to call an ambulance?" asked Emily, alarmed over Sam's heavy breathing.

"Here's a bottle of cool water," said Mark, returning from the cooler in the tent.

After swallowing his pills and taking a sip of water, Sam got attention by coughing loudly.

"Grandpa, I'm sorry I didn't get to the airport to meet you," said Mark, concerned about his health. "I'll take the contract with me and talk it over with Corrine. I'll give you my answer tomorrow morning."

"We're not lingering here another day," announced Sam. "Tomorrow, Renee and I will be leaving on the early flight for Philadelphia."

"Havlett Industries has been producing lethal chemicals and selling them to Iraq for years. Now Sam's biochemists are doing research on germ warfare to destroy the crops of their enemies," stated Renee.

"You promised me you'd keep our government contracts a secret," blurted Sam, leaping from the chair. "Mark, your job is to protect our crops from destruction!"

"Sam, I'll weigh the pros and cons and give you my answer tomorrow," added Mark.

"Tomorrow will be too late!" shouted Sam, rising from his chair with his hands shaking.

"Sam, I hope you don't intend to have a heart attack right here to interrupt Kathy's party," said Renee.

"What do you mean by that, you ugly bitch! You've disclosed confidential information about my contracts. I'm filing for a divorce when we get back to Philadelphia!"

"That's fine with me," uttered Renee, nibbling on a carrot from her paper plate. "Mark should know the truth before he signs papers to work at Havlett Industries."

"Grandpa, I won't work for your company this summer because I don't approve of your research on germ warfare. I don't want to accept any more of your money. I've decided to finish my master's degree without your financial support."

"That's a slap in the face!" shouted Sam. "I've been grooming you for the past five years to take over Havlett Industries. I intended to leave my entire fortune to you! I'm changing my will as soon as I get back to Philadelphia. I've had enough. I'm going back to the hotel," shouted Sam.

"Then go for heaven's sake and leave us alone," said his wife in a perfectly calm voice.

"I've had enough of this family. You can tell Kathy that I'm leaving. I haven't even had a chance to say two words to her. I'm out of here," blurted Sam.

"Mark, I paid for your education for five years at that goddamn university! You owe me, Mark! I'll pursue you wherever you go! You won't escape from me! You've done me wrong and I'll get even with you!"

29

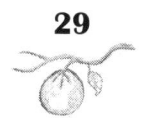

All heads turned toward Sam, who was standing near the entrance of the tent. As he bolted out of the back yard, he shouted, "I'm leaving for the hotel."

"Why are you following me?" asked Sam, glancing over his shoulder as he left the yard.

"Kathy would be disappointed if you left without saying goodbye," said John Brecht. "Here she comes."

"Grandpa! Grandpa! Mom told me you were leaving. Please, don't go now. I want you to meet my friends. They'll be here any minute," said Kathy, taking Sam's arm and leading him toward the band.

"Grandpa, they're playing *Lara's Song* from the movie, *Doctor Zhivago*," said Kathy, offering him a chair next to hers. "Here comes Mom."

"Sam, I could hear you shouting, but I was visting with friends inside the tent," said Barbara. "What's going on?"

"Mark doesn't give a damn about me. He never came to see me in the hospital. No one in this family cares about me," uttered Sam, wallowing in self pity.

"Here's a bottle of water, Sam," said Carl, offering it to him. "Could I get you a plate of food?"

"Get away from me," shouted Sam, turning away from Carl as if he had leprosy. "Barbara, you shouldn't have married that idiot! Just look at this rundown place. It's worse than that disgusting flat you rented at 320 South 42nd

Street when you lived in the slums of Philadelphia."

"Sam, would you like a martini?" asked Barbara. "A drink might calm you down."

"Now you're talking turkey. I haven't had a drink since before going to the hospital," bellowed her father.

"Come to the kitchen with me. It's quiet there and we can talk," said Barbara, turning to Kathy. "Your friends still haven't arrived."

"Mom, don't keep Grandpa in there too long. They'll be here any minute," said Kathy, watching them disappear from the patio into the kitchen.

"Sam, I was worried about your health at the museum last Friday. You did a fine job helping me out because you're an expert on Italian art," reassured Barbara, taking him by the hand and seating him at the kitchen table.

"Somebody complained to the security guard about me. That's when I started having heart palpitations," he gasped, wiping his forehead with a handkerchief.

"Sam, if it wasn't for you I wouldn't be a docent at the Natural History Museum."

"What do you mean?" asked Sam. "I wanted you to finish your MBA at Wharton so you could inherit my business, but you ignored my wishes as if I didn't exist."

"Dad, you and mom took me to Italy several times while I was growing up. I fell in love with Florence, the Uffizi Gallery, and the Santa Maria del Fiore Cathedral."

"Barbara you haven't called me Dad in years," uttered Sam, his voice quivering.

"Dad, you've got to control your temper. Can't you just be ordinary for a change? You don't always have to be the boss. Your responsibilities are making you crazy," said Barbara, mixing her father a martini.

"No thanks, Barbara. I can't have even a single drink," insisted Sam, his hand trembling while he dumped the martini into the sink. "I'm on the wagon. I haven't had a drink or a cigar since I left the hospital."

"That's why you're so angry." said Barbara. "You're used to having cocktails and three or four cigars a day."

"I've quit cold turkey this time. I'm taking medication to stop the cravings for alcohol. The doctor wants me to go to Hazelden in Minnesota to detox. He told me if I go back to my old ways, I'll be dead within a year."

"Dad, come back here and stay with me after you go through treatment. I'm scared to death to live here alone. Carl and Kathy are leaving for Nepal tomorrow, and Mark will be in Colorado."

"Do you really want me here?" asked Sam. "I'm a caged lion without my martinis and cigars."

"Rehab will teach you how to deal with your anger. While you're recovering, you could supervise fixing the roof and painting the house."

"But who will run Havlett Industries while I'm away?" asked Sam, pacing the floor.

"One of your executives can take charge while you're gone," advised Barbara. "You must relax and slow down."

"I've had high blood pressure for years, and I'm tired of taking medications. I shouldn't have gotten so upset with Mark, but he makes me so goddamn mad."

"Dad, you can't control other people," she said.

"I've been angry and resentful for a long time. I need to go to detox," he added. "I don't understand how you can live in this hell hole."

"Our bungalow's a mansion in comparison to the house we had in Pokhara. We lived in a cottage with a tin roof. Our toilet was a hole in the floor. We were fortunate because we had a shower with cold water."

"You gave up everything when you married that worthless anthropologist," sighed Sam. "I know you're in love with Carl, and he really cares about you. I am surprised you don't hate each other after twenty-four years of marriage. I can't stand living with Renee!"

"Going to Nepal changed my life. During the two years I lived there, I saw such stark poverty. I was surprised at the dedication of the medical missionaries, who treated people with typhoid, cholera and leprosy," she said.

"Carl's now involved with a program involving paramedic training for the shamans so they can heal people in remote areas where there are no doctors."

"You've changed, Barbara. You've never been the same since you came back from Nepal with Mark. When Kathy was born, you moved to Chicago. I was heartbroken. I know you left Philadelphia because of me."

"Dad, you've been a successful businessman, but a real failure as a father and grandfather."

"You're right. I have money to burn, but I'm lonely and miserable. I'm angry all the time and addicted to cigars, alcohol, and medications. The doctor told me in that if I don't change my ways, I'll be dead within a year."

"I believe this time you're telling the truth," sighed Barbara, giving her father a hug.

"Renee has stayed with me through thick and thin. I've never told her about my love affairs. They never lasted more than a few months at a time."

"Dad, believe me she knows all about them," said Barbara. "You'll be more relaxed after going to rehab."

"That's why I get so frustrated with everyone. I've been in the hospital three times during the past year. But I always go right back to smoking, drinking, and my medications once I start feeling better," said Sam.

"I've made an appointment for two weeks of treatment beginning the first of June. After that I'll fly back from Minnesota to fix up this place."

"Dad, I'm so proud of you," said Barbara. "We have money saved for the repair work. We won't take a cent from you. Just be here to see that the work gets done."

"I can take you out for dinner every night when you come home from work, Barbara," said Sam.

"That won't be necessary. Let's just live like ordinary people for a change."

"I don't know what that means, Barbara. I've always tried to be extraordinary in everything that I do."

"All that perfectionism and controlling hasn't brought you happiness and it doesn't keep you sober," said Barbara, sitting down with him at the table.

"I hate to admit it, but I'm licked this time. If I go back to drinking and smoking, I'll be dead. My blood pressure was sky high, and I thought I was having a heart attack."

"How about some lemonade?" asked Barbara, removing a pitcher from the refrigerator.

"I shouldn't have threatened to disinherit Mark. I was grooming him to take over my business. I wanted to disinherit you when you married Carl. It's strange how history repeats itself," said Sam.

"It'll keep repeating itself unless you break the cycle. Dad, you have everything but serenity."

"Barbara, you're the only person with enough guts to tell me the truth. Renee's like a stone. She doesn't even talk to me anymore. I swear she has no feelings. At work everyone walks on eggshells when I'm around."

"Dad, you intimidate the hell out of your employees because you brag about your wealth," said Barbara.

Kathy slid open the patio doors and entered the kitchen. "Oh, I didn't mean to interrupt you guys."

"Your mother and I were having a heart to heart talk," said Sam, wiping his eyes with a handkerchief. "I'm coming back to spend some time with her in a few weeks."

"Grandpa will be staying in your room, Kathy. He's going to help me get the house fixed up," said Barbara.

"It's about time," said Kathy. "Cheer up, Grandpa! You look so depressed. All my friends just love your sport shirt and golf cap. They respect you because you don't give a damn what people think. That's why you're so successful."

"Is that what they're saying?" asked Sam. "That's not the whole truth."

"Come on outside and meet my friends. They want to hear all about how you started your company from scratch, without a nickel to your name," said Kathy.

Sam rose from the table and followed Kathy out of the kitchen with Barbara trailing after them.

"Dad, I love you," said Barbara, giving her father a kiss on the cheek in front of the tent.

"I love you too, Barbara. I've got to apologize to Mark," said Sam noticing several guests getting ready to leave.

"You're not going already?" asked Kathy, turning toward her grandparents from Wisconsin.

"We want to get back to Wisconsin before it gets dark. My eyes aren't as good as they used to be for night driving," said Grandpa Brecht shaking hands with Sam and giving Barbara a hug.

"You and Renee have a good flight back to Philadelphia," said Grandma Brecht, giving Kathy a kiss before leaving

30

As the sun set on Arlington Heights, many guests departed from the party. Others lingered listening to the music and dancing under the Japanese lanterns, which illuminated the backyard. All heads turned toward several noisy teenagers arriving late.

"You guys finally got here," said Kathy, introducing her classmates to her grandfather.

"I saw you in the field house with your golf clubs," said Elaine. "I just love your costume. You'd be a lot fun at our Halloween parties."

"The usher ordered me to take my clubs out of the field house," informed Sam. "I wanted to keep them with me."

"I respect you for standing up for your rights. We could all hear you shouting at him," added Fred.

"I'm surprised he didn't call the police to take you to jail in a paddy wagon," said Andrew.

"The police!" blurted Sam. "I'd have called my lawyer and sued the school district."

"You're really cool, Mr. Havlett. I admire you for coming to Kathy's graduation wearing your golf clothes," said Fred. "My father wouldn't have the balls to do it."

"My dad's an attorney. He never goes out of the house unless he's wearing a suit and a tie," claimed Richard. "He's status quo personified."

"Kathy, your grandfather reminds me of Henry David Thoreau," said Marie, removing her glasses. "Everyone made fun of him for being a nonconformist and living at Walden Pond."

"Marie's right although she's a real nerd," agreed Steven. "Mr. Havlett, tell us about how you got rich. Kathy said you're a millionaire."

"Thanks for asking me to talk to you," said Sam. "Well, my father was killed in World War I when I was a child, and my mother died in 1918 from the Influenza. I was raised by my grandparents, George and Ethel Havlett. During the Depression, they sent me to the University of Pennsylvania to get a degree in Business Administration."

Sam told them he worked as a janitor part time at the university because his grandparents insisted he learn the value of money. When they died, he inherited their fortune, which was stock from the British East India Company.

"Grandpa, when did you become the owner of your own business?" asked Kathy.

"After World War II, I founded Havlett Industries. I hired technicians and microbiologists to do research on genetic engineering to improve the rice, and wheat crops and alleviate poverty in India," said Sam, holding the graduates captive for fifteen minutes.

"Thanks for sharing your biography with us," said Marie. "I've never met a grass roots millionaire before."

"You're really cool, Mr. Havlett," said Steven. "I was bored with my graduation party. I got tired of answering the questions of my relatives about my career plans. I never see them except at weddings and funerals."

"Your grandpa's a terrific guy, Kathy. I like him a lot," said Richard. "I didn't expect him to be so down to earth."

Everyone was silent as the band played, *Hey Jude* with the guitar player imitating Paul McCartney.

Renee was surprised that Sam was a hit with the young people. She smiled at him while listening to *Let It Be Me*.

"Would you dance with me?" asked Sam, sitting down next to her and placing his hand on her knee.

"I thought you'd never ask," she said, beaming.

Sam held his wife tightly while dancing to the music. He murmured, "I'm going to Hazelden in Minnesota for a few weeks. When I get out of rehab, I'm staying with Barbara to supervise the remodeling of the house."

Renee was stunned. "Oh, Sam, I'm so proud of you for finally coming to terms with your addiction to alcohol, and medications."

"This fall I thought you and I might go on a cruise to the Greek Islands," suggested Sam. "I always wanted to trace the Voyage of Ulysses."

"Sam, I'd love to go with you, but you've got to promise me that you'll behave. Last time we were on a cruise, you got thrown in jail in Tangiers."

"I...I remember that cruise. I got into a fist fight with the tour guide. I promise I'll be sober the entire trip."

Sam put his cheek next to Renee's and uttered, "I'm sorry for being such an asshole this past year. I'm done with medications, cigars, and booze. I've had enough!"

"I believe you this time," she said, pausing on the dance floor to wipe her tears while he went over to speak with Mark for a few minutes before returning to dance.

"Dad, you won't believe this," said Mark, holding Corrine's hand tightly. "Grandpa actually came over and apologized to me in front of Kathy's friends. I'm still in a state of shock."

"I don't believe Sam's ever apologized to anyone before in his whole life," said Carl turning to ask Barbara to dance with him.

31

Once the band stopped playing at midnight, the remaining guests left, although Sam and Renee lingered. They chatted with Carl and Barbara before departing in the limousine for their hotel.

Carl turned off the patio light and entered the kitchen, where Barbara and Kathy were still putting left overs in the refrigerator.

"Thanks for the wonderful party. I still need to pack my suitcase. I'll see you guys in the morning," said Kathy, giving her parents a hug and leaving to go to bed.

"I never saw Sam have fun before," said Carl, kissing Barbara. "You were marvelous the way you calmed him down. I love you Barbara."

"Thanks, darling," she whispered. "I was surprised that Dad finally came to his senses."

Taking his wife's hand, Carl led her up the stairs to their bedroom. While she was in the bathroom, he removed his clothes, leaving them on the floor.

Carl slid naked onto the bed covering himself with a sheet, his heart beating wildly. Barbara entered the bedroom wearing her pink translucent nightgown and emitting the scent of Este Lauder perfume.

After kissing Barbara tenderly on the lips, Carl caressed her neck and shoulders. She received his kisses, trembling with anticipation. His wife mentioned that the stubble of his beard was scratching her.

"Do you want me to shave?" he asked, enchanted by her perfume and eager to kiss her again.

"No, not now," she whispered, welcoming his tender caresses. "I'll never forget camping with you during the monsoon season when we were trekking in Nepal."

"It took a few days to get use to the rain and the high altitude," he said, kissing her hungrily on the mouth. "We pitched our tent near a stream where the water cascaded over the rocks all night."

"I loved the smell of the pine trees in the forest with the rain dripping from the branches," she gasped as he kissed her again.

Carl recalled another evening when the waterfall was so forceful that it thundered down the mountain, joining the swirling river in the valley near their tent.

Once the intensity of their love making receded, Barbara clung to her husband, her eyes moist with tears. "I'll miss you when you're in Nepal."

"I'll miss you too," he said, kissing her again.

"l will never forget that morning at Gosainkung when the vapors rose from the lake like ghosts. The rising sun awakened the orchid blossoms on the cliffs," said Barbara, reminiscing before falling asleep in Carl's arms.

The next morning Barbara awoke to the ringing of the phone on the nightstand "Oh now who can that be?"

Carl picked up the receiver and handed it to her. "It's Sam. He wants to talk to you."

"What's happening, Dad?" asked Barbara. "Yes, we're planning to meet you at the airport. What? You're about to leave on an early flight to Philadelphia. OK, I'll see you when you come back in couple of weeks. Give my love to Renee. Have a good flight."

After hanging up the phone, Barbara said, "I'm so relieved we don't have to go to the airport. Promise me that you'll be extra careful. I've just had a nightmare."

"I dreamed about a couple strolling through the gardens of the royal palace. They were holding hands and kissing on the bridge over the pond.

"The queen was observing them with disapproval from a window in a tower. She stood near a stained glass window, which had a scene of Sita being kidnapped by Ravana. He took her away in his chariot, drawn by black horses.

"The young lovers strolled toward a statue of the Buddha in the garden below the tower. All of a sudden there were gun shots coming from the garden. The stained glass window in the tower shattered and the queen was screaming.

"That dream really bothers me," uttered Barbara, clinging to her husband and trembling in his arms.

"Do you want me to make love to you?" asked Carl.

"No, I just want to sleep. I'm exhausted," asserted Barbara, annoyed by the sunlight, streaming through the window.

Carl rose from the bed and closed the blinds. He came back to bed and chatted with Barbara for a few minutes until she fell asleep again.

32

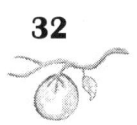

At 10:30 am the phone rang again. This time it was Carl's parents calling to let them know they had arrived safely in Wisconsin. They also wanted to say goodbye to Kathy and Carl before their departure for Nepal.

Around noon Kathy joined her parents in the kitchen for a late breakfast. Afterwards they worked together taking down the tent, putting away the folding chairs, and removing the lights from the tree in the backyard.

"You and Kathy be careful when you're trekking in the mountains," insisted Barbara, helping them fold the tent.

"The Maoists have been very active these past few months. I don't believe the monarchy is doing much to alleviate the poverty in Nepal,"stated Kathy.

"US AID to Nepal was an extravagant waste. In the 1960's our government spent millions of dollars building Himalayan Heights, an isolated American community in Kathmandu, to accommodate agricultural experts, their wives, and children," said Carl. "The experts accomplished very little since they didn't know anything about planting rice or raising water buffaloes."

"John F. Kennedy sent the first group of Peace Corps volunteers to Nepal in 1962," added Carl. "There are rumors that the current volunteers may have to leave the country due to the Maoists activity in the rural areas.

"The wealthy land owners and aristocrats are fearful of the Maoists. They want King Birendra to summon the army and exterminate them," he said, carrying the remaining folding chairs into the garage.

"King Birendra is peace loving. That's why the people love him," added Kathy, helping her mother carry a table.

"The king wants the Prime Minister, M.P. Koirala, to negotiate with the Maoists and solve their differences," said Carl, relieved that everything was finally put away.

After cleaning the yard and carrying the garbage bags to the alley, they returned to the house for a lunch of leftovers from the party.

Barbara spent the afternoon cleaning the house while Kathy and Carl packed their suitcases. While he answered e-mails, and wrote checks for the bills, she chatted on her cell phone for hours saying goodbye to her friends and classmates.

That evening, Barbara drove them to O'Hare. She parked the Honda in the lot. After checking in their luggage, she strolled with Carl and Kathy to the gate of Air India. After many hugs and kisses, she watched them board the plane with tears in her eyes.

Once the plane departed from the runway, Barbara left, sobbing all the way back to Arlington Heights. Upon entering the empty house, she turned on every light, pacing until she turned on the 10:00 pm news.

33

While the passengers were boarding the plane, the flight attendant, Shanta Gupta, glanced at their boarding passes and directed them to the center of the jumbo jet where six seats stretched across the middle of the plane with two more on each side of the aisles.

The flight was filled with Indian passengers wearing business suits, women in saris, anxious children, and bearded Sikhs with turbans.

After they located their seats, Carl and Kathy fastened their seats belts, glancing out the window at the ground crew loading the luggage.

"We didn't have much time to talk at the party," said Kathy. "It's a relief to be leaving Chicago."

"I know what you mean. The change of pace will do us good," said Carl.

"Dad, I'm just exhausted. These past few weeks have been so hectic with final exams. I read in the newspaper that the Crown Prince Dipendra studied at Eaton."

"His father, King Birendra, went there. He also did graduate work at the University of Tokyo and then at Harvard," said Carl.

"The newspaper said Dipendra went to a military academy before he left to study in England," said Kathy.

"That academy is eight miles north of Kathmandu near Budhanilkantha, where a large statue of Vishnu is submerged under water. The sleeping image of the deity rests on the cosmic snake, Ananta.

"According to a legend Vishnu was unable to save the polluted oceans from destruction, so he changed into Shiva. Upon drinking the poison from the polluted oceans, his throat turned blue.

"After penetrating the mountain near Trisuli with his trident and drinking the water, Shiva reclined in the mountainous lake at Gosainkund to rest, where he changed back into Vishnu," said Carl.

"I can't believe that people still believe in those myths these days," said Kathy.

"When Dipendra was studying at the academy, he wasn't allowed to see the image of the sleeping Vishnu."

"Why not, Dad?" asked Kathy.

"The kings of the Shah Dynasty all claimed to be incarnations of Vishnu and were forbidden to look at their own image in the pond or they would die," said Carl.

"What about Prince Dipendra. Did he ever see his image reflected in the pond?" asked his daughter.

"He ignored the prohibition and visited the shrine with his body guard on several occasions," said her father. "He purposely glanced at his reflection in the water, which horrified the priests at the shrine. They were afraid the prince would be struck dead, and they would be blamed by the royal family for his death."

"That's nothing but superstition if you ask me," said Kathy, frowning.

"The Nepalese believe that the king is an incarnation of Vishnu, which is similar to the Divine Right of Kings, believed for many centuries by Europeans. They claimed their authority to rule was God's will," said Carl.

"Many atrocities have been committed in the name of God's will. The massacre of infidels during the Crusades was among them," said Kathy.

Their conversation was interrupted by the pilot. "My name is Chandra Narayan. Welcome aboard Air India Flight 212. The name of our attendant is Shanta Devi. She will go over the rules to make your flight more enjoyable."

"*Namaste*! Good evening ladies and gentlemen. Please be sure that all packages are stowed beneath your seats or secure in the upper chambers," she said, informing them about seat belts, emergency exits, and flotation devices, before wishing the passengers a pleasant flight.

"Now where did we leave off?" asked Carl.

"We were talking about the prince's education."

"Dipendra was trained at the academy by army officers. He was an expert at using weapons including having a Black Belt in karate.

"After finishing his education at Eaton, he returned to Nepal. He often went trekking in the hills and mingled with the ordinary people although he kept his identity secret," added Carl.

"Do you think he'll marry Devyani?" asked Kathy.

"Queen Aishwarya doesn't approve of the marriage. She threatened to withdraw financial support if he marries Devyani and also threatened to put his younger brother, Rajan, on the throne," said Carl.

"She's determined to break up Dipendra and Devyani," said Kathy. "I read that the crown prince drinks heavily, smokes marijuana, and is overweight," said Kathy.

"King Birendra has put him in charge of the summer games scheduled to be held in Kathmandu in June."

"The king might be trying to keep the prince busy so that he won't have time to drink and do drugs," said Kathy, interrupted by a young Indian boy chasing his sister down the aisle of the plane.

"Those children remind me of an incident in India. Some years ago when I was travelling by train, I met a couple with two daughters from the hills of Nepal."

"How old were the girls?" asked Kathy, staring out the window at the clouds that resembled sheep.

Carl told her that Martha was three years old, and Judith five. Neither child spoke a word of English, only Nepali. They were sitting in front of him on the crowded train bound for Kalinagar. At that time Carl was trying to find Nigel, who had been kidnapped by the London Coven and taken to India.

Both of the girls were barefoot, wearing cotton dresses. The older girl was chasing her younger sister down the aisle of the train.

"Judith! Martha! *Yaha chitta, afno mechma basa!* Come here right now and sit down," shouted their bewildered father, who had a beard and long hair.

"Judith! Martha! *Timiharu kaha lukeko chau?"* He asked them where they were hiding as he charged down the aisle in faded jeans and sandals.

"I'm sorry if my children have disturbed you," he said. "My name is James Carlyle. I am a doctor and my wife, Ruth, is a nurse. We've been working as missionaries in the foothills of Nepal for the past six years."

Carl introduced himself, discovering that the couple was from Scotland. James wanted to stay for a second stint as a missionary, but his wife was worried their children were becoming alienated from their own culture and Christian religion. Ruth wanted the girls to attend school and learn to speak English.

The older girl, Martha, stepped into the aisle after pulling her sister's hair. She shouted, *"Timro taukoma dherai sarpaharu chan, kina bhane timi ravana ko chori hau*! Many snakes are living on your head because you are the daughter of Ravana."

Judith, the younger sister, let out a horrific scream and went into a trance.

"Martha! Don't say that!" shouted the alarmed father, rushing toward the girls.

His older daughter screamed at her father in Nepali, "My sister is not a child of God, but a daughter of Ravana, the Demon King."

All heads turned toward the baritone voice coming from Martha. The Indian passengers gasped upon hearing the name, Ravana.

"I was also shocked by the words flowing from Martha's mouth while her sister, Judith, was staring out the window in a trance," said Carl. The incident reminded him of Nigel chasing his brother, Christopher, with a knitting needle on the flight to Kathmandu in 1976."

Judith murmured, "My father is the Demon, Ravana."

Their mother, Ruth, rose from her seat and shouted at them in Nepali, "Judith, Martha, you are daughters of Jesus Christ! May the demons leave you now!"

The girls calmed down instantly and took their seats with their hands folded while their mother read them Biblical passages.

"What a story, Dad! Do you think those children were really possessed by demons?"

"I don't know for sure. What amazed me was the power of their mother's words that settled them down for the rest of the trip."

"As we were leaving the train, Doctor Carlyle asked me if I could help them with their luggage upon reaching Patna. They had to board a ferry and cross the Ganges River before catching a train to Bombay. From there, they planned to take a boat to Scotland. The whole trip would take about a month.

"After sending them on their way, I caught the next train to Kalinagar, where the London Coven had taken Nigel hostage. When I reached my destination, I found out that Indira Gandhi's State of Emergency was going on there.

"I didn't expect to be caught up in the horror of compulsory sterilization in Kalinagar, where Yorg and Myrna had taken Nigel."

"Did you ever hear from Doctor Carlyle?" asked Kathy, concerned about the little girls.

"Yes, I received a letter from him after they got settled in Scotland. He took the girls to their pastor, who was unable to help them. Therefore, he wrote to a Jesuit exorsist in Ireland, requesting him to perform exorcisms on Martha and Judith.

"You don't believe the girls were possessed by demons, do you?" asked Kathy.

"I was skeptical at first, but now I believe they were possessed. Doctor Carlyle told me that a pregnant woman from the village came to their clinic to give birth. She was angry with him and his wife when her infant died two days after being born.

"She blamed the doctor and his wife for killing her baby. Seeking revenge, the mother put a curse on their daughters. A few days after the deranged woman left the clinic, the doctor and his wife noticed that Martha and Judith were behaving strangely so they decided to leave Nepal and return with them to Scotland."

"Wow! That's quite a story, Dad," said Kathy

"I never found out if the Jesuit priest successfully performed an exorcism on the girls or not," said Carl.

34

"I think the Maoists had something to do with the missionaries leaving Nepal," said Kathy, glancing out the window at the dark rain clouds.

"I doubt it. The Maoists usually don't bother people who are helping the villagers. Those missionaries left Nepal because they were concerned about the mental health of their children."

"I don't like the Maoist policy of attacking the police stations and murdering the police," said Kathy.

"It really bothers me that the Maoists are training young children in guerrilla warfare. They teach them to ambush the enemy, strip them, and flee," added Carl.

"Poverty breeds revolution. If people had sufficient food, clothing, and shelter, they wouldn't have to resort to violence," said Kathy.

"That's not always true. There is a lot of violence these days because of alcohol and drug abuse among people from all walks of life, not just the poor," he responded.

"Here comes the Indian stewardess," said Carl, enchanted by her flowing black hair and mango sari.

"May I have a Coke please," requested Kathy, annoyed by her father's interest in the stewardess.

"And what would you like to drink sir?" she asked, smiling at Carl.

"I'll have a tomato juice," said Carl. "What part of India are you from?"

"I grew up in Gujarat" she said. "My name is Lakshmi and I live with my relatives in Mount Prospect, Illinois."

"There's been hostility between the Hindus and Moslems in Gujarat," said Carl. "The Bharatiya Janata Party has its origins in Gujarat, where the nationalist movement originated."

The stewardess agreed with Carl, informing them that the ancient city of Ayodhya in northern India belonged to the Hindus for many centuries, but was taken over by the Muslims. They destroyed the city leaving behind only ruins. The Muslims built a mosque there, which was leveled by militant Hindus from the Shiva Sena.

"I'm fearful that violence will erupt again between the Hindus and the Muslims due to the nationalist movement. Some Hindus even want to drive out the Christians and the Jews from India," said Lakshmi, shaking her head.

Carl mentioned that after Gandhi's death in 1948, the conflict between the Hindus and Muslims intensified, leading to the creation of East and West Pakistan and the massacre of a million people.

"The nationalist movement has united the Hindus, but it has gone too far," said Lakshmi. "The most violent group is Hanuman's Army, trained by fascists."

"It's basically egotism rooted in the belief that one religion is superior to another," asserted Carl.

"What's for dinner?" asked Kathy, weary from listening to the conversation.

"We have vegetable curry or tandori chicken with jasmine rice," said the stewardess, taking their orders.

"Most people in southern India are vegetarians," she commented, pushing her cart forward. "It was so nice to talk to you. I'll be back with your meals shortly."

Carl informed his daughter that many Brahmins in Nepal were strict vegetarians, but most people ate chicken, lamb, or goat. The Newars were fond of water buffalo meat, especially during the Dasain Festival in honor of Durga, the Mother Goddess when thousands of buffaloes were slaughtered.

"Dad, I remember you telling me that your friend Barbara was a strict vegetarian," said Kathy. "Isn't it strange that she has the same name as mom."

"That's right. Barbara Willie and her husband, Angale Lama, were killed in a plane crash with Sir Edmund Hillary's wife and teenage daughter. Their small plane crashed in a wheat field after taking off from the airport in Kathmandu. They were travelling to Angale's estate in eastern Nepal, where he supported a Buddhist monastery."

"How horrible!" sighed Kathy. "When Mark and I were children, you used to tell us a story called, *Barbara and the Wild Boar*. I haven't heard it for years. Do you still remember it?"

Carl told her that Barbara was strolling in the King's Forest in Kathmandu with her boyfriend. All of a sudden a wild boar entered the path several yards away. Jerome panicked. He bolted up the hill and climbed a tree.

Barbara just stood there projecting loving thoughts on the animal. The boar came to a sudden halt six feet in front of her. Rather than attacking her, it turned from the path and darted into the woods.

"What happened to her boyfriend?" asked Kathy.

"Barbara called him to come down from the tree. When she told him about projecting loving thoughts on the boar, Jerome didn't believe that such a thing was possible."

"Dad, do you believe that Barbara was telling the truth?" asked Kathy. "Maybe she made up the story."

"I don't believe she would lie. Barbara was a strict vegetarian. Since she never ate meat, nor wished to harm animals, she had no fear of them," said Carl.

"Barbara had quite an influence on you. Were you in love with her, Dad?" asked Kathy.

"Everyone loved Barbara," said Carl pausing. "I have to admit that she influenced me to become a vegetarian."

"Dad, I remember when you came back from Nepal after doing research. You tried to convince our whole family to become vegetarians."

"I'm sorry about that," said Carl. "I should have learned a lesson from Barbara. When I asked her why she had become a vegetarian, she said that she didn't like the taste of meat and refused to discuss it further."

"Dad, you did just the opposite. You constantly talked about non-violence and animal rights, trying to convert us to vegetarianism," said Kathy.

"Your mother got so angry with me that she threatened to go back to Philadelphia and move in with Sam and Renee. When I saw her packing her bags, I had to redefine my beliefs. She pointed out that I loved animals more than people. I suddenly realized that I was angry and resentful toward human beings who weren't vegetarians," said her father.

The stewardess arrived with their lunches. "Excuse me. Who gets the tandori chicken?" she asked.

"I'll have the vegetable curry," said Kathy. "My Dad has the chicken. He's no longer a strict vegetarian."

"Enjoy your meals," said the stewardess.

"I have a question, Dad. If Barbara Willie had such a non-violent attitude to people and animals, why did she die a violent death in that plane crash?" asked Kathy.

"I really don't know. When the plane crashed in the wheat field in the Kathmandu Valley, everyone aboard died. It's so hard to explain or even understand.

"A Buddhist friend from Hawaii told me that Barbara might have had unresolved karma from her past life, which led to her untimely death," said Carl.

"Do you think that her soul is still wandering up and down the wheat field where that plane crashed?"

"I doubt it. I believe Angale Lama's family performed Buddhist rituals so that the souls of the deceased would continue their journey to their next life."

"Dad, let's talk about it later," said Kathy. "I'm hungry besides they're about to show the movie, *Angels in the Infield.* It's all about angels helping a boy to do incredible things. Even though I don't believe in angels, it's a really good movie."

35

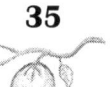

When the flight landed in New Delhi, the passengers were eager to disembark. There were only two jumbo jets in front of them waiting to enter their gates.

"Welcome to the Indira Gandhi International Airport here in Delhi. This is your pilot Chandra Narayan speaking. I hope you had a relaxing flight. Thank you for flying with Air India. Shanta Gupta, your stewardess, has a few words to say to you."

"Good morning. You've been so wonderful on this flight. I want to tell you a little about our airport, named after Indira Gandhi, the only woman ever to become a Prime Minister in India and to serve three successive terms.

"We expect 15 million people to visit Delhi this year. Most people travel here for sight seeing while others come for dental work and surgery for a fraction of the cost they pay for medical procedures in their own countries.

"Our airport is the third largest in the world, and our public transportation system which includes the Delhi Metro, connects the major parts of the city. It will eventually be longer than the Tube in London."

"Dad, I can't believe what's happening here," said Kathy, impressed by the progress.

"About 60% of our people use our air conditioned buses, propelled by energy-efficient compressed natural gas. It's the most popular form of transportation in the city.

"Our information attendants will advise you how to travel efficiently and make bookings at hotels within your price range.

"Now please set your watches. There is a ten and a half hour difference between New Delhi and Chicago. It is now 6:45 am, Tuesday, May 22 here in New Delhi."

"Dad, wasn't Indira Gandhi the daughter of Mahatma Gandhi?" asked Kathy, setting her watch.

"No, Indira was Nehru's daughter. Her father was the first Prime Minister of India. She married a Gandhi."

Carl informed Kathy that Indira would have had a fourth term in office but she was found guilty of election fraud. Instead of resigning from office she declared a State of Emergency in 1975.

Indira got the trains to run on time and government workers to show up for work. She nationalized the press and appointed her son, Sanjay, to be in charge of a family planning program, which eventually got out of control with compulsory sterilization in several communities.

After losing the fourth election Indira Gandhi bounced back. She became Prime Minister again in 1980, but made a fatal mistake by ordering the military to enter the Golden Temple of Amritsar to track down criminals. There was a brutal retaliation by Indira's Sikh body guards, who assassinated her in 1984.

"Dad, everything you said is negative about her. In spite of her mistakes, Indira did a lot of good," said Kathy.

"You're right. She quelled the riots in East Pakistan, which became, Bangladesh, a separate country in 1971."

"The plane has finally stopped," sighed Kathy, listening to the hostess informing them to unfasten their seat belts and gather their hand luggage and parcels.

Everyone filled the aisles and patiently waited to leave the plane. After disembarking, the passengers hurried to catch connecting flights or retrieve their luggage.

The airport was modern and efficient. After obtaining their luggage, Carl and Kathy went through customs. Upon leaving the terminal, they glanced at the long line of taxis and rows of buses, filling with passengers. Some people boarded auto-rickshaws or bicycle rickshaws while others departed in taxis and limousines.

Carl asked a stranger about the location of the Swiss Hotel in Old Delhi. The gentleman with a British accent took them directly to their bus.

Kathy and Carl took their seats among the Indian families with children, relieved by the air conditioning.

"We're lucky we got a seat," said Kathy. "Look, Dad. It's starting to rain."

"The bus is packed," said Carl, taking a deep breath.

There was a horrific clap of thunder and a streak of lightning, followed by a torrential downpour. All heads turned toward the windows, drenched with rain.

The driver used the microphone to reassure the passengers that they were safe on the bus. He started the engine and turned on the windshield wipers.

As the bus pulled away, the passengers chatted, alarmed by another clap of thunder. Everyone murmured when the driver honked the horn to avoid hitting the rickshaws, struggling through the puddles of the flooded road.

The driver's assistant called out the names of the stops on the itinerary, where there was a break for luggage retrieval. Two hours later the bus pulled in front of the Swiss International Hotel in Old Delhi. After getting their luggage, Carl and Kathy hurried toward the entrance.

36

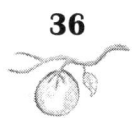

After bringing their luggage to their hotel rooms, Carl and Kathy took a rickshaw to the main street of Old Delhi. They paid the driver and strolled toward the principal mosque of the city, built by Shah Jahan, the emperor responsible for construction of the Taj Mahal. As they approached the sight, they met a young man.

"Good afternoon. My name is Ravi Gupta," he said. "May I be your guide? I'm an archeology student at the university. I have no classes on Tuesday."

Carl introduced himself and Kathy. He chatted with Ravi about the ancient ruins at Harapa and Mohenjadaro along the Indus River before hiring the guide.

"This is the courtyard of the Jama Masjid Mosque, completed in 1656," informed Ravi. "Every Friday 25,000 Muslims gather here at noon to worship. Notice those three domes rising from the roof. The towers flanking the domes are minarets. Please follow me. We'll take the stairs to the entrance of the mosque."

"The steps are very steep," commented Carl. "We're high enough to see what's going on in the courtyard."

"There are several tourists leaving the buses and coming through that main gate," said Kathy.

"The tour guide's speaking in German, using a megaphone," said Carl. "There are Indian students with back packs mingling among the tourists. They must be hawkers selling curios."

"One of the students just bumped into a grey-haired man," mentioned Kathy.

"Why he's snatching his wallet from his back pocket!" blurted Carl. "There's another one reaching for an elderly woman's purse! They're pickpockets working the crowd!"

"Look! Right behind him there's a policeman. He's handcuffing the pickpocket. The other thief is running toward the exit. He ran right past the security guard at the entrance." shouted Kathy.

"I'm sorry you had to witness thieves stealing right here at our most sacred shrine," apologized Ravi.

"What's that building over there?" asked Kathy.

"It's the Red Fort, the palace of Shah Jahan. He moved his capitol from Agra to New Delhi in 1648."

After touring the mosque and the fort, they went to the Lahore Gate and wandered among the craft shops before heading north to the Jain Shrine.

"The Jains are very strict vegetarians," informed Ravi. "Several of them are wearing face masks as they sweep the sidewalks with their brooms. They don't want to injure the ants crawling in front of them."

"After a brief tour of the Jain Temple, they wandered around the outdoor sanctuary for injured birds. Among them were mynahs, parrots, and ducks.

They continued to Esplanade Road, passing a sweet shop, where customers were served purple rice balls, *julebi*, covered with syrup and glasses of steaming tea.

Carl and Kathy observed visitors from different states of India bargaining for gold sold by weight in Hindi, Telegu, Gujarati, and other languages.

Ravi took them into jewelry shops at the Street of the Incomparable Pearl. Afterwards they passed stalls with carpets, leather goods, and aromatic perfumes.

"Here we are at the famous Kinari Bazaar, where you'll find wedding accessories," said the guide pointing to several future brides shopping for red saris and lace veils.

"Over there's another famous sweet shop, called 'Bell Ringer,' where the emperor's elephant used to stop regularly to ring the bell with his long trunk. The shopkeeper would always come out with a treat for both the elephant and the mahout."

The guide led them to Fountain Chowk, where the cascading waterfall offered them relief from the heat. He mentioned that the fountain was near the old police station, where the British massacred the last Mughal Emperor and his children, placing their corpses on display for the public to view during the Mutiny of 1857.

Ravi flagged down a rickshaw, requesting the driver to take his American friends through the bazaar back to the Swiss Hotel. He waved goodbye to Carl and Kathy, thanking them for a crisp twenty dollar bill.

As they travelled in the rickshaw down the lanes and crowded side streets, the driver wove in and out of the traffic, ringing the bell on his rickshaw to warn the pedestrians to step out of the way.

They drove down a side street where prostitutes waved to Carl, trying to encourage the driver to stop. He ignored them moving slowly through the crowded street.

"Dad, those three men over there are carrying an enormous boa constrictor!" exclaimed Kathy. "It reminds me of that movie, *Anaconda*. I hope it doesn't escape."

"Don't worry. They know how to handle that snake," said Carl, amazed by their skill.

"Let's stop at that restaurant," said Kathy. "I'm starving. It looks like there are plenty of seats inside."

Carl requested the rickshaw driver to return in an hour. They entered the restaurant and sat at table next to a Sikh family. The bearded father was sitting across from his wife with their two teenage sons wearing turbans.

"Our house specialty is *tandori* chicken with basmati rice," stated the waiter. "We also have *julebis* and *khir* for dessert with Darjeeling tea."

After placing their order, they began chatting with the Sikh family, who came from the Punjab to visit their relatives in Delhi."

"What's does the word 'Sikh' mean?" asked Kathy.

"It means a disciple who believes in One God and the teaching of *Guru Granth Sahib*, our sacred text," informed Anil Singh, the father.

There conversation was interrupted by the smiling waiter, who set down their steaming plates of rice.

"We believe we are here on earth because of the love of God. Our goal is to seek Him through meditation," stated Anil's wife.

"We don't believe in the teaching from your Bible about turning the other cheek. If we are attacked, we are taught to fight back," said the older son.

"Weren't Sikhs responsible for the assassination of Indira Gandhi?" asked Kathy.

"Yes, that happened 17 years ago," said Anil. "When Indira Gandhi ordered an attack on Sikh militants, they took refuge in the Golden Temple in Amritsar. At that time over 500 people were killed."

"Her bodyguards got revenge for the desecration of the temple by murdering Indira Gandhi. During the retaliation by the Indian Government thousands of our Sikhs were massacred," added Anil. "Most of them were innocent people, who had nothing to do with the assassination."

"Our people have forgotten the incident," said the younger son. "If they remember it, they wouldn't have elected Manmohan Singh to be our Prime Minister.'

Their conversation was interrupted by a crowd in front of the shop. After paying their bill, they followed the Singhs out of the restaurant.

Everyone watched an organ grinder playing *Carnival of Venice* while his monkey danced, wearing a purple hat and a flared red skirt. After whirling around, the monkey changed clothes. He put on a vest and a cowboy hat and amused the crowd by riding an English bulldog.

After the performance, the monkey picked up a tin cup and begged the crowd for money. A few people placed coins in the cup, but most left without giving a donation. The Singh boys each gave a rupee note before departing with their parents.

The disgruntled organ grinder shook his head with disappointment after counting the money. "How can I feed my children?"

Kathy handed him a ten rupee note and said, "We really enjoyed your show."

"*Dhanyavad*," he said, thanking her. "*Om namaha Ganeshaya.* May Lord Ganesh bless you."

The organ grinder picked up the monkey, encouraging him to shake hands with Kathy before she boarded the rickshaw and sat down.

As they were about to depart a beggar using a crutch hobbled toward them. Kathy removed a five rupee note from her purse to give to him.

"Don't give that man any rupees! He's not crippled. He's an imposter," insisted the organ grinder while a crowd gathered to watch the spectacle.

"That poor beggar is wearing a cast with blood stains on it," gasped Kathy. "He can hardly walk."

All heads turned to the policeman pushing his way through the crowd and shouting, "It's against the law to be begging in New Delhi."

The beggar had a grizzly beard and disheveled hair. He wore a black patch over his left eye. He snatched the five rupee note out of Kathy's hand and fled into the crowd.

"Hey you over there," shouted the policeman. "Stop, you won't get away from me this time."

The beggar turned his head squinting at the officer. Unable to see him clearly, he removed the patch covering his eye, lifted his crutch and darted down the street.

"Stop that thief!" shouted the policeman, pushing through the crowd.

The distraught beggar collided into a cart loaded with watermelons, which tumbled to the sidewalk.

"Watch where you're going!" shouted the vendor, alarmed by several melons splitting open on the sidewalk. "Now look what you've done!"

"I wonder if the policeman will catch that beggar?" asked Kathy, noticing barefoot children picking up the split melons and fleeing down the alley.

"I doubt it," said Carl, boarding the rickshaw. "There's never a dull moment here in the bazaar."

A half hour later they arrived at the Swiss Hotel, where they relaxed for several hours at the pool. In the evening they went for a stroll and browsed in the shops near the hotel before retiring.

37

Early the next morning they took a taxi to the Indira Gandhi International Airport. Kathy and Carl hurried toward their gate just in time to board the Royal Nepal Airline's flight destined for Kathmandu. The small jet was filled with numerous Nepalese passengers, tourists, and Indian businessmen. An hour after their plane departed, they approached the mountains of Nepal.

"The Himalayas remind me of grey rhinoceroses. I thought they'd be covered with snow," said Kathy, glancing out the window of the plane.

"The rain has washed away the snow leaving only barren grey peaks," said Carl, thinking about how much he missed Barbara.

Suddenly, there was an unexpected clap of thunder and a streak of lightning, which shook the plane.

"I'm scared," uttered Kathy, seizing her father's hand as the plane vibrated from the air currents.

"Don't worry about the storm," advised a Nepalese passenger, sitting across the aisle from them. "Without the monsoon the rice won't grow in the terraces below."

"May I read you a passage from our sacred text, *The Bhagavad Gita*, 9:19. The verses might calm you down."

"Of course," said Carl, concerned about the turbulence.

"*I Am the heat. I Am the rain; I withhold. I send forth. I Am immortality and death; I Am being and non being, O*

Arjuna. By the way my name is Rishi Lall Shrestha. I'm an accountant for the royal family."

"It's a pleasure to meet you," said Kathy. "I feel better already although I'm still scared."

"I have my office in the royal palace, which is surrounded by 40 acres of land right in the center of Kathmandu. We even have cows, grazing on the premises. The whole area is enclosed by a high brick wall with guards on duty around the clock."

"Tell us a little bit about the royal family," requested Carl. "They've been in the news quite a bit lately."

"I started working at the palace when King Mahendra ruled Nepal. He was the father of our current King Birendra, who married Queen Aishwarya in 1970. Their eldest son, Crown Prince Dipendra, will be thirty years old next month, but he's still not married. He's often seen with his girlfriend, Devyani, at the local restaurants and night clubs," informed Rishi Lall.

"His sister, Princess Shruti, is already married and has two children. His brother, Prince Nirajan, will be coming back from Eton for the summer."

"I read that when Dipendra was studying at Eton, his classmates called him Dippy," commented Kathy. "They teased him because of his strange name, but no one messed with him because he had a black belt in karate."

"His name means the Lamp of Indra. In our mythology Indra was an ancient storm god like Zeus with his lightning bolt," said Rishi Lall.

"I read in the newspaper that Prince Dipendra got into trouble at the university and was almost expelled because he was selling liquor to the students," commented Kathy. "The king and queen bailed him out by flying to England and donating money to the university."

"It's unfortunate how the reporters keep track of every move that Dipendraji makes. He has no privacy," said Rishi Lall, shaking his head with disgust.

"Is it true the prince drinks heavily and smokes hashish and marijuana?" asked Kathy.

"What do you expect? It's the Kali Yuga, the Age of Darkness," said Rishi Lall. "The younger generation is very casual about their use of alcohol and drugs."

"The abuse of drugs is an international problem," added Carl, distracted by the rain splashing against window.

"Do you think the Nepalese government should have stricter regulations on the use of hashish and marijuana?" asked Kathy. "I heard you could buy drugs in the local shops without any problem from the police."

"The police are more concerned about the cocaine and heroin traffic," said Rishi Lall. "Addictive pills are often used by many young people at their rave parties."

As they were talking, the plane began to shudder again from intense wind. The whole cabin vibrated.

Momentarily the lights went out and everyone was in the dark. A few alarmed children screamed while their parents murmured trying to comfort them. Once the lights were restored everyone started chatting about the storm.

"Unfortunately there's a lot of corruption within our society. We have too many self-serving government officials, who don't have the interest of the people at heart.

"Our constitutional monarchy with a quarrelsome parliament hasn't done anything to help the people at the grass roots," complained Rishi Lall. "Many villagers are subsistent farmers barely able to make a living."

"The Maoists are clamoring for representation in the parliament," said Carl. "I understand that King Birendra is loved by the Nepalese people and even by the Maoists."

"The king hasn't been the same since his massive heart attack in 1998. If he should die, his son, Dipendra, will be his successor. The Nepalese are fearful that the prince is not capable of strong leadership."

"What's your opinion of Dipendra?" asked Carl.

"The crown prince has a good heart," said Rishi Lall. "He disguises himself as an ordinary soldier and treks in the mountains, where he listens to the problems of the villagers. He has compassion for the poor.

"Some months ago when he was trekking in eastern Nepal, the Dipendra stayed at the Tengboche Monastery. At that time he met a Buddhist monk, who was born in England and lived at that monastery for the past twenty-four years," said Rishi Lall.

"That monk is Nigel Porter," interrupted Carl. "He was eight-years-old when his brother was murdered in the garden at the Kathmandu Guest House. I was in the garden when his mother, Margaret, collapsed after seeing the corpse of her five-year-old son, Christopher, hanging from the pomelo tree. An ambulance took her to Shanta Bhawan hospital."

"So you know Nigel," said Rishi Lall. "The crown prince brought him to live at the palace several months ago," informed Rishi Lall.

"His mother has been searching for Nigel for many years," stated Carl. "He had been kidnapped long ago by a London coven. I promised Margaret while she was recovering from her nervous breakdown that I would try to find him, but I was unsuccessful."

"Nigel told me that a yogi took him to the Limbu Shaman in eastern Nepal," said Rishi Lall. "The shaman performed an exorcism on him to free his soul from evil spirits. Afterwards he joined the Tengboche Monastery."

"That Limbu Shaman is Moksha," said Carl, surprised. "He will be attending our shaman convention at Bir Hospital with his son, Muktuba."

"Is Nigel still living at the palace?" asked Kathy.

"I believe he's still there. He lives a very quiet life. Nigel spends a lot of time in prayer and meditation. I first met him in April at a party. It's customary for the king and queen to hold a family dinner for all their relatives on the first Friday of every month," said Rishi Lall.

"In fact Crown Prince Dipendra will be hosting the family dinner on June 1st in the Billiards Room across from his apartments on the palace grounds. I've been invited to the dinner. I'm sure Nigel will be there again. If I see him in the near future I will let him know that you're in town. Where will you be staying?"

"My daughter, Kathy, and I are staying at the Kathmandu Guest House. You can leave a message at the desk for us. We'll be attending the shaman convention at Bir Hospital for a whole week."

"That convention is getting a lot of publicity," said Rishi Lall. "The king and queen will be at the opening event with the crown prince at Bir Hospital."

"Do you think Dipendra will marry Devyani? I understand the queen doesn't like her," said Kathy.

"Queen Aishwarya is questioning Devyani's lineage. Her grandfather was Nepalese, but her grandmother was the descendant of a wealthy Maharaja from India.

"The queen doesn't want the prince to marry Devyani. She has picked out a Nepalese bride for him," said Rishi.

Their conversation was interrupted by a stewardess announcing their arrival at the airport.

"Look out the window. You can see the foothills, where our people terraced the mountains centuries ago, and the villagers are planting rice in the flooded paddies.

"There's Bodhnath, our largest Tibetan Buddhist shrine. It wouldn't surprise me if Nigel is there meditating before the image of the Buddha," said Rishi Lall.

"I see the flags fluttering in the wind in spite of the mist. It's still overcast and drizzling," said Kathy. "That domed stupa reminds me of the body of a pregnant woman about to give birth."

"Our country is ready for a rebirth," said Rishi Lall, ponderously. "Nepal has been suffering long enough from the negative karma of our past."

38

After the plane landed at the Tribuwan International Airport in Kathmandu, Carl and Kathy retrieved their luggage and headed toward customs. Rishi Lall was ahead of them in the line arguing with the inspector.

"I must see your passport," said the official.

"Bhima, I've known you for years. Do I really have to show it to you?" asked Rishi Lall. "We've lived in the same neighborhood our whole life."

"I've been ordered to examine every passport and to check the expiration date," insisted Bhima, perspiring from the heat in spite of the whirling fans overhead.

"These are my American friends from Chicago," said Rishi Lall introducing Kathy and Carl. "They're anxious to get to their hotel in Tamel."

Bhima did not acknowledge them, but stamped their passports and handed them back. He insisted that they open their luggage. After rummaging through their belongings, he snapped their suitcases shut and ordered them to depart.

"That man's very rude," blurted Kathy, annoyed by his attitude. "He's angry about something."

"Being a luggage inspector must be a frustrating job," said Carl. "He seems to be under a strain."

"He's very unhappy because his wife had a mental breakdown. She is now living with her parents in Pokhara," informed Rishi Lall.

"Bhima and his four sons live with his sister and her husband with their three children and their aging parents in a crowded house."

"I couldn't stand living with so many people," said Kathy. "They'd get on my nerves."

"They still have the joint family system here in Nepal. However, many couples now live in apartments away from their parents," said Carl, retrieving his luggage and then exchanging traveler's checks into rupees.

As they departed from the airport with their luggage, a group of beggars swarmed them with hands outstretched.

"*Hamilai paisa dinos na*! Give us money!" they demanded in unison with shrill voices. The children had dirty faces, disheveled hair, and scrawny arms.

Kathy felt sorry for them and opened her purse, ready to give the beggars rupees.

"Don't give them any money!" insisted Rishi Lall, yelling at the street urchins. "You'd better leave now, or I'll call the police!"

The barefoot children darted toward a tourist bus filled with grey-haired women looking out the windows. They felt sorry for the children and eagerly handed them twenty rupee notes.

"Why aren't those kids in school?" asked Kathy, noticing a policeman approaching the beggars, which caused them to scatter in different directions.

"Their parents can't afford to pay the monthly fee for their tuition. We don't have free public schools in Nepal although we have many private schools."

"Here's a taxi," said Rishi Lall. A few moments later the driver was putting their luggage in the trunk.

"*Tapai kaha jandai hunuhuncha?* Where are you going?" asked the driver.

"*Waha Tamel jandai hunuhuncha tara ma Rajako Dhawara tira jandai chu.* They're going to the Kathmandu Guest House in Tamel, but I'm going to the Royal Palace," informed Rishi Lall.

As they drove from the airport they passed through Dilli Bazaar, a narrow street crowded with pedestrians shopping, school children in their uniforms, and barefoot porters carrying vegetables in woven baskets, *dokaharu*. The driver slowed down the taxi, beeping his horn at the rickshaw that pulled in front of them.

"Nothing has changed here in Kathmandu," said Carl, smiling at a stray cow snatching a cauliflower from the basket of a shopkeeper.

The angry merchant tried to pull the cauliflower from the cow's mouth, but an elderly woman intervened. She opened her purse and paid the man, scolding him since the cow is an incarnation of the Goddess Lakshmi, the symbol of wealth.

After travelling for another fifteen minutes, the driver turned right on Durbar Marg, the exclusive shopping district leading to the royal palace. A few minutes later the taxi came to a halt. Rishi Lall shook hands with Kathy and Carl, before departing.

As the taxi pulled away, they saw him pass through the guarded gate and ascend the stairs to the main entrance of the Narayanhiti Palace.

They continued down Trideva Marg through the narrow streets of Tamel, crowded with trekkers, tourists, taxis, and rickshaws. After driving through a wrought iron gate, the taxi came to a halt in front of the outdoor café where numerous guests were having lunch at the Kathmandu Guest House.

Carl paid the driver while a porter carried their luggage to the lobby.

39

As they passed through the outdoor cafe, all heads turned toward Carl and Kathy. They couldn't help but overhear the conversation of three tourists seated under a green umbrella, gossiping about the immoral wood carvings on the veranda.

"Mable, just look at that that older man checking into the hotel with that girl. She's young enough to be his daughter," blurted Laura.

"I can't believe, I heard that comment," uttered Kathy. "Those three witches should mind their own business."

"That man looks like John F. Kennedy. He ought to be ashamed of himself. I wouldn't be surprised if he picked up that girl at the airport. She's probably a prostitute," said Mable, adjusting her hearing aid.

"Oh just ignore them, Kathy," said Carl, frowning at the gossiping woman, averting their eyes from the carvings.

"I wished they'd mind their own business," said Kathy. "They're all gaping at the erotic statues of the lions."

"You over there! You ought to be ashamed of yourself travelling with a man old enough to be your grandfather," blurted Roxanne, squinting over her thick glasses.

"He's my father," snapped Kathy, her face flushed.

"That's what they all say," insisted Laura. "The younger generation has no morals."

Kathy and her father hurried past the wood carvings of the rampant lions on the veranda near the entrance.

"Have fun looking at the lions," said Carl, entering the lobby, followed by Kathy.

"Why the nerve of that man," uttered Roxanne, averting her eyes from the lion's erect penis on the nearby column.

"I was shocked by those erotic carvings around those pagoda temples that we saw yesterday. I had to turn my head the other way. Imagine, all those obscene couples having intercourse," said Laura.

"Roxanne, we should complain to the manager to cover up those…those sex organs of the lions on the pillars. They're indecent," sighed Mable. "The Nepalese have no sense of shame!"

"I wouldn't be surprised if they don't have a lot of AIDS and venereal diseases in this country," said Laura.

"You don't think that young girl was telling the truth about that older man being her father, do you?" said Mable, rising from her chair to peek into the lobby. "They're still there at the desk checking into the hotel.

After signing the guest register, Carl and Kathy followed the bellboy with their luggage to their rooms on the second floor.

"Where's the bathroom?" asked Kathy, entering her room opposite her father's. She noticed there was only a sink with a mirror, a dresser, and a bed.

"*Ma angreji bhasha boldaina*. I don't speak English," said the bewildered bellboy, putting down her suitcase.

When he departed, Kathy rushed across the hallway and knocked on the door of her father's room.

"Dad, there's no bathroom in my room," she said, watching her father placing shirts into a dresser drawer.

"Kathy, the bathroom's down the hall. Our rooms are cheaper that way," said Carl.

A few minutes later she came back to her father's room. "Dad, that bathroom's the size of a broom closet. I turned on the shower, but there's no hot water."

"Why don't you just wash your hair in the sink in your room," suggested Carl.

"At least I won't have to worry about lizards this time. There were a half a dozen geckos crawling on the ceiling at our hotel in New Delhi.

"Dad, I'm hungry. Let's get something to eat. I'll meet you in the dining room after I wash and dry my hair. I'll be there in fifteen minutes."

Almost an hour later, Carl glanced up from reading the newspaper, *Rising Nepal*. He noticed that all eyes were focused upon his daughter as she entered the dining room.

Kathy's long black hair cascaded over her shoulders. She wore a low cut orange, sleeveless blouse and blue shorts. Her polished red toe nails protruded from sandals.

The trekkers were enchanted by her appearance, staring with their mouths open; the waiters paused from serving their meals. Even the cooks stepped out of the kitchen to get a glimpse of her, wiping their hands on their aprons.

"I forgot to tell you," announced Carl, agitated by his daughter's outfit." It's not a good idea to wear a sleeveless blouse with shorts. I'd recommend you change into something less revealing."

"Don't be ridiculous, Dad. We're not living in Victorian England," announced Kathy, glancing around the room and smiling at the trekkers and staff.

"But we're in Nepal now," insisted her father. "It's important for us to blend into the culture. We don't want to draw a lot of attention to ourselves. Your outfit's not acceptable. You'll be constantly approached by men."

"You mean they'll try to hit on me?" asked Kathy, noticing that most people were still staring at her.

"Yes, that's exactly what I mean," stated Carl, giving the waiters and cooks a penetrating stare so they'd stop gawking at his daughter and get back to work.

"Order me the cheese sandwich with French Fries, Dad," said his daughter, pushing back her chair. "I'll be back in a few minutes."

Kathy felt uncomfortable and rose from the table, leaving the dining room with everyone watching her.

Ten minutes later she entered the dining room wearing sunglasses and carrying an umbrella. She wore a long sleeve shirt, jeans, and walking shoes. Her hair was in a pony tail. No one recognized her this time.

A few diners glanced toward her, but resumed their conversations. She was no longer a celebrity. Even the waiters only gave her a cursory glance.

During their uneventful lunch, Kathy rummaged through the pages of *Lonely Planet, Nepal*, checking the tourist attractions in the Kathmandu Valley. Carl rose from his chair, paying the waiter and leaving a tip.

"Kathy, I want to show you the garden before we go sightseeing," said Carl, leading her from the lobby.

Kathy followed her father through the double doors into the garden. They walked down the gravel path between the roses and chrysanthemums.

"Over there's the pomelo tree. That's where I saw the corpse of Christopher hanging from a rope in October of 1976," said Carl.

"You told me he was murdered during Dasain when animal sacrifices were offered to the Mother Goddess," stated Kathy.

"That's right. The pomelo tree was blossoming when your mother arrived in the spring of 1977. We sat on that stone bench over there and talked for hours."

Kathy sat down on a bamboo chair in the shade of the tree and unfolded a map. "Why don't we hike to Swayambhu Nath, the Buddhist Shrine? I've heard you talk about it so much over the years."

They both paused upon hearing footsteps on the gravel path. Glancing up, they saw a gray-haired shaman wearing his ritual paraphernalia. His headdress was decorated with a feather, and he had a bandolier of courie shells across his chest. He was carrying a painted drum.

40

"It's Moksha, the Limbu Shaman!" shouted Carl rising from his bamboo chair. "I haven't seen him in twenty-five years! He exorcised demons from Sharon Schliemann's corpse that were tormenting her alcoholic husband, Paul."

"*Namaste, Mokshaji. Tapailai kasto cha?* Hello, Moksha. How are you?" asked Carl, rushing toward him.

"*Malai sanchai cha. Tapai kahile Nepal ma aunu bhaeko ho?* I'm well. When did you come to Nepal?" asked the older shaman.

Moksha shook hands with Carl and bowed to Kathy. As they were chatting in the garden, the doors from the lobby swung open again.

It was Muktuba, the shaman's forty-year-old son. He resembled a Masai warrior charging barefoot down the gravel path, carrying a trident of Shiva. He wore sleigh bells across his muscular chest and a tiger skin loin cloth.

Carl greeted Muktuba, introducing him to Kathy. The younger shaman set down the trident against the tree.

"I'm pleased to meet you. We didn't expect to find you here in the garden, Dr. Brecht," said Muktuba.

"Just call me Carl," he said. "I'm grateful that you'll be attending our shaman convention."

"We arrived at the hotel on Monday," said Muktuba, sitting on the stone bench beneath the tree. "We've been waiting for Margaret Porter. She was supposed to meet us at this hotel, but her plane was delayed due to the weather.

"She hired my father and me to perform exorcisms to put her son Christopher's soul to rest. Margaret believes his ghost is lingering here in the garden," he said.

Moksha, circled the tree examining the flowers and the branches, not paying attention to their conversation.

"Muktuba, what have you been doing since you graduated from the university at Pokhara?" asked Carl.

"I've been helping my father on his farm. He's been teaching me about herbal medicines and how to perform exorcisms for the past five years," he answered.

Moksha interrupted them, requesting everyone to be silent for a few moments. He bent down and picked up the trident and began chanting in Sanskrit.

"What's he saying, Dad?" asked Kathy, puzzled by the strange behavior of the older shaman.

Carl translated, "We worship the Three-Eyed Deity, Shiva, the fragrant one, who grants us prosperity. May He release us from the fear of death like a ripe cucumber falling from a vine, but not from immortality."

"What's Moksha doing with Shiva's trident?" asked Kathy, not understanding the meaning of the prayers.

"He's purifying the tree because there are demons clinging to the branches," commented Muktuba.

"Christopher was only five years old when he was murdered in this tree," added Carl.

"At the time of death, a person's soul leaves the body but hovers over the corpse. It's the duty of the priest to perform rituals for the soul to move on to the next world," added Muktuba, pausing to listen to his father chanting.

"If the family priest doesn't perform the rituals correctly after the cremation of the corpse, the soul won't continue its journey to the next world. That's when shamans are summoned," added Carl. "The ghosts of the dead haunt the relatives if they aren't given a proper funeral."

"*Hera! Tyaha hera! Tyo nilo chara Buddha ko murti tira, udera gayo!*" shouted Moksha, pointing the trident at the statue of the Buddha in front of the prickly pear cacti where a bird had landed.

"What's Moksha saying, Dad?" asked Kathy, noticing dark rain clouds above the garden.

"He said that a bluebird just landed near the statue of the Buddha. It's a sign from the Underworld that Christopher's soul is here in the garden."

"That's nothing but superstition," uttered Kathy. "How could Christopher's soul still be here after so many years?"

"I don't have the answer to your question," said Carl. "What ever happened to Nigel?"

Muktuba informed him that while he was working on his farm twenty-four years ago, a yogi arrived with the eight-year-old boy, who was possessed by several evil spirits. His father performed numerous exorcisms to release Nigel's multiple souls from demonic possession.

"What do you mean by his multiple souls?" asked Kathy, shaking her head with disbelief.

"Nigel was possessed by seven demons. Five of them occupied his sensory souls, which includes sight, smell, taste, sound, and touch. The sixth demon possessed his impression soul, and the seventh his reincarnate soul," informed Moksha.

"Dad, that's impossible. I don't believe we have seven souls," she blurted, alarmed by a crow circling the garden.

All eyes watched the bluebird fly from the statue of the Buddha to a branch of the pomelo tree.

"I've been waiting for a sign from Shiva about the location of the branch where Christopher was murdered. This tree has grown so large since he died that it's been difficult for me to find the exact limb," said Moksha. He spoke in Nepali with his son, Muktuba, translating.

"Yes, that's the branch," uttered Carl, recalling how Christopher was swinging from a rope by the neck when he entered the garden, crowded by spectators that day.

The crow started cawing raucously as it swooped toward the pomelo tree where the bluebird was perched.

Moksha raised the trident of Shiva and shouted at the crow. "*Ravana bahira jau! Tiruntai bahira jau!* Ravana go away. Get out of here now!"

"Ravana is the Demon King that kidnapped Sita," gasped Kathy, trembling at the strident cawing of the crow. She leapt from her chair to get out of the way of the crow swooping down with its talons trying to snatch the bluebird that flew away.

The bewildered crow seized the map with its claws, which Kathy had spread out on a table. It was circling the pomelo tree in the garden.

"That is an inauspicious sign," predicted Muktuba." Our people will mourn like they've never done before in the history of this nation."

Pointing the trident at the crow flying with the map, Moksha recited several mantras. He shouted at his son to stamp his feet and ring the bells on his chest.

"The crow is a messenger of Yama, the Lord of Death," asserted Muktuba. "There will be many deaths and much suffering in Nepal," predicted Moksha.

The crow released the map, which fluttered into the prickly pear cacti behind the Buddha. Moksha rushed to retrieve the map, but it accidentally ripped into two halves.

"Evil things will take place in Kathmandu. Our nation will be divided," predicted Moksha.

"That's ridiculous," criticized Kathy. "It's simply a coincidence that the crow seized the map and it got torn by the thorns of the prickly pears."

"There are no coincidences in this life. Everything happens because of karma," insisted Muktuba.

"Twenty-four years ago, I exorcised the demons from Nigel's souls. Now Margaret Porter has hired us to free Christopher's souls. He is also in bondage and unable to continue his journey to the next world."

"I've had enough of this nonsense. I'm going to the lobby to e-mail mom," said Kathy.

While hurrying down the gravel path, Kathy was attacked by the crow, swooping towards her with its talons. She screamed waving her hands to protect herself.

Moksha rushed toward her, waving the trident at the sinister bird and shouting mantras until it flew away.

Kathy was doubled over, her whole body trembling with fright. Carl rushed down the path and put his arms around his daughter, helping her up.

"I've been trained to examine things scientifically," insisted Kathy, shivering from fright.

"Your lack of faith in the supernatural has caused you suffering. You will endure many hardships during your pilgrimage in our country until you change your attitude," predicted Moksha with his son translating.

"Come back to the garden tonight," requested Muktuba. "You can watch us perform exorcisms to free Christopher's souls from Ravana's demons."

"Margaret Porter sent us a photograph of Christopher along with a box of his clothing. We took them to a Newar artist, who has made an effigy of him. We will bring it to the ceremony at 8:00 pm," said Muktuba.

"We'll see you later. Come on, Kathy. Let's go visit Swayambu Nath," suggested Carl. "It looks like rain. I'll get the umbrella from my room."

41

After leaving the hotel, Carl and Kathy opened their umbrellas and splashed through the puddles, passing through the open gate to the street where empty taxis and rickshaw drivers were waiting for passengers.

They turned south down a vacant street, deserted due to the torrential rain. The tourists and pedestrians had taken refuge in curio shops, restaurants, and bookstores until the storm subsided.

"Dad, I hope you know where you're going?" asked Kathy, noticing a dog shivering in front of a locked door.

They turned right onto Chetrapati, going west for several blocks before arriving at a circular intersection, with streets radiating like spokes on a wheel.

About fifteen minutes later they reached the bridge stretching over the Vishnumati River, where they paused to gaze at the turbulent current flowing south.

"It looks like the rain's finally stopping," said Kathy, collapsing her umbrella "The sun's starting to peek out from behind those clouds."

While standing on the bridge, they observed barefoot women with orange blouses and loose fitting red skirts, carrying woven baskets with seedlings.

"Dad, those women are wading in the water carrying those plants to the flooded field near the river."

"They're returning to the rice paddy to finish planting seedlings by pushing the roots into the mud. Notice the green shoots rising above the water," said Carl.

"They remind me of arrows," said Kathy. "Oh my God! There's a huge snake slithering toward those women."

Carl darted across the bridge and seized loose stones from the footpath which he hurled at the snake.

The women screamed, terrified by the snake swimming toward them. They shouted,"*Sarpa aiyo! Sarpa aiyo!*"

Carl threw more stones at the serpent, confused by the splashing and the ripples of the water in the paddy.

A bold woman with her hair pulled back, removed her machete, *khukari,* from a purple sash and waded through the paddy toward the snake.

Carl threw a final stone at the snake, striking it on the back. The wounded snake writhed before undulating toward the bank, where it slithered into the tall grass.

After inserting the machete into her sash, the women bowed with gratitude to Carl before returning to planting the seedlings with the other women.

"That was a close call," uttered Kathy.

"Every year numerous Nepalese die from snake bites in Nepal," informed Carl. "The shamans at our convention will have a workshop on treating snakebite."

Upon crossing the bridge, they stopped at a temple where a priest was praying before a Shiva Lingam. He was burning incense and reciting the mantra, *Om namaha Shivaya*, I bow to Shiva. Behind the stone lingam was a bronze statue of the Lord of the Dance, *Nata Raja.*

"That statue of Shiva has several snakes on it," observed Kathy. "There's one around his neck, another above his head, and a third around his waist. He even has an earring shaped like a snake."

"The snake is a symbol of male fertility. The cobra circling Shiva's head represents the passage of time."

"Dad, why is Shiva dancing?" asked Kathy, watching the priest circle the three foot lingam.

"Siva's dance symbolizes Creation, Preservation, and Dissolution, which is the cycle of life," said Carl.

The priest stepped forward and offered his guests an oil lamp with a flickering flame. Carl and Kathy stretched out their hands, placing them over the fire for purification. Next he gave them a teaspoon of holy water, which they sipped from their palms.

This was followed by the priest placing a red tika on their foreheads, representing the awakening of the third eye, symbolizing wisdom. Lastly, he gave them each two almonds as a gift, *prasad*.

Carl thanked the temple priest, *pujari,* for allowing them be present during the ceremony and for his blessings.

Before leaving the temple, Kathy said, "I can't understand why God created us with a tendency to do evil and destroy life."

"The innocent die because ignorant people have violated the universal law of karma," responded the priest. "We must always remember, 'As you sow, so shall you reap.'"

"The villagers who don't understand conservation destroy the plants and trees, which eventually leads to the collapse of the mountains," added Kathy.

"That's right innocent people die because of the deforestation and overgrazing of the mountains," said Carl.

"The villagers come to us to pray for the souls of the deceased that are haunting them, but sometimes we can't help them," said the priest. "We don't perform exorcisms."

"That's why the shaman is important. He is a bridge between the soul and its future destiny," said Carl. "Let's go now Kathy. The rain has stopped."

42

"I'm nervous about Moksha and Muktuba performing exorcisms to free Christopher's soul this evening," said Kathy, leaving the temple with her father and heading down the slippery trail.

"The Limbus shamans believe that demons dwell in the sensory souls of the corpse—the eyes, nose, mouth, ears and other apertures of the body," asserted Carl, splashing through a puddle on the trail.

"That seems weird to me," said Kathy.

"When I was young, I didn't believe in the supernatural. Now I'm convinced demonic forces destroy human life. Our shaman friends are worried that Christopher's multiple souls are possessed by poltergeists."

"But Christopher's corpse was buried in London," asserted Kathy.

"Jim Porter flew his son's corpse back to London, where a Requiem Mass was held at St. Paul's Cathedral. Margaret attended the service after she recovered from her breakdown with the help of a psychiatrist."

"You'd think a priest performing a religious service in a cathedral would have been able to put Christopher's soul to rest," added Kathy. "But obviously that didn't happen."

"Moksha was hired to perform exorcisms because Margaret Porter had a dream that Christopher's soul was still in the garden at the Kathmandu Guest House.

"His effigy will be a substitute for the corpse. The shamans believe that Christopher's incarnate soul is clinging to the branches of the pomelo tree, where he died."

"What about his impression soul?" asked Kathy.

"The impression soul dwells on an object that once belonged to the boy. It could be his coat, hat, or a pair of shoes. Muktuba believes that it is in the hotel room where Christopher once stayed with his brother and mother."

"That room is on the second floor near ours. It was shut down by the manager because the guests complained it was haunted by poltergeists," said Carl.

"Dad, that's kind of scary. I mean having our room so close to Christopher's," continued Kathy, noticing a heavy mist settling on the trail.

"Look! The clouds are parting right above the shrine. We'll be able to get a glimpse of Swayambhu Nath, the Self Existent Lord," interrupted her father.

As the clouds drifted away, Kathy was startled by the large eyes peering at her through the mist. They were painted on the four sides of a square block above the domed stupa. A golden steeple soared above the square with colored prayer flags blowing in the wind.

"Those eyes give me the creeps. They're looking right at me," cried Kathy.

"The Limbu Shamans believe in multiple souls, but most Hindus believe in only one soul. Once the shaman exorcises the demons from the soul, it no longer hovers over the corpse but travels to the moon and then goes to the sun for purification. From there the soul travels to heaven until all the good karma is used up before returning to earth to be reborn," said Carl.

"That's nothing but a myth," insisted Kathy, glancing at clouds covering the All Seeing Eyes."

Kathy was startled by the shrill cries of crows soaring over the flooded rice paddies, followed by the rumbling of thunder and lightning.

"Oh my God!" she screamed as lightning struck a tree about a hundred feet in front of them. Her mouth hung open as an enormous branch crashed to the ground.

"I...I shouldn't have doubted your story about the soul's journey," she said, her voice quivering.

"The Tibetan Buddhists believe that the soul must travel for forty-five days before being reincarnated," said Carl.

"I don't want to talk about the supernatural anymore," she said, opening her umbrella.

"We're going to get drenched if we don't find shelter. The wind is terrible," uttered Carl. "We're almost at the base of the hill where the steps lead to the shrine. Let's go into that tea shop over there."

They sloshed through the puddles before entering the crowded tea shop, where German tourists sat at tables, complaining about the storm.

The gracious shopkeeper located seats for Kathy and Carl, bringing them steaming glasses of tea, *chiya*. They listened to the trekkers chatting about their flight to Lukla being cancelled, delaying their trek to Namche Bazaar.

Carl introduced himself and his daughter and joined the conversation. The trekkers teased them about the meaning of their name, since 'Brecht' means 'broken' in German. The topic quickly shifted to politics since the Republicans won the election in 2000, and George Bush, was now president of the United States.

After a half hour Kathy reminded her father that the rain had stopped. Carl took time to shake hands with the Germans before departing with his daughter.

Upon arriving at the entrance of Swayambhu Nath, they were approached by two barefoot boys, begging. Their faces were smudged and clothes tattered.

"Mister, you give us some cigarettes for our mother. She's sick and stays in bed all day," said the older boy with greasy hair.

"If your mother's sick, she shouldn't be smoking cigarettes," said Kathy. "You guys need to wash your face and dirty hands."

"We don't have water in our house. We must borrow it from the neighbor's tap. I can get you marijuana or hashish cheap. Come with us. We take you to our friend's house where you can buy all the drugs you want," said the younger boy, his feet covered with mud.

"We don't use drugs," insisted Kathy, disturbed by their soliciting in the street. They entered through the gate, leaving the boys to accost the German trekkers coming out of the tea shop.

"Those kids should be in school," sighed Kathy as they passed through the entrance arch.

After admiring the statues, they ascended the long flight of cement steps, leading to the stupa. Along the way rhesus monkeys dropped from the trees and leapt onto the steps with their hands outstretched.

"Aren't they cute?" said Kathy. "I have some mints for them in my purse."

"Hang onto your purse. Don't remove it from your shoulder," warned her father. "If they get a chance, the monkeys will steal your purse."

"You're kidding," said Kathy, continuing up the stairs. She was startled when a monkey following her tried to grab her umbrella.

"Get out of here!" she screamed.

Carl whirled around and struck the monkey with the handle of his umbrella. It let out a penetrating squeal revealing sharp teeth before darting into the woods.

As they continued climbing the stairs, another monkey joined them pacing at Kathy's side with his stealthy fingers reaching for her purse.

Carl shouted at the monkey and then snapped open his black umbrella. The frightened monkey backed away, fleeing down the steps.

They paused at the stone image with carvings about the birth of Buddha. According to the legend the newborn infant took seven steps while his mother, Maya, reclined beneath the tree, recovering from her labor.

Kathy read in her guidebook that many centuries after the establishment of Buddhism in Nepal, Mughal soldiers from Bengal invaded the valley and desecrated the Swayambhu Nath Shrine by breaking open the stupa in search of treasure.

"The Nepalese were angry because the stupa was a burial mound for preserving the relics of numerous Buddhas," added Carl.

"Is there more than one Buddha?" asked Kathy.

Her father explained that there were many Buddhas prior to the birth of Gautama Buddha (483-563BC), the founder of the Buddist religion, in Lumbini, Nepal.

Upon reaching the top, they saw two huge stone lions and an enormous metallic thunderbolt. Kathy paused to ask her father about its significance

"The word thunderbolt is *dorjee* in Tibetan and *vajra* in Sanskrit. Its significance goes back to the Hindu god, Indra, a storm deity," said Carl.

"Dad, what's the significance of the prayer flags flapping in the wind?" asked Kathy.

"The flags have mantras written on them to remind the people that the Transcendent Being exists everywhere. Most Buddhists believe that thoughts and words are organic. They have power to hurt or heal people. Therefore, we must watch our words so that we don't inflict suffering on us or others. Once again it is the law of karma."

"Dad, my swimming coach caused our team plenty of suffering. It didn't matter if we won or lost. Regina always screamed at us for not being perfect," continued Kathy.

"Instead of helping you, her constant negative words demoralized the team," stated Carl.

"I wanted to quit the team, but you taught me not to react, but to ignore her harsh comments. Nearly half the team quit during my junior year. We barely had enough swimmers to compete at the meets," said Kathy pausing. "Dad, what are those monks doing over there?"

"They're spinning prayer wheels," said Carl. "Those bronze containers have written mantras in them. Let's join them for a few minutes."

As they circumambulated the shine, Carl and Kathy spun the bronze prayer wheels located on the lower part of the dome at regular intervals.

After completing the circle, they gazed at the clouds drifting over the city below. They paused to locate the central bazaar with its array of Hindu temples, the sports stadium, and the royal palace.

"Where's that chanting coming from?" asked Kathy, turning toward a nearby building.

"It's coming from the monastery. I hear cymbals clashing and trumpets blaring. There must be a ceremony going on inside the Kargyud Gumpa," said Carl.

Sure enough upon entering the monastery, there were fifty monks with their heads shaved, wearing maroon robes and seated on cushions with their hands folded.

Everyone was bowing and chanting in front of the statue of Gautama Buddha, illuminated by butter lamps. The ceremony was interrupted by the clanging of brass cymbals and the abrasive sound of trumpets shaped like elephant tusks.

"We'd better get back to the hotel before it starts to rain again," suggested Kathy, leaving the monastery with her father following her.

"Taxis are parked below," said Carl, heading down the long flight of steps.

"I'm going to e-mail mom as soon as we get back to our hotel," said Kathy.

"I promised your mother I'd e-mail her every day, but I forgot to write to her when we were in New Delhi."

43

That evening Moksha arrived with his son at the garden of the Kathmandu Guest House. The older shaman was dressed in a pleated white skirt with sleigh bells across his chest. His feathered headdress had a daphne pheasant hanging down the back.

Muktuba was muscular and wore only a loin cloth. He trailed behind his father with a stubborn male goat. When the black ram refused to budge, he seized the goat's horns and dragged him down the path, tying him to the trunk of the pomelo tree. He then lighted the sacrificial fire.

Carl and Kathy were seated on the stone bench under the tree waiting for the ceremony to begin.

"Will Muktuba sacrifice the goat to Shiva?" she asked.

"Animals are never sacrificed to Shiva. Blood offerings are only made to the Mother Goddess in Nepal," said Carl.

Moksha adjusted his feathered headdress and requested his son to play the drum, using a drumstick shaped like a snake. Muktuba sat under the pomelo tree, beating the drum and chanting.

His father crushed mustard seeds with a mortar and pestle scattering them in front of the tree and praying to the ancestral spirits. Removing the band of sleigh bells from his chest, he shook them over the fire to purify them.

Moksha recited a prayer in Sanskrit with Carl translating. "*May we know the Lord of the flames. Let us mediate upon the blazing fire. May the Lord of Fire, Agni, impel us toward Him."*

The older shaman danced around the fire, invoking the Mother Goddess Kali while making a large red circle with tika powder around the tree.

"Dad, what's he doing?" asked Kathy, feeling uneasy because the sun had set over the mountains and darkness was enveloping the garden.

"Moksha is praying to the planets so that the exorcism will be auspicious," said her father.

After finishing the prayers, the shaman tied a rope ladder to the tree and a hangman's noose on the branch where Christopher was strangled.

All eyes focused upon Muktuba, who stopped playing the drum. He rose to his feet like Hercules and unfolded the effigy of five-year-old Christopher, dressed in a white shirt and blue shorts with black knee socks. The mask of the boy's face had been made from a photograph.

"Christopher's blond hair and blue eyes are just like his mother's," said Carl, remembering how Margaret entered the garden twenty-five years ago and proceeded down the gravel path. When she saw her son hanging by the neck, she screamed hysterically.

Eight-year-old Nigel hurried toward his stricken mother and handed her a red rose. As she reached for the rose, Margaret collapsed from shock onto the gravel path. A few minutes later an ambulance took her to the hospital.

Moksha circled the sacrificial fire, carrying the effigy of Christopher on his back. It was stuffed with straw with his arms and legs flopping from lack of support.

Curious tourists and guests, hearing the drum beating and the chanting in the garden, appeared on the second storey balconies or entered from the lobby.

Outdoor lights suddenly illuminated the pomelo tree and Buddha's statue in front of the prickly pear cacti. Moksha was distracted by tourists snapping pictures of him with their flash cameras. He danced around the fire with the effigy on his shoulders and the bells ringing from his chest. Moksha paused to chant another hymn.

"*May we know the Goddess Kali. Let us meditate upon the Dweller of the cremation grounds. May the Terrible One lead us toward her,*" translated Carl.

"*Kali Mata, malai choda banayera, ma mathi chadnu hos,*" cried Moksha, requesting the goddess to mount him like a horse.

All eyes were on the shaman trembling before being hurled to the ground. Moksha rolled in the grass behind the fire, convulsing with an epileptic seizure.

The crowd gasped and moaned at the sight of the stiff body of the shaman, writhing and twisting with his eyes rolled back into his head.

"I'll call an ambulance," insisted a waiter, rushing down the gravel path toward the double doors.

"No!" shouted Muktuba. "My father is being possessed by the blood thirsty, Goddess Kali. She will help him drive out the demons."

The crowd murmured due to the intensity of Moksha's convulsions. He writhed, gasping like a fish out of water. More people entered the garden including cooks, bellboys, and clerks, lured by the rhythm of the drums.

After experiencing several convulsions, Moksha lay quietly on his back in the grass. He opened his eyes and rose from the ground, staggering toward the rope ladder.

The shaman trembled while ascending the ladder, fastened to a branch across from the noose. He paused with the effigy hanging from his back.

Moksha shouted in a shrill voice, "*Ravana ko bhut kheta ko atma bata aihile narga ma jau. Tyo ruk ko hangle jau!*" He ordered Ravana's demons to depart from Christopher's incarnate soul, clinging to the branch.

"That's not Moksha's baritone voice. It's the shrill voice of a woman," uttered Kathy, seizing her father's arm.

"Moksha is now possessed by the Goddess Kali. He's a medium with the goddess speaking through him," added her father.

"*Ravanako bhutharu tyo kheta ko atma bata turuntai niskera, Nagarma jauo!*" shouted Moksha, ordering the demons to depart from the boy's soul and return to Hell.

As Moksha ascended the ladder, his whole body shook violently. He clung to the rope ladder with both hands clenched tightly. All of a sudden the ladder began to shake and spin him around.

"What's happening?" cried Kathy.

"The demons are attacking Moksha," uttered Carl.

Muktuba stopped playing the drum and untied the goat from the trunk of the tree, dragging it toward the rope ladder. He seized a bucket of water and threw it onto the goat. The drenched ram shivered from the cold, indicating it was possessed by the goddess and ready to be sacrificed.

Raising the sacrificial knife, Muktuba invoked the name of the Goddess Kali and then chopped off the goat's head with a single blow of the machete. The decapitated head rolled toward the rope ladder where Moksha was still struggling with the demons.

The body of the goat fell to the ground with blood gushing from the neck. Muktuba seized the empty bucket to catch the blood. He splashed some of it onto the branch of the tree where the hangman's noose was dangling.

"*Sabai bhutharu, khasi ko ragat piera, Narga ma jau.*" Muktuba, ordered the demons to drink the blood of the goat and then return to the Underworld.

Within seconds a cold wind stirred the leaves and branches of the pomelo tree. The fire that had been receding suddenly burst into flames.

Muktuba seized the severed goat's head and waved it at his father on the rope ladder. Within seconds Moksha stopped spinning around and climbed down the rungs until he reached the ground, removing the effigy from his back.

All heads turned toward the bucket of goat's blood, rattling on the gravel path. There was an eerie slurping echo coming from the interior of the bucket.

An unexpected clap of thunder shook the tree, followed by a streak of lightning. The terrified guests retreated from the garden as the rain poured down on them.

Muktuba climbed up the rope ladder in the rain, carrying the goat's head, which he secured firmly to the hangman's noose. After chanting several mantras, he came back down.

Drenched from the rain, Moksha informed everyone that Christopher's incarnate soul was freed from the demons, and had been sent back to the Underworld.

The small group remaining in the garden followed Moksha to the shallow grave dug in front of Buddha's statue. The shaman placed Christopher's effigy into the pit, summoning the goddess to remove the demons from the boy's sensory souls.

Muktuba dragged the decapitated body of the goat to the shallow grave, where he sliced open the goat's stomach, covering the effigy with blood and fluids.

Moksha chanted to Kali and ordered the demons to depart from Christopher's eyes, nose, mouth, ears, and hands. After slurping the blood and fluids, the demons left the effigy, departing for Fewa Lake in Pokhara, the entrance of the Underworld.

Moksha removed soft wax from his pocket and knelt down, filling each aperture in the water logged effigy floating in the shallow grave. He then covered the grave with wet dirt and mud using a spade.

"The demons are no longer possessing Christopher's sensory souls," sighed Moksha.

The exhausted shamans, soaked from the rain, gathered their ritualistic paraphernalia and hurried down the gravel path toward the exit. Carl and Kathy followed them through the double doors leading to the lobby.

44

"There's still one soul left," said Moksha, standing in the lobby in his bare feet. His dripping clothing left a puddle on the floor in front of the desk.

"It's Christopher's impression soul," said Carl, who was soaked from the rain.

"I can't stand watching another exorcism," said Kathy shivering in her wet clothes.

Moksha asked the clerk behind the desk for the key to the second-floor room, where Margaret Porter had stayed with her two sons prior to Christopher's death.

"The key is locked in this drawer," said the clerk, consulting with the manager by cell phone.

"We shut down that room years ago because our guests complained that it was haunted. They heard squealing and groaning noises coming from the walls and floor. We tried to use the room for storage, but the staff was afraid to enter due to the peculiar odors."

"Thank you for the key," said Muktuba. "We'll be extra careful when we go into the haunted room

"Let's change our clothes first," suggested Kathy.

"We'll meet you in about ten minutes," agreed Carl.

Moksha informed them that once he found the object with the soul clinging to it, they must return to the garden for a final exorcism.

After changing their clothes, Carl and Kathy joined the shamans in Room 213. Upon entering they winced at the scent of sandalwood incense mingling with the odor of urine, even though the windows were open.

"Have you found anything yet?" asked Carl, recalling how he saw Nigel and Christopher asleep on the twin beds. At that time Margaret led him across the room to the balcony overlooking the garden, where they sat on bamboo chairs. She confessed to him about belonging to the London Coven where Yorg Schmidt offered her son, Nigel, to the Demon King Ravana. She sobbed with remorse, hoping to hire a shaman to liberate her son's soul from demonic possession.

"We searched the dresser drawers and the closets. We've removed the bedding and mattresses and looked under the beds, but we've found nothing," said Muktuba.

"Let's look behind this dresser," suggested Moksha, dragging it away from the wall. Everyone starred at the broken picture frame and glass scattered on the floor.

"Oh!" said Carl. "I remember Nigel smashing that picture of Krishna. "He was so violent after his brother was murdered."

Moksha folded his hands and bowed to Lord Krishna, chanting, "*Om namaha Krishnaya!*"

"Krishna's just a baby in that picture," said Kathy. "Who's that bearded man carrying him in a basket across the river with snakes hovering over them?"

"That's his father, Vasudeva, fleeing with his infant son to escape from being murdered by the wicked king."

"That story reminds me of the Flight into Egypt, when Herod decided to slaughter the infants, or Moses being placed in the Nile before being saved by the Pharaoh's daughter," said Kathy.

Moskha informed them that Christopher's impression soul was not attached to the frame, glass, or picture.

"I remember Iris. She was the nanny watching Nigel when Margaret was in the hospital. When I came to relieve her of her shift, Nigel had locked himself in the bathroom and filled the tub with water."

"Let's go into the bathroom," said Muktuba. "Maybe Christopher's impression soul is still there."

"I kept shouting for Nigel to come out of the locked bathroom. The tub was overflowing and water was seeping under the door. When he finally opened the door, Nigel, was holding a snake puppet," informed Carl. "Within seconds he trashed the bedroom by tearing the drapery from the patio doors."

"*Yaha aunos!* Come here!" shouted Moksha, crouching on the floor. He reaching under the bathtub supported by iron claw feet and pulled out a box of dusty crayons and two wrinkled coloring books.

"I'm surprised those crayons are still here," said Carl, leafing through the coloring book. "This one belonged to Christopher!" He showed the shamans a picture of Jesus, Mary, and Joseph, surrounded by the magi and shepherds in serene pastel colors.

"This must be Nigel's coloring book," said Kathy, paging through it. "Here's the Holy Family scribbled over with black, grey, and purple colors."

"We must return to the garden now," insisted Moksha, leaving the room. "I am certain that Christopher's impression soul is clinging to this coloring book."

Carl and Kathy followed the shamans down the stairs to the lobby, after stopping to get their umbrellas.

A few minutes later they were hovering over the shallow grave where the effigy of Christopher had been buried. In spite of the downpour, Muktuba dug up the mud and placed the coloring book into the grave while Moksha chanted mantras to invoke the goddess to help him.

After the goddess possessed Moksha, he seized a machete, shouting at the evil spirits to leave Christopher's impression soul. The demonic forces attacked him, causing him to stagger and fall head first into the muddy grave.

"What's happening?" asked Kathy, her eyes wide with terror at the sight of the shaman choking in the mud.

Carl yanked Moksha from the mud and splashed water from a puddle onto his face. He shoved his fingers into the shaman's mouth, pulling out clogs of wet dirt.

Moksha shook his head, spitting and then rinsing his mouth with rain water. Upon recovering, he once again ordered Ravana's demons to leave Christopher's soul.

There was a peculiar moaning coming from the grave, followed by a dog howling in the alley behind the brick wall surrounding the garden.

"What's that noise Dad?" said Kathy, shivering under the umbrella.

"The demons that departed from Christopher's soul are attacking the stray dog." said Muktuba, listening to the howling of the tormented animal.

Exhausted from performing the exorcisms, Moksha knelt down and collapsed on the grass. Carl and Kathy helped him get to his feet, leading him down the gravel path and through the double doors into the lobby.

Muktuba followed them carrying their paraphernalia. He requested the desk clerk to remove the sacrificial goat from alongside the grave and donate the meat to a poor family. As they ascended the stairs and headed down the corridors to their rooms, everyone was silent.

"*Hami bholi bihana das baje tira, Bir Haspatal ma betaula,*" said Moksha informing everyone they would meet at Bir Hospital the next morning at 10:00 am.

45

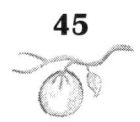

The next morning Carl met his daughter for breakfast at the outdoor café. They sat at a wrought iron table beneath a green umbrella to protect them from the rain.

"It's starting to get cloudy again," said Kathy, smiling at the muscular waiter.

"Your omelet, Miss," he said, setting her plate on a woven mat, and handing Carl toast with orange marmalade.

"By the way my name is Jitesvara," informed the waiter.

"I'm Kathy," she said. "What does your name mean?"

"Jitesvara means Lord of Victory," smiled the waiter. "My ancestors came to Nepal in the 12th century. They fled from the Moslems when they invaded India. We were Brahmans, who settled in the foothills.

"Our town was named after Goraknath, an incarnation of Vishnu. He predicted that the Shah Dynasty would fall after twelve generations," said Jitesvara. "My family is fearful that the prediction will come true."

"I don't believe that Vishnu would disguise himself as a beggar and then curse Prithivi Narayan Shah because he insulted him," said Kathy.

"I'm surprised you know about the curse. God works in mysterious ways. We believe that Vishnu disguised himself as a beggar to remind us that His Presence is found within all livings beings, including the poor and homeless, even the beggars."

"That myth is ridiculous," said Kathy, noticing the dark clouds. "It looks like it's about to rain."

"I'll be right back with more coffee," said Jitesvara, returning in a few minutes to refill their cups.

"Why don't you join us?" asked Kathy, attracted to the young man. "We're the only customers in the café."

"Thank you," responded the waiter, sitting down in the vacant chair next to Kathy.

"Many years ago Goraknath was responsible for a drought, which caused a great famine," said the waiter, gazing into Kathy's brown eyes.

"According to our legends, Goraknath imprisoned nine snake chiefs, *nagas*. He immobilized the snakes by sitting on them, and they became his throne for twelve years.

"During that time the country suffered from drought and famine," said Jitesvara. "We believe that snakes are fertility symbols which bring us the monsoon rains each year so that our rice crops will flourish.

"After many years of hearing prayers from the starving people, *Machendranth*, the Lord of the Fish, arrived in Nepal to visit his pupil, Goraknath.

"When Goraknath saw his teacher, he rose from his throne of snakes and bowed to his guru. The nine snake chiefs slithered away from the palace. As soon as they departed, the clouds formed in the sky and the monsoon rains began. The twelve years of famine came to an end and the people celebrated the victory!"

"Every year during the monsoon season, the people of Nepal celebrate the return of Machendranath at a special festival," said Carl.

"I would like you and your father to come to Gorkha and meet my parents," requested Jitesvara.

"We might be able to make the trip after the shaman convention. It starts at 10:00 o'clock today. It'll be over on Thursday, next week," said Carl.

"May I take your daughter, Kathy, to a club this evening to dance?" asked the waiter.

"I'd love to go dancing. Dad, please let me go with Jitesvara," pleaded his daughter.

"Kathy, I'm worried about you being out after curfew," said her father.

"We can take a taxi back from the club. I'll request the driver to bring us back to the hotel by 11:00 pm," insisted Jitesvara, smiling at Kathy.

"Dad, nothing's going to happen to me. You're being overprotective," asserted Kathy.

"Then it's settled. Kathy, I'll meet you in the lobby at 6:30 this evening," said the waiter.

"I'll be waiting for you to return," said her father, paying the bill. "I want you to check in with me as soon as you get back to the hotel."

"I've got to go now," said Jitesvara. "I'll see you later."

As Carl and Kathy were about to leave the patio, they paused as a taxi came to a screeching halt. The driver got out and opened an umbrella, holding it over the back door as a woman stepped out..

"It's Marilyn Monroe," gasped Kathy. "I thought she died a long time ago."

The blonde woman, wearing a sleeveless black silk dress with a string of pearls, emerged from the taxi. She straightened her disheveled hair with manicured nails.

"It's…It's Margaret Porter," uttered Carl, swallowing at the sight of her cleavage.

"Why Carl Brecht!" exclaimed Margaret, rushing toward him. "It's been so many years since I've seen you."

"I can't believe you're here in Kathmandu," blurted Carl, giving her a hug. "This is my daughter, Kathy."

"We're about to leave for the shaman convention at Bir Hospital," said Kathy, shaking her head.

"That's why I'm here," uttered Margaret. "Muktuba informed me about the convention months ago. I'll join you as soon as I change my clothes."

"My dad said that you were quite an accomplished musician," said Kathy, feeling jealous over the attention her father was giving Margaret.

"Carl, I'll never forget how you encouraged me to sing, *Lily Marlene* at the Royal Hotel when you took me out to dinner that night," said Margaret.

"That was a long time ago," said Carl. "You haven't changed a bit. You're just as gorgeous as ever."

"You've always been so complimentary," said Margaret, reaching into her purse. She extracted a handful of rupees to pay the driver.

Carl intervened and bargained with the taxi driver so that the fee was reduced. While they were talking, a bell boy arrived from the lobby to carry Margaret's luggage.

"I couldn't attend the exorcism in the garden last night because my flight was delayed due to the weather," sighed Margaret, shaking her head. "I really wanted to be there."

"It was quite a ceremony," said Kathy. "It rained the whole time. The shamans put on quite a performance."

"The effigy of Christopher is buried in front of the statue of the Buddha in the garden," said Carl.

"I hired Moksha and Muktuba to exorcise the evil spirits from Christopher's souls because I had several nightmares. My son's ghost kept appearing to me in my dreams saying that he was still in the pomelo tree in the garden here."

"How did you get in touch with Muktuba?" asked Carl.

"Dr. Schiller, a German patron of the museum, informed me about the convention. He had a list of the shamans attending," said Margaret Porter.

"Do you still work at the Albert and Victoria Museum?" asked Carl, escorting Margaret to the lobby with Kathy following them.

"I'm now a docent at the British Museum," she said.

"My mom's a tour guide at the Field Museum in Chicago," informed Kathy.

"How's Barbara doing these days, Carl?" asked Margaret, registering at the desk with the clerk.

"She's fine," said Carl, remembering that he still hadn't e-mailed his wife. "Would you like to have dinner with me at 7:00? My daughter's going to a club, and I'll be here by myself at the hotel.

"Of course, I'd love to go with you to dinner. I'll see you at the convention. I've been invited to sit in the balcony with the king and queen. Crown Prince Dipendra might be there with Devyani. I'm looking forward to seeing my son, Nigel. He will be there with the royal family."

Carl watched Margaret depart for the stairs with her hips swaying. The bellboy with his mouth gaping, trailed behind her carrying the luggage.

"You certainly work fast when Mom's not around," uttered Kathy. "You used to date her, didn't you, Dad?"

"We only went out a couple of times before she had a nervous breakdown," said Carl. "Let's take a taxi to Bir Hospital. It's raining again."

46

The taxi came to an abrupt halt a block away from Bir Hospital. The traffic was horrific due to the arrival of the shamans with their families, the medical staff, and foreign visitors. Carl opened his umbrella as soon as he stepped out of the taxi with Kathy.

They joined the crowd heading toward the hospital while the rain poured down. Everywhere pedestrians were colliding into each other with open umbrellas.

The traffic on Kanti Path had come to a halt because the shamans were crossing the crowded street with their wives and children, carrying their drums and paraphernalia.

A bus was stranded in front of Ratna Park with medical students in white coats streaming out. Impatient taxi drivers were honking their horns at the stalled traffic.

Upon entering Bir Hospital, the shamans were already registering at the tables. A Nepalese woman stood behind a podium with a microphone speaking to the crowd.

"After finishing your registration, please go to the auditorium for orientation," she announced.

"I didn't expect to see so many shamans wearing their ceremonial costumes," said Kathy, amazed by their bells jingling from their chests, wrists, and ankles and their feathered headdresses.

"Here come, our friends, Moksha and Muktuba," said Carl, signaling to them and bowing with his hands folded.

"We're both tired out from last night's ceremony at the hotel. We met Margaret Porter going to her room before coming here," said Moksha.

"She wants all of us to fly with her to Pokhara next Thursday after the workshop to perform an exorcism. She'll pay for our expenses. We'll be staying overnight at the Third Eye Hotel at Fewa Lake," added Muktuba.

"Not another exorcism. I'd like to just relax at the hotel," said Kathy. "I'm getting tired of the monsoon."

"We won't have time to relax. Margaret wants us to go to Dr. Bhinna Atma's cottage to perform exorcisms to put Yorg Schmidt's and Myrna Reynolds' souls to rest," continued Muktuba.

"How odd, I thought Margaret came to Kathmandu to find her son, Nigel. She hasn't seen him for twenty-five years," said Carl.

"Nigel's staying at the royal palace. He's a guest of Crown Prince Dipendra. Margaret is worried because she saw Yorg's ghost in her dream. He told her that Ravana's demons want to possess Nigel," said Muktuba.

"We'll discuss the trip to Pokhara later," said Carl. "You guys better get registered. It's getting late."

Upon entering the auditorium, they observed the families of the shamans filling the vacant seats. The speaker behind the podium on the stage turned on the microphone and spoke.

"My name is Dr. Raj Pandey, the chairman of the convention. All shamans attending the workshop should be seated on the stage. It is not necessary to bring your ritual paraphernalia with you. Drums and cymbals may be left behind with your family in the audience."

Kathy followed her father up the steps to the stage, followed by Muktuba and Moksha.

"Dad, you told me that the police exhumed the corpses of Myrna and Yorg and had them flown to London and Berlin to be buried," said Kathy. "I can't understand why Margaret wants to go back to that cottage in Pokhara."

"Yorg died there when a huge stone lingam fell on him during a barbaric ceremony performed by the coven," said Carl. "Myrna was killed when the roof of the cottage collapsed on her."

"They both were never properly buried," insisted Moksha. "They died violent deaths while worshipping powerful demons. Now their souls are possessed by them."

"Margaret is fearful that these demons will come back to harm Nigel since he is no longer staying in the shelter of the monastery at Tengboche," said Muktuba.

"I think Margaret should just mind her own business and not stir up trouble," insisted Kathy.

"Yorg and Myrna need to be redeemed. Once the evil spirits leave their souls, they will be free to continue their journey to the next world. They may have to spend time in Hell, *Narga*, because of their evil *karma* before being reborn," added Muktuba.

"They don't deserve to be saved. They were responsible for Christopher's death," insisted Kathy.

"Even the souls of evil people and demons are entitled to be redeemed because they are God's creation," insisted Muktuba, surprised by Kathy's comment.

"You mean Satan and his devils can be redeemed?" asked Kathy. "According to the Christian beliefs, they were cast into Hell for all eternity."

"We believe that Ravana (Satan) will be saved by the Lord's mercy. All of God's creatures are destined to evolve through many incarnations until they unite forever with the Transcendent Soul, *Parmatama*."

"Carl, it is such a pleasure to see you," interrupted Dr. Pandey, leaving the podium to shake hands with him. "This must be your charming daughter, Kathy. She's just beautiful. Welcome to Kathmandu."

"Here's a list of the shamans from the various regions of Nepal," he said. "Now that everyone is seated, I will introduce you."

Carl approached the podium and stood next to Dr. Pandey, who requested that everyone stand while he recited a prayer to Ganesh for the success of the convention.

"*Vakra tunda Mahakaya surya kothi samaprabha/ nirvignam kuru me deva/ sarva karyeshu sarva da.* We invoke the curved tusk deity with the great elephant body, which radiates light like a thousand suns. We request Him to remove the obstacles from all of our affairs, especially at this convention.

"Now I would like to introduce you to Dr. Carl Brecht, who teaches anthropology at the University of Chicago. His specialty is Shamanism in Nepal."

"Thank you so much, Dr. Pandey for inviting me to speak at this wonderful gathering of shamans from different regions of Nepal. Most of you have come to Kathmandu from remote areas. Let's give the shamans a round of applause for being willing to undergo medical training here at Bir Hospital.

"I've noticed that the royal family has just arrived and are about to take their seats in the upper balcony of the auditorium. Please stand to greet them," said Carl.

King Birendra, Queen Aishwarya, Crown Prince Dipendra, Devyani, and a Buddhist monk bowed and waved to the audience from the balcony.

"Will everyone remain standing while Gita Sharma sings the Nepalese National Anthem," requested Carl, pausing until she was finished.

After the song Carl informed the audience that the shaman convention wouldn't have taken place without Dr. Pandey, who was responsible for the paramedic training of 1000 shamans, *dhamis/jankris,* in 1980, followed by dozens of workshops since that major event.

He stated that in the future the shamans would not only treat spiritual and psychological illnesses, but they would combat diseases by using antibiotics and other scientific medical procedures.

Carl thanked Dr. Widmar and Dr. Kroll from Heidlberg along with the German patrons for financing the workshop.

"And now it's time to introduce the shamans. Please reserve your applause until all them have been recognized," he said.

"Let's begin today with the Shaman from Sabra in eastern Nepal. Next is the Shaman from the Thulung Rai Community. He is followed by the Sherpa Shamans from Namche Bazaar and Solo Khumbu."

After introducing several districts, Carl paused to give the names of the shamans. As he was about to continue with the program, a loud clap of thunder shook the ceiling of the auditorium as if a bomb had detonated.

Momentarily the lights went out and the microphone went dead. The audience gasped and murmured sighing with relief when the electricity and sound were restored.

While her father continued introducing the shamans, Kathy whispered to Muktuba, who was sitting next to her.

"Do you recognize that Buddhist monk sitting next to Prince Dipendra and Devyani in the balcony? asked Kathy, removing opera glasses from her purse. "Could that monk be Nigel Porter?"

"Let me take a look. I haven't seen him for some years now. I'm sure my father would recognize him," said Muktuba, passing the glasses to Moksha.

Moskha glanced toward the balcony. He said, "*Tyo bhikshu niscaya nai Nigel ho!*"

"My father said that the monk is definitely Nigel. He performed exorcisms on him when the yogi brought him to our home twenty-four years ago."

"Nigel seems very calm," said Kathy getting a glimpse of him. "Why, he's getting up and leaving the auditorium with the prince and his girlfriend. The queen seems very angry over their departure."

"I will now introduce my good friends, Moksha and Muktuba," said Carl. "They are Limbu Shamans from Terhathum in eastern Nepal. I also want to introduce my daughter, Kathy. She accompanied me to Nepal to attend this convention."

The three guests stood and bowed, returning to their seats on the stage.

"Let's give a final round of applause to all the shamans and their families, attending this convention."

After the round of applause, Kathy glanced through her field glasses toward the balcony. "It's Margaret Porter! She finally arrived wearing a low cut yellow sundress. Why she's shaking hands with the queen," gasped Kathy.

"Now here is Dr. Pandey," said Carl. "He will inform you about the procedure for the convention."

Dr Pandey read the titles of the workshops and their room numbers to the audience.

1. *Family Planning and Venereal Diseases* (204)
2. *Pharmaceutical and Herbal Medicines*, (208)
3. *Gastro-Intestinal Diseases and Parasites* (212)
4. *Tuberculosis, Asthma, and Allergies* (216)
5. *Bleeding and Urinary Tract Infections* (218)
6. *Setting Bones and Making Casts* (102) *Emergency Room*

He informed the shamans they were to leave the auditorium and go to their classrooms for medical training, escorted by medical students. The workshops would rotate for the next six days. All classes would be held daily from 9:00 am-5:00 pm and terminate on the following Thursday. At that time the shamans would receive their certificates, followed by a farewell luncheon.

"The families of the shamans will be boarding the tourist buses, waiting in front of the hospital. Today's tour will be to our ancient city of Patan, culminating with a picnic at the zoo," said Dr. Pandey.

"I'll be spending the day with Moksha in the Emergency Room 102," said Carl. "I understand we'll be making splints and plaster casts most of the afternoon."

"I'm going with Muktuba to study *Pharmaceuticals and Herbal Cures*," said Kathy.

As Kathy and Carl left the auditorium, they ran into Margaret Porter in the crowded corridor.

"I'm...I'm so grateful that I've caught up with you," sighed Margaret, covering her shoulders with a white shawl. "I feel so conspicuous in this sundress. I really shouldn't have worn it."

"It's very beautiful," said Carl, starring at the golden cross suspended between her breasts. "You remember my daughter, Kathy."

"I certainly do. She's stunning just like Barbara. You sent me photographs of your wedding here in Kathmandu and then again when your son, Mark was born," said Margaret, smiling at Carl.

"Perhaps you would like to join my daughter and me for lunch. We'll be leaving around 12:30," asked Carl.

"I'd love to go with you, but King Birendra and Queen Aishwarya invited me to the Royal Palace for lunch. I was hoping to see Nigel at the convention, but he left a few minutes before I arrived."

"Nigel was sitting in the balcony next to the Crown Prince and Devyani. They left rather abruptly," said Kathy.

"I haven't seen Nigel since he was kidnapped. He's coming back to the palace with the Crown Prince for afternoon tea," said Margaret on the verge of tears.

"Muktuba said that you want us to go with you to Pokhara," said Carl, glancing at Margaret's figure.

"I took the liberty to make bookings on a flight to Pokhara for Thursday, May 31. We'll go directly to Dr. Bhinna Atma's cottage so that the shamans can perform the exorcisms. We'll stay at the Third Eye Hotel overnight and then catch an afternoon flight on Friday to Kathmandu."

"I must go now. King Birendra's limousine is waiting for me in front of the hospital. I'll see you later, Carl," she said, high heeling toward the exit.

"I'm sure you will," said Kathy, scowling as she departed. "Dad, did you send Mom an e-mail yet?"

"Oh, I forgot to write to Barbara," said Carl. "I'll e-mail her this evening."

47

After attending the afternoon workshops, they returned to the hotel. Kathy went directly to her room to get dressed, anticipating her date with Jitesvara. However, Carl was stopped in the lobby by the desk clerk, who gave him a note from his mailbox.

Carl entered the garden through the double doors and hurried down the gravel path. He sat under the pomelo tree to read the message.

Dearest Carl, 5/24/01
Please forgive me for not being able to join you for dinner tonight. I enjoyed the company of the king and queen including several family members during lunch. Everyone was so gracious.
After lunch we waited for hours for Prince Dipendra and Devyani to bring Nigel to the palace. They promised to come for afternoon tea, but they didn't show up. I was terribly disappointed since I haven't seen Nigel since he was kidnapped by Yorg twenty-five years ago. I'm too disturbed to go out tonight. I'll see you tomorrow at the convention.
Affectionately yours,
Margaret

Carl rose from the chair and paced in front of the pomelo tree, deciding to send an e-mail to Barbara. Upon returning to the lobby to use the computer, he saw his daughter coming down the stairs.

Kathy's black hair flowed down the back of her tropical print dress with her high heels clicking from each step. She smiled at her father, covering her bare shoulders with a tangerine shawl.

Jitesvara arrived wearing a black suit with a red tie. He was carrying a gift with a pink bow.

"Oh, you're so sweet," sighed Kathy, opening the present and placing the coral and turquoise bracelet on her wrist. "I just love it. It's gorgeous."

"Our taxi's waiting to take us to the disco," said Jitesvara. "Don't worry Dr. Brecht. I'll have your daughter back at the hotel by 11:00 pm. We'll be at the Thunderbolt Club in Lazinpat."

"Dad, I hope you'll enjoy your date with Margaret Porter," said Kathy. "I suppose you're going back to the Royal Hotel to dance for old time's sake."

"Margaret's not feeling well. We're not going out this evening. She spent the afternoon at the royal palace," said her father, explaining to her that she hadn't seen Nigel and was too upset to have dinner with him.

"Don't worry. I've got plenty of notes to type about the convention," he added waving to them as they left the lobby to get a taxi, parked in front of the hotel.

After a light meal in the restaurant, Carl spent a restless evening typing at his desk. He was preoccupied with his daughter being out for the evening with the waiter.

It was 10:30 pm when he went down to the lobby to send Barbara an e-mail. Carl finally wrote a lengthy letter to his wife, informing her about the shamans performing the exorcisms in the garden the previous evening and the first day's activities of the convention. A half hour later, he returned to the deserted garden, where he sat on the stone bench under the pomelo tree, thinking about how much he missed Barbara.

48

When Crown Prince Dipendra returned to the royal palace, he went directly to his living quarters. He was exhausted and wanted to go right to bed. He left Nigel to meditate in front of the statue of the Buddha in the garden near the pond.

Upon opening the door of his apartment at the top of the stairs, he was alarmed at the sight of his mother, Queen Aishwarya, waiting for him inside. She was pacing in front of the fireplace like a lioness about to pounce on her prey.

"Why mother, what are you doing here?" asked the crown prince, trying to conceal his annoyance by pouring himself a drink of *The Famous Grouse*.

"I'm very disappointed that you didn't show up for tea. Your father and I had to entertain Margaret Porter the whole afternoon without you. She came all the way from London to meet her son, Nigel.

"Margaret informed me that she wants to take him back to Britain with her. Good riddance. I'm tired of him hanging around the palace grounds," asserted the queen.

"I completely forgot about the afternoon tea," said Dipendra. "When I finally checked my mobile phone, it was too late to join you."

"I don't believe you're sorry at all," snapped his mother. "Where have you been? Devyani's mother telephoned three times, interrupting our conversation with Margaret and our relatives. That woman has a lot of nerve calling us during the tea to speak to her daughter. Why didn't you show up like you promised?"

"We left the convention early to go out to Godvari on a picnic," said Dipendra. "Afterwards I took Devyani and Swayambhu on a tour of Bhaktapur. We spent the afternoon admiring Newar artists' tapestries, *tangkas.* Later in the evening we stopped at a club for a few drinks."

"You broke your promise. I felt so embarrassed when you didn't show up. You told me that you'd be there with Nigel. If it wasn't for your aunts being so gracious the gathering would have been ruined. Your grandmother asked about you constantly. Margaret Porter was on edge the whole time, expecting to see Nigel. She finally left with a headache, worried that something happened to him."

"I'll invite her to attend our family dinner next Friday evening. I've already told Swayambhu and Devyani that I want them to join us. I'm hosting the party here at Tribhuwan Sadan in the Billiards Room," announced the crown prince finishing his drink and lighting a cigarette.

"I don't know why you call Nigel, Swayambhu. It's not right. You act as if he's a yogi or a bodhisattva. I don't want him at our family dinner. I've also had enough of Margaret Porter, and that girl friend of yours.

"Margaret doesn't know how to dress properly. Her outfits are indecent. You'd think she was attending the Academy Awards in Hollywood and not an afternoon tea. I forbid you to bring Devyani to any more family gatherings!"

"I don't want to discuss this tonight. I spent all day yesterday at boring meetings with the Maoists," said Dipendra. "I was with Uncle Dhirendra and the generals."

"I don't know why we're even negotiating with them. The Prime Minister, G.P. Koirala, wants to deploy the

Royal Nepal Army and rid the capitol of the Maoist insurgents," said the queen. "I agree with him totally, but I can't convince your father to do this. He never listens to me anyway. After all, he's the King of Nepal."

"We're going to meet with father tomorrow afternoon to give him a full report about the Maoists," said the prince, pausing to replenish his drink. "I'm exhausted. I wish you'd leave now, Mother."

"You're terribly rude, Dipendra. It's because you've been drinking and smoking marijuana again. If you don't do something about your addictions, I will. I'm fed up seeing your picture in the newspapers with Devyani.

"I don't want you spoiling our family dinner party next Friday by being high. You were slurring your words last month at the party. Dipendra, you must get a grip on yourself. I'm arranging for you to go to Switzerland for rehab right after the Summer Olympics."

Dipendra walked to the door and held it open, waiting for his mother to depart. The queen refused to go. She parted the curtains, glancing down at the garden from the second story. Nigel was sitting in front of the statue of Buddha, meditating.

"I don't know why you ever brought Nigel here from Tengboche. If Margaret Porter doesn't take him back to London with her, you must send him back to the monastery. I don't want him staying at the palace any longer. It's time for him to leave!"

"Yes, Mother," said Dipendra. "Thanks for stopping by for such a pleasant visit."

"You're being sarcastic again," said Queen Aishwarya, picking up her purse. "I know when I'm not wanted. I'm going to have a chat with your brother, Rajan, when he gets back from Eaton. At least he's cooperating with me about his wedding plans."

The angry queen left her son's living quarters and headed down the stairs. She paused shaking her head at Nigel, who was holding his beads and chanting.

Dipendra waited until his mother was out of sight. He called his servant, Krishna, on his cell phone requesting him to bring Nigel to his room from the garden. When the monk entered his living quarters, the crown prince asked him to be seated near the fireplace.

"Swayambhu, I have a severe headache. I'm very disgusted with my mother. She wants to control my life," said Dipendra, pouring another drink. "I'm thirty years old and she treats me like a child. I'm tired of her interfering with my life. I'm also sorry she's been so rude to you."

"Your mother doesn't want me staying here at the royal palace," said Nigel. "The queen refuses to even speak to me. I don't want to create problems for you. I would like to go back to the Tengboche Monastery."

"No! I need you here at the palace. You're the only person I trust," insisted the crown prince. "My mother finds fault with everything that I do. I can never please her. Please don't leave the palace until after our family dinner party on Friday, June 1st."

"I'd rather not come to the party, but I'll stay in the garden and meditate," agreed Nigel.

"That's very kind of you, Swayambhu. I'm sorry I didn't bring you back to the palace for tea to meet your mother. I didn't mean to upset her."

"I haven't seen my mother in years. I'm afraid her negative karma is preventing us from getting together. She still believes that I'm responsible for my brother's death," said Nigel, fingering his beads.

"I've forgiven her many years ago for not being a loving mother. She's suffered from bipolar depression. When she went off her medications, my mother used to take my brother and me on long trips. That's why we came here in 1976. Enough about my past, why are you so disturbed tonight, Dipendraji?"

"I'm uneasy about the Maoists. They've taken over the police stations in Western Nepal and are causing trouble at the university in Pokhara. Their leaders are demanding representation in parliament," said Dipendra. "I believe they should be allowed to have seats in the parliament. My father wants to negotiate with them and restore order. However, there are strong factions that want the Maoist exterminated."

"Negotiation is the first step toward peace. We must be willing to allow the Spirit to transform us so that we can bring about a new society. The old order is decadent, not only in Nepal, but throughout the world," said Nigel, pausing. "By the way how did your meeting go about the Summer Olympics?"

"It was tedious. The Fifth National Games will be held here in Kathmandu on June 3rd," stated the prince, nervously pacing in front of the fireplace.

"Some months ago you mentioned you wanted to compete in the karate competition," said Nigel.

"Just look at me," blurted Dipendra. "I'm grossly overweight. I had a black belt in karate when I attended Eaton. Now, I'm totally out of shape. I'd be the laughing stock of the competition if I tried to compete.

"I find it hard to breathe when I'm trekking in the mountains. I shouldn't be smoking these damn cigarettes," he said, crumpling the packet and hurling them into the fireplace. The prince also removed his cigarette case and dumped the hashish along with some black substance into the blazing fire.

"You have forgotten your true nature," said Nigel. "*Om Mane Padme Hum*! Behold the Jewel in the Lotus

Blossom. Your true nature is wholeness. We're all blinded by the illusion that we are superior or inferior to others."

"I know all about illusion, *maya*. My yogi teacher used to tell me that my body was an illusion, and that the only true reality was my soul. One day I grabbed him by the throat and started to choke him. He finally confessed that the pain was real and not an illusion," laughed Dipendra.

"Dipendra, the body is just as real as the soul. *Maya* does not mean illusion. It is the creative aspect of reality, the cause of illusion. Maya is the belief that something impermanent is permanent. Most people seek relief from feelings of inadequacy and inferiority by turning to addictive substances and pleasures. They want to fill their emptiness, unaware of the truth about themselves."

"Swayambhu, I've tried to quit smoking and drinking, but I can't do it. Recently, I saw my doctor. He told me I have high blood pressure and high cholesterol. I've been taking medications to control these problems. I've got them right here." He removed his prescriptions from his coat pocket and handed them to Nigel.

"It says here on the labels: Do not use with alcohol or dizziness may occur. It also says do not drive while taking this medication," stated Nigel.

"That's why I have a chauffeur. I wish my mother would just leave me alone," asserted Dipendra. "I haven't told her that I'm planning to marry Devyani in December. I've already rented the ballroom at the Royal Hotel for the reception. When I hinted at using the Grand Hall at the Narayanhiti Palace, she was furious. That was a week ago.

"My mother's doesn't want me to marry Devyani. She believes that Devyani is unable to produce male heirs because she doesn't have any brothers in her family.

"She wants me to marry Supriya Shah, my former girlfriend. Her second choice is Garima Rana. I dated both of them, but we mutually decided to break up."

"You are blaming your mother and rebelling against her control. You equivocate between obeying her and having your own way. This equivocation creates constant tension within you," said Nigel.

"You might want to come with me to Bodhnath on a retreat after the Olympic Games. It will help you to relieve your stress so you can make the right decisions about your future," suggested Nigel.

"I don't care what my mother said. I'm going to marry Devyani! My mother told me that if I married without her consent, she would take away my monthly living allowance and disinherit me."

"Dipendra, you must straighten out your life or you'll not only lose Devyani but your sanity," asserted Nigel.

"My mother is already making plans for my brother's wedding. I'm so angry! I just don't know what to do anymore. I'm so exhausted. I just want to sleep!"

"I'd better go to my room down the hall," said Nigel, rising from the chair. "I'll pray to Avalokitesvara and the Bodhisattvas to give you guidance so that you will be free from the bondage of your addictions."

"You're…you're right. I'll go with you to Bodhnath on a retreat. I've got to stop drinking, smoking, and eating so much. Good night, Swayambhu. I'll see you in the morning," yawned the crown prince.

49

Dipendra woke up with an excruciating headache the next morning. He was suffering from a hangover from the previous evening at the nightclub. The prince felt burdened by the responsibilities and obligations placed upon him. More than anything else he wanted to marry Devyani; yet he had to play the role of the oldest son, who would inherit the throne and become the future king, a responsibility that he dreaded.

The crown prince rose from his bed in his living quarters at Tribuwan Sadan. He squinted from the light streaming in through window. Seizing his cell phone, he dialed his servant, requesting him to come immediately to his room.

"*Subha Kamana, Birendraji,*" uttered Ram Krishna, opening the bedroom door and bowing to his master.

"I need all the blessings I can get. Mix me a drink. I've got a terrible headache," uttered the prince, pacing in front of the window.

"*Ek chin pachi, ma rakshi liera, farkinchu,*" said the servant. "I'll return with the liquor in just a moment."

Ram Krishna hurried across the room to the liquor cabinet and removed a bottle of *The Famous Grouse*. He placed it on a silver tray. Filling a tumbler with ice from the refrigerator, he mixed a sizzling drink.

"*Rakshi piera, Dipendraji, tapai ko tauko dukhdaina.* After drinking the liquor, your head won't hurt," said the servant, handing the drink to the prince.

Dipendra's hand trembled as he picked up the glass and swallowed the liquor in a single gulp.

The servant, knowing the prince's routine, removed a large bath towel from the cupboard and handed it to him.

"Please ring up Nayan Raj Pandey, my astrologer. I want to consult with him to see if Devyani and I should get married in December. I also want to know if I'm destined to be the future king of Nepal."

After making the appointment for a visit to the court astrologer, the servant helped his master get dressed in tight fitting Nepalese pants and a long white shirt which hung almost to his knees.

"*Hajur bihana ko khana khaibaksincha?*" Ram Krishna asked Dipendra if he wanted to eat breakfast.

The prince informed him he only wanted more liquor. He requested the servant to bring him his horoscope prepared by his father's astrologer.

The crown prince gulped down his drink, asking for his cigarette case. He had forgotten that he emptied the contents in the fireplace the night before. The servant immediately replenished the silver case with the prince's cigarettes along with a fresh supply of marijuana, hashish, and a black substance.

Dipendra tucked the case into an inner pocket of his jacket and left the bedroom. Carrying his astrological chart under his arm, he hurried through the living room and then down the hallway and out the door. His shoes thudded on the stairs leading to the garden.

Outside the prince lit a pipe of hashish, exhaling a cloud of smoke which circled his head. In the distance he noticed his limousine had arrived with the driver waiting for him.

Dipendra meandered toward the bridge which separated his living quarters from the Billiards Room. He paused on the bridge to observe the lotus blossoms in the water.

Glancing toward the statue of the Buddha, he saw Nigel wearing his maroon robe, sitting on a bench with his hands folded. Dipendra observed that the French doors of the Billiards Room had been opened by a servant, who was vacuuming the hall.

"Swayambhu, come over here!" shouted the prince, observing the monk hurrying toward him.

"I hope you slept well, Dipendra," said Nigel, his footsteps echoing on the wooden bridge.

"I'm embarrassed to say this, but my mother did a background check on you. The other evening she informed me that you were kidnapped by a coven when you were ten-years-old."

"That's true," said Nigel. "I was traumatized by the London Coven during their sinister ceremonies."

"The coven was responsible for murdering a dear friend of my mother's. His name was Yorg Schmidt," informed the crown prince. "He donated a great deal of money to the *Save the Rhinoceros Fund*. Each year he funded a young man's college education from the Paroparkar Orphanage Did you happen to know Yorg?"

"Of course, he was the leader of the coven. He owned a chain of jewelry stores in Berlin. He's was responsible for murdering my brother," said Nigel.

"The coroner's report stated that Yorg's naked body was found at Dr. Bhinna Atma's cottage. He had a terrible bruise where he had been struck on the head. He died from hemorrhaging," said the prince.

"The authorities also found an anthropologist standing on the pier, handcuffed. He informed the police that a renegade yogi had saved your life by pulling you out of the cottage just before it collapsed."

"The anthropologist is Dr. Carl Brecht. He was a friend of my mother. Yorg was planning to sacrifice him to the demons in the cottage, but he managed to escape when a whirlwind destroyed the building."

Nigel mentioned that the yogi took him across Fewa Lake in the boat. From there they trekked for nearly two months before reaching Terhathum. Yogi Parshamsa Dev took him to Moksha, who performed numerous exorcisms on him. Finally, he was liberated from the demonic forces that held him in bondage.

"Did the exorcisms work?" asked Dipendra. "Perhaps Moksha could help me."

"Yes, Moksha and his son, Muktuba, are attending the shaman convention at Bir Hospital," informed Nigel.

"Maybe I could get in touch with them," said Dipendra, glancing at the Billiards Room.

"Why do you keep looking over your shoulder, Dipendraji?" asked Nigel, noticing the agitation of the prince, who was pacing up and down on the bridge.

"I feel uneasy about hosting the family dinner in the Billiards Room," admitted Dipendra. "It's not important. I want you to come with me to Dilli Bazaar. I've got an appointment with my astrologer. I don't want to go there by myself."

"I'll be glad to go with you," said Nigel.

"Let's go right now," said Dipendra. "I have a copy of my horoscope with me. I want the astrologer to check the calendar for my wedding in December."

"You and Devyani certainly are star-crossed lovers," said Nigel, entering the backseat of the limousine and sitting next to the prince.

"Love is a smoke made with the fume of sighs;

Being purg'd, a sea nourishe'd with loving tears. What is it else? A madness most descreet," said the prince reciting a passage from *Romeo and Juliet.* "I'd rather die than break up with Devyani. She's the only woman that I have ever truly loved."

"You're stressed over hosting the dinner party," said Nigel. "You need to go on a retreat before the event so that you won't be so tense."

"That's impossible. I've got too many obligations. I must meet with my father to discuss the negotiations with the Maoists and the committee about the Summer Games."

"Let me take a look at those astrological charts," insisted Nigel. "I studied astrology at the monastery."

Dipendra opened the charts, handing them to Nigel. He then ordered the driver to take them to Dilli Bazaar to the home of his astrologer.

"Your chart, Dipendra, indicates unusual movement among the stars and planets during the later part of the month of May and the first week in June. In fact the astrological disturbance will have a great affect on the entire nation," said Nigel.

"How about during the autumn and winter?" asked Dipendra. "What's going on?"

"There will be a catastrophic event on September 11, 2001, which will have global consequences," said Nigel.

"Just focus upon my horoscope," advised Dipendra, glancing out the window. "I hate those huge fruit bats, hanging from the palm trees."

"I woke up startled the other night when you were in the garden shooting at them," said Nigel.

"It's the only way I have to release my rage. I shoot at the crows and the bats because I'm overwhelmed with responsibilities these days.

"I fear, too early; for my mind misgives. Some consequences yet hanging in the stars shall bitterly begin his fearful date. With this night's revels, and expire the term. Of a despised life clos'd in my breast, By some vile forfeit of untimely death," recited Dipendra.

"You're being influenced too much by Shakespeare. Your life doesn't have to become a tragedy. You don't have to be victimized by the stars. They are merely guideposts, warning you to be vigilant," said Nigel.

"You don't understand, Swayambhu. I have no control over my destiny," uttered Dipendra, pointing a finger out the window at a crow pecking at the carcass of a dead rat lying in the street.

The driver swerved the limousine through the palace gate and then south on Durbar Marg past Tri Chandra College, turning left.

"Dipendra, you always have a choice. You live too much in the future. It's important to stay in the present moment," said Nigel.

"My mother threatened to disinherit me if I marry Devyani," uttered Dipendra. "She'll take away my monthly living allowance."

"That might be a good thing. You will then be totally independent of her control over you," said Nigel.

"Stop the limo, Mohanji," shouted Dipendra, opening the door and getting out.

He walked toward a beggar woman with her bony hand outstretched, asking for money. The pitiful woman was barefoot, wearing a faded sari. She had disheveled hair and was clinging to an emaciated infant.

"*Ke bhayo?*" asked the crown prince, touching the baby, who was pale and lifeless.

"*Nani birami bhaeki cha.*" The mother said that her child was terribly sick.

"Please come with me. We must go to the hospital. The doctor will give your baby medicine," said Dipendra.

The driver opened the front door of the limousine for the woman and her infant. When the distraught mother entered the vehicle, everyone winced from the body odor of the mother and the stench of the baby's diaper.

Mohan drove the limousine directly to the Emergency Room of Bir Hospital. The crown prince departed from the vehicle with the beggar woman and her infant. They hurried past a room, where the shamans from the convention were receiving instruction on setting bones.

At the circulation desk, the prince spoke to the nurse about having a doctor examine the sick child immediately. Once the woman was registered, Dipendra paid cash for the treatment of the sick infant.

When the crown prince returned to the limousine, he sat next to Nigel. I see you're studying my astrological chart."

"I'm pleased that you helped that poor woman and her baby. You and Devyani have some issues to work out according to your chart. December isn't an auspicious month for you to get married," said Nigel.

"But I already gave a deposit for the ballroom of the Royal Hotel for our wedding in December," said Dipendra.

"You are doing this to defy your mother. Instead of controlling your own destiny, you are placing it in her hands," informed Nigel.

"If I bring Devyani to our family party, my mother threatened to have a guard remove her from the premises. I'm angry with my mother. She's a control freak!"

"Here we are at Dilli Bazaar," said the driver pulling up in front of the home of the astrologer.

"Mohan, go back to the hospital and check up on the mother and the baby. Take them to the shelter for the homeless near Shanta Bhawan in Patan.," said the prince.

50

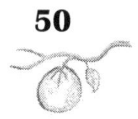

After knocking on the door several times, Dipendra and Nigel were admitted to the home of the astrologer by the servant. They followed him down the hall and then up three flights of stairs.

"Welcome to my humble living quarters," bowed Nayan Raj Pandey, rising from a large red cushion on the floor. "I'm honored that the future King of Nepal has come to my humble dwelling place to pay me an official visit. You will be the next incarnation of Lord Vishnu."

The gray-haired astrologer stretched out, prostrating himself at the feet of the crown prince.

"I'm only an ordinary man and not a god," insisted Dipendra. "I don't want you to put me on a pedestal."

"But your father King Birendra is an incarnation of Lord Vishnu," informed the obsequious astrologer. "When your father dies, the Divinity will leave his body and enter yours. You will be the next Living Temple of the Lord."

The wrinkled old man rose from the floor and kissed the prince's ring. "I have been the Court Astrologer for the past three generations of kings. I was appointed by your great grandfather, King Tribuwan. By the way, who is your new travelling companion?"

"This is my friend, Swayambhu. I brought him to Kathmandu from the Tengboche Monastery. He's my spiritual director."

"Would you kindly tell me your real name?" asked the astrologer, scrutinizing the stranger as if he were a specimen under a microscope.

"My name is Nigel Porter," he said. "I don't deserve the title that Prince Dipendra has given to me. The Self Existent One is the essence of all living beings."

"I finally get to meet the long lost son of Margaret Porter," sneered the astrologer, reaching for the charts with his arthritic hands.

"Have you met my mother?" asked Nigel, handing the astrologer the prince's charts.

"Of course, Margaret Porter came here to visit me last night. She was disturbed because you didn't meet her for tea yesterday afternoon. She came with a shaman named Muktuba and his father, Moksha."

"What did they want with you, Nayanji?" asked Dipendra, lighting a cigarette.

"Margaret wanted to know if it was auspicious for them to fly to Pokhara next Thursday. I checked my charts and told her I saw no problem with them travelling at that time although more rain is predicted."

"Your mother informed me that many years ago Moksha had performed exorcisms to liberate you from demons," commented the astrologer. "I see you are a convert to Tibetan Buddhism. I despise those ugly maroon robes."

"The past is gone forever. I prefer to focus upon the present moment," stated Nigel.

"Why is Margaret going to Pokhara?" asked the prince.

"I'm not free to discuss Margaret's horoscope with you, Dipendraji. It is confidential information," uttered the astrologer, opening the charts. He placed them on the floor to examine them.

"Don't change the subject. I asked you a question and I expect a straight answer," demanded Dipendra, throwing his cigarette on the wooden floor and crushing it out with the heel of his shoe.

"There's an ash tray on the coffee table," snapped Nayan coughing from the smoke. Rising from his cushion he opened a window to ventilate the room.

"Margaret hired the shamans from the convention to perform exorcisms at Dr. Bhinna Atma's cottage. She wants them to liberate Yorg Schmidt's soul from the evil spirits," said the astrologer, shaking his head.

"Yorg Schmidt was a friend of my parents. He often came to our family dinners. I was only a child when I first met him. He brought a woman with him named Myrna. I believe she was British," said the crown prince.

"Yorg was a great philanthropist. He paid for the construction of a whole new dormitory at the orphanage," said the astrologer.

"Yorg was the leader of the London coven, and he married Myrna Reynolds," informed Nigel. "They kidnapped me and brought me to Pokhara".

"I can't believe those rumors about Yorg and Myrna. I'm afraid you've made a terrible mistake," snapped the astrologer, ignoring Nigel's comment.

"I was at the Dr. Bhinna Atma's cottage at Fewa Lake where Yorg and Myrna were preparing to sacrifice Carl Brecht to the Demon King Ravana when the roof collapsed and killed them," insisted Nigel.

"Oh," gasped the astrologer, clutching his heart. His eyes were wide with terror upon hearing the name Ravana. He stared fixedly at Nigel. "You're mother told me something about you that I can't repeat. It is confidential."

"I could use a drink, Nayanji. You got any liquor in the house? You're as pale as a corpse," said Dipendra.

The astrologer removed a bottle of whiskey from the cupboard and poured two drinks.

"I want to make a toast to celebrate my marriage to Devyani," announced the crown prince. "Give, my spiritual director, Swayambhu, a drink."

"No thank you," said Nigel. "I've taken a vow to abstain from drinking for the rest of my life."

"I guess you and I will have to finish the bottle ourselves," said the crown prince.

"No more for me," said the astrologer. "A shot of whiskey is more than enough, but help yourself. There's more where that came from in my kitchen."

"I've had enough for now," said Dipendra, setting down his glass next to the charts. "Nayanji, please tell me the secret that you refused to talk about earlier."

"It's strictly confidential," said the astrologer, his hands trembling as he held a chart.

Dipendra seized the astrologer by the arm and twisted it. "I want you to disclose what you know about Swayambu."

"Of course, I'll tell you everything, Dipendraji. I will have to break my promise to Margaret Porter, but you are entitled to know the truth.

"That's better," said Dipendra, releasing his grip on the astrologer's arm.

He informed them that when Nigel was an infant Margaret dedicated him to the Demon King Ravana at a ceremony held by the London coven. At that time Yorg was the leader of the coven, who claimed that Nigel was the son of Ravana and Sita. He believed the dormant seed of Ravana had been passed on to numerous women through many incarnations, finally manifested itself through Margaret's pregnancy.

"The coven's conclusion was due to distorted thinking from the use of drugs," announced Nigel. "I was present at the cottage in Pokhara when Yorg and Myrna distributed heroin, cocaine, LSD, and other drugs to the members."

The astrologer commented that the traditional scriptures and the epics did not agree with the conclusion of the coven. *The Ramayana* explicitly stated that Sita was never violated by Ravana in spite of his attempts to seduce her.

"Your mother, Nigel, still believes that you were involved with the murder of your brother Christopher," said the astrologer.

"She's partially correct. Yorg placed the noose in the pomelo tree in the garden and taught me a game about putting my head in the noose. When we experimented with the game on my brother, he was strangled by the rope.

"I had no intention of murdering Christopher. Yorg deceived me into being an accomplice in the crime because of his perverse desire to punish my mother for fleeing from the London Coven," sighed Nigel.

"My mother made a serious mistake by offering me to the coven when I was an infant. She tried to correct her error by fleeing. Yorg caught up with her, killed my younger brother, and then kidnapped me," said Nigel, gazing out the window at the storm clouds drifting over from the mountains toward Kathmandu.".

Dipendra said, "Swayambhu, I had no idea that Yorg Schmidt was so evil. He was always pleasant at our family dinner parties. My mother just worshipped him."

The astrologer dropped to the floor, stretching his hands toward Nigel's feet. "If you are the son of Ravana, the Demon King, please spare my life!"

"My dear Nayanji," uttered Nigel. "Yorg lied about me. I am definitely not an incarnation of Ravana. You don't have to be afraid of me. I am just an ordinary monk."

"Margaret informed me that she had a Newar artist make an effigy of you. She plans to take it to Fewa Lake and have the shamans perform an exorcism to free your soul from demonic forces in the palace," uttered the astrologer, prostrating at Nigel's feet. "Please do not injure me, son of Ravana and Sita."

Dipendra seized the astrologer by the collar and pulled him up from the floor. "You asshole, don't call my spiritual director a son of Ravana! He told you that Yorg lied to the coven about him."

"I'm...I'm so sorry Dipendraji, the future King of Nepal. Please forgive me," begged the astrologer.

"I don't know why my mother wants the shamans to perform more exorcisms in Pokhara. I was liberated from demonic possession many years ago," asserted Nigel.

"Moksha informed me that corpses of Yorg and Myrna were never flown to Berlin for a proper burial. They are still buried beneath the ruins of the collapsed cottage at Fewa Lake," blurted the astrologer, still trembling. "Your mother is fearful that demons are hovering over their remains seeking to possess you again."

"Nayanji, I thought you didn't believe that Yorg was the leader of the coven," asserted Dipendra, replenishing his glass with whiskey. He glanced out the window at the congestion in the street. A taxi driver was honking his horn at a stray cow blocking the traffic.

"Most people wear a mask covering up their thoughts and feelings. It's difficult to know the truth because we are all actors on the stage of life. Only during a crisis or at the time of death is the mask completely removed," said Nigel.

"All the world's a stage, And all the men and women are players: They have their exits and entrances; And one man in his time plays many parts," continued Dipendra, quoting Shakespeare.

"Have another drink Nayanji. You look like you can use one. I understand you're having an anniversary party here next week on Friday afternoon. You'll be married seventy years," said Dipendra.

"I was married when I was ten years old," informed the astrologer. "My bride was only eight at the time. My parents arranged the marriage."

"That was a long time ago. Things have changed now. Arranged marriages are rarely accepted without the consent of the couple," uttered Dipendra pouring another drink. "We came here to find out if Devyani and I are compatible to be married."

"I need a few moments to study the astrological charts to see if you are compatible," said Nayan trembling.

The astrologer studied the charts and then removed several volumes on astrology from his shelves. He checked and doubled checked his sources.

"I have found that December 7, 2001 will be an auspicious day for your wedding. There is no doubt that you will become the next king," said the astrologer.

"What about the prediction of Goraknath that the Shah dynasty will end after twelve generations?" asked Dipendra, pacing in front of the window.

"I wouldn't pay attention to that prediction. We will deal with it when the time comes. I hope Queen Aishwarya will be pleased with the wedding date," said Nayan Raj Pandey. "She's been so anxious to have you married."

"That is not an auspicious day for a wedding. I read the charts this morning," asserted Nigel. "Dipendraji, you must go on a retreat and then to the hospital for detox."

"You are right, Swayambhu," uttered the crown prince. "I'm suffering from alcohol and drug addiction. I can't go on like this. I often think of commiting suicide!"

"I've heard complaints from neighbors in the vicinity of the royal palace that you've been shooting at the bats in the trees. They are alarmed by the sound of your machine gun late at night," stated the astrologer.

"I've also been awakened many times by the noise," said Nigel. "Substance abuse has caused your thinking to become distorted."

"I get so depressed at times that I just want to die. I'm filled with shame and remorse. I feel trapped in a vicious cycle," uttered the crown prince, lighting a cigarette.

"I feel so empty. I can never smoke enough, drink enough, or eat enough. I suffer from a constant desire to have more of everything. I feel so inadequate," confessed the crown prince.

"You are getting to the source of the problem that we must all face. All human beings feel inferior or superior to others because of the ego," said Nigel.

"You are truly, Swayambhu, the Self Existent One," cried the astrologer, getting down on his knees.

"I am only a ray from the light of the Self Existent One. But you are also a ray, and so are all living beings on this planet and throughout the universe," said Nigel.

"*I am the moon and Juliet is the sun,*" uttered Dipendra, quoting Shakespeare again. "Without Devyani, I have no reason to live. She's the light that dispels my darkness."

"Devyani's love is also a ray from the Source of Light," mentioned Nigel.

"I will definitely go on the retreat with you after the games next week. You and Devyani can come to visit me while I go through detox," agreed the prince.

"Swayambhu, I want you to be the best man in my wedding at the Royal Hotel in December. If my mother disinherits me, I'll get a job working for a travel agency, and take trekkers to the Everest region. I don't care about becoming the next king."

"Your future wedding is written in the stars," said the astrologer. "Please stay for tea and biscuits."

"I'd rather have another glass of whiskey," stated Dipendra, pouring another drink.

"But Dipendraji, you've already had several drinks this morning," said Nigel.

"You're right," said Dipendra, setting down the glass. "I'll smoke a cigarette instead."

"Your driver has just arrived with the limousine," said the astrologer, glancing out the window.

"Come on Swayambhu. It's time to go," insisted the crown prince, exhaling a cloud of smoke.

"Don't forget to come to my 70th Wedding Anniversary next Friday afternoon," said the astrologer, coughing.

"I'm coming here with my parents," said Dipendra. "Swayambhu, I want you to join us."

"I plan to go to Bodhnath for a few days. I'll be back in the evening before your dinner party on June 1st to meditate in the garden," informed Nigel.

51

The convention continued through Saturday at the hospital in the center of town near the royal palace. Each day the shamans rotated their schedules by attending a different medical training session. On Sunday they joined their families to tour the sights of the valley.

The shamans had three more days of training the following week, returning on Thursday, May 31st for the final day of the convention. They gathered with their families in the auditorium to receive their certificates, followed by a luncheon at the hospital.

Carl and Kathy left the convention early. They took a taxi to Tribuwan Airport, where they met Margaret, and the Limbu Shamans. Early that afternoon, they boarded the plane for Pokhara.

Margaret sat in the aisle seat next to Carl, who gazed out the window at the clouds hovering over the mountains. They were barely visible due to the fog.

"I never saw so many shamans before in my whole life," commented Margaret, wearing a sheer blouse and a tight black skirt.

"I'm relieved the convention's finally over," said Carl. "Those workshops kept us busy the whole day."

"I'm so pleased we could get away early today," said Margaret, smoothing her hair with manicured nails. "I found Moksha's farewell address stimulating."

"Muktuba did a fine job translating his speech for the audience," added Carl, glancing over his shoulder at the shamans dozing in the seat behind them.

"He's a very attractive man and so is his elderly father," stated Margaret.

"They're both married men," stated Kathy sitting across the aisle. "And so is my dad! Don't forget mom's coming to Nepal in September."

"When are you expecting Barbara to arrive?" asked Margaret, reaching for the pink shawl in her handbag and covering herself.

"I just got an e-mail from her yesterday. She'll be departing from Chicago after Labor Day. Barbara is lonely living alone in our house because everyone's away for the summer," said Carl.

"I know just how she feels. I was lonely after I got my divorce from Jim. It was bad enough losing my youngest son, Christopher, but then Nigel was kidnapped."

She informed Carl that she had tried numerous times to contact Nigel over the past several years, but he never responded to her letters and e-mails. However, she got several replies from the abbot at the monastery, who said he was doing well.

"My mother is a tour guide at the Field Museum of Natural History in downtown Chicago," mentioned Kathy.

"I'd love to meet Barbara. Your parents were married in the garden beneath the pomelo tree at the Kathmandu Guest House," sighed Margaret. "That's where my son, Christopher, died. I...I saw him hanging in the tree with a noose around his neck."

"His soul is finally at rest," said Carl. "Moksha buried his effigy at your request in the garden. He also put his sensory souls and impression soul to rest."

"He told me all about it," sobbed Margaret, wiping her tears with a handkerchief. "I wish I could have been there for the ceremony last week. I spent a whole hour the other day at his grave. Maybe we could have a prayer service for him when we return from Pokhara."

"That's a good idea," said Carl. "We could invite Father Kent to bless the grave and offer some prayers for him."

"I am hoping to meet Nigel at the royal palace when we get back from Pokhara. The prince sent me an invitation to come to their family dinner party tomorrow evening, but the astrologer, Nayan Raj Pandey, told me I shouldn't go because it wasn't auspicious. I'm not sure what to do."

"Is Nigel still staying with Dipendra at the royal palace?" asked Kathy, suddenly feeling sorry for Margaret over Christopher's death.

"Yes, he's still there. It's been so many years since I've seen Nigel. I can't wait to spend some time with him. Dipendra told me that if I didn't want to stay at the party, I could meet with Nigel in the royal garden."

"Birendra started the custom of family dinners when he became king," contributed Carl.

"Will Devyani be there?" asked Kathy

"I doubt it. The court astrologer informed us that Queen Aishwarya doesn't approve of her," said Margaret.

"Why are we going to the cottage at Fewa Lake?" asked Kathy, interrupting the conversation. "The whole idea of performing more exorcisms gives me the creeps."

"I had a dream that evil spirits left the ruins of the cottage and were preparing to attack Nigel. He's been living for years in the shelter of the monastery.

"However, for the past several months he's been staying with Crown Prince Dipendra away from the security of the Buddhist community," stated Margaret, clutching a golden cross, suspended between her breasts.

"Moksha believes that the burial of Nigel's effigy will prevent the demons from attacking him," said Muktuba.

"I can't understand why demons want to possess Nigel's soul again," said Kathy.

"Some people are plotting against the monarchy; others against the Maoists. The forces of darkness congregate wherever conspirators intend to murder the opposition." added Muktuba.

"After I liberated the demons from Nigel's soul, they travelled back to Fewa Lake. Some of them returned to the Underworld. Others settled in the collapsed cottage where the coven worshipped their images," informed Moksha while his son translated for him.

"We must protect Nigel from being attacked by the demons," sobbed Margaret, wiping her eyes with a lace handkerchief.

"I'm tired of exorcism," confessed Kathy. "Dad, look out the window. There's a temple on that hill."

"It's the Manakamana Temple, built in honor of the goddess Bhagwati, another name for Shiva's wife, Parvati. The goddess is known for granting wishes to newlywed couples and barren women requesting sons," said Carl.

"There is a sacrificial area behind the temple where goats and pigeons are offered to the goddess," said Kathy, reading from the guidebook. "In the distance is Gorkha, which used to be the capitol of the Shah Dynasty. It is a four hour trek from the temple."

"I've heard rumors that the Maoists are planning to take over that entire town," said Muktuba.

"I hope not," said Carl. "I know they've been active among the university students in Pokhara."

"It says here that the view of Annapura and Ganesh Himalaya are exceptional during the fall and spring," added

Kathy. "It's too bad we can't see them today due to the rain clouds."

"There's a mountain emerging through the fog. It looks like the tail of a huge gray whale," cried Margaret.

"That's Machhpuchare, the Fish Tail," uttered Carl, glancing out the window.

"I haven't seen it since I was a student here at the university," said Muktuba.

"Attention passengers, please fasten your seatbelts," interrupted the stewardess. "We are about to arrive in Pokhara. Be sure to check the overhead carrier for parcels and hand luggage before disembarking."

As the plane circled the airport, Carl glanced out the window, pointing to the Tribuwan University Campus, where he lived with Barbara and their son, Mark, was born.

"My son, Om, is now studying on that campus," stated Muktuba. "He will join us for dinner at the hotel this evening when we return from Fewa Lake."

52

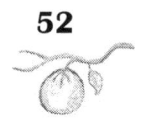

Upon leaving the airport, everyone crowded into a taxi and headed toward the Third Eye Hotel. Along the way, the driver informed them about the area's main attractions.

He recommended they take a boat across Fewa Lake and trek to the World Peace Pagoda, where there were splendid views of the Himalayas.

"We won't have too much time to spend here. We're returning to Kathmandu tomorrow afternoon," said Margaret. "Maybe we could come back another time to see the sights around the town."

"The best time to return is August, when we're celebrating the Tiger Festival, *Bhag Jatra*, and the Cow Festival, *Gai Jatra*, honoring the Goddess Lakshmi," mentioned the taxi driver.

"Here we are at the entrance to the Third Eye Hotel," said Carl. "It's been a long time since I've set foot in this place. Yorg and Myrna were staying here with Nigel, when I checked in years ago."

"Just look at that gorgeous fountain," said Margaret. "It's surrounded by replicas of Michelangelo's statues, *Dawn & Dusk* and *Night & Day* from the Medici Chapel."

"What a magnificent hotel," said Kathy, impressed by the Greek columns soaring from the veranda with a beach leading to the lake.

A few moments later, they were ascending the steps shaded by palm trees in terracotta pots. Upon entering the lobby, they admired the crystal chandelier but were startled by the head of a bull elephant with enormous tusks mounted on the wall behind the main desk.

Before checking into their rooms, Margaret paused to admire a reproduction of Cellini's sculpture of *Perseus*, holding the head of the Medusa, writhing with snakes.

Everyone walked across the polished marble floor, heading toward the elevator. Moksha was annoyed by the delay and burdened from carrying his drum and ritualistic paraphernalia. He mumbled that they'd better depart for the cottage before the next cloudburst.

After checking into their rooms and changing clothes, they ordered box lunches from the restaurant, which they ate on the veranda overlooking Fewa Lake. After lunch they went down to the beach and boarded a motor boat.

Carl recalled being handcuffed by Yorg, who took him hostage at gun point on the pier. This was followed by a turbulent boat ride involving Durga drowning in the lake without anyone from the coven trying to save her.

Once everyone was seated in the boat, Carl started the motor. A few moments later they were travelling over the choppy waves toward the cottage.

They were in awe when the clouds parted and the sun appeared, revealing the grandeur of Machhapuchare, located between the Annapurnas.

Upon reaching the crumbling pier near the ruins of the cottage, Carl continued steering the craft along the bank, the length of a soccer field before docking.

Muktuba leapt out and anchored the boat, helping the passengers up the steep embankment. He led the way down an overgrown path toward the collapsed cottage.

"We forgot to bring the sacrificial goat," said Muktuba, worried that the ritual would not be successful.

"Don't worry about it. Lord Shiva will provide us with the goat," informed Moksha.

"The mosquitoes are terrible here," cried Margaret, regretting that she wore shorts and sandals.

"I've got some insect repellent in my backpack," informed Carl, pausing on the path to retrieve it for her.

"Thanks," said Margaret, dousing her arms and legs with the repellant. She passed it to Kathy, who also was wearing shorts and a sleeveless blouse.

When they reached the site, the cottage was scarcely visible due to overgrown weeds, bushes, and trees. In the distant meadow a white-haired man with a mustache was grazing a herd of goats.

Moksha went directly to the goat herder and bargained for a medium seized ram. He returned with the goat and tied it to the trunk of a scrawny tree.

Muktuba requested Carl to help him build a fire from the boards protruding from roof of the ruins. He asked the goat herder to take Kathy and Margaret to locate the entrance to cave of the Underworld.

The two women followed the herder down the path where weeds and briars scratched their legs.

"My legs are bleeding," cried Margaret, rubbing them with her fingers.

"Raksha ko gupha tyaha cha." The goat herder said that the cave was over there, pointing to the entrance between two boulders covered with moss.

The women followed him through the gnat infested weeds toward the cave. Kathy tripped when her canvas shoes became tangled in the vines.

The irritated herder removed a machete from his sash and chopped the sharp briars and brush blocking the path.

Upon arriving at the entrance of the cave, he hacked away the overhead vines freeing them to go inside.

Kathy and Margaret followed him into the dark cave, where hundreds of bats were hanging from the ceiling. Hearing the footsteps of the strangers, the bats squealed, flapping their wings and swooping down at them.

"Oh my God!" screamed Kathy, turning around and fleeing with a bat tangled in her hair while several landed on her back.

Margaret gave a shrill cry, covering her head with her arms as bats clung to her blonde hair. She fled from the cave with the goat herder following them.

Kathy was crouched on the ground, her hands covering her face as the herder pulled the bats from her hair and back. He then turned to help Margaret, who was screaming in agony from being covered by them.

After the goat herder released the squealing bats from the trembling women, he stood watching the bats circle the cave several times before returning to the dark entrance of the Underworld.

"We'd better get back or we'll miss the exorcisms," groaned Margaret. "I'd rather be sipping lemonade and relaxing at the hotel pool."

When they returned to the cottage, Moksha was already possessed by the Goddess Kali and leaping among the ruins. His son was beating the drum while Carl was tending the sacrificial fire.

Moksha paused to clear away several decayed boards. Eventually, he located a large stone phallus covered with fungus. He removed the sleigh bells from his chest and shook them over the stone image, summoning Ravana's demons to leave the cottage. He leapt back and forth over the lingam protruding from the cottage ruins.

"Ravanako bhutharu, Narga ma jau!" he shouted, sending Ravana's demons back to the Underworld.

Moksha's face, arms, and clothing were soaked with perspiration. In spite of his efforts to exorcise the demons, he was unsuccessful. There was only a slight puff of dust around the boards near the phallus.

Muktuba dragged the trembling goat through the weeds toward the cottage. The goat's legs became ensnared by weeds grasping like fingers. The shaman chopped at the vegetation with his machete, dragging the braying goat over the collapsed roof of the cottage.

Carl was busy ripping boards from the roof and feeding them into the fire. He shouted to Muktuba, "I've just removed a rafter that's pressing on a skeleton."

"Let me see it!" exclaimed Kathy, hurrying toward him, but tripping on vines.

"The back bone of this skeleton is broken! It must be Myrna Reynolds' remains!" exclaimed Carl, recalling how she had screamed when the rafter fell from the ceiling, pinning her to the floor before the roof collapsed.

"Oh my God!" gasped Kathy, shocked at the sight of the human skeleton."

Moksha came over to examine the bones. He informed everyone that the dead woman's soul was possessed by demons because she died a violent death and was never given a proper burial.

"Be very careful and don't move the woman's skeleton," he shouted. "The demons are still hovering over her bones, ready to attack."

Carl helped Margaret climb over the rubble to get a glimpse of the skeleton. She screamed at the sight of Myrna's broken spinal column.

"I had a dream about a British woman crying for help from the ruins of this cottage. It was just awful," shuddered Margaret, covering her face with her hands.

"*Yaha aunuhos! Sabai taruntai yaha aunos!* Come here. Everyone come here now!" insisted Moksha, digging with a spade around the stone lingam. He got down on his knees and removed the earth with his hands, uncovering another human skeleton.

"It's Yorg!" shouted Carl. "I remember Myrna was about to sacrifice me with a knife and offer me to the demon, Ravana, right in front of that phallus. She dropped the knife when Yorg seized the stone lingam, which struck him on the head and killed him."

"Look at his crushed skull," insisted Moksha, removing it from the ruins and holding it up for everyone to see. "We must now liberate the souls of Myrna and Yorg from the demons that are holding them in bondage with the intention of harming Nigel."

While Muktuba dug a shallow grave for Nigel's effigy, Moksha chanted and beat on the drum. He carefully lifted the bones from the ruins and placed them on the grass next to the grave.

Margaret and Kathy gasped when Muktuba sacrificed the goat by decapitating it with a single stroke of the machete. He sprinkled the blood onto the skeletons and the effigy, reciting mantras.

Moksha, wearing his headdress and a band of sleigh bells across his chest, invoked the Goddess Kali. *"Ravanako bhutharu gupha ma gaiera, Narga ma jau!"* The shaman commanded the evil spirits to leave the skeletons and go back to the Underworld.

While he chanted and leapt across the grave, dark clouds moved over the ruins of the cottage. Moksha advised everyone to take shelter in the nearby woods, including the herder with his bleating goats.

Margaret was trembling with fright as the black cloud settled over the cottage and nearby graves. Carl took her by the arm, leading her into the woods with Kathy following.

Moksha held the severed head of the goat, commanding Ravana and his army of demons to leave the skeletons of Myrna and Yorg. Having plugged the apertures of the effigy of Nigel with wax, he also ordered the demons to leave the boy's sensory souls forever.

Dancing around the grave, Muktuba beat the drum, pausing to clash the cymbals. As he continued with the ceremony, granules of sand rose from the bank of the lake.

"It's a whirlwind!" screamed Kathy as the sand stung them like bees defending their hives.

Margaret threw herself into Carl's arms, burying her face in his chest to prevent the sand from stinging her face.

Moksha ordered the demons to leave, holding the goat's head toward the whirlwind. The demons rattled the skeletons on the grass and stirred the effigy in the grave before attacking the shaman and hurling him to the ground.

"The skeletons are rising from the grass," gasped Kathy, observing the whirlwind swoop down, lift the bones, and cast them into the turbulent waves of the lake.

"I've never seen anything like that before," uttered Carl with Margaret, clinging to him and trembling.

Muktuba rushed toward the herder and spoke to him. The white haired man grabbed the fishing net and black plastic bags and hurried toward the Fewa Lake.

Moksha rose from the ground and shouted mantras in a final attempt to drive the demons back to the Underworld.

"There's Nigel's effigy rising from the grave!" shouted Kathy, as the whirlwind seized the image, flinging it into the meadow. The current of wind circled the ruins of the cottage before heading across the lake north to Kathmandu.

All of a sudden there was silence as the dust and sand settled. Moksha said, "This is not a good sign. Thousands of demons have departed from the Underworld in that whirlwind. Many of them had been dwelling in the ruins of the collapsed cottage."

"We must bury Nigel's effigy and offer prayers for his protection," uttered Muktuba, picking up the image from the meadow and carrying it back to the shallow grave.

Everyone observed Moksha praying and chanting while his son beat the drum and clashed the cymbals.

"Oh, I feel so badly," sobbed Margaret, knelling down and kissing the mask of Nigel. His effigy was dressed in a white shirt, blue shorts, knee socks, and shoes.

"Nigel wore these clothes when he was at boarding school in London. He was only eight-years-old when he was kidnapped," cried Margaret.

"The Newar artist did a good job. The effigy looks just like Nigel," said Carl, helping Margaret to her feet. She wept profusely during the ceremony.

Even though Kathy resented Margaret, she suddenly felt compassion for her over Nigel.

After the burial of the effigy, everyone headed back to the boat. Muktuba helped his father, who was so exhausted he could scarcely walk. Carl consoled Margaret, assisting her into the boat followed by Kathy. Everyone felt weary from the turbulence of wind and waves.

They were about to leave when the goat herder appeared with two black plastic bags. His white hair, mustache, and clothing were dripping wet. He spoke to Moksha in Nepali and handed him the bags.

The shaman gave him a ten rupee note and promised to pray for him. The herder bowed and waved to them, heading toward his goats grazing in the meadow.

"Oh my God," uttered Kathy, glancing at the gray clouds above them. "It looks like another storm!"

"I'm terribly worried," cried Margaret. "I hope Nigel's going to be all right."

"He'll be fine," consoled Muktuba, pausing. "My father predicts there will be a disaster in Kathmandu when the whirlwind releases the demons in the city."

"I hope good will triumph over evil," said Carl, trying to console Margaret, who was trembling. "We better get back to the hotel before the rain."

"What's in those plastic bags?" asked Kathy. "I saw the goat herder diving in the water with his net during the burial of the effigy."

"He fished out Yorg and Myrna's bones from Fewa Lake," said Muktuba.

"It was bad enough to dig them up, but now we've got them in the boat," muttered Kathy, shivering from the fog.

"We'll bring them to the morgue in Pokhara so they can be given a proper burial," said Carl, overhearing Muktuba speaking to his son, Om, on his mobile phone.

"Their skeletons should be cremated, or they will attract demons again," insisted Moksha.

"I don't believe in all those superstitions," said Kathy, opening a plastic bag to get a glimpse of the remains. "Oh my God! It's Yorg's crushed skull!"

"Ke gareko? What have you done?" shouted Moksha rising from his seat in the boat.

"What's wrong?" screamed Kathy, noticing a puff of dust rising from the bag and mingling with the fog.

"Bhut aiyo!" shouted Moksha, informing them that an evil spirit was hovering over the boat.

"I didn't mean to do anything wrong," apologized Kathy, tying the black bag shut.

"What's that horrible noise?" asked Margaret, her teeth chattering.

"It's only crows flying above us in the fog," said Muktuba, beating on the drum while his father chanted to drive away the evil spirit.

53

As they continued across Fewa Lake, Carl was worried about storm clouds moving toward them from the mountains, now shrouded in mist. He had difficulty steering the motorboat due to the turbulent waves. Kathy and Margaret sat together shivering. Behind them the shamans were dozing from exhaustion in spite of water splashing on them at regular intervals.

"This is the spot where Durga freaked out from using drugs and fell overboard," announced Carl.

"Dad, why didn't you try to save her?" asked Kathy, feeling sorry for the old woman, who drowned.

"I was handcuffed the whole time," said Carl, reflecting upon the incident. "I yelled at Yorg to stop the boat, but he ignored my request."

"How horrible!" shuddered Margaret. "Nigel was at that cottage, witnessing the sinister ceremonies of the coven. He was a disturbed child long before Yorg kidnapped him. It was my fault for offering him to the coven when he was a baby. I'm afraid something terrible will happen to him!"

Moksha advised Margaret to stop blaming herself for Nigel's demonic possession. He encouraged her not to harbor resentment against Nigel because her negative karma was preventing her from meeting him.

Margaret placed her hands over her face, sobbing. "All these years I've blamed Nigel for murdering Christopher."

"I exorcised the demons from Nigel long ago. He totally forgave you for offering him to the coven" said Moksha. "The time has come for you to forgive yourself and him."

"I've tried over and over to forgive him, but my thoughts always go back to the pomelo tree in the garden, when Christopher was hanging by the neck."

"You must make a decision to reject that image and forgive Nigel. Forgiveness means releasing the thoughts that are disturbing you," stated Moksha.

He stood up in the boat praying to the Transcendent Soul, *Parmatama*, to free Margaret from her negativity. While he was chanting everyone was startled by a clap of thunder and a sudden cloudburst.

Margaret felt cleansed by the rain as the tears streamed down her cheeks, releasing her fear, guilt and shame. She finally was liberated from her anger and resentment toward her son, Nigel.

"Oh! Thank you!" cried Margaret "I feel as if a millstone has been removed from my neck. Carl, you were there when I needed you the most. If it wasn't for you visiting me in the hospital, I wouldn't have gotten well."

"Dr. Manandar, the psychiatrist, deserves the credit not me. He helped you to accept Christopher's death and to deal with Nigel's kidnapping."

"You must know the truth," interrupted Moksha. "Nigel's at risk of being possessed again. I'm fearful the whirlwind is transporting an army of demons to the royal palace in Kathmandu."

"There's the Third Eye Hotel," interrupted Kathy, trembling from the chill. "It looks like the House of Usher, shrouded in fog."

"We're finally approaching the dock," said Carl, tying the boat to the pier while the passengers disembarked.

"The fog is so thick on the beach, I can barely see my feet," said Margaret, watching Kathy disappear into the mist in front of her.

"My son, Om, should be at the hotel. He wants to take us on a tour of the university tomorrow before we leave for Kathmandu," said Muktuba, carrying the plastic bags with skeletal remains.

Carl walked behind Moksha, almost invisible in the mist. The shaman was still wearing his headdress and carrying his drum while the band of sleigh bells jingled in the heavy fog.

On the steps leading to the entrance of the hotel, a handsome young man was waiting for them with Mr. Shrestha, the Chief of Police, and a forensic anthropologist.

Muktuba embraced his son, who bowed to his grandfather, Moksha.

"Om, I want you to meet our friends, Dr. Carl Brecht, his daughter, Kathy, and Margaret Porter," said Muktuba."

After chatting with them for some time, Om escorted the women to the lobby, leaving the men talking about the skeletal remains.

"We'll take the bones to Kathmandu for examination," said Dr. Thapa, the anthropologist. "There's a helicopter waiting for us at the airport."

"After we photograph Yorg Schmidt's skeleton, it will be flown to Berlin for a proper burial by his relatives. Myrna Reynold's remains will be sent to her family in London," said Mr. Shrestha.

Carl gave them a detailed report about the exhuming of the skeletons and his past experiences with the coven before returning to the hotel with the shamans.

In the lobby they were surprised to see Kathy and Om sitting on a leather sofa in front of the nude statue of

Perseus. Om had his arm around Kathy and was pressing his cheek against hers and whispering in her ear.

"I'll be starting my freshmen year at college," laughed Kathy, amused by a joke that Om had just told her.

"I'm almost finished with my sophomore year. "I'm majoring in biochemistry and anatomy," said Om.

Carl was annoyed by the young man's display of affection toward his daughter, who was totally mesmerized by his charming personality.

"Dad, I'm starving. I just invited Om to have dinner with us," said Kathy, holding his hand.

Carl noticed that Kathy's sleeveless blouse and tight shorts were getting Om's undivided attention.

"Where's Margaret?" asked Kathy, irritated by her father's disapproval of Om.

"I think she went to her room. She was complaining of a headache," said Carl, scowling at his daughter for sitting so close to Om.

"Margaret's sleeping on the sofa over there," said Om.

"*Ke bhayo waha lai?* What happened to her?" asked Moksha setting down his drum and cymbals. He shook his head upon seeing his grandson with his arm around Kathy.

When Muktuba arrived he cleared his throat and stared fixedly at Om, who removed his arm from Kathy's shoulder and slid away from her on the sofa, leaving a space between them.

"Kathy, I think you better go to your room and change for dinner. We don't want to offend the Nepalese by inappropriate clothing and behavior," insisted Carl.

"But we are at a resort and it's summertime," said Kathy, aware of everyone's disapproval of Om showing her affection.

"I'll go wake up Margaret and encourage her to change for dinner," said Carl, noticing the bell boys were straightening out the magazines on the coffee table in front of the sofa where she was reclining while staring at her sensuous figure.

"We could all use a shower before we meet in the dining room," said Muktuba. "Om, you can come to our room and watch television while we get cleaned up."

"I'd rather take Kathy for a stroll around the veranda of the hotel," he insisted, rising from the sofa.

"We'll join you for dinner later," said Kathy, ignoring the disapproval of her father and the shamans.

"Your grandfather wants to spend some time with you, Om," said Muktuba, noticing that Margaret had risen from the sofa and was not wearing a bra. She limped toward them carrying her shoes.

"Kathy, you must change for dinner! We'll meet in the dining room in an hour. It's already almost 6:00 o'clock," said Carl, leading the way to the elevator.

"If you could stay in Pokhara for a few days, Kathy, I'll take you to the Buddhist Peace Pagoda," suggested Om.

"I'd love to stay here for a week and then join you in eastern Nepal," said Kathy.

"I don't think that's a good idea. Om has a research paper to finish," interrupted Muktuba.

"Once the term paper is done, I'll be free to spend the rest of the summer with you, Kathy," said Om.

"That's not a good idea!" said Carl, angry with him for flirting with his daughter. "We're returning to Kathmandu together tomorrow. Moksha and I will be flying to Terhathum to do further research on the shamans."

Margaret yawned, interrupting them. "I can't wait to see Nigel at tomorrow night's dinner party at the royal palace. I've decided to go in spite of the astrologer's warning."

"I'm taking Kathy to the Tengboche Monastery to study medicinal plants. The monks have an extensive herbal garden there," said Muktuba.

"I could help you with the research. I have a biochemistry major!" insisted Om.

"You must finish your research paper. If you're done with it on time, maybe you can join us," said Mukthuba. "We're leaving Kathmandu on Monday morning."

"Kathy, I've decided that you must come with Moksha and me to Terhathum," insisted Carl.

"Oh no, you promised that I could travel to Tengboche with Muktuba and Margaret!" she asserted.

"That's right," said Margaret. "I need to get permission from the abbot to take Nigel back to London with me."

"Don't worry Carl. I'll keep my eye on these two love birds. Kathy and Om will be with me all day in the greenhouse working at the computers. In the evening I'll have Buddhist monks chaperoning them," said Muktuba.

Moksha, heading toward the elevator said, "Come on, Om. I want to talk to you about the marriage that we have arranged for you in Terhathum."

"An arranged marriage?" gasped Kathy, staring at Om.

"Om's wedding will take place in November during the Festival of the Lights, Tihar," said Muktuba.

"I'm definitely not marrying that Limbu girl. I don't believe in that outdated custom," said Om. He stepped aside allowing Carl and Margaret to enter the elevator.

"There's not enough room for all of us in this elevator," announced Muktuba, standing beside Kathy. "Om, you'll have to get out and take the next elevator."

"Oh no," said Kathy feeling tense as the doors of the elevator closed, leaving Om behind in the lobby.

54

Later in the evening the men returned to the lobby waiting patiently for Margaret and Kathy to join them. They strolled across the marble floor, pausing to get a glimpse of *Hercules Fighting the Centaur, Nessus.*

"I don't remember this statue being here years ago," said Carl. "It's a replica from the Florentine collection. The centaur has the upper body of a man, but the lower body of a horse. The hero is fighting a mythical beast."

"We need to control our animalistic nature rather than fight it," said Moksha.

"Our mind is a tiger wandering in the past, or a goat grazing in the future. The ego is never satisfied to stay in the present moment," added Muktuba.

"Here comes Kathy," said Carl, shocked by her appearance as she stepped out of the elevator. She was wearing black slacks with a tangerine blouse and high heels that echoed on the marble floor.

"Your daughter's very beautiful," said Om, his mouth gaping at her figure. He hurried toward Kathy, giving her a hug in front of everyone and reaching for her hand.

A few moments later Margaret arrived in an aqua blue silk dress with golden earrings. All eyes focused upon her cleavage, which she covered with a peach shawl.

"Would you prefer the main dining room or the veranda facing the lake?" asked the head waiter, approaching them with menus.

"It's chilly outside," insisted Kathy, smiling at Om. "We've had enough rain and fog for today."

"We'd prefer to eat in the dining room," insisted Om, whispering in Kathy's ear. "You're beautiful in that outfit."

Margaret reached for Carl's arm. "I'll be your date for the evening," she said. "I hope Barbara doesn't mind. I won't tell her if you don't."

Carl cleared his throat. "I plan to e-mail Barbara this evening after dinner."

Everyone followed the waiter into the dining room where the polished silverware and crystal goblets glistened among the china plates. Each table was covered with a linen cloth with a red rose soaring from a vase. The waiter seated them near a window facing Fewa Lake and then handed the guests menus.

"This place is so elegant," said Margaret, removing her linen napkin from a silver ring.

"Kathy, I want to take you dancing at the ballroom of the hotel this evening. I'll introduce you to my friends from the university," announced Om.

"I'd love to go dancing with you," said Kathy, opening the menu.

"You need your rest," asserted Carl, worried about the safety of his daughter. "We're returning to Kathmandu tomorrow afternoon."

"But I'm not tired," insisted Kathy. "I'm eighteen years old, not ten. I'm going to the dance with Om."

"Om, you've got to finish your research paper if you want to travel with us to Tengboche," insisted Muktuba.

"I come here to the dance every Thursday evening because the entrance fee is half price. On Friday night the ballroom's really crowded," said Om, ignoring his father.

"You shouldn't be dating after all your engaged to be married to a young woman in Terhathum," said Moksha.

"I'll never marry an uneducated village woman! "If you try to force me to get married, I'll stay here in Pokhara for the rest of my life. I'll never go back to Terhathum," asserted Om, shocking everyone at the table.

"I don't believe parents have the right to arrange a marriage for their children," asserted Kathy, deciding to have vegetarian meal of rice.

"Sir, may I take your order now?" asked the waiter.

"I'll have the chicken curry, *kukhura ko masu*, with the rice and lentils, *dal bhat*," said Carl, shaking his head.

"That's a good choice," said Om. "The curry is made with a stick of cinnamon, cardamom, and cloves."

"You really know a lot about cooking," said Kathy, placing her order.

"I work part time in the kitchen here preparing our traditional dishes. It helps me pay for my expenses at the university," said Om.

"What's the best dish on the menu?" asked Margaret, removing her reading glasses from her purse.

"Most tourists prefer the spiced almond chicken, *masaledar bijami kukhura,*" said Om.

"I'll try that spiced almond chicken," smiled Margaret, handing the waiter the menu.

"I'm going to have the Gundruk Soup. It's made from spinach leaves," said Muktuba, scowling at his son.

"I'll also have the soupwith smoked fish," said Moksha, squirming in his chair because of Om's defiance.

After dinner Kathy and Om departed for the dance. Carl and Margaret followed them to the ballroom to chaperone, leaving the shamans watching TV in the lobby.

The next morning at breakfast, the manager of the hotel announced that the airport had shut down due to the storm, leaving everyone annoyed because of the weather.

55

After a turbulent day of rain, the family members and guests began arriving at the royal palace on Friday at 6:30 for the dinner party. Crown Prince Dipendra was the host, greeting everyone as they entered the Billiards Room after crossing the wooden bridge opposite his living quarters.

"I'm so pleased you could join us this evening, Maheswar Singh. What will you have to drink?" asked Prince Dipendra.

"I'll have a lemon squash. Who's your friend wearing the saffron robe?" he asked, scowling at Nigel, who stood beside the prince.

"I want you to meet my spiritual guide, Swayambhu," said Dipendra. "I met him at the Tengboche Monastery and brought him to Kathmandu this past April."

"*Namaste*, I'm pleased to meet you, Maheshwar Singh," said Nigel, feeling out of place in his saffron robe.

"Queen Aishwarya told me all about you staying with the crown prince at the palace," said Maheswar, shaking his head with disgust.

"My mother doesn't approve of my friends," asserted Dipendra, changing the subject. "Here comes Uncle Rabi. He's now retired from the army."

"Good evening, Dipendraji. You're looking well tonight. Where's your fiancé, Devyani?" asked his uncle.

"She may come later for dessert," informed Dipendra. "I hope she'll wear her red dress like Scarlet O'Hara in *Gone with the Wind*. That'll give my mother and aunts something to talk about."

"Uncle Rabi, I want you to meet my friend, Swayambu. He's been my house guest for the past few months," said Prince Dipendra, turning to the bartender to order a drink.

"Swayambhu indeed! The Queen doesn't like having Nigel Porter at our family gatherings. I've seen his picture in the newspapers with you and Devyani," said Uncle Rabi, asking the bartender for a martini with a twist of lemon.

"Nigel, I met your father, Jim Porter, many years ago. In fact I hired a private plane so that he could fly your brother's corpse to London," informed Maheswara.

"My brother's death was a terrible tragedy," said Nigel, glancing at his watch. "I wonder what's keeping my mother. She should be here by now."

"Dipendraji, don't tell me you invited Margaret Porter to the dinner party?" asked Uncle Rabi. "The queen will be furious if she comes here. Your mother had a headache after entertaining Margaret for lunch last week,"

"Please excuse me. I'll wait for my mother in the garden," said Nigel, leaving through the French doors.

"Why are you associating with Nigel Porter, your Highness?" asked Uncle Rabi. "He looks foolish in that saffron robe from Thailand. At Tengboche the monks all wear maroon robes."

"He's my spiritual advisor and my friend," defended Dipendra, sipping his drink. "Devyani likes to see Nigel in a saffron robe. She's thinks it's more fashionable than those ugly maroon robes."

"Many years ago I took Nigel's father, Jim Porter, to Shanta Bhawan Hospital to visit his wife, Margaret. She had a nervous breakdown after Christopher's death. At that time Jim told me that Margaret was mentally ill," stated Maheswar Singh.

"Nigel murdered his brother and got away with it by blaming Yorg Schmidt," said Uncle Rabi. "He was only a child at the time, but he should have been incarcerated. He's also mentally ill and can't be trusted since he's from the Tengboche Monastery, which is under surveillance.

"You're wrong about Nigel," insisted the crown prince. "Swayambu's a very spiritual man."

"He's an imposter," insisted Uncle Rabi, pacing the floor.

"Something wicked this way comes," said Dipendra quoting *Macbeth*. He raised his glass to toast his mother and his aunts, entering the room through the French doors.

Uncle Rabi hurried to greet the women. "Good evening Queen Aishwarya, Princess Shanti, Princess Shrada, and Princess Shobha. You're lovely in your new evening gowns. You must have got them in Europe."

"We bought them in Paris," said Queen Aishwarya, coming to the bar with her relatives.

"'Double, double, toil and trouble…Here comes mother and the three witches. They're busy plotting my wedding," uttered Dipendra, gulping his drink.

"I heard that remark," snapped Queen Aishwarya. "No one's plotting anything. Your aunts and I are concerned about the future of our monarchy."

"Good evening, Mother," said the crown prince, bowing to her and his aunts. "What would you like to drink?"

"Nothing right now," uttered the queen. "Has your grandmother arrived yet?"

"I just called my driver, requesting him to bring her to the party in my limousine. Would you mind if Margaret Porter joins you and the queen mother? I believe she met grandma at your afternoon tea."

"I can't believe you invited Margaret!" shouted the queen. "She won't be coming here tonight. I found out she's in Pokhara with the shamans from the convention.

They're staying at the Third Eye Hotel. All flights to Kathmandu have been delayed due to the rain until tomorrow afternoon."

"I was shocked by the low cut gown that Margaret wore at the luncheon the other day," said Princess Shrada.

"I'm sure Margaret dyes her hair," said Queen Aishwaraya. "Of course, she could be wearing a wig."

"Margaret's plunging neckline got the attention of the men all right. Even the waiters and cooks came from the kitchen to stare at her cleavage," remarked Princess Shanti.

"She doesn't know how to dress appropriately. Margaret reminds me of a gypsy," snapped the queen, placing an order with the bartender. "Have a waiter bring our drinks to the sitting room. We always have gin and tonics with twists of lemon."

"Come on girls. We'll wait for the queen mother in her sitting room," said Queen Aishwarya departing from the Billiards Room with the king's three sisters.

"Good evening Dipendraji," said Krishna, the prince's servant. "The monk in the garden is wondering if his mother, Margaret Porter, arrived yet."

"Tell Swayambhu that his mother won't be here tonight. She's delayed in Pokhara due to the storm," said the crown prince, setting down his drink.

All heads turned toward the queen mother entering the Billiards Room through the French doors. She was wearing a bronze sari and an Egyptian necklace glistening with diamonds.

Dipendra greeted his grandmother and requested his servant, Krishna, to escort her to the sitting room.

The crown prince left the room to smoke a joint on the bridge. Upon returning, he went straight to the bar to replenish his drink. He set down the glass to play a game of billiards while his bodyguard, Major Bohara, fed him the balls. He was interrupted by his servant.

"Dipendraji, should I inform Swayambhu to join us for dinner? He's meditating in the garden."

"No, Krishna. Nigel's not welcome here," insisted the queen, who had just returned with the women from the sitting room. "Dipendra, I want to speak to you privately."

"What the hell's so urgent, Mother?" slurred Dipendra, setting down his cue and picking up his drink.

"Alcohol always makes you defiant," insisted the queen. "You've had enough to drink tonight. We'll talk outside on the veranda. I don't want to create a scene in here."

56

Queen Aishwarya hurried across the Billiards Room with her black velvet dress sweeping the floor. She fingered her ruby necklace, reflected in the crystal chandelier.

"What do want from me this time, Mother?" asked Dipendra, following her through the French doors onto the veranda. He paced in front of her, smoking a cigarette.

In the distance Nigel was sitting beneath the statue of the Buddha. His saffron robe was illuminated by the setting of the sun on the palace grounds.

"I don't approve of Nigel Porter being at our family gathering," stated the queen. "Your aunts are embarrassed by his presence in the palace. All of Kathmandu is gossiping about your relationship with him."

"Let them talk. You didn't want me to invite Devyani either. She won't be at the party tonight, but might show up later for dessert," said the prince.

"I invited Supriya Shah and her family," informed the queen. "But they declined the invitation as well."

"You never liked Supriya when I was dating her. Now you're trying to match me up with her again," blurted the prince. "I wish you'd mind your own business."

"Dipendra, I'm not going to argue with you. I just wanted to inform you that I called Gurima Rana and asked her to join us for dessert with her mother."

"You did what?" bellowed the crown prince, flushed with anger. "I dated her a long time ago. I'm not even mildly interested in her."

"I thought you might reconsider. I know she's busy with her career as a lawyer, but she told me on the phone she was still fond of you."

"Please, Mother! I wish you would stop interfering with my life!" shouted the crown prince, pacing up and down on the veranda like a rampant lion.

"Interfere! I'm concerned about your health. I got a report from your physician today. He told me that you have high blood pressure, high cholesterol, and you're grossly overweight. He said you drink and smoke too much! Just look at yourself! You're not fit to be the next ruler of this country!" screamed the queen.

"I'm going on a retreat with Swayambhu right after the Summer Games. I'm planning to quit smoking and drinking. I'm even going on a strict diet."

"You never follow through on your promises. I've arranged for you to go to a clinic in Switzerland for six weeks. You'll come back a new man, totally free from addictions," insisted the queen.

"No, Mother," argued Dipendra. "I plan to go to rehab at Shanta Bhawan in Patan after the retreat."

"I'm sure Nigel advised you to say here in Kathmandu. I don't know why you call him Swayambhu. I had detectives do a background check on him.

"He's was kidnapped by a London Coven, who were performing sinister rituals at Doctor Bhinna Atma's cottage on Fewa Lake many years ago," said his mother.

"Nigel told me all about being held hostage there," said Dipendra, pacing on the bridge.

"I just got news from palace security that a forensic anthropologist brought the remains of Yorg and Myrna back to Kathmandu from that cottage. You will never guess who was responsible for digging up their skeletons?"

"Who was it?" asked Dipendra, gulping his drink.

"It was Margaret Porter! Everyone knows she's having an affair with Carl Brecht, the anthropologist. She hired shamans to perform exorcisms at the collapsed cottage.

"I'm telling you, Dipendra, that your friend, Nigel, sitting over there pretending to be a Buddhist monk, is an imposter. He murdered his brother under the pomelo tree at the Kathmandu Guest House in October of 1976."

"You've got everything wrong. Swayambhu told me Yorg Schmidt staged Christopher's death," said the prince.

"That's nothing but a lie. Yorg was my friend. He used to attend our family dinners. I was shocked that his remains were never properly buried because of corruption in the police department in Pokhara. They forged the records about removing his remains and sending them to Europe.

"I forbid you to associate with Nigel any longer. I want him out of the palace by tomorrow morning!" screamed the queen. "He's been lingering here getting attention long enough! You shouldn't have brought him to Kathmandu!

"Our family astrologer told me all about your visit to his quarters with Nigel," continued the angry queen. "You certainly weren't hospitable when we took you to celebrate Pandey's 70th wedding anniversary this afternoon. You were busy smoking marijuana with your cousin, Paras."

"What did the astrologer tell you about me?" asked Dipendra, lighting another cigarette.

"He told me you intend to marry Devyani in December. When he double checked your chart, he found out that the date was inauspicious."

"What?" asked Dipendra. "That dirty rat! He lied to me. When we were there, he told me that it was an auspicious day because our marriage was made in heaven."

The queen laughed maniacally. "Well, he occasionally makes a mistake. Here come your aunts. I also found out you rented the ballroom at the Royal Hotel for your wedding reception. But I took the liberty to cancel the reservation. The manager agreed to refund your deposit."

"I don't care what you say. I'm going to marry Devyani whether you approve or not," insisted the prince.

"If you marry her, you won't become the next king. I've already talked to your brother Nirajan about this. He's agreed to marry the bride that I've chosen for him without resistance. I'll see that he inherits the throne."

"But I'm the oldest son. I'm next in line for succession," shouted Dipendra, flushed with rage.

"I'll reconsider, if you to go the clinic in Switzerland for six weeks. Let me know about your decision early next week so I can book the flight."

"Don't worry," asserted Dipendra, his fists clenched. "My decision is that I'm not going!"

"I've had enough of your reckless living. The whole family is ashamed of your behavior and scandalous life.

"Here comes your sister, Princess Shruti with her husband Kumar Gorakh," said the queen. "Shruti, Shruti, come over here. I want you to say hello to your brother, who intends to be the future king of the Shah dynasty."

"Hello Mother," said Shruti. "Dipendraji, it's wonderful to see you. I understand you'll be competing in karate at the games on Sunday."

"He's not fit for that competition," uttered the queen. "Just look at him. He needs to lose a hundred pounds."

"Good evening, Kumar," said Dipendra, turning toward his sister's husband and ignoring his mother's comment. "Why don't you have a game of billiards with me?"

"Of course I'll join you, Dipendraji. I haven't had a good game of billiards since our last family dinner," stated Kumar, giving his wife, Shruti, a kiss on the cheek.

"How are my nieces doing?" asked Dipendra, turning toward his sister.

"The girls are doing fine. We had a party for them last week," informed Shruti. "I'm sorry you weren't there."

57

Kumar and Shruti sipped their drinks, chatting with Dipendra about their recent trip to Italy. The queen interrupted their conversation to inform them more guests had just entered through the French doors.

"Here comes your brother. He came all the way from Britain so that he could be here for our family dinner," said Queen Aishwarya, waving to her son.

"Good evening, everyone," said Prince Nirajan. "It's so nice to see you, Dipendraji. My flight from London was delayed for hours in Delhi due to the monsoon."

"Congratulations for finishing your studies at Eaton," said Dipendra. "Are you going back to do graduate work?"

"Not if I can help it," announced the queen. "I have other plans for Nirajan. We have an appointment to see the astrologer next week to set his wedding date."

"I'm going to be held hostage at the palace while Mother makes arrangements for my wedding," smiled Nirajan. "I'm so happy to be back in Kathmandu."

"I don't trust the astrologer. He's a dirty rat," asserted Prince Dipendra, gulping his drink.

"What nonsense are you talking about now?" asked Queen Aishwarya. "You better go easy on the liquor this time. I don't want you embaraassing me again."

"The astrologer is a lying bastard," asserted Dipendra.

"How you talk about Pandeyji," defended the queen. "He's been with our family for three generations."

"The problem is that mother hates Devyani's family because they are wealthy industrialists from New Delhi with more money than the entire Shah dynasty," announced Crown Prince Dipendra, slightly inebriated.

"Don't talk nonsense!" uttered Queen Aishwarya.

"I have to admit that my marriage to Kumar was made in heaven," commented Princess Shruti.

"It's because your sister had enough sense to listen to me. I'm the one who arranged her marriage," said the queen, scowling at the crown prince.

"But Dipendra's in love with Devyani," defended Shruti. "He's old enough to make his own decision about his marriage, Mother."

"Here comes my cousin, Prince Paras, with his wife, Himani," said Dipendra. "Aunt Kamal is with them but not Uncle Gyanendra".

"Where's Gyanendra?" asked the queen. "He never misses our monthly dinners."

"He's at the Chitwaun National Park and won't be back until Sunday," responded his wife.

"Your son, Paras, is still sowing his wild oats even though he's married," informed the queen in a hostile tone.

"Mother, you better not talk so loudly," whispered the princess. "Cousin Paras will hear you."

"Everyone knows Paras is a womanizer. That's why your aunt has grey hair," snarled the queen. "I know she did everything possible to raise your cousin properly, but your philandering uncle undermined her authority."

Dipendra bowed to his relatives. "I'm so pleased to see all of you. How about a drink? Paras, why don't you join us for a game of billiards?"

"Dipendra, more guests are arrving," shouted the queen. "There's your father's older brother, Prince Dhirendra. He hasn't been the same since his divorce."

"I'll be right back," said the crown prince, replenishing his drink at the bar.

The queen greeted Mrs. Ketaki Chester, her mother, Princess Helen, and her sister, Princess Jayanti. She encouraged them to greet the queen mother in her chamber after getting a drink at the bar.

Dipendra sighed with relief when the queen left the room with the women trailing after her. "Paras, would you like to have a drink with me? It looks like you could use one."

"Not tonight. I'll just finish this Coca Cola," said his cousin, setting his glass on the corner of the billiards table.

"I'm relieved my mother's with grandmother. They'll be returning for dinner in a half hour," said the crown prince, gulping his drink.

"There's nothing like a game of billiards to relieve stress after a busy day," said Kumar, pausing after taking a shot at the balls. "Dipendra! What's wrong with you?"

The crown prince stumbled, dropping his cue on the floor. He seized the rim of the billiard table with both hands saying, "I'm feeling dizzy right now."

"Did you trip on something?" asked Paras

"No, I'm fine," insisted Dipendra, trying to stand up straight while clinging to the table. He grabbed the cue and then stumbled backward again.

"Are you all right, Dipendraji?" asked Uncle Dhirendra, taking the prince by the arm. "Surely you're not drunk. You know how to hold your liquor like a gentleman. I've never seen you like this before."

"I'm all right," uttered Dipendra, trembling.

"We better take you outside to get some fresh air," said Paras. "It's stuffy in here."

"A little exercise will do me good. We can go to the garden and chat with Swayambhu for a few minutes. He's mediating in front of the statue of Buddha. I could use another drink," insisted Dipendra.

"You'd better slow down," advised his uncle. "You don't want to be drunk before dinner tonight."

"I can walk just fine," said Dipendra, breaking away from them and staggering across the room toward the exit.

"Have you been arguing with your mother again, Dipendraji?" asked Paras.

"My mother's trying to control my life. She has threatened to take away my monthly allowance and give the throne to my younger brother, Nirajan, if I marry Devyani," blurted the crown prince.

"What does your father, King Birendra, think about your relationship with Devyani?" asked Paras.

"He's too stressed about the Maoists to be concerned about my marriage," said Dipendra, leaving the veranda and pausing on the bridge to take deep breaths.

"You've got to stand up for yourself," advised Paras. "You can't let your family push you around. You're not a child anymore. You're a man destined to be the king."

Uncle Dhirendra insisted that Queen Aishwarya was bluffing about putting Prince Nirajan on the throne and that she would be forced to follow the protocol. There was no doubt in his mind that succession to the throne must go to the eldest son.

"My mother has always liked my brother and my sister more than me," sighed the crown prince.

"You need some allies to put the queen in her place!" advised Paras. "I'll tell you something. I don't let my parents control my life! I do what I please! You need the support of the queen mother."

"I've already tried that, but she refuses to talk about my marriage. Every time I bring up the topic, she changes the subject," said Dipendra.

"What's that British monk doing over there next to the statue of the Buddha?" asked Paras. "Your mother wants him out of here."

"Hey! Swayambhu! Come over here. I want to introduce you to my dinner guests," shouted Dipendra, holding the railing of the bridge to steady himself. A few moments later, he opened his cigarette case and removed the remaining hashish and a black substance.

"This is my cousin, Paras, and Uncle Dhirendra, my father's brother," said the crown prince lighting a pipe and exhaling a cloud of smoke.

"It's a real pleasure to see both of you again," stated Nigel, shaking their hands.

"I'm the unruly and disobedient cousin," laughed Paras. "You're Nigel. I met you at the dinner party last month."

"Look over there. It's a whirlwind rising from the bank of the pond near the statue of the Buddha," said the prince.

"We'd better take shelter inside the Billiards Room," shouted Uncle Direndra"

"Please excuse me, Dipendraji. I'm going to your apartment to pack my things. I must leave the royal palace so that the queen won't create more problems for you. I'll take a taxi to the monastery and stay with the monks at Bodhnath," insisted Nigel.

"I'll join you at the monastery later," said the prince, crossing the bridge with the others following him.

58

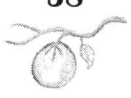

The sand from the whirlwind was stinging Nigel's face as he rushed toward the stairs leading to the crown prince's apartments. The force of the wind was so strong he could scarcely go up the steps. A horrific clap of thunder was preceded by a torrential downpour.

Dipendra glanced over his shoulder, noticing that Nigel was struggling to open the door to his apartments at the top of the stairs. Once Nigel was safe inside his quarters, the prince returned to the Billiards Room.

Paras approached him saying, "Devyani wants you to call her. Here come the waiters with the hors d'oeuvres. It won't be long before the women join us for dinner."

Dipendra removed his cell phone from his pocket and dialed Devyani. He listened to her for sometime before responding in a loud voice.

"I don't care what my mother said about you to her sisters. I want you to join us tonight for dessert…I understand you're busy right now…No! I don't care about her at all," said the prince listening for a few moments before terminating the conversation.

"What's going on, Dipendraji?" asked Paras, returning with a plate of shrimp and cocktail sauce.

"Devyani doesn't want to come here for dessert because my mother makes her feel uncomfortable. I'd like to have another drink."

"You'd better eat something first. It's not good to be drinking on an empty stomach," said his cousin.

"I'm not hungry," said the crown prince. He went straight to the bar for a glass of *The Famous Grouse*, a blended Scotch malt whiskey.

Opening his silver cigarette case, Dipendra discovered that it was empty. He called his personal servant on his cell phone. "I need a fresh supply of everything."

Dipendra walked over to Paras, who was chatting with his mother's three sisters at the hors d'oeurvre table. He hurried toward them, interrupting the conversation.

"Excuse me, Paras," said Dipendra whispering to his cousin. "Please do me a favor. Here's my cigarette case. Go to my apartments and have Krishna replenish it with five joints and some black bullets? He'll be waiting for you at the door."

"You're not still taking black bullets, are you? No wonder you're stumbling all over the place. I quit using them a long time ago. They made me dizzy."

Dipendra paused to remove his ringing cell phone from his coat pocket. "It's Devyani... I...I can't talk now. I'm busy with my guests. No, I'm not mad at you. I'll call you after the party."

The crown prince headed for the billiards table and continued the game with his guests. He paused when Paras arrived with his cigarette case and slipped it into his pocket. His cousin then joined them at billiards.

A few minutes later Dipendra began sweating, claiming he was dizzy. He dropped the cue and clung to the side of the table, claiming his legs were limp. Within a short time he collapsed on the floor with a loud thud, bumping his head. The prince was sprawled out, unconscious with his eyes closed, breathing heavily through his mouth.

"We've got to bring him to his quarters before King Birendra arrives," shouted Paras, hovering over the prince.

Kumar and Major Bohara set down their cues to help. They each lifted the crown prince's shoulders while Paras took his feet. The three men carried the overweight prince from the Billiards Room, across the bridge, and up the stairs to his living quarters. Upon entering his apartments, they found Nigel about to leave with his suitcase.

"You can't go now," insisted Paras. "You've got to stay to take care of Dipendraji."

"You'd better put him on the bed in his room," insisted Nigel. "I'll get a bag of ice from the refrigerator for that bruise on his head."

"Maybe you can sober him up enough to meet his father. King Birendra will be furious if he finds out that Dipendra collapsed because he was drunk."

"I warned him not to smoke so much," said Paras. "He'll be all right after he takes a cold shower. Krishna's already making him some black coffee."

"We'd better get back to the party," said Kumar. "Shruti will be coming for snacks with Queen Aishwarya and the queen mother at any moment."

59

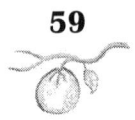

Nigel was disturbed by the moaning coming from the next room. Leaving his suitcase in front of the fireplace, he entered the bedroom, where the crown prince was propped up on the bed, and his servant was giving him coffee.

"I hope you're feeling better, Dipendraji," said Nigel, handing Krishna the ice pack. "That was quite a fall you had in the Billiards Room. You've got to be more careful."

"I'm all right," uttered Dipendra. "Krishna, go ahead and turn on the shower. I've got to get back to the dinner party. My father will be angry with me if I'm not there to greet him when he arrives."

"You've got to stop smoking and using that black substance," advised Krishna, returning from the bathroom.

"I don't remember taking a black bullet tonight. I have a funny feeling that something terrible is going to happen," said the prince.

"Stop worrying," said Nigel, quietly reciting the Gayatri Mantra to calm Dipendra.

"My grandmother taught me that prayer when I was a little boy. I used to recite it daily," sighed the crown prince. "I have to confess, I did smoke hashish on the bridge, but I really didn't drink very much tonight."

"But Dipendraji, you must be honest, if not with me, at least with yourself," insisted Nigel. "I saw you drinking with your guests. Socrates once said that we tell ourselves lies and believe our own lies," said Nigel.

"I'm telling you the truth, Swayambhu," said the crown prince, removing the ice pack from his forehead. "I had the bartender give me only a half a glass of liquor each time I went to the bar. He usually fills my glass."

"I think somebody slipped a drug into my drink. I suddenly got dizzy at the billiards table and collapsed on the floor. I don't remember anything after that.

"I'm angry with my mother. She's turned my family against me. I'm still dizzy from hitting my head on the floor," said the prince, rising from the bed. He got up and glanced at himself in the mirror.

"My clothes are wrinkled. I need to take a shower. Krishna, get me a tuxedo."

The servant informed the prince that his suits and tuxedos were at the cleaners, but his three army uniforms had come back yesterday afternoon. He also said two soldiers were looking for him earlier while he was visiting the astrologer.

"I was surprised to find them in the living room when I came upstairs to change the sheets and vacuum the carpet," said Krishna. "You must have given the soldiers a key to your apartments?"

"I don't remember giving them a key," said Dipendra, opening the door to his wardrobe. "Sure enough, two of my new army uniforms are gone! That's strange. Krishna, I want you to call the laundry service. I don't trust them. There's always something missing."

"Dipendraji, drinking and smoking makes you either grandiose with unlimited power or remorseful and feeling inferior. It also causes memory loss," asserted Nigel.

"Let's leave the dinner party early and go to Bodhnath. We'll stop on the way and get Devyani. Wait for me behind the statue of the Buddha, Swayambhu," asserted the crown prince. "After the retreat, I will go to treatment."

"Krishna, why were the two soldiers in Dipendra's living room?" asked Nigel.

"They wanted the prince to donate money to the Gurkha Veterans Fund. I told them to come back this evening before the dinner party," said Krishna, pausing. "Your bath is ready Dipendraji. I'll bring you fresh towels."

Dipendra removed his clothing and put on a terrycloth robe, leaving his wrinkled tuxedo in a heap on the floor. He ordered the servant to get his army uniform from the wardrobe and leave it on his bed.

"It wouldn't be proper for you to wear your army uniform to the family gathering," advised the servant.

"I don't have anything else to wear," insisted the prince, heading toward the shower. "My two new uniforms are missing. I thought you said they came back from the cleaners."

"Dipendraji, I hope you will keep your promise about going to detox at the hospital," said Nigel, concerned about the prince's health.

"Why should I lie to you, Swayambhu?" asked the crown prince. "You're the only person around here that I can trust although I also confide in my cousin, Paras."

"It was strange to see that whirlwind earlier this evening," said Nigel, puzzled. "The last time I saw such a whirlwind was at Dr. Bhinna Atma's cottage when I was kidnapped by the coven."

"Krishna, I want you to make an appointment for me to go to rehab on Monday, June 4th at Shanta Bhawan Hospital. This time reserve a plain room for me, not the royal suite," insisted the crown prince.

"I will make the appointment the first thing in the morning," said the servant.

The crown prince entered the bathroom. About ten minutes later he emerged with his hair combed.

"Here's your army uniform," said Krishna, helping the prince get dressed.

"Swayambhu, why are you staring out the window so intensely?" asked the crown prince.

"Your father, King Birendra has just arrived. He's getting out of the limousine and going toward the bridge," said Nigel, pausing. "He's now crossing the bridge and entering the Billiards Room."

"He was working late with Mohan Bahadur, his press secretary on an article for *Newsweek*. My father's been making a real effort to negotiate with the Maoists," said the prince, putting on his army boots and uniform.

"There's something strange going on outside," said Nigel, glancing out the window. "Someone is hiding in the bushes over there. He's wearing an army uniform just like yours. That soldier even looks like you, Dipendraji. He could be your twin."

"That's impossible," said Dipendra, crossing the room with his boots striking the polished oak floor. "Let me have a look...I'll be damned. That soldier does look like me! He's wearing my uniform and holding a submachine gun just like mine."

"He's now going toward the other soldier, who just came out from behind those bushes with two guns," said Nigel, still standing at the window.

"That second soldier is also wearing my uniform and holding an assault rifle and a twelve gauge pump action shot gun!" shouted Dipendra.

"I...I wonder if I gave those two men a key to my apartment the other night when I was at the rave party in the warehouse. I must have blacked out," said the crown prince. "Maybe I told them we'd stage a little drama at our family dinner party."

The prince turned to his servant coming out of the bathroom with the wet towels for the laundry.

"Come over here, Krishna," said Dipendra. "Take a good look out of the window at those soldiers below. Were those the two men who were in my apartment asking for a donation earlier?"

"That man doesn't look like you anymore," said Nigel, his eyebrows raised. "There's something strange going on out there in front of the Billiards Room."

"Those are the two men that were here," said Krishna. "They wanted me to donate your old clothing to their organization. I told them you didn't have any clothing to give away."

"They obviously helped themselves to my uniforms," said Dipendra. "I wonder if they borrowed my guns."

The crown prince hurried over to his gun collection and opened the glass case. "They've got my MP5K submachine gun, my colt M-16, my twelve gauge SPAS. The rest of my weapons are still here."

"Dipendraji, I don't think you should go back to the dinner party tonight," advised Nigel. "We should leave immediately for the monastery. Just look at the wind stirring the trees again."

"I'm sure I met those two men at the rave party," said Dipendra. "I must have given them my spare key."

"Krishnaji, I want you to go down there and tell those two soldiers to come to my quarters....Krishna? Where did that stupid servant go?"

"I saw him go out the back door with the laundry while you were talking, Dipendraji," said Nigel.

"Those soldiers are standing on the bridge smoking cigarettes. They seem to be planning something. I'm going to find out what's going on," insisted the prince, putting on his camouflage vest and black gloves.

"Don't go Dipendraji!" said Nigel. "Look over there! A whirlwind is stirring up the pond.

"Those two soldiers are standing in front of the French doors, looking into the Billiards Room," said Dipendra. "Now I remember. We planned to have a mock attack on the royal family to add some excitement to the family dinner party. They're always so boring," said Dipendra.

"I beg you to come with me," said Nigel, picking up his suitcase in front of the fireplace. "We must flee from the palace grounds. Let's go now."

"Don't worry about me. I can take care of myself," said the crown prince, leaving his living quarters. He headed down the stairs toward the bridge.

A few moments later Nigel hurried out the door and stood at the top of the stairs. He saw a soldier with a weapon open the French Doors and enter the Billiards Room. The other soldier was nowhere in sight. Dipendra had also disappeared.

In the distance the whirlwind was gaining momentum, hurling sand and water onto the bridge. Nigel hurried down the stairs carrying his suitcase.

All of a sudden one of the soldiers seized him by the arm. "Queen Aishwarya wants you to leave the palace grounds immediately. She's not pleased with you living here any longer. Get into that limousine and the driver will take you to the Kathmandu Guest House for the night."

"Don't be ridiculous," said Nigel. "I can't leave now. Prince Dipendra wants me to meet him in front of the statute of the Buddha. We're going on a retreat to Bodhnath after the dinner party."

"Dipendra went inside the Billiards Room. Go over there and wait for him," said the soldier with the twelve gauge pump action shot gun.

"Why are you wearing Dipendra's uniform and using his gun?" asked Nigel.

"We're rehearsing a combat in case terrorists invade the palace. The crown prince gave us a key to his apartments. He told us at the warehouse that we could borrow his uniforms and guns anytime we wanted to practice."

"Was it a rave party?" asked Nigel, recalling the prince's conversation.

"Yes, we often see him at rave parties. My boss and I are employed by the Royal Nepalese Army to conduct this mock attack. Don't be alarmed if you hear shots. They're not real bullets. I've got to go now," said the soldier.

Nigel was bewildered as he hurried with his suitcase toward the statue. The whirlwind was spinning sand in his face until he took refuge behind the Buddha, covering his head with his arms.

60

Inside the Billards Room King Birendra was surrounded by the older men chatting about whether the army should be deployed against the Maoists. Uncle Rabi, the retired general, was supportive of the move, but Maheswar Singh was against it.

"I'm not only concerned about the Maoists," said the king, "but I'm worried about the influence of the Hindu Nationalist Movement, the *Bharatiya Janata Party*."

"I'm more concerned about the militant splinter group, the *Shiva Sena* which controls most of Mumbai like the mafia in Chicago," said Maheswar Singh.

"A few years ago the *Shiva Sena* destroyed the mosque built over the ruins of the ancient Hindu palace in Ayodhya, where Lord Rama was born," said the king.

"Islamic terrorists from Pakistan retaliated by attacking several train stations in Mumbai, massacring the Hindu passengers," announced Maheswar.

"I've heard from a reliable source that the Islamic terrorists were plotting to destroy the Taj Mahal Hotel in Mumbai," said King Birendra, sipping his lemonade.

"All of our attention has been on the Maoists here in Nepal. We've ignored dissident groups from India like the *Shiva Sena*, which may be active here in Kathmandu."

"Our local Muslim community is concerned about prejudice and hostility from Indian gangs in Kathmandu," said Uncle Rabi.

"It was a mistake to open our country to unlimited immigration from India," asserted Uncle Rabi. "Nearly all of the Indians came here from northern India"

"Their shops are an eyesore. Crime has gone up since they settled here. The hoodlums wander around the city dealing in drugs and intimidating our people," added Maheswar Singh.

"Who is that dark figure hovering in the doorway?" asked King Birendra. "He's been standing there for a long time. He's now turning toward us ."

"It's your son, Crown Prince Dipendra. He's wearing his army uniform and combat boots. He's staging some type of maneuver," said Uncle Rabi.

"Ever since he was a child, Dipendra liked to wear military costumes and perform for us," smiled King Birendra.

"Our family dinner has become a masquerade party," announced Mrs. Ketaki Chester, moving away from the bar and heading toward the crown prince.

"Dipendra always played with toy guns when he was a child," said King Birendra. "He loved going to the military academy, where he became an expert marksman."

"He might be practicing a maneuver in case we're attacked by terrorists," announced Uncle Rabi.

"Dipendra excelled at karate when he was at Eaton. We're proud of his Black Belt status," informed the king. "Please excuse me. I've got to talk to him about changing his clothes for the dinner party. His mother will be angry if she sees him in his army uniform."

"Dipendra, why on earth are you dressed in those army fatigues and combat boots?" asked the king, approaching his son with his hands outstretched.

The soldier raised the submachine gun and fired two bullets at his father. King Birendra just stood there with blood gushing from his side and neck.

"*Ke gardeko?* What have you done?" questioned the king, collapsing onto the floor.

"It must have been an accident!" screamed Princess Shobha, the king's youngest sister.

"Someone ring up an ambulance!" shouted Uncle Rabi.

All eyes were wide with horror as the crown prince fired two more rounds of ammunition into the ceiling before turning around and leaving through the French doors.

Upon hearing the shots coming from the Billiards Room, Nigel rose from behind the statue of the Buddha in the garden and hurried toward the bridge.

He was shocked to see Dipendra standing on the bridge, holding a submachine gun. The prince was gazing at the whirlwind churning up the waves on the pond.

"Dipendraji come over here. We must leave for the monastery right away," shouted Nigel.

The armed soldier lifted the rifle and fired at him from the bridge. Nigel was startled as the bullets whizzed past him, striking the Buddha and chipping the statue. He threw himself onto the ground. Raising his head, Nigel saw Dipendra return to the Billiards Room.

Rising from the ground, he hurried toward the scene of the crime. Glancing through the French doors, he saw the crown prince hurl the MP5K submachine onto the floor. This time he was holding the Colt M-16, an assault rifle.

Princess Sobha, snatched up the submachine gun from the floor and then picked up the magazine that had fallen out. She shouted, "We've had enough violence for one day!"

Dipendra raised the assault rifle and shocked everyone by firing again at his father, King Birendra. The king's brother, Dhirendra, stepped forward trying to stop the violence but was shot in the chest. Taking aim at his brother-in-law, the crown prince fired at Kumar Gorak who collapsed in front of the billiards table.

Princess Shruti screamed, dropping her dinner plate of food. It crashed to the floor shattering into several pieces. She rushed toward her bleeding husband, Kumar, trying to comfort him, but was shot by her brother.

Upon seeing his sister bleeding on the floor, Dipendra backed away and left the Billiards Room. He was unaware that Nigel was hiding behind a potted plant on the veranda.

A few moments later Crown Prince Dipendra returned to the room, where he opened fire on his relatives, incuding Princesses Shanti, Princess Shrada, Princess Jayanti and Paras' mother, Aunt Kamal.

During the entire massacre, the crown prince had a peculiar frozen smile. There was no sign of anxiety on his face, only a fixed jack-o-lantern grin. He alarmed the survivors when he hysterically kicked the bloody corpses on the floor of the Billiards Room.

Horrified at seeing the murders through the window, Nigel fled across the bridge to hide behind the statue of the Buddha. He was trembling from shock.

The deranged prince left the room for a few minutes and returned with his hat pulled down over his eyes. He raised the collar of his uniform to conceal his face.

"Dipendraji, you've come back. I'm your cousin, Paras. I've been your friend ever since we were children. Please, we wish you no harm."

"Who's that hiding behind the sofa?" asked the crown prince in a barely audible voice.

"They are your relatives, who agreed to attend your wedding to Devyani at the Royal Hotel in December," stated Paras, his voive quivering.

"Who are they? I want to know their names," insisted Dipendra, his face still expressionless except for the sinister smile.

"Your cousin is hiding there. She's Uncle Dhirendra's daughter," said Paras, concerned about her safety.

"I want to see her," demanded the crown prince.

Sitosna rose from behind the sofa because she was the bravest of the three relatives.

"She just returned from Scotland where she's been studying," said Paras, his voice quivering.

"Who else is hiding there?" asked the prince, elevating his rifle, ready to fire another round of ammunition at his relatives.

"My wife, Himani. She's always been kind to you. Uncle Rabi and Maheswar Singh are also here. They've been faithful to you ever since you were born."

"Where's your mother, Paras?" asked Dipendra.

"She's over there. I think she's dead," said Paras, forcing himself to remain calm.

"I've got to go now. All of you may live," informed Dipendra, backing out of the room through the French doors and onto the veranda.

61

Dipendra paused on the bridge for a few moments before heading toward his apartments. He was half way up the stairs when he heard a shrill voice coming from the veranda.

"Dipendra! Dipendra! *Ma tapai sangha ahile kura garnu man lagcha.* I want to speak with you right now," screamed Queen Aishwarya, crossing the bridge with Prince Nirajan following her.

"We just came from Grandmother's sitting room. She's waiting for you to come and visit her. Come down here and join us," shouted his brother.

"I'm busy," uttered the crown prince. "I've got a lot of things to do yet tonight."

"Dipendra! You filthy bastard! What have you done?" shrieked the queen. "You're a murderer!"

"Give me that rifle," shouted Prince Nirajan, stepping in front of his mother to shield her. He hurried toward the stairs with his arms outstretched.

The killer stood on the steps, his face paralyzed with a maniacal grin, illuminated by the outdoor floodlight. He raised the assault rifle and opened fire repeatedly on his brother. The unarmed Nirajan fell to the ground, his torso gushing blood from a dozen bullet wounds.

From behind the statue of the Buddha, Nigel squinted at the slaughter of Prince Nirajan. He was terrified as another whirlwind rose from the bank of the pond, whipping sand at the base of the stairs, where the queen was standing immobilized.

"You monster! You've shot your brother. You dirty bastard. You've killed the future king of Nepal! Give me that rifle," demanded the hysterical queen.

Dipendra hurried up the stairs and flung open the door to his quarters He rushed inside, leaving the door half open.

The queen gathered up her black velvet gown and hurried up the stairs with her high heels clicking. She screamed repeatedly, "Dipendra, Dipendra, give me that rifle! Give it to me right now!"

When she reached the seventh step, her eyes were wide with terror. She saw her son coming through the open door with the rifle. The desperate queen turned around to flee down the stairs but it was too late.

"You can have my rifle now," muttered the killer, shooting the queen in the head, blowing her brains out. Blood and gore were splattered on the stairs as the grinning murderer riddled her body with bullets.

Nigel observed the violence, followed by the whirlwind flinging sand onto the corpse before spinning over the roof of the Billiards Room into the clouded sky.

He saw Dipendra come down the stairs and kick the twisted body of Queen Aishwarya causing it to tumble down the remaining stairs.

"You can get up now," shouted a soldier, wearing the prince's army uniform. He came out of the bushes with a duffle bag, pausing to remove the gag from the mouth of the hostage, whose hands were tied with ropes. The soldier gave the heavy-set man a shove forward.

"Hariyo, take our prisoner to the statue of the Buddha. There's someone there waiting for him. I'll join you shortly," said the assassin, going up the stairs into the living quarters.

"What's happened? I heard the queen screaming a few minutes ago and then gun shots," said the overweight Dipendra, tied up and wearing his old military uniform. He stumbled across the lawn. "Before that I heard the voice of Nirajan followed by more bullets."

"Prince Nirajan foolishly tried to defend his mother," uttered the soldier, pushing the perspiring hostage forward with a rifle against his back.

"Why are you wearing my new army uniforms? I remember you now. You're the fellow I met at the rave party with your other friend," said Dipendra, his hands still tied behind his back.

"I don't have time to talk now," said Hariyo. "Here we are at the statue of the Buddha.

"My boss just murdered your brother, Prince Nirajan, and your mother, Queen Aishwarya," laughed Hariyo. "We like wearing your uniforms."

"What are you talking about? When I came down the stairs earlier this evening someone knocked me out and dragged me into the bushes over there. I've been lying there unconscious until a few minutes ago. I woke up when I heard my brother shouting and my mother screaming," said Crown Prince Dipendra, still stunned. "I've been tied up. My hands hurt from these ropes. Please untie me."

"Here comes my boss, Yama Raj. You can talk to him about untying your ropes," said Hariyo.

"I finally get to meet Crown Prince Dipendra, who was once destined to be the future king of Nepal," said Yama Raj. "But not anymore."

"Just look at him now, tied up with a rope," laughed Hariyo. "Here's his pistol that we stole from his gun collection."

"He's now destined to die!" said Yama Raj, wearing the prince's army uniform. Raising his rifle, the killer struck the crown prince on the head with the butt.

Dipendra collapsed on the ground with his hands still tied. After untying his hands, Yama Raj shot Dipendra in the head and then inserted a pistol into the prince's hand to make it look like suicide. The bullet penetrated his skull. The two men left him bleeding on the ground.

Yama Raj, the assassin of the royal family, removed the rubber mask that he had been wearing of Crown Prince Dipendra, and stuffed it into his uniform's pocket. He turned toward his partner, Hariyo. "Here come the palace guards. Keep your mouth shut and let me do the talking."

The two soldiers heard an ambulance arriving and then the footsteps of guards coming toward them.

"What's going on here?" asked a palace guard. "We heard a shot coming from the statue of the Buddha. "My God! Not another murder. It's Crown Prince Dipendra!"

Yama Raj told the guard he and Hariyo were soldiers from the army hired by the royal family for the evening to keep watch.

"Unfortunately, we were unable to prevent Prince Dipendra from killing his family and dinner guests," stated Yama Raj. "It was terrifying to see such a slaughter!"

"We followed the disturbed prince to the statue of the Buddha. By the time we got there, it was too late. He had pulled the trigger, killing himself," added Hariyo, pacing in front of the statue.

"What do you mean?" asked the security guard, hurrying toward the bleeding body of Crown Prince Dipendra.

"It's not too late. The prince is still alive! He's still

breathing," said the security guard, shouting to the ambulance attendants to bring a stretcher while he tried to stop the bleeding.

"There's a noise coming from behind the statue," stated Hariyo, searching the bushes.

"What are you doing here, Nigel?" asked Yama Raj. "The queen told me that if you were found on the premises of the palace grounds during the dinner party, I should arrest you."

Yama Raj seized Nigel by the arm and took him behind the bushes with Hariyo following him.

"I saw you murder the royal family. You were wearing a mask of Dipendra. You struck him with the butt of your rifle and then shot him in the head with his own pistol," blurted Nigel.

"You'd better keep your fuckin' mouth shut. You're the brains behind the conspiracy," shouted Yama Raj.

Nigel yanked the mask out of the assassin's pocket "Here's proof that Dipendra's not the killer! You're both wearing his military uniforms that you stole from his wardrobe closet in his living quarters."

"I told you to keep your fuckin' mouth shut," shouted Yama Raj, seizing the mask from Nigel and stuffing it back into his coat pocket. "Gag this fool!"

Hariyo shoved a large handkerchief into Nigel's mouth, nearly choking him in the process. He then pushed him toward the Statue of the Buddha."

The security guard, who had been hovering over Dipendra the whole time gasped, "I've stop the bleeding. Here come the relatives of the wounded prince."

Paras hurried across the lawn with Maheswar Singh and Uncle Rabi. Yama Raja stepped forward and informed them that Dipendra attempted suicide after massacring his family and dinner guests.

"Why do you have Nigel gagged and tied up?" asked Paras. "He's Prince Dipendra's only real friend."

Yama Raj explained that Nigel Porter was the brains behind the conspiracy to assassinate the royal family.

He also informed them that the Tengboche Monastery was harboring Maoist terrorists. The police had arrested three Tibetan Buddhist monks from that monastery and a yogi, who were now prisoners at the downtown jail.

"All of them including Nigel confessed that they wanted to destroy the Shah Dynasty," lied Hariyo.

"I can't believe Nigel is a terrorist," said Paras, pausing as the ambulance pulled up near the bridge.

"There are wounded people inside the Billiards Room," shouted Paras to the paramedics arriving with stretchers. "We'll take the crown prince to Chunnai Hospital in my limo," insisted his cousin.

Maheswar Singh and General Rabi helped Paras carry the wounded Crown Prince Dipendra to his limousine, followed by placing the corpse of Nirajan in the trunk.

"What about Nigel?" asked Paras, bewildered.

"Don't worry about him. We'll bring him to jail, where the other conspirators will keep him company," insisted Yama Raj. "I'm still in shock from the brutal murders."

Sitting in the backseat of the police car, handcuffed and gagged, Nigel glanced out the window. He saw the ambulance attendants carrying the wounded out of the Billiards Room on stretchers. Next came the mutilated corpses of the royal family and the king's three sisters. He wondered if there were more bodies still lying in the Billiards Room.

62

The clerk in the office of the jail patiently waited to record the charges against Nigel Porter presented to him by Yama Raj with Hariyo as a witness. After completing the report, the two soldiers departed. The clerk spoke to Nigel, who was still handcuffed and sitting on a chair.

"You have been accused of conspiring to murder the royal family, leading to the brutal massacre at the palace," said the clerk.

He ordered Tej Bahadur Shah, the security guard to remove the handkerchief from the prisoner's mouth.

"I'm innocent," uttered Nigel. "Dipendra didn't assassinate the royal family. He was knocked out by the assassins, who were wearing masks. I saw them shoot the crown prince in the head with his own pistol. It's a miracle that the prince survived the bullet wound."

"I will note that in my report. Are you able to identify the soldiers who wore the masks?" asked the clerk.

"Yes, the assassin was Yama Raj, the security guard who just brought me here. He was wearing a mask of Dipendra, which he stuffed into his pocket," said Nigel. "His companion, Hariyo, also wore a mask of the crown prince. They were both wearing the prince's military uniforms, and they used his stolen weapons to murder the royal family," asserted Nigel.

"I've written everything in this report," said the clerk. "Yama Raja is a highly respected officer in the Royal

Nepalese Army. He and his partner were hired by the king to be present at their family dinner for security reasons."

"Tej Bahadur, you may take the prisoner to his cell now. Put him in with the monks and the yogi," said the clerk.

"It was Yama Raj, who shot Prince Nirajan and Queen Aishwarya in cold blood on the stairs leading to the prince's apartments," said Nigel being led from the room.

"He told me that you were the brains behind the assassination of the royal family and must be charged accordingly," shouted the clerk.

"I'm a Buddhist monk. I would never do such a thing," said Nigel, refusing to leave the office.

"Yama Raj told us you were Dipendra's lover. He also said the crown prince loved you more than Devyani. I understand he ordered you to wear that silk saffron robe instead of your maroon robe because it made you look more sensual," added the desk clerk.

Nigel was stunned by the accusation. He recited a mantra so that the truth would be revealed.

"Tej Bahadur, take this murderer to his cell right now. I've had enough of this conversation," said the clerk, sitting down to type at the computer.

As they walked down the corridor, Nigel asked the guard if the crown prince had died. The guard said he was still alive at the hospital. The rumor was that he would be proclaimed the next King of Nepal by the Privy Council, even though he was seriously injured.

The guard led Nigel past cells filled with political prisoners, including university students who had been arrested for being Maoist sympathizers or members of the Communist Party, trying to overthrow the monarchy.

At the end of the corridor, the security guard reached for the keys and opened the door to a cell. He gave Nigel a shove inside with the butt of the rifle.

"Here's your friend, Nigel Porter, who drugged the crown prince and encouraged him to murder his relatives along with several dinner guests," shouted Tej Bahadur.

Nigel shook his head, refusing to defend himself. Upon entering the cell, he was surprised to find Yogi Parahamsa, who had rescued him from the cottage at Fewa Lake when he was eight-years-old.

"*Tapai kahile yaha aunubhaeko cha?*" When did you come here?" asked Nigel, gaping at the seventy-five-year old yogi, who was barefoot and wearing only a loin cloth.

"*Ma ek hapta agari yo bhikshuharu sangha yaha aiye.* I came here a week ago with these monks," said the yogi, stroking his white beard.

Nigel bowed to the three monks from the Tengboche Monastery: Ratna, Vairocana, and Dorjee, whom he recognized immediately.

"*Namaste! Om Mane Padme Hum,*" they recited in unison, inviting him to sit down next to them on the floor.

They informed Nigel that they had been arrested and brought to Kathmandu because of saving the life of a wounded Maoist terrorist. The Maoist had been brought to the Tengboche Monastery because he was suffering from bullet wounds. After being healed, he departed from the monastery and was never seen again.

"Because we saved the life of a wounded terrorist, we've been accused of being Maoist sympathizers," said Ratna, the oldest monk.

"Guards from Kathmandu have been stationed at our monastery for several weeks now. They found out that you were living at our monastery as a monk and were staying at the royal palace. They accused us of being conspirators, intending to overthrow the Shah Dynasty with the help of the Maoists," stated Dorjee, the youngest monk.

"The soldiers burst into the medicine cave above the monastery where I was meditating and arrested me. They found out that I rescued you twenty-four years ago," added Yogi Paramhamsa.

"It's so good to see you all again," said Nigel. He explained to them how he witnessed the assassination of the royal family and their guests by Yama Raj and Hariyo, including the shooting of Crown Prince Dipendra, who had been knocked out and dragged into the bushes in the garden of the palace.

"I was there. I saw everything through the French doors of the Billiards Room and from behind the statue of the Buddha in the garden," informed Nigel. He told them that a whirlwind stirred up the pond prior to the assassination.

"I remember that a fierce whirlwind caused the cottage to collapse on Fewa Lake. That's where the coven was worshipping powerful demons many years ago," said the yogi, his brow wrinkled from anxiey.

The yogi insisted that the whirlwind of demons circling the pond at the royal palace was Ravana's army from the Underworld. He said that the astral bodies of the royal family and their relatives would not be able to rest.

"The souls of the dead are bewildered by their sudden and violent deaths and are hovering over the corpses in the morgue, unable to continue their journey," said Dorjee.

"Unfortunately, the demons from Fewa Lake are still loose in Kathmandu, seeking others to torment," added Variocana, fingering his raksha (rosary) beads.

The yogi added that the souls of the royal family will hover over the corpses until their bodies are cremated at Pashupati Nath, where the priests will perform rituals to liberate them.

"The whole nation will be grieving the loss of our beloved King Birenda, Queen Aishwarya, and their son, Prince Nirajan, and daughter, Princess Shruti," said Dorjee.

"We're not safe in this jail," stated Ratna. "We must bribe the guard and flee from Kathmandu."

"Yama Raj and Hariyo will come here to kill us," predicted Vairocana.

The monks prayed for guidance from *Avalokitesvara,* the Lord Looking Down with compassion. They recited mantras for their enemies to be delivered from the forces of evil, which hold them in bondage, including the souls of the royal family and the assassins.

"Let's not forget those people, who have suffered from violent deaths during the monsoon season," added Ratna.

"We must pray for all human beings including the plants and animals," concluded Dorje.

"Does anyone have any money to bribe the guard so that we can escape," asked the yogi.

"I have no money, only a jewel," said Nigel. "*Om Mane Padme Hum.* Behold the Jewel in the Lotus Blossom."

63

The news of the assassination of the royal family travelled swiftly throughout Nepal and was transmitted to the major newspapers, radios, and TV stations of the world.

The rumors were rampant as shopkeepers opened their doors in the three cities of the valley, Kathmandu, Bhaktapur, and Patan. The streets were crowded with flower vendors, selling wreaths of marigolds and bouquets to grieving customers to be offered at the numerous shrines and temples.

Every restaurant and shop in the towns, villages, and hamlets of the nation were bustling with Nepalese crowded around the radios or television sets to find out the latest news about the survivors and the gruesome deaths.

Some believed that Maoist terrorists had entered the palace and bribed the crown prince to murder his parents and relatives. Others claimed the palace guards were in a coup to place Gyanendra, the king's brother, on the throne. Many Nepalese concluded that the CIA had plotted to overthrow the monarchy. Very few believed that the crown prince assassinated his family and guests.

No one knew that two renegade soldiers were expelled from political organizations in India: Shiva's Army, the National Peoples Party, and Hanuman's Army.

After their expulsion, Yama Raj and Hariyo had joined the Nepalese Army and were now members of K*alo Hasta*, the Black Hand. They despised the monarchy and had personal grudges against the Shah Dynasty for confiscating their family property and wealth during the reign of Pritivi Narayan Shah, when he was unifying the tribal peoples to conquer the Kathmandu Valley.

"Just listen to those rumors spreading about the assassination," laughed Yama Raj, sitting in a tea shop with members of the Black Hand.

"We finally got even with the Shahs," uttered Hariyo, bragging that they had knocked out Dipendra and tied his hands, hiding him in the bushes during the assassination.

"It won't be long now before the Shah Dynasty collapses," stated Yama Raj, pausing to listen to the radio. "You guys better shut the fuck up so I can hear the news."

The Privy Council met this morning and has announced that Dipendra is now the King of Nepal, the eleventh successor to the throne of the Shah Dynasty. Last night, Crown Prince Dipendra was wounded during the attack on his family at the Narayanhiti Palace. He is now recovering at Chhuani Hospital.

The assassin wearing a military uniform shot and killed King Birendra, Queen Aishwarya, Princess Shruti, and Prince Niranjan along with the three sisters of the king.

Among the wounded who survived was Princess Komal. Her husband Prince Gyanendra was not present at the family dinner. He arrived by helicopter early this morning from Pokhara and is helping with the funeral arrangements.

The gate of the royal palace will be open to mourners tomorrow on Sunday, June 3rd from 8:00 am. to 5:00 pm, where the people will be able to pay their respects to the deceased prior to their cremation along the Bhagmati River at the Pashupati Nath Temple.

"The Privy Council doesn't have the balls to announce that Dipendra was the assassin," blurted Yama Raj, his face flushed with rage.

"That's because Dipendra's innocent. He never killed anybody at that dinner party," said Hariyo.

"You're an idiot," shouted Yama Raj, knocking his partner off his chair while everyone laughed at him sprawled on the floor.

"Get the fuck up, Hariyo! It's time for us to visit the jail. The clerk telephoned me last night and said Nigel's been spreading rumors among the prisoners that Dipendra is innocent and that I was the mass murderer of the royal family," said Yama Raj, rising from the table.

"You made a mistake by not getting rid of Nigel," said Hariyo, getting up from the floor and rubbing his head.

"You're right. I should have killed that bastard in the palace garden," insisted Yama Raj, saluting his friends from the Black Hand before leaving the tea shop.

"You made another mistake by not putting a second bullet in Dipendra's head," asserted Hariyo. "You should have made sure he was dead. If he lives, he'll tell everyone that we're the assassins," said Hariyo.

"He won't survive. We have friends at the hospital, who will take care of him. I only have to call them on my mobile phone," asserted Yama Raj.

"We also have friends here in Kathmandu, who buy illegal weapons from us," said Hariyo.

"Stop bragging! People will hear you!" shouted Yama Raj. "We'd better go to the jail and get rid of Nigel, his monk friends, and that yogi," advised Yama Raj.

They hurried past a woman weeping. She was holding the hand of her sobbing daughter, who was clinging to a picture of the king and queen.

"You should be celebrating, not weeping," blurted Hariyo. "Nepal is better off without the Shahs ruling!"

"You're a fool for saying that," reprimanded Yama Raj, slapping his partner on the side of the head. "You're stupid like your name implies! No sane person would name their child, Hariyophal. It means Green Fruit. I shortened your name to Hariyo so people wouldn't tease you."

"My parents were poor villagers from the hills of Nepal. They couldn't read or write," whimpered Hariyo, his head aching from the blow.

"You don't know your ass from a hole in the ground," said Yama Raj, slapping him again on the head.

"I...I wish you wouldn't hit me like that. You're always hurting me," pleaded his partner.

"I'm just trying to toughen you up. You need to be hard as steel if you're going to help me destroy the Shah Dynasty," insisted Yama Raj.

"What does *Kalo Hasta* mean?" asked Hariyo.

Yama Raj informed him the Black Hand was the name of a fascist group from Serbia, responsible for assassinating the Arch Duke of Austria, which precipitated World War I. Later they were the ruthless supporters of Mussolini who tortured or exterminated the opposition.

Yama Raja told his partner that the staff of the royal family would be gone within twenty-four hours. They would either be on the evening buses for India or they would be dead. The rest of the security guards would be fired for allowing the massacre to occur.

"Did you have the Newars make the mask of the crown prince?" asked Hariyo.

"Hell no, I had them made in China. It cost me a small fortune because they're rubber. Not a single person at the dinner party recognized me. They all believed that I was Prince Dipendra," laughed Yama Raj. "I stuffed my stomach with a pillow so I could look like that fat slob."

They paused at a procession of grieving women, taking garlands and flowers to the Taleju Temple, which was open for mourners.

"I never thought we'd get away with the assassination of the royal family," blurted Hariyo.

"Keep your voice down, stupid," insisted Yama Raj. "I'm sure that the Maoists will be blamed."

"When did you become a hit man?" asked Hariyo, scratching his head.

Yama Raj told him that he was in Mumbai in 1993 when the Muslims attacked the city to destroy the Stock Exchange. He had already been thrown out of the Bharatiya Janata Party, the Shiva Sena, and Hanuman's Army, where he learned to shoot.

"Do you think the Maoists will take over Nepal?" asked Hariyo as they approached Durbar Square with its array of temples and shrines.

Yama Raj said that Dipendra wouldn't be alive much longer. Once the prince died, his uncle Gyanendra would become king of Nepal, and there would be a bitter struggle for some years until the Maoists attained representation in the parliament. Their ultimate goal was to take over the whole country.

"In the meantime we're going to make a fortune selling weapons to the Maoists," said Hariyo.

"Where do we get the weapons to sell to them," asked Hariyo, scratching his head.

"We get them from the United States, Dubai, and Russia. We buy them at a discount from the manufacturers, not their governments," informed Yama Raj.

"When is our next shipment of rifles expected in Kathmandu?" asked Hariyo.

"They'll be arriving at the end of June. We'll sell them to the Islamic terrorists. They're plotting to attack the train leaving for Ayodhaya from Gujarat and then the Taj Mahal Hotel in Mumbai," stated Yama Raj, approaching the statue of Kalo Bhairava.

The enormous black statue of Shiva was engulfed in painted orange flames. His vampire-like teeth protruded from his curved red mouth. Six huge arms stretched out from his monstrous body with hands clutching a trident, a shield, and a sword. His feet were trampling a demon.

"My boss and I worship the Lord of Destruction," uttered Hariyo, bowing to the image where several older women had placed flowers and were burning incense.

"Shiva is the Creator, the Preserver, and the Destroyer of life on this planet," commented a devotee, wiping her eyes. She placed a bouquet near the statue's feet.

"Hariyo, come over here this minute!" demanded Yama Raj. "Please excuse my friend. He's mentally disabled."

"You're...you're mean," stuttered Hariyo. "I don't like the way you insult me."

"Shut the fuck up! Those women are grieving and you're interfering with their worship," snapped Yama Raj.

"I didn't say anything wrong. It's true we do worship Shiva, the Lord of Destruction," said Hariyo.

"No, we don't, you fool. We worship Ravana, the Demon King," insisted Yama Raj. "He was present in that whirlwind with his demons at the palace during the assassinations. They came from the Underworld at Fewa Lake in Pokhara."

"That's right. I forgot. We used to worship Shiva, but we don't anymore. Now we worship Ravana," said Hariyo.

"In a few minutes we'll be at the police station," said Yama Raj, noticing a procession of school children wearing white shirts and blue shorts. They were placiing garlands of marigolds on the pictures of the royal family.

"You're awfully smart, Yama Raj. That's why your name means the King of Death," said Hariyo.

Yama Raj informed his partner that he graduated from the university with a master's degree in economics. Since there were no jobs available, he sold postcards to tourists, but he was unable to earn a living that way.

His wife was always angry because they didn't have enough money. She tried to make ends meet as an elementary school teacher, but she didn't earn enough to educate their sons at a private school. After a bitter divorce, she took their two sons to live with her parents in Pokhara.

That's when he left for India and joined the Hindu Nationalist Party. But he was only a petty clerk, not earning enough to survive. He got into a fist fight after stealing money and was thrown out of the organization.

"No one really knows that we belong to the Black Hand," asserted Hariyo.

"If the Nepalese Army found out the truth, we'd be thrown in jail," said Yama Raj. "That's why we must keep it secret. So keep your fuckin' mouth shut!"

They both paused near the jail at a tea shop to listen to a radio broadcast.

The entire country and the world are mourning the death of our beloved King Birendra and Queen Aishwaraya. The assassination of the royal family took place last night at the monthly dinner party hosted by Crown Prince Dipendra. He has now been appointed the King of Nepal.

Upon leaving the shop, they paused at a shrine of Ganesh, where devotees were leaving bouquets of flowers near pictures of the king and queen. Several elderly couples burned incense while their grandchildren offered tangerines and mangoes to the deity.

"Birendra had a lot of nerve claiming to be an incarnation of Vishnu," blurted Yama Raj.

"I feel like smashing the king's picture with my pistol," he continued. "I was expelled from the Shiva Sena for beating a soldier to death, who owed me fifty rupees and didn't pay me back like he promised," said Yama Raj, irritated by the crowd.

"I didn't know that," said Hairyo, fearful that his boss might hit him again.

"Are you listening to me?" asked Yama Raj. "After that I joined the Hanuman Army, a youth movement composed of men between fifteen and thirty. Our training was similar to the facists in Italy.

"We were taught that anyone who was not Hindu, deserved to die. Our goal was to drive the Christians, Moslems, and Jews out of India. If they refused to go, they were to be exterminated."

"Don't you remember? That's where I met you. Later on we became roommates," said Hariyo.

Yama Raj informed Hariyo that the primary purpose of the Hanuman Army was to make the youth of India into men. The Indian male had become weak and effeminate during the British occupation because of Gandhi's foolish beliefs about non-violence.

The young men wore black belts, yellow socks, and black shoes. They trained rigorously from early morning to late at night and were forbidden to smoke, drink liquor, and eat meat. In addition they slept on hard beds and were to remain celibate.

Yama Raj claimed their mission was to kill or be killed since they were the Spartans of India. They led the riots in Ayodhya with the help of the Shiva Sena and slaughtered 3000 Muslims, destroying the Mosque of Babur in 1992.

"The leader of Hanuman's Army, Sushil Kumar, knew I was filled with rage toward the Shah monarchy. He encouraged me to joined the Black Hand and become a member of the Royal Nepalese Army, " said Yama Raj.

"Did he tell you to assassinate the royal family?" asked Hariyo, scratching his head.

"No, it was strictly my idea. I, Yama Raj, alone am responsible for assassinating the royal family of Nepal. Of course you helped me, but you don't deserve to get the credit because you're mentally handicapped.

"Once the monarchy has been destroyed, we'll leave Nepal and go either to Italy or Serbia. There are still members of the Black Hand in those countries," said Yama Raj, hurrying toward the jail with Hariyo following him.

64

Early on Saturday morning Tej Bahadur Shah, the security guard at the jail, ordered the servant to bring a tray with tea and biscuits to the prisoners. After going down a long corridor, they arrived together at their cell. The guard opened the door with a large key.

Inside the cell the three Buddhist monks and Nigel were seated in the lotus position on the floor, praying to the compassionate, *Avalokitesvara.*

The Hindu yogi was standing at the window facing east and bowing to the sun, rising over the mountains. He was reciting the Gayatri Mantra, *"Om bhu bhuvaha svaha/ tat savitur varenyam...* I bow to the venerable planet, the Sun, the giver of life, the remover of suffering, the bestower of happiness on all beings..."

All heads turned toward the security guard and barefoot servant with the breakfast tray. The yogi continued with his chanting, *"Bhargo devasya dhimahi /dhiyo yo naha,* Let us meditate upon the remover of sin and may our intellects be ..."

"You'd better stop praying," interrupted the guard. He seized a glass of steaming tea and handed it to the bewildered yogi, who was wearing only a loin cloth.

Yogi Parahamsa reached for the glass with his claw-like hand but was unable to hold it firmly. The glass shattered on the cement floor. The security guard backed away from him as the sunlight filtered through the bars onto the broken glass.

"It's bad luck to interrupt a yogi when he's reciting the *Gaytri Mantra*," said Dorjee. "It's a serious sin."

"*Ravana ko rakshas ahile hamro kotha aieko chan*, Ravana's demons have now come into the room!" shouted the yogi. "They will try to possess you."

"I'm getting out of here," blurted the servant, his eyes wide with terror. He released his grip on the bronze tray, which fell to floor, shattering the glasses. The tea sprawled on the cement like the tentacles of a squid.

"*Bhut aiyo! Bhut aiyo!*" yelled the servant claiming that an evil spirit was present. He fled through the open door down the corriodor, awakening the prisoners in their cells.

The security guard backed away from the steam rising from the tea as if it were alive.

"You should be afraid," shouted the yogi. "A demon intends to harm you. You must release us immediately!"

"Look over there," shouted Dorjee, pointing to a foot-long rat crawling out from a dark corner. It rose on its hind legs, bared its teeth and shrieked, scampering through the open door of the cell.

"If you don't release us, Ravana will attack you and your family," informed the yogi.

"No! No!" shouted the guard. "I had nothing to do with the assassination of the royal family.

"But you are a relative of the royal family. Your name is Tej Bahadur Shah," insisted Dorjee.

Nigel stared at the image of a serpent appearing in the steam. He shouted, "Beware of the snake! It's going to attack the guard."

"O Goraknath! We invoke you to remove your curse from Tej Bahadur and his family. Do not allow Ravana and his demons to torment them," cried the yogi.

"Stop, stop!" gasped the guard. "I can't breathe. Get this invisible snake off my chest! It's strangling me. I beg you not to harm my pregnant wife and my three-year-old son."

"If you free us from jail now, the curse of Goraknath will be lifted," shouted the yogi.

"I'll free you at once," informed the guard, his voice hoarse from the attack of the demon in the steam.

"I have a cure for your sore throat," said Vairocana. "Take these medicinal herbs. You will feel better."

As the guard chewed the herbs, he staggered in the cell and collapsed on the floor. The yogi quickly picked up his ring of keys.

"Tej Bahadur will wake up in a few minutes. The herbs won't harm him. Let's lock him in our cell and leave through the side door of the prison."

While hurrying down the long corridor, they heard the cries of the prisoners. "Help us! Please release us. We've been in jail long enough!"

"The same key opens all the doors," informed an elderly man, sentenced for rebelling against the government.

The prisoners shouted with joy when Nigel opened their cells. They flooded down the corridor and through the back door to the street where they mingled with the crowd heading toward the temples.

In the street the monks, the yogi, and Nigel overheard mourners speculating about whether Crown Prince Dipendra would survive the bullet wound to his head. The people were worried that Gyanendra would become the next king and his son, Paras, the crown prince.

The Nepalese knew that Paras was speeding in his automobile when he struck down a little girl, killing her. He was never arrested because the incident was covered up by the royal family.

"Now where do we go from here?" asked the yogi, shaking his head.

"I'm afraid Yama Raja and Hariyo will be coming after us," said Nigel "Let's make our way to the Bodhnath Monastery. We should avoid the main streets where the police might see us."

"We should trade our maroon robes for some plain clothes," suggested Dorjee. "I see a shop over there."

Ratna went inside the clothing shop while the others waited outside. He pleaded with the owner to exchange their robes for shorts and t-shirts. The monks rejoiced when he returned with street clothes for them.

The proprietor allowed them to change in the corridor of his shop. However, Nigel refused to surrender his saffron robe because it was a gift from Dipendra. Instead he gave the shopkeeper, a golden chain with an image of the Buddha engraved on it. The proprietor wrapped the saffron robe in a newspaper for Nigel to carry with him.

They bowed to the family and then departed for Durbar Square, mingling with the grieving crowd.

Dorjee said, "We need to get sunglasses so that we won't be recognized. I see a vendor over there."

They continued down Makantole until they found a vendor willing to trade their raksha beads (rosaries) for sunglasses.

As they proceeded through Durbar Square, they paused to listen to a radio coming from a tea shop.

Attention! Attention! Three monks wearing maroon robes and a yogi have escaped from the Basantapur Jail, along with a British monk, Nigel Porter, in a saffron robe. These criminals are Maoist sympathizers who conspired to assassinate the royal family.

Upon departing from the shop, they were accosted by a police officer. "Where are you fellows going in such a hurry?" asked the officer, putting away his cell phone.

"We're going to the Kathmandu Guest House to pack our clothes," said Vairocana. "We're supposed to leave on the morning flight to Darjeeling."

"I'm looking for the criminals who just escaped from the Basantapur jail and released dozens of political prisoners," informed the officer. "They are conspirators involved with the assassination of the royal family."

"We saw them a few minutes ago heading toward the Taleju Temple," said Ratna. "There were three monks and a yogi with a British monk in a saffron robe."

"Where's that bearded man going?" asked the officer, observing the yogi about to board a rickshaw."

The officer ran toward the rickshaw, where the yogi was bargaining with the driver to reduce the fee.

"Why are you in such a big hurry to leave?" asked the officer, removing a pencil and a pad.

"I'm meeting our friends who are arriving from Pokhara on the afternoon flight," said the yogi.

"The flights have been delayed due to the weather. We're concerned about Maoists taking over the city," said the officer, informing the yogi to continue his journey.

"That was a close call," said Ratna. "Let's catch the bus at Ratna Park. It will take us to the Bodhnath Monastery,"

"We'll stop at the hotel first," said Nigel. "I have a message to leave at the desk for my mother."

65

"Here we are at the Kathmandu Guest House," said Nigel. "We should split up. I'll meet you at Bodhnath. I hope the abbot can hide us there for a few days."

"That's a good idea. After the cremation of the royal family tomorrow evening at the Pashupati Nath Temple, we'll leave for eastern Nepal," suggested Vairocana. "We're not safe here in Kathmandu."

"It will be a long trek to the Tengboche Monastery," said the yogi. "It'll take us several days to get there. You should leave now for Bodhnath. Nigel and I will join you there later."

As soon as the three monks departed, the yogi said to Nigel. "I wouldn't go inside the hotel if I were you. I'll take your message for your mother to the front desk. You wait for me here by the entrance gate."

Nigel paced nervously waiting for the yogi to return. He was startled when a taxi swerved through the gate, coming to a halt in front of the restaurant. German trekkers stepped out wearing backpacks and heading toward the entrance. They almost knocked over the yogi, who was leaving the crowded hotel.

"Nigel, I gave your note to the clerk," said the yogi. "He told me that your mother will be arriving at the airport this afternoon from Pokhara."

"I haven't seen my mother since I was a child. She wasn't in Kathmandu when the shamans performed exorcisms to free Christopher's souls from demons."

"You suffered a long time over the death of your brother," said the yogi, moving down the crowded street.

"If it wasn't for you, I would have died in Dr. Bhinna Atma's cottage at Fewa Lake. You saved my life by pulling me out before the roof collapsed," recalled Nigel, glancing at the dark clouds above them.

"It was my destiny to help you," said the yogi, pausing as a rickshaw driver swerved to avoid hitting them. He squeezed the bulb of his rubber horn emitting harsh blasts, warning the pedestrians to step out of the way.

"There's quite a line of mourners in front of the royal palace. The street is blocked by Gurkha soldiers," said Nigel as they crossed Kanti Path.

"The palace is open for mourners, who wish to view the remains of the royal family, but they won't be cremated until tomorrow night," said the yogi, putting on his sunglasses.

"Maybe we could join the crowd to pay our respects to the deceased," said Nigel, feeling agitated by the noise.

"Definitely not," stated the yogi. "If the police recognize us, we'll be arrested and murdered by Yama Raj. Let's take the bus from Ratna Park directly to Bodhnath," advised the yogi.

"The whole valley is heading toward the royal palace to grieve over the loss of the royal family," observed Nigel.

66

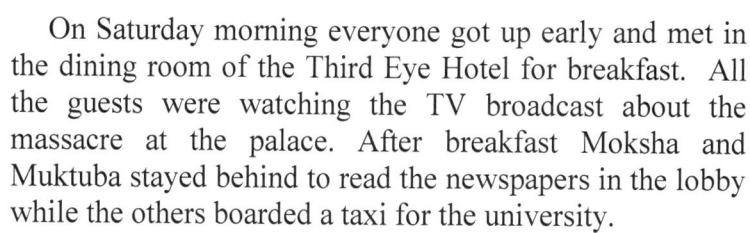

On Saturday morning everyone got up early and met in the dining room of the Third Eye Hotel for breakfast. All the guests were watching the TV broadcast about the massacre at the palace. After breakfast Moksha and Muktuba stayed behind to read the newspapers in the lobby while the others boarded a taxi for the university.

During the entire ride, they discussed the assassination. Margaret was worried about Nigel's safety. She sat in the front seat between the driver and Carl while Kathy and Om were in the backseat holding hands.

Upon reaching the campus, Om took them on a tour. The first stop was the cottage where Carl and Barbara lived many years ago. The professor, who was now occupying the cottage, came out to shake hands. He invited them inside to meet his wife and daughter.

The cottage had a tin roof and indoor plumbing, but no hot water. The kitchen, living room, and two bedrooms were small. The most impressive feature was the veranda overlooking the garden with a view of the Fish Tail Mountain, *Machapuchare.*

While Carl and Margaret were busy chatting with the professor, Kathy and Om went to the veranda to admire the view. They noticed poinsettias growing along the wall enclosing the garden, where banana, papaya, and mango trees flourished. A solitary pomelo tree soared in the center offering shade to cucumber and pumpkin vines.

"This place is so peaceful," sighed Kathy, enjoying the beauty of the tropical vegetation. "Look, there's Machhapuchare peeking out from behind the clouds."

"The mountains are even more beautiful during the fall and spring when they're covered with snow. You must come back and spend some time here," insisted Om.

"I wish you were coming with us on the flight to Kathmandu this afternoon," said Kathy.

"The tickets are sold out for today," said Om. "A lot of important people are arriving in Kathamndu this weekend to attend the cremation of the royal family."

"I'll miss you, Om," sighed Kathy. "I hope you can book a flight and join us. We're leaving on Monday."

"I'm almost done with my term paper. I'll have to stay up all night typing it on my computer. I really want to go with you and my father to the Tengboche Monastery."

"The Fish Tail Mountain is disappearing behind those grey clouds. I hope it doesn't rain," said Kathy, wiping her tears with a handkerchief. "I'm worried that I'll never see you again."

"Of course, we'll meet again soon," promised Om, taking her hands and kissing Kathy firmly on the lips.

"Om, I...I really don't know what to say," she gasped, allowing him to kiss her again. She broke away from him upon hearing footsteps on the veranda.

"We have a view of the Himalayas from the garden," said the professor coming outside with Carl and Margaret.

"Oh, how gorgeous," said Margaret. "I just love your garden. Carl, you and Barbara must have been happy, living in this tropical paradise."

"We were very happy here," said Carl, recalling how he sat with Barbara on the veranda in the moonlight, enchanted by the grandeur of mountains and the sent of roses in the garden.

After leaving the cottage, Om took them to the university. They went to the anthropology department where the janitor opened the door to Carl's office. Once inside Margaret found a dusy copy of *Spirit Possession in the Nepal Himalayas,* edited by John T. Hitchcock.

"Are you familiar with this article about the Mahakala Ceremony?" asked, Margaret, opening the text. "The Tibetan deity reminds me of Kalo Bhairava in Kathmandu.

"I remember standing in front of his statue with Iris, the nanny. We were nervously waiting for you to arrive with news about my runaway sons. They had escaped from the nanny, and I was terrified they had been kidnapped."

"Of course, I remember the incident. That's when I found Nigel in a trance at the Taleju Temple, holding a goat's head and stamping his feet in a pool of blood. It was during the animal sacrifices to Kali," said Carl.

"I was shocked as we rode back to the hotel in the taxi because Nigel wouldn't let go of the goat's head. I was worried because the upholstery in the backseat was covered with blood," sobbed Margaret.

"I…I didn't mean to upset you," said Carl, distracted by Margaret's voluptuous figure. He wanted to take her into his arms and hold her tightly.

"I've also seen the ceremony to Mahakala, the ferocious deity with 16 arms," said Om.

"Why do the Tibetans want to worship such a fierce god?" asked Kathy.

"Maybe it's because life and death can be brutal at times," sighed Margaret. "We must pass through darkness before reaching the light."

"Tibet has a harsh climate during the winter; the single road from Lhasa to Kathmandu is always buried in snow while the temperature is below zero," said Om.

"Tell us more about the ceremony," requested Margaret, putting away her handkerchief.

Carl informed them that the Tibetan priest invokes the wife of Mahakala, inviting her to possess him to cleanse his chakras from delusion, lust, hatred, pride, and jealousy.

Once his body has been cleansed, the priest transfers the purified vibrations to the suffering person brought to him with an illness. This is followed by a sacred meal of rice, bread, and fruit.

"The Tibetan priest is like a shaman. The Mahakala Ceremony treats psychological, emotional, and spiritual illness, but not severe injuries or diseases," said Carl.

"People can become physically ill from their negative feelings. Too much stress affects the immune system so that the body is vulnerable to diseases," said Margaret remembering her hospitalization after Christopher's death.

"We must leave for the airport shortly. Let's have a quick tour of the museum built by Dorothy Mierow. She lived in Pokhara for years teaching at this university and publishing several books," said Carl.

Om led the way across the campus past the dormitories and vacant classroom. In a few minutes they arrived at the museum with carvings of deities on the veranda.

"I like those statues of Rama and Sita. Lord Rama was separated from his wife, Sita, for many years after she was kidnapped by the Demon King Ravana. Rama grieved a lot when he was separated from his wife," said Om.

"I know exactly how she felt," said Margaret taking Carl by the arm as they entered the museum.

"Dad, I hope you e-mailed Mom before we left the hotel this morning?" asked Kathy, reaching for Om's hand.

67

As Nigel and Yogi Parahamsa Dev pushed their way through the crowd going toward Ratna Park, the mourners were irritated with them for going against the flow of the pedestrian traffic.

"You're going the wrong way, you fools," shouted an angry mourner, wearing white clothing. "You should be coming with us to see the remains of the royal family."

"Sorry about that. We're heading for the Bodhnath Monastery," sighed Nigel, weary and stressed out from witnessing the assassination and the now the grieving.

"When I first met you many years ago, I couldn't speak a word of English," said the yogi, trying to console him. "You taught me your language while we were trekking to Terhathum to meet Moksha."

"You were a good pupil," said Nigel. "You also taught me a lot of Nepali on that long journey from Pokhara.

They paused crossing the street, darting between taxis and rickshaws. Arriving at Ratna Park where the buses were parked, they were accosted by street vendors selling pictures, and postcards of the royal family.

Upon boarding the bus, Nigel and the yogi bargained with the driver to take their sunglasses in exchange for a ride since they didn't have any rupees for the fare. The reluctant driver agreed.

"When will we be leaving for Bodhnath?" asked Nigel, feeling exhausted. He noticed that there was a long line of mourners gathering to board the bus.

"We won't leave until the bus is filled," insisted the driver. "Please be seated in the back."

Nigel and the yogi went down the aisle and took their seats, observing that many grieving Nepalese passengers were silent although a few chatted in Newari.

A half dozen retired American school teachers boarded, filling the seats directly in front of them. The women wore straw hats with matching handbags bought in the bazaar. They had cameras hanging from their shoulders and wore tropical blouses, white slacks, and canvas shoes. Once the bus was filled the driver departed, inching his way down the crowded street to Ring Road.

"You girls better be careful with your cameras and your purses," advised Mary, their guide. "There are lots of pickpockets in Nepal.

"It says right here in my guide book that Bodhnath is the largest shrine in Kathmandu Valley, where the Tibetan culture is still vibrant."

"I can't wait to see some real Tibetans," said Lorna, wiping her forehead with a lace handkerchief. "Mary, will you please read louder?"

"I can hardly hear a word you're saying. There are too many natives mumbling in strange languages around here. You would think it was the end of the world the way they're weeping and wailing everywhere we go these days," complained Julia.

"The natives should be more considerate of tourists from other countries," added Emily, fanning herself with a Time magazine. "It's awfully hot in here. Mary! Tell the driver to turn on the air conditioning!"

"How you talk," admonished Lorna. "These poor people are grieving the death of the royal family!"

She began reading from the newspaper the names of those who were murdered and the survivors of the massacre, stumbling over the pronunciation of the names.

"We heard all about it at breakfast this morning," interrupted Emily, "We didn't come to Nepal to grieve over the assassination of the royal family. We're here to relax on our vacation. We are still stressed out from teaching all year in the public schools."

"It says the whole conspiracy was planned by Buddhist monks from the Tengboche Monastery," continued Sylvia. "They've been harboring wounded Maoist terrorists for several months now."

"Enough! Enough!" screamed Mary taking control of the discussion. "Emily is right. We're not here to get involved with politics. We're here to learn about the culture, art, and architecture of Nepal."

The driver located a side street leading to Ring Road, constructed with money given to the Nepalese Government by China.

Mary removed her straw hat to fan herself as she read from the guide book to the women.

"Many of the Tibetans living in Nepal are refugees, who fled from Tibet following the unsuccessful uprising against the Chinese Communists in 1959.

"While living at Bodhnath, they produce quality carpets, tangka paintings, and colorful tapestries for the tourists. Their homes surrounding the monastery are centers of culture and learning."

"You told us at breakfast that we're going to stay for the evening prayer service at the monastery I'm looking forward to the Tibetan Buddhist ceremony," said Lorna, removing her handkerchief from her purse and wiping her forehead.

"The prayer service tonight will be for the royal family and their murdered guests," said Mary, standing up in the aisle, fanning herself with her straw hat.

"Tell the driver to turn on the air conditioning," shouted Sally. "It's suffocating on this crowded bus. You can all go to that prayer service, but I'm not setting foot in a Buddhist monastery. I'm a Christian. I don't worship false gods!"

Nigel was annoyed by the comments of the woman sitting in front of him. He turned to the yogi and whispered, "I wonder what time my mother's flight will be arriving this afternoon. I'm worried that she'll be detained at the airport with her friends."

A few minutes later the driver announced that they had arrived at the Tribuwan National Airport, which was crowded with dignitaries arriving from every country of the world to attend the funeral of the king and queen. The driver left the bus to help a few passengers with their luggage, eager to catch their flight.

The tourists glanced out the windows at the passengers boarding limousines sent from the embassies in Kathmandu with chauffeurs hovering over them with umbrellas.

"Oh my God! It's starting to rain again. I hope you gals brought your umbrellas," announced Mary.

"Look at all those drenched German trekkers with back packs boarding that bus. You'd think they have enough sense not to come here during the monsoon," stated Lorna.

"Mary, you never told us we'd be here during the rainy season," complained Emily. "It's bad enough we have to deal with mourners. Now we have to worry about carrying umbrellas. This is the worst tour that I've ever taken."

"Emily's absolutely right. Mary should have warned us ahead of time about the monsoon," complained Julia.

"My guide book says the best time to travel to Nepal is before the monsoon starts in May or when the rainy season's over in middle of September," complained Sally.

The driver returned and continued their journey. A few minutes later he announced, "Here we are at the most sacred Hindu temple in Nepal, Pashupati Nath. Tomorrow evening the entire valley will be attending the cremation of our beloved king and queen here. Be sure to come early or you won't even have a place to stand."

"It says here that the cremation ghats are right on the Bhagmati River, behind the temple. Foreigners are not allowed to go into the temple unless they are Hindu," read Mary, standing up in the aisle.

"Mary, just sit down. You're giving me a headache," announced Emily. "It's hot in here and you're jabbering away. Why isn't the air-conditioning on?"

"Just be patient. The driver said that it broke down yesterday and needs to be repaired. We'll be at Bodhnath in a few minutes," said Mary, fanning herself.

When they finally reached the Tibetan Buddhist Stupa, everyone vacated the bus. The rain had stopped and the sun was peering through the clouds. Mary led the teachers toward the shrine with the All Seeing Eyes.

Nigel and Parahamsa Dev departed from the bus and went to the monastery, where the abbot admitted them to the entrance of the prayer hall.

"Your friends are waiting for you," said the abbot, *rinpoche*, taking them inside.

They were in awe at the sight of a 30 foot bronze statue of the Buddha, soaring toward the ceiling. The statue was illuminated only by flickering butter lamps.

As they approached the image their footsteps echoed throughout the vacant hall. When their eyes adjusted to the darkness, they noticed monks meditating in the lotus position on cushions.

After praying for some moments before the Buddha, the abbot took them behind the statue, where he rolled up a prayer rug covering a trap door. The abbot handed the yogi a flashlight, removed from the inner pocket of his maroon robe. He then opened the trap door which squeaked loudly.

"You can find your way down the stairs. Your friends are staying in the underground chamber. You must go through the tunnel and then take the path to your left until you come to their room. It will be illuminated by lamps.

"After you change into your robes, please join us at the prayer service for the departed souls of the royal family. They are beginning their 45 day journey before they return to earth in their next incarnation," said the *rinpoche*.

Nigel followed the yogi down the winding, stone stairs until they reached the dirt floor of the tunnel. The yogi turned on the flashlight, where a rat scampered into the darkness of the crypt.

The basement of\the monastery was damp with mold growing on the walls of the tunnel. They hurried past monuments containing the ashes of abbots with inscriptions in Tibetan and Sanskrit. Next was a row of funerary urns with the remains of monks. At regular intervals a human skull was embedded in the crumbling wall.

They continued down the tunnel, finally reaching an underground room. Inside they found Dorjee, Vairocana, and Ratna seated on cushions playing a game of cards to pass the time before dinner. They were pleased to be reunited with Nigel and Yogi Parahamsa Dev.

"There are robes for you in the closet," said Dorjee. "If you'd like to wash your hands and face before dinner, we've got a bucket of water and a towel over there.

"I've got a terrible headache," said Nigel, informing everyone that he was disturbed over the assassination of the royal family, especially by the whirlwind over the pond.

They all prayed over him before changing into their robes for dinner. A few minutes later they returned to the dining room.

The entire community of monks wore maroon robes. They sat on wooden benches drinking their salted, barley tea, *tsampa,* and eating their wheat tacos, *chapattis*. During the meal an elderly monk read passages from the *Tibetan Book of the Dead*.

The room was dark except for the oil lamps flickering at intervals on the wooden table. Shaded electric lights illuminated the walls, covered by rich tapestries.

"What's wrong with you, Nigel?" asked the yogi in a whisper. "You haven't touched your meal."

"I'm feeling rather strange," uttered Nigel, staring vacuously at the nearby tapestry of the Wheel of Life.

"Perhaps, if you eat something, you'll feel better," recommend Ratna.

"I have a stomach ache," said Nigel. "I must use the toilet. I think I've got diarrhea."

"The restroom is down the hall to the left," said a monk, overhearing the conversation.

Nigel rose from the table concealing his distress. He gently bowed to everyone at his table, excusing himself as he backed out of the room. Once he reached the corridor, he hurried toward the restroom.

After dinner the monks left the dining room and took their seats on their cushions in the prayer hall. The abbot bowed to everyone and led the prayers to the Radiating One, known as the Illuminator.

"I should go check on Nigel," said Ratna, concerned that he hadn't returned.

"I don't think he's still in the restroom. If he doesn't make an appearance within ten minutes, I'll go with you to look for him." said the yogi.

"Nigel was pale when he arrived at our room in the basement. I'm sure he's suffering from the shock of the massacre at the palace. He was a good friend of Crown Prince Dipendra," stated Dorjee.

68

The flight from Pokhara to Katmandu was turbulent due to the monsoon. Carl sat next to Margaret, who was gazing out the window at dark clouds forming over the Himalayas.

Across the aisle a businessman and his wife were reading a newspaper about the assassination.

Kathy was seated behind her father, leafing through her guidebook. Next to her a Limbu woman was rocking a sleeping baby. Moksha and Muktuba were behind them dozing in cramped seats.

All the other seats were taken by tourists and relatives of the royal family returning to Kathmandu for the cremation scheduled for Sunday evening, June 3.

"I'm concerned about the weather. I hope we're not heading into another storm," said Carl, his shoulder touching Margaret, who wore a sleeveless sundress.

"What did you say?" she asked. "I really wasn't paying attention. Look at those drifting clouds. They remind me of wild elephants trampling everything in sight."

Margaret shivered, removing a lavender sweater from her handbag to cover herself. "It's cold in here. I was at the palace only a few days ago having lunch with the king and queen. And now they're dead!"

"I'm worried about Nigel because he was at the family dinner hosted by Crown Prince Dipendra," said Carl.

"I don't want to talk about it," asserted Margaret. "When is Barbara coming to Nepal? You told me, but I forgot the time."

"Not until September," said Carl, mentioning that Barbara's father was still in treatment for alcoholism and planned to stay with her for some weeks once he got out.

"At least she won't have to be alone for the summer while you're here doing research. I hate being alone at night. When I'm in London, I play the piano for hours, or read until I fall asleep."

"I thought you'd be remarried by now," said Carl.

"I was engaged several times, but I couldn't commit myself to a long term relationship. I made a mistake marrying Jim Porter. He lived for a few years with his secretary, Craig. Their relationship ended when Jim left him for Norman, a night club dancer. Craig was so depressed that he committed suicide."

"I remember Craig. He was a rather pleasant fellow. At that time Jim was enraged over Christopher's death and Nigel's disappearance," said Carl.

"I'm so worried about Nigel," sobbed Margaret. "I hope he's safe. The queen mentioned at the luncheom that he was planning to go on a retreat with Prince Dipendra at Bodhnath."

"Excuse me," uttered the Nepalese businessman sitting across the aisle, introducing himself as Joshi Shah. "We heard on the radio this morning that Nigel Porter was the primary suspect in a conspiracy to destroy the Shah Dynasty. He was disguised as a Buddhist monk when he was arrested at the palace."

"You must be mistaken," gasped Margaret. "My son, Nigel, was a friend of Prince Dipendra. He was present at the family dinner last night."

"A soldier named Yama Raj handcuffed him at the royal palace near the statue of the Buddha, the very spot where the crown prince shot himself in the head," informed Sushila, sitting beside her husband.

"Oh no!" cried Margaret. "It can't be true. Not Nigel! He's been living at the palace since April."

Joshi informed her that Yama Raj escorted Nigel to the jail in Basantapur, but he escaped this morning with a yogi and three Buddhist monks from the Tengboche Monastery. They were conspirators, giving asylum to wounded Maoist terrorists who were planning to overthrow the monarchy. The monks and the abbot at Tengboche were currently under surveillance by the government.

"That monastery should be shut down permanently. It's only because of the Germans that it's thriving," said Sushila. "They rebuilt the prayer hall after it was destroyed by fire in 1989. Tengboche was burnt to the ground because it was a center for Maoist activity."

"But Sushila, that's only a rumor. It's more accurate to say that a tourist left a kerosene space heater in his room too close to the bedding," said Joshi.

Sushila informed them that the whole country had been alerted about the conspirators escaping from the jail in Kathmandu after clubbing the guard and freeing the political prisoners. The government was offering 100,000 rupees to anyone with evidence leading to their arrest.

"Let's not discuss this any further," insisted Carl, trying to calm Margaret, who was trembling next to him.

"We're about to arrive in Kathmandu," said Sushila glancing out the window. "There's Pashupati Nath Temple. Deer Park is across the river over there. It will be packed with mourners attending the funeral tomorrow evening."

"My cousin, King Birendra, and his family will be cremated there tomorrow," said Joshi. "I hope the police arrest those assassins and bring them to trial. They all deserve to be shot for murdering my relatives."

"Nigel is innocent!" sobbed Margaret, clinging to Carl, who helped her unfasten her seatbelt.

"Oh my God," said Kathy glancing out the window as the plane landed. "There are squad cars coming toward us on the runway."

As the passengers were leaving the plane and heading down the metal stairs, they were surprised that two uniformed soldiers were hurrying toward the passengers.

"You must be Carl Brecht with your daughter, Kathy," said Yama Raj. "You're obviously, Margaret Porter. Please come with me to the squad car. I have a few questions to ask you about your son, Nigel."

"What about us?" asked Muktuba, turning toward Moksha, who was puzzled by the presence of the soldiers.

Yama Raj removed his pistol from the holster and pointed it at the shamans. "You'd better not interfere, or you'll be arrested. Now get the hell out of here."

Muktuba and Moksha turned around quickly and departed for the terminal.

"You don't have to be so rude," uttered Kathy, entering the squad car and sitting between her father and Margaret.

"We have some questions to ask you," said Yama Raj, putting his pistol back into the holster. He sat in the front seat next to Hariyo.

"I was recently at the Kathmandu Guest House. The clerk at the desk gave me this note from your son, Nigel," said Yama Raj, reading it to Margaret.

> *Mother,*
>
> *I'm so pleased you've come to Kathmandu. I was at the hotel last week hoping to meet with you, but you weren't there due to the rain. I saw the shamans performing the exorcism to put Christopher's soul to rest from an upper balcony. The clerk told*

me you went to Pokhara. Please come to Bodhnath this evening when you return from Fewa Lake. There will be a prayer service for the royal family at the Gelugpa Samtenlang Gompa. I hope to see you there later.

Your loving son, Nigel   6/02/01.

"I'm so relieved that he's safe at the monastery," uttered Margaret. "I've been worried about him."

Yama Raj reiterated that Nigel, the monks, and the yogi were conspirators involved with Maoist terrorists to overthrow the Shah Dynasty.

"No! No! Moksha, the Limbu Shaman, healed my son many years ago," blurted Margaret, bursting into tears.

"What do you mean? Why did a shaman have to heal your son?" asked Yama Raj, jotting down notes.

"It's…it's because he was kidnapped by the London Coven and possessed by evil spirits," blurted Margaret, her voice quivering from shock.

"Why don't you leave Margaret alone? Can't you see she's stressed out with worry about Nigel," said Kathy.

The driver turned on the siren, drowning out further questioning. A few moments later he stopped in front of the terminal. They hurried into the building and headed toward customs. Upon their arrival, the Chief of Police was waiting for them.

"Dr. Brecht, we meet again," said Mr. Shrestha shaking Carl's hand. "And here's your lovely daughter, Kathy, and Margaret Porter. How nice to see you, but under such unfortunate circumstances."

"Mr. Shrestha, I remember you came to the hospital in Patan to visit me a long time ago," sighed Margaret.

"You were heavily sedated because of the death of your son, Christopher," he said, requesting that they follow him to a nearby office.

Once inside the room, Mr. Shrestha asked everyone to be seated before continuing with the investigation. Yama Raj and Hariyo paced the floor, smoking cigarettes during the interrogation.

"Margaret, when did you last see Nigel?" asked the Chief of Police, speaking in a gentle tone.

"It's been twenty-five years ago," she said. "I came to Kathmandu because I saw a picture of him with the crown prince. I...I have the newspaper clippings with me here in my purse."

"I'm familiar with the publicity. I saw Nigel's picture in our newspapers with Dipendraji at least half a dozen times before the assassination," said Mr. Shrestha.

"Nigel was wearing a saffron robe when I arrested him in the garden of the palace on the evening of the assassination," interrupted Yama Raj. "Crown Prince Dipendra enjoyed seeing him in that translucent silk robe when Devyani wasn't with them."

"What do you mean by that?" asked Margaret, her voice quivering with fear.

"Most people thought it peculiar that Nigel was living in the same quarters with the crown prince," said Yama Raj.

"I saw Dipendra murder the queen. He shot her in the head on the steps of his living quarters. We were there in the garden when it happened," added Hariyo.

Mr. Shrestha was annoyed by the interruptions. "Please keep silent while I'm questioning Margaret."

"You'll have to excuse my partner," laughed Yama Raj. "He's not all there. His brain was damaged years ago from a blow to the head."

"You always say nasty things about me," pouted Hairyo, his fists clenched with anger.

"Margaret, why didn't you communicate with your son on a regular basis?" asked Mr. Shrestha.

"For some years I believed that Nigel was dead," sobbed his mother. "My husband, Jim, had hired private detectives to find him, but they didn't have any luck."

Margaret informed them that Nigel had become a monk at the Tengboche Monastery. She wrote to him several times, but he never answered her letters. She even travelled to the monastery twice, only to find out that her son had left a few days before her arrival to go on a retreat or study herbal medicine in Lhasa.

"Why are you in Kathmandu during this inauspicious time?" asked the Chief of Police.

"I came to here to meet Nigel and bring him back to London with me for a few weeks," said Margaret.

"I doubt whether that will be possible, Mrs. Porter," sighed Mr. Shrestha, adjusting the patch over his left eye.

Yama Raj informed them King Birendra hired him and Hariyo as palace guards. On the tragic evening of the massacre, he overheard the queen inform the prince that she wanted Nigel removed from the palace grounds.

"Rather than obey his mother, Dipendra brought him as a guest to the dinner party," added Yama Raj.

"Nigel made an appearance in a saffron robe, which shocked the guests. However he didn't stay long. Instead he left to guard the weapons hidden in the bushes on the veranda, which Dipendra used to assassinate his family and guests," continued Yama Raj.

"Oh no!" screamed Margaret. "Stop! I can't listen to anymore of this horror."

Carl pleaded with Mr. Shrestha to allow Margaret to lie down on a cot in the inner office, where he helped her get settled before returning.

Yama Raj stated that Nigel had packed his bags in Dipendra's quarters when a servant arrived to replenish the prince's cigarette case. The servant said that he saw Nigel lying on the crown prince's bed in his translucent robe, high from smoking hashish.

"That black substance was a drug similar to LSD. We found it in Dipendraji's cigarette case," informed the Chief of Police.

"We believe that Nigel was supplying the crown prince with hallucinogenic drugs, made from herbs raised at the Tengboche Monastery. The drugs caused Dipendra to become insane," insisted Yama Raja.

He also reported that Dipendra was hallucinating on the evening of the the dinner party. The prince thought that evil spirits from the Underworld had invaded the Billiards Room, which led him to open fire on the demons so they wouldn't harm his family.

"Each time Dipendra left the Billiards Room, Nigel was there handing him another weapon---the machine gun, rifle, and pistol. After he massacred his family and relatives, the crown prince attempted suicide with his pistol," said Yama Raj, pacing the floor nervously and smoking a cigarette.

"We saw a whirlwind spinning around the pond from the bridge leading to the Billiards Room," contributed Hariyo. "Ravana's demons were in the storm."

"Oh my God!" blurted Kathy. "There were whirlwinds hovering over the skeletal remains at Fewa Lake."

"How interesting," uttered Mr. Shrestha. "Our forensic anthropologist brought Yorg's and Myrna's remains to our morgue here in Kathmandu. Carl, you were there with the shamans and Margaret at Dr. Bhinna Atma's cottage.

"We must interrogate those shamans," asserted Yama Raj. "It wouldn't surprise me if they are conspirators, working with the Maoists to assassinate the royal family."

"Don't be ridiculous," insisted Carl. "Moksha and Muktuba were attending our shaman convention at Bir

Hospital. They were with us in Pokhara during the assassination of the royal family."

"I heard Nigel chanting mantras behind the statue of Buddha to the Demon King Ravana," said Yama Raj.

Overhearing the conversation in the next room, Margaret rose from the cot and opened door. She screamed, "Nigel didn't do it! He's innocent!"

Everyone was startled as she stumbled toward them, collapsing on the floor.

"Call an ambulance!" shouted Carl. "Margaret's not well. We must take her to the hospital!"

69

In the oldest monastery at Bodhnath, the abbot led the evening prayers by ringing a hand bell in front of the enormous statue of the Buddha. Two monks standing on each side of him were blowing six foot horns that touched the floor.

This was followed by a purification ceremony led by the Vajrayana priest, making an offering to *Mahakala*, the ferocious aspect of the Buddha.

"Have you seen Nigel?" whispered Dorjee, sitting on a cushion next to a monk meditating.

"I saw him leave the restroom with two monks holding him by the arms sometime ago," said the monk..

Vairacana said, "They must have taken him to the underground room."

All the monks seated on cushions were reciting the mantra, *Om Mane Padme Hum* to cleanse themselves from egotism and their negative karma.

The Vajrayana priest and the abbot walked around the enormous statue carrying incense. When they returned, they bowed to an attendant arriving with a bronze candelabrum, which illuminated the pictures of the deceased members of the royal family. The colorful photographs were located at the feet of the Buddha.

While the entire community was chanting to liberate the souls of the royal family from demonic influences, a shadowy figure stepped out from behind the bronze statue.

The monk's head was covered with the hood of his maroon robe. While holding a machete, he rushed toward the framed pictures, slashing at the images of King Birendra and Queen Aishwarya, then smashing them.

The abbot dropped his bronze tray, scattering the incense and red tika powder onto the floor. The metallic thud of the tray on the floor echoed through the hall.

"Put down that weapon now," shouted the abbot, approaching the monk. "Give it to me!"

The monk pulled back his maroon hood and stepped in front of the candles which illuminated his face. All the monks and tourists gasped with horror as he charged toward the abbot.

"It's Nigel!" shouted the yogi. "What's happened to him? He's insane!"

"He's got the most hideous frozen smile. We've got to stop him," said Ratna, startled by someone taking pictures with a flash camera.

Nigel raised the machete and struck the abbot on the neck and then plunged the blade into his stomach. He laughed manically as the abbot collapsed on the floor. He then turned to attack the Vajrayana priest, who had raised his hands to cover his face.

"Stop it Nigel! Don't do it!" shouted Dorjee, pushing his way through the crowd with two monks following him,

While the abbot lay bleeding on the floor, Nigel attacked the Vajrayana Priest, who fell to his knees bleeding from his arms. He then laughed hysterically, smashing the pictures of Prince Nirajan and Princess Shruti, placed at the feet of the Buddha.

A camera flashed several times before Nigel covered his head with the maroon hood, fleeing toward the rear of the statue and disappearing from the prayer hall.

The three monks and the yogi hovered over the bodies of the abbot and priest, trying to stop the bleeding by putting pressure on their wounds.

"Someone call an ambulance!" shouted Vairocana.

"The killer's Nigel Porter!" shouted a stranger from the prayer hall. "Those monks attending the abbot and priest are Maoist terrorists!"

As the camera flashed again, Yogi Parahamsa Dev winced from the light. "There's nothing we can do for the abbot. He's going to die from loss of blood."

"Someone call the police! Those monks are assassins and so is that yogi. Stop them!" shouted another voice coming from the crowd.

The three monks and the yogi hurried behind the statue, where the trap door was left open. The last person going down the cement steps pulled the door shut, locking it with a wooden board. They hurried past the crypts and through the dark tunnel to their room.

Everyone changed from their robes into their street clothes. They paused, listening to Gurkha guards striking the trap door with the butts of their rifles.

As they were about to leave the room, they heard a moaning coming from the closet. Vairocana opened the door, sliding the robes aside. He was startled by movement on the floor.

"What are you doing in here?" asked Vairocana, his eyes wide with terror.

"Who's in that closet?" asked Dorje, packing his robe into a gym bag.

"It's Nigel!" shouted the yogi, glancing into the closet.

Everyone gasped as Nigel crawled out of the closet holding a bloody machete tied to his hand with a rope. His saffron robe was drenched with blood stains.

The horrified monks backed away, fearful of being attacked. They were alarmed to see Nigel drooling as he stared vacuously at the machete in his hand. He was stunned, unaware of his surroundings.

"Nigel's possessed by demons again!" asserted the yogi, recalling how he pulled him out of the cottage at Fewa Lake before it collapsed.

"No! No! I'm not possessed," uttered Nigel, the saliva oozing from the side of his mouth. "I was in the bathroom when I heard footsteps. I tried to escape from those two monks, but they knocked me out and tied me up. They locked me in the closet. Please, you've got to help me."

Nigel raised his arm with the bloody machete hanging from his wrist. Seizing the handle, he raised the blade and said, "Someone tied this knife to my hand. Dorje, you can help me."

Stressed out and disoriented, Nigel rose and stumbled toward Dorjee with the blade raised as if he were going to strike him. "I have to get rid of this heavy machete."

The yogi intervened by pushing a chair between Nigel and Dorjee. "Put that machete down, Nigel!"

"Let's get out of here," shouted Vairocana. "The guards have broken through the trap door. I can hear them coming down the tunnel."

"Bring your maroon robes," shouted the yogi. "We can exchange them for food before we leave for Tengboche."

Vairocana led them out of the room, illuminating the way with a flashlight. They hurried down the dirt path, leaving Nigel behind.

The yogi glanced over his shoulder at Nigel, who stood bewildered in the doorway. He shouted at them, "Why are you running away from me? I didn't do anything wrong."

"We must find Moksha, the Limbu Shaman. He can perform an exorcism on Nigel and restore him to sanity," said the yogi, shaking his head.

"It's too late now to help Nigel. He'll be arrested and taken to jail for killing the abbot and wounding the priest. He's possessed. There's nothing we can do to help him," said Dorjee.

"I...I hear sirens. It must be the ambulance arriving. I hope the paramedics can save that priest," added the yogi.

"It's a shame that Nigel relapsed and became so violent. He was sane when he was with us in jail. He was always talking about spiritual things," said Dorjee, nearly out of breath from running.

"I hear a single set of footsteps coming after us. "It could be Nigel. He might try to attack us like he did the abbot and that priest," said Vairocana.

"No, just listen," said the yogi, pausing "There are several sets of footsteps. It must be the Gurkha guards from the entrance of the monastery," said the yogi.

"Hurry, we've got to get out of here," uttered Dorjee.

Vairocana told them that the tunnel was an abandoned sewer winding from Bodhnath to the Bhagmati River with an outlet at Deer Park across from the Pashupati Nath Temple.

"My shoes are starting to get wet," mentioned Dorjee. "There's water dripping from the bricks in the ceiling and the sides of the tunnel."

"I'm already up to my ankles in water because of the monsoon rain." said Vairacana, splashing through the water, which had a putrid smell. Everyone was exhausted from the force of the current increasing as they struggled through the tunnel.

"There's a stairway over there," said Vairocana, shining the flashlight onto the stone steps.

The water was waist high before they reached the stairs. As they climbed the stone steps, they were startled by a dozen rats scurrying ahead of them into the entrance of small brick monument.

"This place must be a tomb for a king," said Ratna.

"No, it's a shrine, *Shivalaya*," said yogi, casting a beam from his flashlight onto the six-headed stone sculpture of Lord Shiva's warrior son, Shanmukha.

Vairocana brushed away an enormous cobweb woven over the stone image. Instantly a large black and yellow spider scurried toward the ceiling.

When the yogi pushed open the rotted wooden door, his companions were relieved as they entered an extensive garden covered with memorials, Shivalayas, and stone lingams.

They saw numerous yogis with their bodies covered with ashes, sitting in the lotus position meditating. Others were gathered around bonfires, waiting for their rice and lentils to cook in iron pots. The monks and the yogi were welcomed by the yogis, who shared their food with them.

Later that evening Yogi Parahamsa took the three monks across the bridge to the Pashupati Nath Temple, where they bowed to the images of Shiva and the ancient statues of the Mother Goddess.

Afterwards the yogi took them to a shelter to spend the night. Since they had no money, they slept without mosquito netting or bedding on the veranda across from a clinic, where the infirm came to die prior to being cremated along the Bhagmati River.

70

Early the next morning as the sun was rising hundreds of devotees were bathing in the river, followed by worshipping at the Pashupati Nath Temple. The three monks and yogi woke up from the sound of chanting and prayers for the deceased members of the royal family.

"Why is Shiva so popular among the Hindus? Pilgrims come to this shrine from all over India to worship him," said Dorjee, impressed by their devotion.

"It is because Shiva assumed the form of a deer to redeem us from our animalistic nature," said the yogi.

"We have more in common with animals than we want to admit," agreed Dorjee, bewildered by the number of families with their children hurrying toward the park.

"The people are arriving early to find a place to sit so they can witness the cremation of the royal family tonight," said Ratna, who hadn't slept very well.

The monks and yogi left the shelter amazed by the crowd crossing the bridge and ascending the hill on the other side of the Bhagmati River.

While drinking their morning tea at a nearby stand, they observed hundreds of families settling into Deer Park with folding chairs, blankets, and picnic baskets.

The men wore long shirts, vests, and topis; the women, colorful silk saris with jewelry. Their children chased each other around the Shiva lingams, playing tag in their school uniforms while grandparents took naps on blankets enjoying the sunshine while it lasted. Everyone had umbrellas or rain coats, anticipating a cloudburst.

"We better move along and join the crowd before the officers close the bridge from further traffic," suggested Yogi Parahamsa, leading them across the river.

"Look over there," said Ratna. "Those guards are coming out of the monument, where we pushed open the door yesterday. They finally made it through the tunnel from Bodhnath."

"They're wearing rubber suits," said Dorjee. "The water in the tunnel must be awfully high by now since it rained heavily last night."

"I didn't get much sleep because of the thunder and lightning, not to mention the mosquitoes," said Vairocana.

The yogi asked an elderly woman when the cremation ceremony would start. She said the parade from the royal palace would take place late in the afternoon before the sun went down, but the cremations wouldn't occur until after dark. She turned to console her daughter's crying baby.

"We'd better split up so those guards won't recognize us," said Dorjee, noticing that a squad car had arrived with half a dozen police to close the bridge from pedestrian traffic since the park was filled.

"Let's meet at the monument before the ceremony begins." suggested Vairocana.

The yogi and the monks wandered among the families, the whole day chatting with the local people about their theories regarding the assassination of the royal family.

At dusk they gathered near the place where they surfaced from the tunnel. The monks and yogi paused to listen to a transistor radio belonging to a nearby family.

The funeral procession began at the Chhuani Hospital over two hours ago. There are an estimated 20,000 grieving people, who are following the palanquin of Queen Aiswaraya. The corpses of King Birendra, Prince Nirajan, and Princess Shruti are being carried on plain bamboo poles behind the queen.

The Priviy Council has appointed Crown Prince Dipendra to be the King of Nepal, even though he is still in the hospital recovering from being shot by the assassin. Survivors of the massacre at the palace have informed the media that Dipendra was responsible for the slaying of his parents due to the influence of conspirators from the Tengboche Monastery. The prisoners responsible for the assassination have escaped from the Basantapur Jail. They are a British monk, a yogi, and three Buddhist monks....

"We loved our king and queen," uttered a tearful teenage girl, sitting on a blanket with her family attentively listening to the radio.

"We don't believe that Prince Dipendra would kill his own parents. He loved them dearly," said the girl's brother.

"Be quiet! The Brahmin priests are starting to chant across the river at the ghats," scolded the grandmother.

Everyone paused to listen to the priest reciting Vedic Prayers to Agni, the fire god as they stood in front of the four wooden pyres, where the royal family would be cremated on individual ghats.

The cement stairs leading from the Pashupati Nath Temple was crowded with tearful mourners, anticipating the arrival of the corpses.

"I hear some noise coming from the steps connected to the tunnel," said Vairocana, encouraging his friends to move away from the monument.

"Dorjee led the way, pushing through the crowd, followed by Ratna, Vairocana, and Yogi Parahamsa Dev.

"Hey, watch where you're going!" You're stepping on our blanket," shouted a little girl.

"*Kasto kisimko mancheharu chan?* What kind of men are they?" mumbled a weary grandfather. "Those four people look like they're running away from the police. They might be pickpockets. Watch your wallets!"

"*Bhuwa! Bhuwa!. Ma pisab garnu parcha*," cried a frightened little boy. "Grandfather, I have to pee."

The old man told him to urinate behind the nearby Shiva lingam.

"Let's stand next to these yogis," insisted Vairocana. "We can hide behind them."

"It's starting to get dark. We'd better stay away from their fire, or we'll be recognized," said Dorjee.

He glanced over his shoulder at the two guards coming through the rotted door of the monument from the tunnel. They were asking questions of the family seated on the blanket, where a little girl was jumping up and down, and pointing her finger toward them.

"I see them! I see them! They're over there next to those yogis. They were over here only a few minutes ago!" she shouted loudly, drawing a lot of attention to herself.

The police pushed their way through the crowd. By the time they reached the fire, the three monks and the yogi had disappeared into the crowd.

As darkness enveloped Deer Park, a band played the Nepalese National Anthem with the arrival of the corpses.The guards holding flaming torches encouraged the people on the stairs leading to the river to make room for the pall bearers. They were carrying the palanquin with the queen, followed by the corpses of the king, prince, and princess.

At the sight of the four corpses, the grieving relatives showered them with flowers, vermillion, and holy water. Within moments the pall bearers placed the deceased family members on separate funeral pyres, *ghats*, stacked with sandalwood.

Brahmin priests surrounded each pyre, chanting Vedic hymns so the souls of the departed would not cling to the corpses but continue their journey.

"Because the members of the royal family died violent deaths, their souls were unprepared to make their journey to the next world," stated the yogi. "After spending some time on the moon, their souls will travel to the sun for purification before going to *Swarga,* the Heavenly Planet."

"If they have done evil in this life, their souls will go to the Underworld and remain there until their negative karma has been used up. Then they will be reincarnated in a lower form of life," continued the yogi.

The conversation was interrupted by a twenty-two gun salute. The echoing of the rifles reverberated across the river, startling the spectators. At precisely 9:46 pm Sahibja Dipak Shah lit the funeral pyres. As the flames devoured the corpses of the royal family, the mourners wept, wailed, and sobbed.

The crowd became silent as thousands of Nepalese watched the fires consume the remains of the royal family.

It was after midnight when the yogi and the three monks left the crowd. They slowly departed going north. After walking for several hours, they found the east trail.

"I'm exhausted," said the Yogi Parahamsa. "We're coming to a village. We'll ask the farmer if we can sleep in his barn near the buffaloes. At least we will be sheltered if it starts to rain."

"It will take us about a week to reach the Tengboche Monastery," said Ratna. "Maybe even longer if the trails are washed away due to flooding."

71

Mr. Shrestha located a hotel for Carl and Kathy near the airport. He also contacted a medical doctor from Shanta Bhawan, who arrived on Saturday afternoon to examine Margaret. The doctor recommened that Margaret stay overnight at the airport with a nurse monitoring her since the hospitals in the city had no beds available. Kathmandu was overcrowded with people arriving to attend the funeral of the royal family

On Sunday afternoon Carl and Kathy returned to the airport to visit Margaret. The nurse was with her in the inner office, when she had regained consciousness. Kathy joined them after a few minutes with a bottle of cold water for Margaret.

They waited for an hour for an ambulance to arrive, but it was delayed because the road was congested with spectators heading toward Pashupati Nath to attend the cremation ceremony.

"Maybe we can take a taxi back to the Kathmandu Guest House," suggested Carl, helping Margaret get up from the cot.

"I'm still dizzy. I can't remember what happened," she uttered. "I was standing on the bridge over looking the Thames near West Minster Abbey when I fainted."

"Margaret, you're in Kathmandu, not London," said Kathy, concerned about her mental health.

"What on earth am I doing in Nepal?" she asked. "Oh, that's right. I came here to bring Nigel back to London. I was supposed to meet him at the royal palace for afternoon tea, but he never showed up."

"Kathy, wait here with Margaret and the nurse. I'll see if I can find a taxi," said Carl leaving the terminal.

Since there were no taxis or buses available, Carl returned to the office, requesting Mr. Shrestha to give them a ride to hospital in his squad car.

The Chief of Police informed them the main road into the city was blocked with 20,000 mourners. They were following the pall bearers, who were carrying the corpses of the royal family from the palace to the cremations ghats. The entire police force was occupied trying to control the grieving crowd.

"We could take the Ring Road back to the city," suggested the nurse. "Margaret needs to be hospitalized. There's finally a room available for her at Shanta Bhawan. You'll be responsible if something happens to her."

"Of course, I completely forgot about the Ring Road. I can drive you myself to the hospital."

"Let's get going then," insisted Carl, helping Margaret get up from the cot with the nurse's assistance.

"Before you leave, I have something important to tell you," shouted Yama Raj, hurrying toward them while talking on his mobile phone.

"Margaret's dizzy. She must sit down now," insisted the nurse annoyed by the intrusion.

"She can sit here at my desk," said Mr. Shresthra, adjusting the patch over his left eye. "What is it this time, Yama Raj?"

"I want to speak to you privately," insisted Yama Raj, glancing at Margaret, who was pale.

"Something has happened to Nigel," gasped Margaret, rising from the chair. She seized Carl's arm. "Tell me the truth. What's happened to him?"

Yama Raj said, "There was another brutal murder at Bodhnath. The killer was a Buddhist monk. who struck and killed the abbot. He also wounded the Vajrayana priest."

"Margaret's in no condition to deal with another tragedy. She should be in the hospital. She's had enough trauma for one day," defended Kathy.

"We're leaving for the hospital," insisted the nurse.

"No! I want to hear the truth," uttered Margaret, struggling to get up from the chair.

"All right," said Yama Raj. "If you want to know the truth, I'll tell you what happened."

He informed them that about the details of the murder of the abbot and that some tourists had taken pictures of the murderer.

"We took the films to be developed at a shop near the monastery," added Hariyo. "That's how we found out the identity of the killer."

"I'm sorry to tell you that the murderer of the abbot was your son, Nigel," stated Yama Raj. "His picture will be on the front page of every newspaper in the morning. We've also released the photos to the international press."

"You're lying! I don't believe you," gasped Margaret, placing her hands over her face. "Nigel was a good friend of Crown Prince Dipendra. We must ask him to help us."

"Dipendra's in the hospital, dying from a bullet wound," said Yama Raja. "He can't help Nigel. Your son was involved in the conspiracy with the Maoists to assassinate the royal family."

Margaret screamed, clawing at her face with her sharp fingernails. "No! You're lying! Nigel is a Buddhist monk!"

"Stop that," shouted the nurse, pulling Margaret's hands behind her back and leading her back to the inner office.

"Did you have to tell her about Nigel?" asked Kathy. "That was terribly cruel of you. You're a monster!"

"She wanted to know the truth," asserted Yama Raj.

The Chief of Police telephoned the First Aid Office in the terminal, requesting assistance. A few minutes later a paramedic arrived to give Margaret a sedative and stop the bleeding on her face. She sobbed hysterically, blaming herself for Nigel's violent behavior.

Once she was settled down, Mr. Shrestha advised Carl to bring Margaret to his squad car. It had finally arrived at the entrance to the airport.

The paramedic took Margaret in a wheelchair to the parked car. She sat in the back seat between the nurse and Kathy, where she fell asleep. Carl sat next to Mr. Shrestha in the front seat. A few minutes later they departed for the hospital in Patan.

"I'm so sorry I'm late. I wanted you to know that I received information from Yama Raj that the guards at the monastery broke open the trap door behind the bronze statue of the Buddha," said the Chief of Police.

He informed them that when the guards arrived at the room where the three monks and yogi had been hiding, they found a saffron robe with blood stains on it. They also found the machete that Nigel used to kill the abbot and injure the priest."

"Did they find Nigel and arrest him?" asked Carl, noticing that Margaret moaned upon hearing her son's name although she didn't open her eyes.

"No. He wasn't there," said the Chief of Police.

Mr. Shrestha told them that the guards pursued the monks and the yogi through an abandoned storm sewer from Bodhnath to Deer Park. They planned to continue the search, believing that Nigel was with the conspirators, hiding among the spectators, who came to witness the cremations of the royal family.

There was silence as the driver paused due to the traffic. The Ring Road, circling the capitol city, was crowded with rickshaws, taxis, buses, and pedestrians, heading toward Pashupati Nath to see the cremations.

The driver of the squad car honked the horn several times to warn the pedestrians to step aside. Margaret awoke from the blaring of the horn as several stray cows and a Brahma bull blocked traffic.

"We've got to find Nigel," uttered Margaret. "I made a mistake by getting involved with that London Coven."

Mr. Shrestha said, "I remember when Nigel was kidnapped by the coven after Christopher's death at the Kathmandu Guest House."

Carl explained to him about what had transpired since he and Kathy arrived in town for the shaman convention.

"Dr. Brecht, you certainly get around. Several years ago we found you in front of that collapsed cottage on the pier at Fewa Lake with your hands tied. At that time a yogi had rescued Nigel from the London coven and had taken him away in a boat.

"Now you're in Kathmandu where Nigel's accused of murdering the abbot at Bodhnath and conspiring to assassinate the royal family. You're always in the right place at the wrong time," laughed Mr. Shrestha. "Here we are at Shanta Bhawan Hospital."

"The last time I was here, Margaret was admitted over Christopher's death. Now she's here because of Nigel's criminal behavior," said Carl, helping Margaret out of the squad car while Mr. Shrestha went to register her.

A few minutes later paramedics arrived to take her into the emergency room, where the doctor on duty checked her blood pressure and pulse.

"She's suffering from shock," insisted the doctor, asking for more information about her condition. Carl then told him about the death of Christopher, and Nigel being accused of plotting to assassinate the royal family and murdering the abbot.

"No wonder this poor woman has had a mental breakdown," commented the doctor, shaking his head.

"Dr. Manandhar, the psychiatrist, helped Margaret deal with Christopher's death. Maybe, he can help her face Nigel's tragic relapse," said Carl.

"I'll call Dr. Manandhar since he's a friend of Margaret's," said the doctor, requesting the nurse to bring an IV for the patient.

"Have you heard any news about how the crown prince is doing?" asked Kathy.

"My friends at the Chunnai Hospital informed me that they don't think he'll live. Gyanedra will surely be the next king," said the doctor.

"I just heard from Yama Raj that the cremation fires won't be lit at Pashupati Nath until after nine o'clock," said the Chief of Police, entering the emergency room."

Mr. Shrestha spoke to Carl and Kathy, "I'll take you back to the Kathmandu Guest House. We must leave before the mourners return by the thousands from the cremation grounds."

As they departed from the emergency room, they heard the doctor say, "Nurse, please take Margaret Porter to room 112. Give her another sedative in four hours. I'll be back to check on her at midnight. I contacted Doctor Manandhar. He agreed to see Margaret early tomorrow morning."

72

After a restless night at the Kathmandu Guest House due to the heavy rain, Carl shaved at the sink in his room, took a shower down the hall and finally got dressed. A few minutes later he met his daughter in the dining room of the hotel for breakfast

"I could hardly sleep last night," said Kathy, yawning. "The thunder and lightning woke me up several times. I was petrified!"

"The rain poured down against my window so intensely that I thought it would break the glass," said Carl.

"The whole garden was illuminated by lightning," said Kathy. "I swear the demons had returned from Fewa Lake and were trying to get into my room."

"I was worried about Margaret. She was so pale when we left her at the hospital last night," said her father.

"You're still in love with her, Dad," concluded Kathy. "I can tell by the way you look at her."

"Don't be ridiculous Kathy. Of course I'm attracted to Margaret," admitted Carl, haggard from a lack of sleep. "I wish your mother was here with us. I really miss her."

"Margaret's beautiful in spite of her wrinkles," said Kathy. "I can see why you're attracted to her. She looks like Marilyn Monroe.

"I sent a message to your mother last night before going to bed," said Carl. "I received an e-mail from her this morning. She bought paint for the house and was looking at roof samples. Your mother reminds me of..."

"I know, Audrey Hepburn," said Kathy, glancing at the menu. "You told me that a thousand times."

The waiter arrived to take their order after pouring them cups of coffee. He paused beneath the TV set for a few minutes to watch the latest news with the guests.

The ashes from the funeral pyre of our beloved King Birendra and Queen Aishwarya will be transported from Kathmandu to Gorkha, where the ancient palace of the Shah Dynasty is located 150 kilometers west of Kathmandu. The remains of the king and queen will be stored there in the temple.

Condolences are pouring into Kathmandu from around the world. "India grieves with Nepal as a close neighbor. The government and people of India are stunned at the tragic and untimely demise of the king and other members of his family," said Mr. Jaswant Singh.

A spokesman from the UK stated, "Queen Elizabeth II and Prince Charles were deeply shocked by the massacre of the royal family in Nepal. Prime Minister, Tony Blair, also expressed sympathy over the deaths of the royal family which he called a 'dreadful tragedy.'"

The Chinese President, Jiang Zemin, expressed his regret and grief over the demise of the royal family. The Dalai Lama also sends his condolences to the bereaved survivors of the massacre and the people of Nepal. The Russian Foreign Minister, Igor Ivanov sends condolences...

"Dad, I thought we were supposed to catch the afternoon planes for eastern Nepal," interrupted Kathy as the waiter arrived with their omelets and toast.

"The flights may be delayed because of the departures of foreign dignitaries today," said Carl.

"Look who's here! I can't believe it," said Kathy leaping from her chair and rushing toward the young man.

"I caught the morning flight from Pokhara," said Om. "I stayed up all night working on my research paper and took it to my advisor. He told me that Tribuwan University will be shut down for the next 13 days to mourn the deaths of the royal family."

Kathy hugged Om, kissing him on the cheek. She took him by the arm and led him to their table.

After shaking hands with Om, Carl left to check with the desk clerk about the flight schedules. Upon returning to the restaurant, he said, "We won't be leaving Kathmandu until Tuesday for Lukla and Terhathum."

"Om, do you have your ticket yet?" asked Kathy.

"No, I must get it this morning," he replied. "I'm looking forward to going with you and my father to the Tengboche Monastery for the next two weeks."

"The monastery is under surveillance by the Nepalese army," said Carl. "The government believes that the monks are harboring Maoist terrorists. Kathy, I'd like you to come to eastern Nepal with me and Moksha."

"Dad, you promised I could go with Muktuba and Om to Tengboche. Now you're breaking your promise," complained Kathy.

"I'm worried about your safety. There's a lot of unrest in Nepal over the assassinations," said Carl.

"I must get my ticket this morning at the Guida Travel Agency" interrupted Om. "Have you seen my father and grandfather this morning?"

"Muktuba and Moksha left the hotel an hour ago. They were summoned to perform exorcisms at the palace in the Billards Room and Dipendra's apartments."

"I'll bring Om's luggage and computer to my room," insisted Carl, rising from the table. "Kathy, please get me a copy of *Rising Nepal*. There's a paper boy out on the veranda of the hotel."

When Carl returned to the table, he noticed that Kathy and Om were hovered over the newspaper. Kathy read him the initial headline, *Royal Family Cremated at Pashupati*. Halfway down the page was the second one, *Murder of Abbot at Bodhnath by British Monk*.

"I can't believe it!" blurted Carl. "It's Nigel's picture! He is wearing a maroon robe and holding a machete!"

"Yama Raj told us his picture would be in all the papers. That's why Margaret's in the hospital again. She's had a nervous breakdown," said Kathy reading the article to her father.

A British monk from the Tengboche Monastery, Nigel Porter, attacked and killed the Abbot at Bodhnath last night after smashing the pictures of our beloved King Birendra and Queen Aishwarya during a purification ceremony. He also severely wounded the Vajrayana priest with his machete. The priest is recovering at Shanta Bhawan Hospital in Patan.

Yama Raj, a palace security guard, reported that Nigel was arrested during the dinner party for conspiring to assassinate the royal famiy on Friday night.

On Saturday morning Nigel escaped from the Basantapur jail with three monks and a yogi. After killing the abbot, they fled from Bodhnath through an abandoned sewer ending at Deer Park, where they hid among the mourners during the cremation of the royal family last night. The police believe the conspirators escaped to the hills beyond the Kathmandu Valley.

If anyone has information leading to the arrest of these assassins, they will be given 100,000 rupees informed Mr. Shrestha, the Chief of Police.

"I feel sorry for Margaret," said Kathy. "It will take her a long time to recover from this tragedy."

"Dr. Manandhar, her psychiatrist, should be able to help her," reassured Carl.

"How awful," said Kathy, reading that the assassination at the palace was the worst since the Kot Massacre in 1846 when the Ranas slaughtered one hundred supporters of the king and took over the monarchy.

"It was as brutal as the murder of the Romanov Family in 1918, when Czar Nicholas II, his wife, and children were massacred," said Kathy.

"Just look at that hideous expression on Nigel's face," said Om. "It's enough to terrify anyone. I hope Margaret doesn't see the newspaper or she'll never recover."

"Nigel looks deranged. It's horrifying to see him with that bloody machete," said Kathy. "Om, I need some fresh air. Let's go for a stroll."

"I'll take you for a tour of the city," said Om. "You can come with us, Dr. Brecht."

"I'll come with you for a short walk. I have things to do," said Carl, worried about Kathy's safety.

Upon leaving the Kathmandu Guest House, they encountered a crowd of protestors, marching through Tamel carrying portraits of the deceased king and queen.

While hurrying down Tridev Marg, they noticed hundreds of men squatting in the street, getting their heads shaved by the local barbers to mourn the deaths of the royal family. Even foreign trekkers and tourists submitted to being tonsured to express their grieving.

Upon reaching Kanti Path, they observed that the mood of the protesters had shifted from grieving to anger and frustration. "Remove Prime Minister Girja Prasad Koirala from office," they chanted in unison.

As they passed Bir Hospital, students were shouting, "*Yo sarkar chaindaina. Juto prachaar chaindaina!* We don't want this government. We don't want false news!"

"Those protestors are really angry," commented Kathy, holding Om's hand tightly with her father beside them.

"*Satya chaincha. Jutho prachaar chaindaina!* We want the truth. We don't want false news," shouted more protestors with shaved heads, carrying placards. Others held up posters of King Birendra and Queen Aishwarya.

"I'm scared. We need to get away from the protestors," insisted Kathy.

"After I get my ticket at the travel agency, I'll take you to a restaurant," said Om.

"I won't go with you. I want to take a taxi to the hospital to see how Margaret's doing. I'll meet you later in the garden at the Kathmandu Guest House," stated Carl.

"Be extra careful because the people are angry and blaming the foreign press. The Maoist leaders have openly admitted that they want the monarchy to end," added Carl.

As he searched for a taxi, Carl heard a wave of people gathered at Ratna Park, shouting, "*Hatyara lai fashi de! Bideshi hamro des chora!* Hang the murderers! Foreigners must leave Nepal."

Upon reaching New Road, Carl went into a bookstore, and bought a copy of the *Times of India*. "I'm sorry to hear about the massacre," said Carl, offering his condolences to the proprietor and the Nepalese customers.

"We are angry because our government has deceived us. Nepal is a puppet manipulated by foreign lands," asserted the proprietor.

Carl left the shop feeling disturbed. He located a taxi and went directly to Shanta Bhawan Hospital.

73

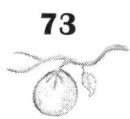

While travelling in the taxi to the hospital, Carl was chatting with the driver, who was angry over the events that had transpired since the assassination on Friday evening. Their conversation came to a halt when the driver turned on the radio.

We interrupt this broadcast about the Summer Games in Kathmandu to inform you that Crown Prince Dipendra died this morning at 3:45. The prince had a black belt in karate when he was studying at Eaton.
Dipendraji was the King of Nepal for only three days. His tragic death was due to a bullet wound in the head by the assassin on Friday night during the family dinner at the royal palace. Prince Gyanendra, a brother of the deceased King Birendra, will be coronated King of Nepal at the ancient royal palace on New Road. Please stay tuned for further news...

"I'm worried about the future of our country. When Gyanendra becomes the king, his son, Paras will be in line for the succession to the throne," said the taxi driver. "Paras' crimes are unforgivable.

"Not too long ago he went to a bar in Chitwaun, where he beat up a man because he didn't like his looks," continued the driver. "The stranger died from internal hemorrhaging, and Paras got away with the murder," continued the driver, turning up the radio to hear the details about the cremation from the previous night.

"Our future is now uncertain," said the driver, crossing the bridge into Patan. "Gyanendra has no interest in negotiating with the Maoists. He wants to drive them out of the country with the help of foreign governments. I'm afraid there will be a revolution here in Nepal."

"Here we are at Shanta Bhawan Hospital in Patan. Could you come back in an hour?" asked Carl, paying the driver and hurrying into the hosptial.

At the information desk, Carl spoke to the receptionist about seeing Margaret Porter. He was told that a doctor was with her and to be seated.

When Carl entered the crowded waiting room, no one noticed him. All eyes were focused on the TV with the current news.

According to the physicians at Chhuani Hospital, Princess Komal, the wife of the Regent Gyanendra, is now in satisfactory condition after being wounded during the massacre at the palace. Princess Shobha, the deceased king's sister, has also survived. Other survivors of the brutal slayings are: Kumar, the husband of Princess Shruti and Mrs. Ketaki Chester. Prince Dhirendra Shah, the older brother of the deceased king, is still seriously wounded.

The coronation of Gyandendra will take place at 10:30 a.m. today, Monday, June 4th, at Hanuman Dokha, the traditional palace of the Malla Kings.

Carl watched the news about the cremation of the royal family. A few minutes later he was surprised to see the doctor coming down the hallway.

"Doctor Brecht, it's a pleasure to see you again," said the psychiatrist, shaking his hand.

"Just call me Carl. How's Margaret doing this morning Dr. Manandhar?"

"You need not be so formal. Please call me Krishna. She's better now, but I'm afraid she's suffering from shock over the massacre at the palace. She is still in denial about Nigel murdering the abbot at Bodhnath. Margaret insists that he wasn't in the prayer hall during the time of the murder and the assault of the priest."

"I saw Nigel's picture in the newspaper this morning." said Carl, his brow furrowed.

The psychiatrist informed Carl that Margaret regretted going to Fewa Lake, and she blamed herself for hiring the shamans, who released the demons responsible for the assassination of the royal family and the possession of Nigel. She is filled with fear, guilt, shame, and remorse over the deaths.

"May I see Margaret?" asked Carl, worried about her.

"Of course, I'll take you to her room," agreed Krishna, leading the way down the corridor.

Upon entering the room Carl was surprised to find her sitting up in bed, wearing a hospital gown.

"Carl, I'm so thrilled to see you," said Margaret, "I was just reading Psalm 107. *O give thanks to the Lord, for he is good; for his steadfast love endures forever! Let the redeemed of the Lord say so...*You're a gift from God. Thanks so much for coming to visit me."

"Margaret, you're looking well," said Carl, amazed by her recovery after a single session with the psychiatrist.

"I must speak to Moksha in the near future," said Margaret. "I'm worried because the exorcisms he performed at Fewa Lake didn't protect Nigel."

"Margaret had a dream that Nigel was being attacked by the demons, exorcised by Moksha from that cottage in Pokhara," said Dr. Manandhar.

"Tomorrow, Moksha and I will be flying to Terhathum to do research on the implementation of the paramedic training of shamans," announced Carl.

"How about Muktuba?" asked Margaret. "I was planning to go with him and Kathy to the Tengboche Monastery. I must get permission from the abbot to bring Nigel back to London with me."

"Muktuba will fly to Lukla tomorrow with Kathy and Om and trek to Namache Bazaar. The following day they'll depart for the Tengboche Monastery to record data about medicinal herbs," informed Carl.

"Something's happened to Nigel. I must go with you. I can't stay here any longer," cried Margaret.

Dr. Manandhar approached her bed. "I'm sorry for interrupting this conversation Carl, but it's time for you to be going. Margaret, you're in no condition to leave."

"It's my fault that Nigel is possessed again," she said.

"Margaret, you must rest now. I've asked the nurse to bring you another sedative. I don't want you becoming overly stimulated," said Krishna.

"I don't want a sedative. I want to go to the hotel to get my clothes. I would like to go out to dinner with you and Carl this evening," she insisted.

"I believe Margaret's well enough to go out this evening if she rests this afternoon. I can take her to the hotel to get her clothes and meet you for dinner," suggested the doctor.

"I'll join you at the Kathmandu Guest House in the lobby at 7:00 tonight." said Carl.

Margaret seized Carl by the hand and said, "Thank you. We'll see you later this evening."

Carl departed from the hospital in the taxi. When he returned to Kathmandu the streets were blocked. He walked from the stadium pushing his way through the crowd. Eventually he arrived at the ancient palace to witness the coronation of Gyanendra. Several hours later he returned to the hotel to work on his research. Later that evening he met Margaret and Krishna, in the lobby.

"You look gorgeous," said Carl, distracted by her low cut tropical gown accented with pearls. Her pink toenails protruded from white sandals.

When Carl gave Margaret a hug, she whispered in his ear, "Thank you for inviting me to dinner. You've always been so kind to me. I remember when you took me to the Royal Hotel dancing."

"That was a long time ago," said Carl, noticing Kathy and Om entering the lobby.

Carl blushed with embarrassment when Margaret suddenly kissed him on the cheek in front of them.

"Why, Kathy?" said Carl, clearing his throat. "Why don't you and Om join us for dinner here at the hotel."

"We've already eaten at a Tibetan restaurant," said Kathy, scowling at Margaret. "We're going for a stroll in the bazaar. We'll be back later."

"I have two handsome men to escort me to the dining room," said Margaret, taking their arms and entering the dining room.

The room was filled with tourists who spent the day visiting the major shrines of the valley in spite of the protesters and mourners. All heads turned toward Margaret being seated with two men. Some of the travelers whispered among themselves about her blonde hair, clothing, and sensuous figure.

"Were you detained after leaving the hospital because of the coronation?" asked Margaret, glancing at the menu.

Carl said, "When I finally got to the ancient wooden palace, I had to push my way through the crowd to see the king being crowned. The spectators were silent except for the protesters who were shouting that the government was a false democracy."

"I watched the coronation on the TV in my room at the hospital," said Margaret. "I saw protestors arrested by the police. They were trying to incite a riot."

"After the arrest of the protestors the crowd settled down. There was a brooding silence when Gyanendra was crowned at the traditional palace of the Shah Dynasty," added the psychiatrist.

Carl said he observed the priest putting the golden crown loaded with jewels and a white plume on Gyanendra's head. The future king sat on an elevated throne wearing traditional Nepali clothing, a long shirt, a vest, and a coat.

After the coronation, King Gyanendra boarded the royal chariot, which was pulled by six white horses. A military band wearing red uniforms led the way back to the royal palace. There were thousands of people crowded on the sidewalks along the way silently watching.

"The whole event was like a fairytale. It reminded me of Cinderella going to the royal ball," said Margaret, turning to the waiter, who took their orders.

"The odd thing about the ceremony was that the crowd was so solemn. There were no protestors shouting or creating a disturbance. No one cheered the new king along the way," said the psychiatrist, nodding to the waiter and ordering the tandoori chicken with jasmine rice.

"That's because the whole country is grieving the death of Dipendra, and the hasty cremation of the royal family," said Carl, handing the waiter the menu. "I'll have the barbecued chicken with fried potatoes."

"I'll have the same," agreed Margaret, smiling at the waiter, who was staring at her cleavage.

Their conversation was interrupted by a TV broadcast announcing the death of Dipendra.

"Nigel was staying with Dipendra at the royal palace when the assassination took place," recalled Margaret, seizing Carl's arm.

"Margaret, do you recall going to Fewa Lake with the shamans to perform the exorcisms," asked the psychiatrist.

Carl and the doctor listened to her tell them about finding the skeletons, the performance of exorcisms, and the whirlwinds leaving the lake with Ravana's demons.

"Ravana was the Demon King who abducted Sita and carried her off to Sri Lanka," said Margaret. "Before Nigel was born, Yorg told me that I was an incarnation of Sita who carried the dormant seed of Ravana in my womb through many incarnations."

"Did you believe that Yorg was telling you the truth?" asked the doctor.

"Yes, I believed him at that time. After Nigel was born, I foolishly offered him to Ravana at a special ceremony of the London Coven," said Margaret. "I made a terrible mistake by joining the coven.

"I came to Nepal because I believed Nigel was possessed by evil spirits. I wanted a shaman to perform an exorcism on him. I'm...I'm terrified evil spirits from Fewa Lake have possessed Nigel once again," uttered Margaret.

"Then you don't believe that Nigel is the son of Ravana," said the psychiatrist, nodding to the waiter as he set down their plates.

"No! When I read *The Ramayana,* I found out that Sita never yielded to Ravana during her captivity. She was always faithful to her husband, Rama. I realized that Yorg had lied to me about being an incarnation of Sita," said Margaret, turning toward the TV set.

The three Tibetan Buddhist monks and the yogi were last seen at Pashupati Nath last night during the cremation of the remains of the royal family. They fled from jail with Nigel Porter, the murderer of the abbot at Bodhnath. He is also wanted by the police for conspiring with the Maoists to destroy the Shah Dynasty. Here is a photograph of him, dressed in a maroon robe and holding a machete...

"No!" screamed Margaret rising from her chair at the table. "That's not my son! It can't be Nigel! "

"Sit down, Margaret," insisted the psychiatrist taking her by the arm.

All heads turned toward Margaret, sobbing hysterically with her hands over her face.

"We must go back to the hospital," insisted Dr. Manandhar. "I'm sorry, Carl, that we haven't had a chance to enjoy our meals with you."

"If Margaret calms down, I might be able to bring her to the airport tomorrow to say goodbye to you and Moksha," said the psychiatrist taking her by the arm and leaving the restaurant. But I can't promise you anything," said Krishna.

Carl left his meal untouched and followed them through the lobby to the exit. They continued through the deserted patio where a taxi was waiting to take them back to the hospital.

Margaret rolled down the window and sobbed, "Carl, please come and visit me once you return from Terhathum."

"I'll be back in Kathmandu in a couple of weeks," said Carl. "By then you'll be well enough to travel."

After the departure of the taxi, Carl went back to restaurant to pay the bill. He sat down at a table and took a deep breath, reflecting upon everything that had happened since he and Kathy arrived in Kathmandu.

74

Upon returning to the desk Carl asked the despondent clerk for his room key. The clerk was preoccupied and hesitant about speaking to him.

"I'm very sorry to hear about the death of Prince Dipendra," said Carl.

"You mean King Dipendra," said the clerk, his face tense. "He only ruled for three days. The Privy Council shouldn't have appointed him king. It was a mistake."

"I attended the coronation of the new king this morning," said Carl. "It was a very solemn ceremony."

"That's another mistake. Our country will never recover from the assassination of our royal family," uttered the clerk. "By the way, your daughter and her boyfriend are waiting for you in the garden."

Carl entered the garden through the double doors. He hurried down the gravel path, noticing Kathy and Om sitting on bamboo chairs beneath the pomelo tree.

"What are you studying so intensely?" asked Carl.

"I learned a lot about snakebites in the workshop at the convention," said Kathy, leafing through her notes. "I'm sharing notes with Om."

"There are more snake bites in the *terai*, the southern plains, than anywhere else in Nepal," recalled Carl.

"You're right," said Kathy, reading from her notes. "Most snake bites occur in the villages of the *terai* and the middle regions of Nepal rather than at higher altitudes. There are 77 different species of snakes in Nepal, but only 21 are poisonous. They include the cobra, coral, krait, and the viper family."

"We learned how to use a tourniquet when treating poisonous snake bites. If the wound is neglected, it will become gangrenous," continued Kathy.

"*Nagpanchami* is our Five Day Snake Festival. It always takes place in July. At that time we paste flyers with snake designs on them over the entrance of our homes and shops for protection against snake bite," stated Om.

"Why are you so interested in snakebites?" asked Carl.

"Dad, we'll be hiking all the way from Lukla to Namache Bazaar and then to the Tengboche during the monsoon season when snake bites are more frequent," said Kathy, frowning at her father.

"There are more snake bites during the monsoon season than any other time of the year," agreed Om.

"I put a snake bite kit in my backpack," said Kathy. "Dad, you'll also need one when you're trekking with Moksha to Terhathum."

"My kit is already packed" said Carl. "Excuse me. I'm going to go to the lobby to check my e-mail."

Carl went directly to a guest computer to open his e-mail. He was pleased to find a message from Barbara.

Dearest Carl, *June 3, 2001*
   I miss you so much even though you've only been gone two weeks. I've been counting the days since you left, marking them on the calendar. Sam will be arriving at O'Hare tomorrow. He's agreed to supervise the crew while they fix up the house.
   Kathy e-mailed me that Om arrived from Pokhara and will be travelling with her on Tuesday. His father, Muktuba, will be the chaperone. I'm terrified about her going to the Tengboche, now under surveillance because the monks have been accused of

harboring terrorists. I hope you have enough sense not to let Kathy go there.

Nigel Porter has made headlines in the Chicago Tribune for murdering the abbot at Bodhnath. His picture has been flashed across the evening news on TV. I'm stressed out over the assassination of the royal family with Nigel right in the thick of things. I feel sorry for Margaret Porter. Kathy told me that Margaret's in love with you. I hope not.

I also watched the cremation of the royal family on TV. The crowd was filled with grieving mourners. Some of them were very angry.

Please keep an eye on Kathy. I'm scared to death that something might happen to her. Mark is at Outward Bound and sends his love. I'm so lonely in this house without you.

With all my love,
Barbara

Carl printed out his wife's e-mail and took it to the garden to read to Kathy.

"Your mother's also concerned. I'm going to check with the American Embassy about you travelling to the Tengboche Monastery," said Carl.

After contacting the embassy, Carl felt reassured. He was told that the tourists and research teams would be allowed to visit and perform their tasks without interference from the security guards at the monastery.

He e-mailed Barbara to reassure her that everything was under control and not to worry about Kathy. Upon returning to the garden, Kathy and Om were gone.

The desk clerk informed him, they had gone out to dance at a club and would be back early.

"Dr. Brecht, I also have a message from the airlines. You will be departing at 8:00 am if the weather is good. You should check in your baggage at 7:00 tomorrow."

75

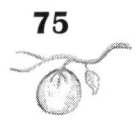

On Tuesday morning it was raining heavily when Carl and Kathy entered the taxi in front of the hotel. As they travelled to the airport, the streets were crowded with mourners in spite of the downpour.

"What time did you get in last night?" asked Carl, noticing that Kathy was yawning.

"Oh for heaven's sake, Dad, we got back to the hotel before 10:30 and watched TV in the lobby. The film was in Hindi, and I didn't understand a word of it.

"We finally went for a walk in the garden. I swear I was in my room by midnight. I even reminded Moksha and Muktuba about our morning flight when Om joined them in their room," said Kathy.

"I didn't sleep the whole night, worrying about you. I was hoping you'd knock on my door and let me know that you were back in the hotel," said Carl.

"Dad, you still treat me like I'm ten-years-old," she snapped. "Don't worry. I won't do anything foolish."

"I'm worried about your safety. The Nepalese are angry with foreigners. Some of them want us out of the country permanently," said Carl.

"I'm disgusted about your relationship with Margaret Porter," said Kathy. "I saw her kissing you in the lobby."

"I didn't expect her to do that. She's taking an awful lot of medication," said Carl, wondering if he should tell his daughter that he knew she was taking birth control pills because he overheard her conversation with Mark on the patio before leaving Chicago.

"I'm shocked by the way she clings to you constantly in front of everyone," continued Kathy. "I told Mom that Margaret's in love with you in my e-mail."

"I wish you wouldn't have done that. Mom's already suffering from the empty nest syndrome. She'll be more stressed with Sam staying with her to supervise the remodeling of the house."

"There's nothing going on between Margaret and me. She's in shock over Nigel. I was only trying to console her. Doctor Manandhar was there the whole time. They just arrived from the hospital when she kissed me. She's not well enough to be going to the Tengboche Monastery."

"That's a relief. I'm sorry for being overly critical of her," said Kathy, noticing the taxi was slowing down. "Those protestors are really angry. They're coming toward us with their signs. What are they chanting?"

As the taxi headed past the royal palace, young men with shaved heads banged on their roof, shouting at them, "*Hatyara lai fashi de*! Death to the murderers!"

"Oh God!" gasped Kathy. "Here come more protestors with posters of Nigel in his maroon robe with a machete!"

"Margaret finally came to terms with Christopher's death by having exorcisms performed. Now she must deal with Nigel murdering the abbot," said Carl.

The driver blasted the horn several times and then crept forward through the unruly crowd.

"Om and the shamans are in the taxi right behind us," screamed Kathy, her eyes wide with terror. "No one's pounding on their roof."

The protestors kept waving the posters of Nigel and shouting, *"Bideshi dabad chaindaina. Jhuto prajatantra chaindaina*! We don't want foreign pressure. We don't want a fake democracy!"

"Can you understand why I was so worried about you last night?" asked Carl. "The Nepalese are furious over the assassination of the royal family."

"Dad, I'm really sorry. I should've called your room when we returned at 10:30. I didn't want to say anything to you about what happened to us. We came home early from the club because some students high on drugs were causing trouble at the dance."

"What happened?" asked Carl, his brow furrowed.

"Some angry students wanted to know why Om was dancing with a foreigner. He almost got into a fist fight with them. I insisted that we leave. We were lucky to get a taxi right in front of the club.

"I was very upset by the incident," blurted Kathy. "Om asked me to watch TV with him in the lobby to calm down, but it didn't help. I walked around the garden several times to try to get over my fright. I…I wanted to tell you not to worry about me because I'm taking birth control pills."

"Kathy, I know you're 18 years old and that all the girls in your graduating class were taking birth control pills. I overheard you talking to Mark about seeing the doctor to get the pills. I just hope if you decide to have sex, you'll be sure you take the necessary precautions."

"Don't worry, Dad," she said. "I've been too tense to even think about having sex with Om. He's been very understanding. That's why I like him."

As the taxi finally drove past the palace and turned onto Durbar Marg, the crowd separated due to the presence of numerous policemen. The driver was finally able to continue at a reasonable speed to Dilli Bazaar.

A few minutes later the taxi slowed down at the bridge where a barefoot farmer was crossing with a huge water buffalo. He was followed by villagers carrying bundles of freshly cut grass. On the banks of the river several *dobhis* were washing clothes in the rain.

After crossing another bridge over the Bhagmati River, they followed the Ring Road until they arrived at the Tribuwan International Airport.

While checking in their backpacks, they saw Moksha, Muktuba, and Om enter the terminal, drenched from the sudden cloudburst.

"Your flights to Lukla and Terhathum are scheduled to depart on time," said the clerk, looking over their passports.

"Will you promise to take good care of my daughter?" asked Carl, shaking hands with Om and Muktuba. They chatted together about the possibility of meeting Maoists on the trail from Namche Bazaar to Tengboche.

"Here we are at our gate," said Om. "Our flight to Lukla takes only thirty-five minutes. If the storm gets worse we may have to stay there overnight in a hotel."

"We might be able to trek to Namche Bazaar, the Base Camp of Mount Everest yet this afternoon," said Muktuba. "The accommodations are good there because the Sherpas are used to dealing with trekkers."

"Excuse me," said a bearded trekker approaching them. "I overheard your conversation. The German ambassador was quoted in today's newspaper that Tengboche is no longer under suspicion for harboring terrorists."

He informed them that the German patrons of the Tengboche Development Project were offended by the rumor that the monastery was harboring Maoists. They denied that the monks there were conspiring to destroy the Shah Dynasty.

"What about Nigel Porter? He lived at that monastery for several years," said Carl.

"Ambassador Herr Halsted was shocked when he saw Nigel's picture in the newspaper. He had no comment to make about the deranged monk, but agreed to cooperate with the authorities to have him arrested and brought to trial for the murder of the abbot at Bodhnath."

"Will all passengers departing for Lukla please board their aircraft now," announced the attendant.

Carl gave Kathy a hug. "I'll meet you at Tengboche in two weeks. Please e-mail to let me know that you got there safely."

"I'll e-mail you," said Kathy, hugging her father.

Carl and Moksha watched them board the plane along with numerous trekkers, waving to them as their plane departed from Kathmandu.

76

After watching the plane take off for Lukla, Carl and Moksha headed toward their gate for departure to Terhathum. The flight was delayed for an hour due to an inspection of the engine and the equipment, waterlogged from the rain.

"I heard the security guard knocking on your door last night while I was working late at my desk," said Carl. "After you left the hotel, I took a taxi to witness the cremation of Dipendra and the Katto Ceremony at Pashupati Nath."

"Muktuba and I were summoned to the royal palace by King Gyanendra to perform exorcisms to get rid of the evil spirits inhabiting the Billiards Room and the crown prince's living quarters" said Moksha.

"We chanted and burned incense for several hours," said Moksha. "Afterwards a palace guard took us in the royal limousine to see the ceremony at the river."

Their conversation was interrupted by a radio broadcast.

This is Mohan Lall with the latest news about the massacre at the palace. Last night after the cremation of Crown Prince Dipendra, those attending stayed to witness the Katto Eating Ceremony.

This event was scheduled to be held eleven days after the cremation. However, King Gyanenda decided to perform the ceremony on Monday evening.

The crowd was small in comparison to those attending the cremation of the royal family on Sunday evening. The funeral of Dipendra was private and limited to relatives and friends.

Everyone gathered to listen to the priests chanting to liberate Dipendra's soul from negative karma and evil spirits so he could continue his journey to the next world.

Once the cremation was over, the first Katto Eating Ceremony was successfully performed for the passage of King Birendra's soul to the next world. It was followed by a disastrous second ceremony for Dipendra, which shocked the spectators.

"Will all passengers flying to Terhathum now board their flight," announced the clerk.

"I feel badly that the exorcisms at the royal palace were a failure," said Moksha. "The evil spirits left the Billiards Room and went directly to the cremation ground where they attacked a priest and his elephant."

Carl and Moksha paused before boarding to listen to the broadcast along with some German trekkers.

The Katto Eating Ceremony for King Birendra was performed by Durga Prasad, a 75-year-old Brahmin priest, who came by helicopter to Kathmandu. This priest was a strict vegetarian He was served a total of 84 dishes; some of them contained pieces of sacrificial goat.

The priest was instructed to sample the dishes. Upon eating the goat meat, he was no longer pure (suddha) but became impure (katto).

By eating the meat, Durga Prasad assumed the sins of the deceased King Birendra, enabling his soul to continue its journey. Because of his fall from grace, the priest was exiled forever since Brahmins are forbidden to eat meat.

The priest was given $1700 US dollars, a TV set, a radio, and furniture of the dead king. Wearing the king's sun glasses, his clothing, and crown he boarded the elephant and crossed the turbulent Bhagmati River without any difficulty. He then departed from the city on the back of the elephant with an entourage carrying the gifts and furniture.

"This is the last call for passengers to board the plane for Terhathum," announced the clerk.

"We'd better get going," said Carl, following Moksha, who was carrying his shamanic paraphernalia.

Once they were seated, they could hear the animated conversation of the trekkers. All eyes were on the TV above the entrance to the cockpit

Unfortunately the Katto Ceremony for Dipendra was not as auspicious. The second priest named Devi Prasad was not so fortunate. While the mahout was bringing his elephant to Kathmandu, a pregnant village woman foolishly believed that if she crawled under the belly of the elephant, her infant would be born a male. The startled elephant panicked from the intrusion and trampled the woman to death.

"I'm sorry for interrupting the broadcast," announced the stewardess, snapping off the TV. "Please fasten your seat belts. Be sure that your luggage is stored beneath the seats or in the upper compartments."

"We want to know more about the second ceremony," shouted Hans, a German trekker.

Moksha interrupted the stewardess and obtained her permission to speak to the passengers because he was present at the cremation grounds and could tell them about the second Katto Ceremony for Crown Prince Dipendra once they were airborne.

Ten minutes later, Moksha was in the aisle speaking to the passengers in Nepali, with Carl standing behind him translating.

"After becoming impure from eating goat meat (katto), the second priest, Devi Prasad, tried to board the elephant. The restless elephant didn't cooperate with him. Rather than crossing the river, it reared up hurling the priest into the swirling river.

"The trumpeting elephant whirled around and charged in the opposite direction, threatening the lives of the guests and relatives along the river bank.

"Several people fled from the enraged elephant, fearful of being trampled to death. Finally policemen and several university students pelted the raging elephant with stones and forced the beast to cross the river," said Moksha.

He informed them that demons, exorcised from the royal palace, were responsible for attacking the elephant and the priest, who nearly drowned in the river.

"Does anyone have any questions?" asked the shaman.

"Do you know anything about Nigel Porter?" asked Siegfried. "We saw his picture in the newspaper. He was a friend of Crown Prince Dipendra."

"Yes, I met Nigel many years ago," said Moksha, telling them about how he performed exorcisms on him before he became a Buddhist monk.

"Nigel's insane! He's wanted for the murder of the abbot of Bodhnath," asserted Siegfried. "The reputation of the monastery has been tainted because of him!"

The conversation came to a halt due to turbulence from heavy rain clouds which caused the plane to shake.

When the storm subsided, the stewardess announced. "Will all passengers please fasten their seat belts. We will be landing in Terhathum in a few minutes."

77

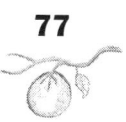

When the plane landed at Lukla, the German trekkers were the first to disembark. They put on their backpacks and departed from the airport, heading toward the trail to Namache Bazaar.

The rest of the passengers took refuge in a local restaurant, complaining about the turbulent thirty-five minute flight. They were angry because the pilot circled for an additional twenty minutes before landing in the fog.

After breakfast several tourists checked into the hotels although Muktuba, Om, and Kathy didn't stay with them. They followed the German trekkers toward the steep trail.

Unaccustomed to hiking, Kathy was soon out of breath and stopped to rest. Om agreed to stay behind with her on the trail, where drifting clouds obscured the view of the mountains. Nearby they could hear the thunderous roar of the Dudh Koshi River.

Muktuba was reluctant to leave them alone, so he lingered admiring the plants, pausing to check the map.

"I'm sorry to cause the delay," apologized Kathy. "I didn't realize the trail would be so steep."

"We need to pace ourselves by climbing slowly but steadily," recommended Om. "It's important to rest for ten minutes after trekking for an hour."

"If it doesn't rain, I'm sure we can arrive at Namache Bazaar before it gets dark. It's a gradual ascent to 11,000 feet. We'll just take our time," said Muktuba.

"Tell me about the yeti," requested Kathy, putting on her backpack and following Om up the mountain.

"The yeti is the abominable snowman," said Om. "Most Sherpas are afraid of them because of their height. A full grown yeti is at least three meters tall."

"The yeti is brown and hairy like a huge gorilla. He emits a repulsive odor and is a carnivore, attacking sheep, yaks, and people. After sucking the victim's blood, the yeti eats their brains and inner organs," continued Om.

"The abbot at Tengboche claims that the yeti isn't an animal but a human. He has the brain capacity of a genius although he behaves like a wolf," said Muktuba.

"My Sherpa friends believe the yeti is clairvoyant with supernatural powers. He mimics nocturnal animals so he can prey on them," added Om.

Muktuba told them that two monasteries in Nepal possessed yeti skulls, and the scientists, who examined them, claim that they resemble human beings.

"We'd better go a little faster. Or we'll never get to Namche Bazaar before it gets dark. It looks like it might rain," added Om.

They trekked for another hour before taking shelter in a hamlet because of the rain. A hospitable Sherpa from Chaurikhara allowed them to stay on his veranda, offering them glasses of tea. He informed them that the German trekkers had stopped there over an hour ago.

When the rain finally ceased, they continued climbing until they arrived at the confluence of two streams pouring into the Dudh Koshi River.

"We're not too far from our destination," said Muktuba, listening to the river thundering against the boulders.

They continued north on the trail until they finally got their first glimpse of Namche Bazaar with tiers of stone houses rising up the side of the mountain.

"Namche is the main hub of the Solo Khumbu region," announced Moksha. "Most of the Sherpas of Nepal live in this area."

"I certainly could use a shower," said Kathy.

"The town has several small hotels with electricity and hot water because of a hydro-electric plant. There are restaurants, shops and video parlors. The friendly Sherpas earn their living by helping trekkers," said Om.

"I'll get our trekking permits. We'll need them to go to the Tengboche Monastery," said Muktuba, heading toward a district office.

"I'm starving," said Kathy. "We didn't eat much at the restaurant in Lukla."

Upon entering a nearby restaurant, the waiter seated them at a table. Everyone ordered yak momos and *tsampa*, the salted Tibetan tea with barley.

"What is the meaning of the word, Sherpa?" asked Kathy as the waiter returned with their dinners.

"Sherpa means the people from the east. Our ancestors immigrated from Eastern Tibet many centuries ago. We were farmers, traders, and yak herders," informed the waiter, smiling at Kathy.

"I hope you can stay for our Saturday Market, when the villagers come to Namche Bazaar from the mountains to sell fresh fruits, vegetables, and their coral and turquoise jewelry," continued the waiter.

"I wish we could stay, but we have to leave tomorrow," sighed Kathy. "I would really like to see the area."

"Excuse me. My name is Pemba. I overheard your conversation," he said, approaching their table. "I would like to be your guide for the afternoon. Since the sun is finally shining, I could take you on a hike to Kunde and then to Kunjunk. These settlements are at 13,000 feet with spectacular views of the mountains.

"If you have a few more days we could trek to the glacier then drop to 16,000 feet and visit the Tibetan Plateau," he suggested.

"We are here only to get acclimated. We're not equipped for a high altitude trek to Tibet," asserted Muktuba, frowning.

"Our agency will provide everything for you, sleeping bags, tents, a cook, hiking boots, and food. We have Sherpa porters to carry your backpacks. The only thing you need is your camera," said Pemba.

"No! We're leaving tomorrow for Tengboche! Since the sun is out, we'd like you take us to get a glimpse of Mt. Everest before it gets dark. First we need to find a reasonable hotel," said Muktuba.

"I'll take you to an inexpensive hotel where you may leave your back packs," insisted Pemba.

"I can't wait to see Mount Everest. We'd better get going before it clouds over," agreed Om, offering to carry Kathy's backpack.

"We have a cheap hotel next to the video parlor," said the guide, leading the way from the restaurant.

After checking into their hotel, the guide led them through the terraced town, where the stone houses were close together.

"What are those peculiar animals?" asked Kathy as they hiked away from the settlement.

"They are yaks and dzoms. The herder is bringing them to the lower altitude to be sold at Saturday's Market," informed Pemba.

"Why do some of them have such big horns while the others are so small?" asked Kathy.

"The smaller hairy animals are yaks. When they are bred with cattle, the calves are called dzoms," informed the guide. "Both are pack animals and carry loads of potatoes, buckwheat, and barley to Tibet, where we trade them for salt and kerosene. Please follow me down this trail."

After trekking for about an hour, they saw an awesome view of Mount Everest, which silenced everyone.

"I can't believe it," whispered Kathy. "I wish we could stay here forever."

"For centuries the Sherpas were forbidden to climb Mount Everest," said Pemba. "Tensing Norgay Sherpa was the first Nepalese to reach the summit with Sir Edmund Hillary in 1953.

"Over the past several years so many people have climbed Everest that it's difficult to keep track of them. Many trekkers are careless these days. They leave debris on the mountain, including tin cans, plastic bottles, and empty oxygen cylinders that contaminate our rivers and streams," continued Pemba.

"Even Sir Edmund Hillary is disturbed by the pollution of the Everest Region. He was the first to open schools in this region with the help of Jim Fisher, who is now an anthropologist teaching at Carleton College."

"I visited that campus in Northfield, Minnesota, and met Jim Fisher," commented Kathy. "He took several of us on a tour of the campus."

"It's time to be heading back. But let's get some good pictures before we leave," said Muktuba.

"Kathy, I'd like you to come with me to the video parlor after dinner tonight," requested Pemba.

"We'll all go there with you," suggested Muktuba, concerned about the guide's interest in Kathy and Om's jealousy of him.

78

The following morning everyone was up early at the hotel in Namche Bazaar. They went into the dining room for breakfast, where their guide joined them. Pemba wanted to take Kathy shopping for jewelry before they left town. She agreed to go with him while the others stayed behind to pay the bill and pack their clothes.

Kathy purchased a coral and turquoise necklace. Upon leaving the shop, Pemba was surprised to find the group ready to depart for the monastery.

"We're leaving for Tengboche in a few minutes," said Om, handing Kathy her backpack.

"Let's get going before it starts to rain again," said Muktuba, adjusting his backpack.

Kathy was annoyed with them because she wanted to spend more time shopping. She thanked Pemba for taking her to the bazaar, inviting him to visit her in Tengboche.

"It's a four hour trek from here," asserted Om, jealous of Pemba for giving Kathy his undivided attention.

"I might visit you on my day off, stay overnight, and return the next morning," said Pemba.

"We're going to be busy recording data on the computer for the next two weeks," asserted Muktuba, leading the way toward the trail.

Kathy lingered chatting with Pemba before catching up with them. They slowly ascended the mountain by pacing themselves and taking a break every hour.

By early afternoon they had reached the Tengboche Monastery. The abbot invited them into his living quarters, where a young monk served them tea and tangerines.

"I've been expecting you," said the abbot, sitting in the lotus position. He chatted with them about the slippery trails due to the monsoon.

"I was informed that you are here to study and record data about our herbal medicine. I have a laboratory set up for you in the greenhouse. Nima Lama will take you on a tour of our buildings and get you settled in your quarters."

Kathy kept staring at the enormous woven tapestry hanging on the wall behind the abbot. She was alarmed by the ferocious image of the deity with huge vampire fangs, holding the Wheel of Life with claw like hands.

The abbot said, "Don't be frightened by Mahakala, Great Time. We are slaves of time because we always have too much time or not enough."

"That's very true," agreed Muktuba. "We usually live with regret about the past or anxiety over the future. Rarely are we content to live in the present moment."

The abbot explained that the animals in the center of the painting represent our major character defects: the pig was delusion, the rooster attachment, and the snake hatred.

"Oh look," blurted Kathy, setting her cup down. "There are soldiers standing at the window with guns. They're spying on us!"

"Don't pay any attention to them. They've been asking our monks a lot of questions because we once helped a wounded Maoist terrorist recover from his injuries," said the abbot, shaking his head.

He pointed to the tapestry with six spokes radiating from the center which represented the human condition in conflict with its opposite polarity.

"Our basic problem is feeling separated from others rather than united with them. Notice that each spoke in the wheel has the guiding light of a Buddha," said the abbot.

"Please excuse me. I must talk with the Sherpas waiting outside to see me. The villagers are quarreling because a herd of yaks broke loose and destroyed a field of barley. Here comes your guide. He will take you on a tour of the monastery," stated the abbot.

"This way to our prayer hall," said Nima Lama, bowing to the abbot and leaving his quarters. A few minutes later they entered the vast hall.

"This building is called Dokhang. The enormous bronze image is the historical Buddha, Sakyamuni."

"What are the names of the statues on each side of the Buddha?" asked Kathy.

"This statue is Manjushri, the Bodhisattva of Wisdom," pointed Nima. "And here is Maitraya, the Future Buddha. Our sacred scriptures are located in the glass case."

"Please excuse me," interrupted Muktuba. "I must go now to the greenhouse to set up the computers. I'm taking an inventory about the medicinal plants growing here."

"Dad, I'll join you later with Kathy," said Om.

"The greenhouse is only a ten minute walk from here," informed Nima Lama. "I'll bring them there after the tour."

"Manjusri radiates a golden light. He holds a flaming sword which cuts through ignorance." said Nima Lama.

While listening to their guide Om reached for Kathy's hand in the dark prayer hall, illuminated only by butter lamps. He squeezed her hand, kissing her on the cheek.

All of sudden the front door of the monastery flung open and a soldier bolted into the hall with a machine gun. He looked around and then departed quickly.

"What's going on here?" gasped Kathy, clinging to Om.

"Those guards have been searching the premises and harassing our monks, hoping they'll confess that we are harboring Maoist terrorists," said their guide.

Nima Lama ignored the intrusion, trying not to alarm the guests. "There's a legend about Manjusri. Many centuries ago a Serpent King ruled the Kathmandu Valley when it was submerged in water. Thousands of snakes lived in the vast lake among the aquatic plants."

"What's happening?" gasped Kathy, turning toward the entrance, where armed guards entered again.

They slammed the door shut and were heading toward them with their boots striking the wooden floor and echoing throughout the empty hall.

"They look like the Gestapo with their guns raised," said Om, feeling nervous.

"It's Yama Raj and Hariyo! What are you doing here in Tengboche?" asked Kathy, frowning with disgust.

"We're here to arrest Nigel Porter and the three monks who escaped from the Basantapur jail with that yogi," asserted Yama Raj.

"The Sherpas in Namche Bazaar informed us that they saw Nigel slaughter a yak and drink its blood near a monastery in Kumjung," continued Yama Raj.

"Nigel ripped out the entrails and ate them raw because he's possessed by evil spirits. That's why he killed the abbot at Bodhnath," added Hariyo.

"I have some questions to ask you," insisted Yama Raj.

Kathy said, "I have nothing to say to you. We're leaving now to help Muktuba in the greenhouse."

"You're not going anywhere. You're coming with us to the convent," insisted Yama Raj.

"But first I want to show them the kitchen where they'll be taking their meals," said Nima Lama, leading the way.

79

Upon leaving the prayer hall, Yama Raj was anxious to get to the convent. He was angry with Nima Lama for taking them to the kitchen. Everyone ignored him, admiring the spectacular views of the mountains as they strolled between the buildings.

"I'm impressed with the architecture of the monastery. It's a real paradise," said Kathy. "How many monks do you have staying here?"

"We have twenty-five ordained monks and ten students here. Another nine are studying in India," said Nima Lama.

"Here's the kitchen," uttered Hariyo. "I'm hungry. I didn't have much to eat for breakfast."

"You fat slob," uttered Yama Raj. "I saw you gulp down two glasses of tea and eat a dozen donuts."

"You always criticize me," blurted Hariyo, clenching his fists. "I only ate nine donuts."

"We're here too early for lunch, but we can have some Tibetan tea," said Nima Lama, heading toward the cook.

Yama Raj rushed ahead of everyone toward the stove, where the chef was stirring a pot.

"Give us some of those momos," he demanded, lifting the lid on the kettle with a pot holder.

"You heard my boss. We want something to eat!" shouted Hariyo. "We're hungry!"

"I'm sorry, but the momos aren't quite ready. Our community dinner will be served today at 12:30 pm. We have plenty of *sampa*," said the chef, pouring the thick tea for them into wooden bowls.

"I hate that shit," shouted Yama Raj, knocking the bowl from his hands. It crashed to the floor with a thud.

"If you'll...you'll come back in fifteen minutes the meal will be ready," stammered the fearful cook.

Yama Raj snatched a dipper from the counter and removed steaming vegetable dumplings from the kettle. "I'll have some of these right now."

"We're guards from the royal palace," announced Hariyo. "We saw the crown prince murder his family."

"Did you ever meet Nigel Porter when you were at the palace?" asked Kathy.

"Of course we met him," insisted Hariyo. "We arrested Nigel and slammed him in jail with his friends from this monastery. They were all conspirators, even the yogi."

"I told you to shut up, you fool!" shouted Yama Raj, sitting down at a table with his bowl of momos. He glanced out the window at the soldiers, smoking cigarettes.

"Nigel Porter's crazy," said Hariyo. "He's been killing yaks and drinking their blood."

"He's with those three deranged monks from this monastery and that perverted yogi," informed Yama Raj, stuffing his mouth and spitting the momos onto the floor. "What the fuck. This dough's still raw. That asshole chef doesn't even know how to cook!"

"Nigel murdered the abbot at Bodhnath," said Om, disgusted by the security guard's crude behavior.

"That's why Solu Khumbu is under surveillance," said Yama Raj, dumping the momos on the floor. "The Royal Nepalese Army is guarding every shrine and monastery in this area and patrolling the hills."

While they were talking, the chef came over with steaming bowls of *sampa* for Kathy, Om, and Nima Lama.

"What's that loud noise?" asked Kathy, glancing out the window. "It sounds like a helicopter landing."

Yama Raj and Hariyo hurried toward the exit, opened the door, and stepped outside.

"It's a helicopter all right. There are more in the distance scouring the mountains. They're searching for Nigel and the conspirators," informed Yama Raj returning to the dining room. "If they spot the murderers, the guards will shoot to kill."

Nima Lama mentioned, "Our monks, Vairocana, Ratna, and Dorjee, have taken vows to practice nonviolence. They are strict vegetarians and won't even slap a mosquito.".

Yama Raj said, "Those three monks murdered the guard at the jail. They clubbed him to death, stole his keys, and stripped him of his clothes."

"We found his naked body on the floor with his head bashed in," added Hariyo.

Nima Lama denied that they were responsible for the slaying of the guard because they were ordained red cap monks who took vows of celibacy.

"That makes them even more dangerous," asserted Yama Raj. "I know all about the vow of celibacy. I once belonged to the Shiva Sena and then Hanuman's Army."

"We were expelled from Hanuman's Army because Yama Raj killed a soldier for insulting him," blurted Hariyo, pacing the floor.

"I told you to shut the fuck up!" shouted Yama Raj, striking his partner with his fist.

"I'm bleeding," sobbed Hariyo, rising from the table. The blood gushed from his nose onto the wooden floor.

"Stop being such a bully," shouted Kathy, rushing to the sink to get a wet cloth. "Yama Raj, you've really gone too far this time!"

"It's time to go to the convent," announced Yama Raj, removing a knife from the sheath on his hip. "The next time Hariyo opens his mouth, I'll cut out his tongue!"

"We're not going anywhere with you," announced Kathy, placing a wet cloth on Hariyo's nose and tilting his head back to stop the bleeding.

"I said we're leaving right now," insisted Yama Raj, waving the knife at them.

"We better go with him to the convent," advised Nima Lama, trying to remain calm.

Everyone was silent as they left the kitchen and walked down the winding trail toward the convent. They passed two monks carrying baskets of fresh vegetables to the kitchen. Others followed them with bundles of wood.

"Look," gasped Kathy. "There are more soldiers leaving the helicopter that just landed below the monastery."

"We know that the monks are holding secret meetings here to overthrow the government. That's why the royalists burned this place to the ground in 1989," said Yama Raj.

"You guys shouldn't be bandaging wounded Maoists," added Hariyo. "You should just let them bleed to death."

"If you open your mouth again, I'll knock your fuckin' teeth out," shouted Yama Raj, striking him on the head with his fists.

"Sorry, I won't say another word. I promise you. I'll be quiet," uttered Hariyo, covering his face with his arms.

"Here we are at the convent," said Nima Lama, approaching a dilapidated building.

The abbotess with her head shaved was in the garden hoeing cabbages. She approached them, reminding Nima

Lama that the roof needed to be repaired and the crumbling bricks replaced.

"We want a place where we can speak privately to these people," insisted Yama Raj.

The abbotess bowed to the soldiers and led them into the prayer hall, where her little community of nuns was seated at the feet of a statue of Gautama Buddha.

"Tell the nuns to get out of here," ordered Yama Raj, annoyed by their chanting.

The alarmed abbotess informed the women to vacate the building. A dozen trembling nuns rose from their cushions, bowed, and departed with their hands folded.

Yama Raj ordered Nima Lama, to wait outside because he wanted to question Kathy and Om privately. He bolted the door and ordered Hariyo to search Om for weapons before handcuffing him.

"What do you want with us?" screamed Kathy, backing away from them, terrified.

"You'll find out soon enough," asserted Yama Raj, thrusting a letter and a pen at her. "Now sign this."

"I'm not signing anything," she blurted, fleeing across the room toward the window.

Yama Raj charged her like a rampant bull. He seized Kathy by the arm and slapped her across the face. "You bitch. I told you to sign this letter!"

Yama Raj released his tight grip on her arm and led her to a table. Kathy was trembling with fright when she begged him to read her the message. He lit a cigarette and read it to her.

June 6, 2001
Dad, please come at once to the convent at the Tengboche Monastery. I've become ill with a high fever. The abbotess thinks I have hepatitis, but don't worry. The nuns are taking good care of me.

I'll probably be flown by helicopter to Kathmandu and taken to Shanta Bhawan Hospital as soon as you arrive. The soldiers guarding the monastery will send a helicopter from the Royal Nepalese Army to transport you from Terhathum to Tengboche. Bring Moksha with you.

I'm sorry for interrupting your research, but it's important that you come here immediately.

"You've forged this letter. It's a lie," interrupted Kathy. There's nothing wrong with me," blurted Kathy.

"You'll really be sick when we're done with you," threatened Yama Raj, crushing the cigarette with his boot.

Kathy wanted to protest, but she was terrified. She picked up the pen and signed it.

Yama Raj refused to read the second page of the letter to her. He went to the door and stepped outside where he spoke to Nima Lama. He was standing next to the nuns, who were waiting to return to the shrine room.

"Take this message to Muktuba in the greenhouse. He must e-mail it to Carl Brecht in Terhathum."

"Of course," said Nima Lama, startled. "When will you bring Kathy and Om to the greenhouse."

"I'm afraid Kathy's running a high temperature. It came on rather suddenly," said Yama Raj.

"That's odd. Kathy was perfectly healthy when she went into the shrine room," said Nima Lama.

"This new strain of hepatitis comes on quickly," insisted Yama Raj. "Don't worry. The nuns will take care of her."

"I'll take the note to Muktuba right away," said Nima Lama, hurrying up the trail toward the monastery. He paused on the way to read the letter. He was especially disturbed by the message on the second page.

Dad, the nuns decided to take me and Om to a higher altitude, where the air and water are purer. I will be staying in a

Medicine Cave, where herbs are dried before they are processed into medications. The place is also a sanctuary where injured Sherpas come for rest and recuperation.

It's easy to get to the cave. Just follow the trail north of the monastery. After passing through a Sherpa village, you take the trail to the right for about ten minutes. Maybe I'll be fully recovered by the time you get here. I'm feeling better already knowing you're on your way.

    Your loving daughter,
    Kathy Marie Brecht

After Nima Lama departed, the guards chatted in front of the convent with the abbotess and nuns listening.

"You really pulled the wool over their eyes this time, Yama Raj," laughed Hariyo.

Yama Raj turned toward the abbotess and handed her a 100 rupee note. "This is a donation for your new roof. Don't spend it all in one place."

"No, thank you," said the abbotess bowing. "We can't accept your money or participate in your deceitful scheme. You lied about Kathy being sick with hepatitis. She's perfectly well. There is no need to bring her father here by helicopter! I overheard your conversation while I was working in the garden because you left the window open in the prayer hall."

"You deceitful bitch," shouted Yama Raj, seizing the abbotess by the arm. "You will do exactly as I say or I'll kill you and your nuns."

"You may kill me, but please spare the nuns. They are innocent," insisted the abbotess.

"I'll break their legs and then bash their heads with the butt of my rifle," shouted Yama Raj, shoving a terrified nun to the ground and threatening to rape her.

"No! Please stop!" screamed the Abbotess. "Do not hurt the nuns. They've done nothing to harm you."

"If anyone asks you any questions, tell them that Kathy is recovering from hepatitis in the Medicine Cave."

"I'll do exactly as you wish," uttered the abbotess.

Upon returning to the shrine, he handcuffed Kathy, who was sitting next to Om on the floor. Yama Raj said, "It's time for us to go now."

"Where are you taking us," sobbed Kathy, trembling with fright. "These handcuffs really hurt."

"We're heading for the Medicine Cave," informed Yama Raj. "It's a forty minute walk from here."

"Please remove these handcuffs. We promise we won't give you any trouble on the trail," begged Om.

"I'll take them off later," promised Yama Raj.

As they left the shrine, the nuns and abbotess bowed to them before returning to their prayers. They promised Kathy and Om, they would recite mantras for their safety and protection.

.

80

While Muktuba read about the history of the medicinal garden and the origin of Tibetan medicine, he sat at the computer in the greenhouse near the herbal garden. It was surrounded by a stone wall to protect the plants from stray yaks and goats.

His research was interrupted by Padma, who was a botanist sent by the abbot to help him record data.

"How long have you been here at the monastery?" asked Muktuba, grateful for his arrival.

"I've been here for over twelve years," said Padma, informing him that the monastery sold their herbs to the Namche Healing Center, a clinic with a doctor and a pharmacy, patronized by the Sherpas and trekkers.

Muktuba learned from the botanist that Nepal has 7000 species of plants, but only 600 were medicinal herbs of which 150 grew in the Solu Kumbhu region.

"I wonder what's keeping Kathy and Om. They agreed to help me record the names of the herbs on the computer."

"I saw them leave the kitchen with two guards. They were going to the convent," said Padma, offering to help him with the data.

"I'm annoyed by helicopters flying over the monastery and armed guards entering the greenhouse to search for Maoists," said Muktuba.

"The soldiers are trying to find our three monks, the yogi, and Nigel Porter, who have been accused of being conspirators. I know them all personally. They wouldn't hurt anyone," said Padma.

"We were told that the monastery would be perfectly safe for us to do our research. I didn't expect constant interruptions from soldiers," said Muktuba.

"Our abbot wants us to ignore the soldiers and their false accusations," stated the monk.

"Please tell me about the origins of Tibetan medicine," requested Muktuba, ready to take notes on the computer.

Padma said, "Many centuries ago Quan Yin, the Goddess of Mercy, instructed two physicians from India to go to Tibet and teach the people about herbs.

"They were experts in Ayurvedic Medicine, who taught the Sherpas about medicinal herbs. The physicians are now 2000 years old and live at a hermitage in the Sandalwood Forest in India. They are called Masters."

"It's seems like a myth rather than reality," said Muktuba. "How about the theory of the three humors that cause illness? We learned about them at our shaman convention."

"The humors are wind, bile, and phlegm. They must be in balance to avoid illness. Our main concern at this high altitude is phlegm, which is the source of lung and respiratory diseases," stated the monk.

He informed Muktuba that each year 35,000 trekkers visit Tengboche and many of them need to be treated for pneumonia, bronchitis, or the common cold. Their conversation was interrupted by the arrival of a monk.

"The abbot requests you to help a sick village woman. She's waiting outside the greenhouse. Sorry to disturb your work, but our clinic is overloaded with patients."

Muktuba left the greenhouse with Padma. He removed his stethoscope from his backpack and asked the woman if he could listen to her breathing. The frightened woman agreed to allow him to examine her.

"She's suffering from congestion," said Muktuba, setting down the stethoscope. He removed a tongue depressor from his medical kit and examed her throat.

The elderly woman said, "I've had a sore throat for three days. I'm unable to sleep from coughing."

"It might be strep throat, which could turn into scarlet fever," said Muktuba. "It doesn't look like tonsillitis. I recommend 500 milligrams of amoxicillin for ten days. I have them here in my kit."

"We have herbs raised in our garden. Their roots heal respiratory illness. We should give this woman rhodiola and sedum erythrosticum. The two herbs are mixed with licorice to treat lung infections. We have the liquid medicine in our dispensary at the clinic," said Padma.

"Then give the woman the herbal medicine. If she's not better in five days, she should come back and get the amoxicillin," agreed Muktuba, returning to his work. While he was typing, Nima Lama entered the greenhouse.

" I have an urgent message from Yama Raj," he said.

Muktuba read the letter from Kathy. He was shocked that she had come down with hepatitis and was being transferred to the Medicine Cave. He typed the letter and e-mailed Carl and Moksha in Terhathum informing them that a helicopter was on the way to transport them to Tengboche.

81

Carl and Moksha arrived at the airport in the Terhathum region around noon. Upon leaving the plane, they stopped for lunch at a nearby restaurant. A half hour later they located the winding trail in the valley near the Tambar River.

As they began their ascent of the mountain, they paused to listen to the stream thundering against the boulders.

"Moksha, tell me more about the Limbu culture since I've never been to eastern Nepal," requested Carl.

"We have about 250,000 Limbus in this region," he said "I'll tell you a myth about how we came into existence.

"The Creator of the Universe, *Tagera Hingwaphuma*, made the sun, wind, earth, and water. He also created plants and animals, including good and evil spirits before resting. He inspired the Grandmother Spirit to come to Tibet centuries before Buddhism arrived. She was nonviolent, preferring offerings of fruits and flowers and not animal sacrifices.

"Hindu priests from Bengal eventually arrived here and taught us to worship Shiva, *Mahesvara*, who was also nonviolent. Later on the priests introduced the Mother Goddess, who preferred animal sacrifices," said Moksha, interrupted by a herder coming on the trail with his yaks.

The yak herder's voice was strident and tense. "Have you heard the news about a yeti attacking animals in Solo Khumbu? I'm worried that a yeti might attack my herd."

"No, we haven't heard any news about a Yeti," said Carl. "We just arrived about an hour ago at the airport."

"My neighbor is a retired Gurkha soldier, who has a transistor radio from Hong Kong. This morning we heard on the news that a yeti killed yaks at a Sherpa settlement in Tengboche."

"Oh no," said Carl, worried about Kathy's safety. "My daughter's staying at the monastery there."

The terrified yak herder was paranoid when he heard a rustling in the bushes. Moksha intervened and tried to calm him down. "You must pray to Vishnu for protection."

The herder said, "Yama Raj, a security guard, stationed at the Tengboche Monastery spoke on the radio. He insisted that it wasn't a yeti killing the yaks, but an insane monk, named Nigel Porter."

He also told them that Nigel had been seen by Sherpa villagers carrying a machete and wandering in the mountains, covered with blood.

The terrified herder refused to stay any longer. He departed swiftly with his yaks down the trail.

After he departed, Moksha said, "Whenever there is political unrest, evil spirits are present. They seek out people, who are using drugs and alcohol. Many of them are addicts, prone to demonic possession."

"Dipendra drank heavily and used drugs," said Carl.

"I don't believe the prince assassinated his family. His addictions weakened him so that he was victimized by by evil spirits influencing the security guards from the royal palace." claimed Moksha. "I'm fearful our monarchy is on the verge of collapse."

82

After hiking in the mist, Carl and Moksha put on their raincoats and continued climbing the slippery trail, hoping to find a hamlet around the bend. They were disappointed because there was no shelter in sight. The storm became fierce with gusts of wind and torrential rain.

An hour later they came to a settlement on the side of the mountain, where herds of yaks and goats were kept in pens. Upon arriving at the stone house, the owner was standing on the veranda with his Tibetan mastiff, barking and snarling.

"It's a relief to see you, Okwanama. May we take shelter on your porch?" requested Moksha.

"Of course," he shouted, silencing the ferocious dog by chaining him. "No doubt, you have been sent to us by the Grandmother Spirit."

Upon ascending the steps to the porch, Moksha and Carl exchanged greetings and removed their rain coats and backpacks.

"Who is your friend?" asked Okwanama, noticing that the rain had subsided before taking them into the house.

Moksha introduced Carl Brecht, telling the host about the shaman convention in Kathmandu where he and his son received paramedic training.

"Maybe you can help my wife," requested Okwanama entering the living room and introducing them to his teenage son, tending the fire, and his nine-year-old daughter, weaving a rug beneath the window.

"My wife fell down and injured her leg two nights ago. "Hey! *Manju, utta ujallo bhayo, gham udana lagyo.* Manju, get up, there is light; the sun is shining."

Carl glanced through the window, noticing that the rain had stopped. A feeble sun was peering from behind the dark clouds.

Manju was lying on a blanket in front of the fire and moaning from pain. She opened her eyes and turned her head toward the strangers, greeting them with a *Namaste.*

Her husband removed the blanket from her and showed them his wife's swollen leg. Carl examined her leg while Moksha hurried back to the porch, returning with the medical kit from his backpack.

After taking Manju's blood pressure, Moksha advised her to stop eating *sampa*, due to the salt and to drink black tea with goat's milk.

Moksha listened with the stethoscope to the woman's breathing and heart rate, concluding she had congestion from bronchitis. He requested the son to bring him hot water from the kettle in the fireplace to wash his hands.

"Manju, tell us how you injured your leg?" asked Carl, recording her testimony in a notebook.

"A few days ago I was carrying grass on my back to feed the yaks and goats. The bundle was large and the grass hung over my eyes so that I had difficulty seeing the trail. I lost my balance and fell down. Since I couldn't get up because of the pain, I just lay there and wept," uttered Manju. "My husband came searching for me and carried me back to the house."

"Did you fall on a sharp stone or a protruding rock?" asked Moksha, pressing his hand on the swollen bone.

Manju moaned and winched from the pain. "No, I fell on the gravel in a puddle of water."

"You probably have a simple fracture from the fall. I don't feel any bone protruding. Of course, I don't know for sure unless we take you to a clinic for an x-ray. We will have to carry you down the mountain to the clinic near the airport," continued Moksha.

"No, I will stay here and die," gasped the desperate woman, her eyes clouded with tears.

"Manju you're not going to die. I will give you an injection for pain, and pills to prevent infection for the next ten days. My friend Carl Brecht and I will make a plaster cast for your leg."

Carl found some bamboo in the back yard and sawed a section of it in half. He fitted the bamboo halves on the woman's leg, binding them with gauze. Moksha mixed a small bag of plaster with water and sealed the cast, informing the woman to wear it for six weeks.

They sawed a branch, made crutches and taught her to use them by hobbling around the room.

"Manju, you are only to do household chores. No more climbing the mountains to cut grass for the animals. Your son and daughter will take over your chores," said Carl.

Moksha informed her that she was not to put pressure on the injured leg at all. He insisted that after the cast was removed, the skin should be bathed with soap.

"The Forest Spirits caused me to fall down and break my leg," said Manju, sleepy from the injection and the weight of the cast. "I don't know why they attacked me?"

"Do you know of anyone who died on this mountain recently?" asked Moksha.

"Yes, my uncle. He fell from the mountain two years ago," she said. "He lived about a mile from here."

"Maybe his *sogha*, a demon ridden ghost, attacked you," suggested Moksha.

Manju claimed that her uncle was an evil man. He never married, but lived with her parents when she was a child. Her uncle was drunk all the time and chased her and her younger brother when they were home alone. This happened once a month while their parents took the yaks and goats to market.

"We were terrified of him and climbed up the ladder into the attic of our house. When he came after us, we pushed the ladder down, causing him to fall. When my parents came home, they found him naked and drunk on the floor. They finally told him to leave our house and never come back."

"Do you have anything that belongs to your uncle?" asked Moksha.

"We still have his woolen hat hanging on a hook behind the door," said Manju, her eyes tearful.

"Give me the hat," insisted the shaman. "Your drunken uncle's souls are not able to rest. They are possessed by demons. What else do you have that belongs to him?"

"My uncle was expelled from the Gurkha army because of drunkenness and then came to live with us. We still have his army uniform and his boots in that trunk in the corner. There's also a picture of him in the wooden chest."

Moksha made an effigy of the uncle by stuffing straw into his army uniform. He removed his picture from the frame and wrapped it around the head adding the wool cap. After he punctured holes into the effigy, he place wax in the apertures.

When the effigy was finished, he performed a cleansing ritual in the living room, followed by exorcisms to liberate the uncle's souls from demons. The effigy was cremated in the fireplace because the ground was too wet for a burial.

Manju sobbed during the exorcisms, releasing her pent up rage. When the ceremony was finished, she confessed to Moksha that her uncle had sexually abused her and her brother several times prior to their parents sending him away from their home.

Moksha told her that she was finally free from the influence of the uncle's ghost and evil spirits. Her uncle had no more power to hurt her.

"Whenever you think of your uncle, Manju, you must recite the mantra, *Om Mane Padme Hum*. Then pray to the Grandmother Spirit for protection," said Moksha.

Manju thanked them for mending her leg and liberating her soul from the evil spirits that were trying to destroy her.

The next morning Carl and Moksha left at dawn. They hiked for nearly three hours on the muddy trail before reaching Moksha's farm, where his wife served them a lunch of rice with a vegetable curry.

Moksha didn't have electricity on his farm, but his neighbor had a generator run by a gas engine. It was brought by his son when he came home on leave from the Gurkha Army.

In the evening Moksha took Carl to his neighbor's farm, where he e-mailed Barbara and then opened his e-mails. Carl was alarmed when he read that Kathy had hepatitis and had been transferred to a Medicine Cave.

He wondered if the army helicopter would be able to find Moksha's remote farm. After the neighbor gave him the exact location, Carl sent the directions to Muktuba at Tengboche.

The next morning Carl and Moksha were having breakfast when they heard the droning of a helicopter. It landed in the pasture some distance from Moksha's farm. A few minutes later they saw two guards wearing military uniforms coming toward them.

83

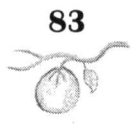

After reading the note about Kathy's illness, Muktuba consulted with the abbot about sending Nima Lama to the Medicine Cave to bring Kathy and Om to the clinic at the monastery.

Nima Lama departed with the message even though it was raining and getting dark. Upon reaching the Sherpa village, the rain had subsided. He was surprised to see a campfire blazing with several people warming themselves.

"Hello! Hello!" he shouted gasping for breath from trekking. "I have a message from the abbot."

Yama Raj removed a pistol from his holster and approached Nima Lama, ordering him to hand over the message and come with him.

Upon reaching the fire, he was surprised to see Kathy and Om handcuffed, hovering over the fire.

"I thought you'd be at the Medicine Cave by now," he said "What's going on here?"

"We're being held hostage," blurted Kathy, trembling from fright.

"The abbot sent me to bring you back to the monastery to recover from your illness," said Nima Lama.

"She's not sick," insisted Om, standing next to Kathy. "We're being held hostage."

Yama Raj crumpled the note and threw it into the fire. He shouted, "Hariyo, handcuff this monk. He's coming with us to the Medicine Cave."

"That won't be necessary," insisted Nima Lama. "I give you my word. I won't try to escape."

"We've got a surprise for you," said Hariyo, pointing into the darkness.

"There's a dead monk behind those rocks," asserted Kathy, her voice quivering. "He was murdered by a Yeti."

"I'm sure you know him. He's a monk from your monastery," informed Hariyo, turning on a flash light and taking Nima Lama to see the corpse behind the boulders.

"It's Vairocana! He's been murdered! His throat's torn and he's been ripped open!" shouted Nima Lama, shocked.

"It wasn't a Yeti who mutilated his body and sucked his blood. It was Nigel Porter. He's gone mad!" informed Yama Raj, hurrying toward them.

"Vairocana was a friend of mine. He was a very spiritual man," sobbed Nima Lama. "I sat next to him every morning during prayer and meditation. I don't believe Nigel would do such a thing. He was always kind to everyone at our monastery."

"Hariyo, you must talk to the Sherpas. Give them some rupees to carry the corpses back to the monastery for burial along with Nigel's other victims," ordered Yama Raj.

"What other victims?" asked Kathy, her mouth gaping.

"They're over here," announced Yama Raj, leading the way with a flashlight. Everyone followed him into a wooded area about twenty feet away.

Yama Raj beamed the flashlight on the vultures flapping their wings and the crows taking flight into the darkness. Everyone gasped upon seeing the mutilated corpses that were still recognizable.

"It's Ratna and Dorjee! They were such good monks," sobbed Nima Lama, grieving over the loss of his friends.

"I can't look," screamed Kathy, clinging to Om for support. "I've never seen anything so horrible!"

All heads turned to Hariyo arriving with several villagers from the settlement. The Sherpas immediately wrapped the corpses of the three dead monks in canvases and slung them over their shoulders. Within moments they departed barefoot down the slippery trail, carrying the bodies to the monastery.

"Why are you taking us hostage?" screamed Kathy, unable to control her pent up rage over the deaths.

"Those monks were conspirators working with Nigel Porter to assassinate the royal family. They had escaped from jail in Kathmandu. Twenty-four years ago Nigel murdered his brother, Christopher. This time he killed the abbot at Bodhnath and these three monks in cold blood," informed Yama Raj, lighting a cigarette. "Nigel's a psychopathic murderer."

"Don't forget Yogi Parahamsa Dev was also involved with them," added Hariyo."We haven't found his corpse. It might be near the Medicine Cave."

"These handcuffs are hurting my wrist," blurted Kathy, her voice quivering. "Please remove them."

"Her wrists are black and blue," complained Om.

"Yama Raj wants to use you and Om for bait to lure Nigel to the cave," informed Hariyo.

"Hariyo's telling the truth for a change. I'm trying to get him to come back to the scene of the crimes. Let's get going. The cave is only a ten minute walk from here."

"Thanks a lot for using us for bait," cried Kathy, fearful that Nigel might be lingering in the shadows.

After ascending the slippery trail for about ten minutes, Yama Raj advised everyone to be alert, especially if they heard any noise coming from the bushes on the trail.

"We believe Nigel will try to rip us apart like he did those monks," said Hariyo.

"For once you're talking like a logical human being, Hariyo," said Yama Raj.

As they approached the Medicine Cave, they heard footsteps coming from the trail above them. Everyone froze expecting Nigel to appear with a machete to attack them. They were surprised to see a herder, his son, and several yaks and dzoms.

The yak herder was trembling with fright. He informed them that earlier in the day, he sent his son to get permission from the the headman of the Sherpa settlement to stay there over night with their animals.

His son returned in a state of shock after seeing a crazy white man attack three monks and mutilate their corpses, hiding them behind the rocks on the trail.

"Oh no," gasped Kathy, feeling sick to her stomach.

"That crazy monk is Nigel Porter, and he's wanted for murder," said Yama Raj. "If you see him again, come and tell us, and I'll give you ten rupees. We'll be staying here in the Medicine Cave with our friends."

"Of course," uttered the nervous yak herder, bowing and disappearing into the darkness with his traumatized son and their yaks.

"Here's the cave. Let's go inside," said Hariyo. "It looks like it will rain again any minute. He paused to listen to a clap of thunder followed by a lightning bolt.

Prior to entering the cave, Yama Raj removed the handcuffs from Kathy and Om. They thanked him as they walked cautiously through the cavernous entrance.

Hariyo turned on his flashlight to illuminate the walls, where stalactites hung from the roof like mastodon tusks, and stalagmites soared from the ground. As they continued they heard the squealing and fluttering of hundreds bats, clinging to the ceiling of the cave.

Eventually they reached a clearing, where the medicinal herbs were drying on frames, suspended from ropes, or like fish caught in enormous nets. A sleepy servant approached them with a lantern, leading them toward the dark ceremonial chamber, where the statue of Buddha was surrounded by flickering butter lamps.

The servant stepped aside and turned on a generator. Instantly, the cave was illuminated by electric lights and space heaters emitting waves of heat.

"This is how we dry the herbs. I'm sure you must be tired and hungry after your trek up the mountain. I'll bring you tea with rice and lentils, *dal/bhat,*" said the servant.

After they ate, Nima Lama said, "I should return to the monastery now and tell Muktuba and the abbot that you're safe here. I don't want them to be alarmed. He was very worried when he sent the message to your father in Terhathum, Kathy."

Yama Raj said, "I arranged for a helicopter to transport Carl Brecht and Moksha from Terhathum to the Tengboche Monastery. You must bring them back here to comfort Kathy and Om."

Nima Yama said, "The abbot will contact the police in Kathmandu about the brutal slaying of the three monks. I'm sure the police will come with reporters from Kathmandu to take photographs and investigate the murders. I'll inform the abbot that everyone's safe here. Of course I will bring Carl and Moksha back to the cave."

"Tell my father not to worry," said Kathy.

After Nima Lama departed, Yama Raj ordered Hariyo to keep watch at the entrance of the cave with his rifle loaded in case Nigel made an appearance..

"You and Om are free to wander around the ceremonial cave," smiled Yama Raj, finishing his rice and lentils.

"We have a small library here," said the servant. "I'll take your guests to see some of our traditional texts."

Kathy and Om followed the servant to the library separated from the ceremonial hall by a curtain. He left them to examine the books on the shelves.

After leafing through the Sanskrit, Pali, and Tibetan texts, Kathy whispered, "There's something fishy going on here. I'm terrified! I don't trust Yama Raj."

"I'm worried about him using us as bait to attract Nigel," said Om, taking Kathy's hand and kissing her tenderly on the lips.

Kathy clung to him, holding him tightly until she stopped trembling.

Om kissed her again passionately and led her behind the book case. He removed his shirt and let it fall to the ground, revealing his bare chest. Kathy pressed her head against his chest, listening to his heart beating.

"I love you, Kathy,' he whispered, guiding her to the floor. When he kissed her again passionately, she broke away from him to catch her breath.

"Om, I love you too," said Kathy, suddenly aware of footsteps on the other side of the curtain.

"I shouldn't have opened that plastic bag in the boat," whispered Kathy. "I must have released evil spirits."

"It wasn't your fault. You didn't mean to hurt anyone," said Om, groping for his shirt.

"Sometime we hurt other people because of our carelessness," insisted Kathy, rising from the floor.

Suddenly a hand pulled back the curtain linking the library to the ceremonial hall. It was Yama Raj. He was standing there with a yogi, who was naked except for a loin cloth, holding a trident of Shiva.

"What are you two whispering about? Come out from there this minute," ordered Yama Raj, observing Om buttoning his shirt.

"Now tell these lovers what you just told me," said Yama Raj to the naked yogi, wearing only a flimsy loin cloth. His face was hidden by long strands of hair and his entire body was covered with ashes.

The yogi spoke to them in Nepali, which Om translated for Kathy. "I was in the woods meditating behind the Medicine Cave when I saw a white man murder three monks and then chop them up with his machete."

"Oh my God!" gasped Kathy. "That was Nigel!"

"Is this the man you saw killing the monks?" asked Yama Raj, removing a newspaper clipping of Nigel from his pocket.

"That's him! I saw him murder the monks," said the yogi. "I can show you where he hid the corpses."

"That won't be necessary," said Yama Raj. "You may go back to prayer hall now and continue your journey to the monastery. But first get something to eat from the servant in the prayer hall."

"Come this way," said Yama Raj, ordering Kathy and Om to follow him. "I don't want you having sex behind my back. Next time we'll invite Hariyo to participate in the act with you. We don't want him to be left out just because he's mentally handicapped."

"That's disgusting," said Kathy, feeling uneasy about Yama Raja's comment. She noticed that the yogi forgot to take his trident with him, leaving it propped up against the feet of the Buddha.

84

Yama Raj's plan unfolded flawlessly. On Thursday morning the helicopter circled the Tengboche Monastery, searching for a place to land. The pilot finally descended in a field near the convent. Carl and Moksha disembarked, wearing their back packs. Coming down the trail toward them were Nima Lama and the abbot.

"We are so pleased to meet you," said Carl, bowing to both of them. "How's Kathy?"

"I want to reassure you, Dr. Brecht, that your daughter, Kathy, doesn't have hepatitis. I got back from the Medicine Cave late last night," said Nima Lama.

"I requested Yama Raj to bring Kathy and Om back to our clinic, but he ignored my message," said the abbot.

"Not Yama Raj! He was the security guard from the palace who arrested Nigel after the assassination of the royal family! We met him at the airport in Kathmandu with his partner Hariyo," shouted Carl, his brow wrinkled.

"Kathy was perfectly fine when I left the cave," reassured Nima Lama. "Om's all right too."

"What the hell's going on here?" asked Carl.

"I'm confused," said the abbot. "I don't think Yama Raj is honest. He accused me of harboring wounded Maoists, insinuated that our monks are conspiring to destroy the Shah dynasty."

"Why are helicopters flying around the mountains above the monastery?" asked Carl.

"They're searching for Nigel Porter," said Nima Lama.

"Last night around midnight Sherpas were pounding on the door of the monastery. I woke up from a sound sleep to admit them. I was shocked when they showed me the mutilated corpses of our monks, Vairocana, Ratna, and Dorjee," informed the abbot.

"They are the monks, who escaped with Nigel and the yogi from the jail in Kathmandu," said Carl, alarmed.

"Nigel killed them," blurted Nima Lama. "He shot them in the back, mutilated the corpses, and hid their corpses behind rocks on the trail near the Medicine Cave."

"How do you know that Nigel is the killer?" asked Carl, worried about Kathy's safety.

"A yak herder's son saw him shoot and hack the corpses with a machete. I met him yesterday," said Nima Lama.

"Why are Kathy and Om in that cave?" said Carl, removing her letter from his pocket and reading it to them.

"I got this e-mail last night to come to the Medicine Cave. Now what the hell's going on here!"

"Yama Raj brought Kathy and Om to that cave as decoys. He wants to lure Nigel to come out from hiding so he can capture him," informed Nima Lama, his voice quivering with fright.

"Decoys? You mean he's risking my daughter's life so that he can capture Nigel for the reward money," asked Carl, pacing nervously.

"Yama Raj cannot be trusted. Please excuse me," said the abbot. "I must arrange for the funeral of the monks. They are wrapped in canvases in the prayer hall. Then I will speak to the reporters and the police, who just arrived by helicopter from Kathmandu. They want to interview me about the murders. Several of them have already left for the Sherpa settlement."

"Nima Lama, please take us to the Medicine Cave immediately," insisted Carl, raising his voice.

"Where's my son, Muktuba? He should be coming with us," insisted Moksha. "I hope my grandson is safe."

"The abbot asked Muktuba to give first aid to the villagers injured by landslides," stated Nima Lama.

"He can join us later," said Carl, following him down the trail toward the convent.

The abbotess informed Carl and Moksha that Yama Raj had handcuffed Kathy and Om and led them from the convent at gun point. Prior to leaving Yama Raj had threatened to kill her entire community if she didn't cooperate with him.

"Yama Raj removed their handcuffs before I left the cave last night. He seemed more relaxed once a yogi arrived who had witnessed Nigel murdering the three monks," added Nima Lama.

"I wonder if that was Yogi Parahamsa Dev? Let's not waste any more time," insisted Carl. "We must leave now."

Nima Lama led the way up the mountain. They hiked until they came to the Sherpa settlement, where reporters from Kathmandu were questioning the villagers about the death of the monks.

The yak herder was also there with his son being photographed. When they saw Carl and Moksha, the reporters snapped pictures of them and requested statements. However, they refused to be interviewed.

After leaving the village they paused to rest on the trail, where the monks had been murdered. They were surprised when armed guards stepped out from behind the rocks, carrying rifles.

"*Ke chaiyo*. What do you want?" asked Moksha, who refused to be intimidated by them.

"We are Maoists," said the older soldier, wearing a faded army uniform. "Give us each a thousand rupees, and you may continue your journey."

"Bhishma, I recognize you," said Nima Lama. "You're the wounded Maoist who came to our monastery two years ago. You were shot in the chest. I remember changing your bandages several times at the clinic."

"You have a good memory," said Bhishma. "Your abbot contacted a doctor in Namche Bazaar, who walked for four hours to Tengboche to remove the bullets from my chest."

"That incident got a lot of publicity in the newspapers," said Carl. "I read about it in the Chicago Tribune."

"It's unfortunate that our monastery got the reputation of being a refuge for terrorists because we helped to save the life of a Maoist." uttered Nima Lama.

"We should let these people continue their trek without demanding money from them," stated the other soldier.

"You're right, Bharat. I wouldn't be alive if it wasn't for your monks tending my wounds," said Bhishma.

"Do you happen to know Nigel Porter?" asked Carl, concerned about his destructive behavior.

"Of course," said Bhishma, his eyes moist with tears. "He stayed with me all night chanting mantras when I was wounded. He brought my fever down with cold wash cloths placed on my forehead. Nigel was the kindest monk in the whole monastery."

"We heard gun shots yesterday and later found out from a yak herder that Nigel had shot and disemboweled three monks. It happened right over there on the trail behind the boulders," added Bharat.

"Nigel's been accused of plotting with Maoists to destroy the Shah Dynasty," stated Carl.

"We heard about those rumors," said Bhishma. "Even though we are opposed to the monarchy, we weren't involved with the conspiracy to massacre the royal family."

"King Birendra always cooperated with our leader, attempting to negotiate with us so that we could have representation in the Parliament. Prince Dipendra was present during those meetings," added Bharat.

"We're concerned that King Gyanendra is not willing to negotiate with us, which can only mean more bloodshed and violence," said Bhishma.

"But you have been systematically slaughtering the police and taking over their stations," said Carl.

"The police stations are symbols of the status quo and our corrupt government. We belong to the Communist Party of Nepal-Maoist, but we are not influenced by the communists of India or China. We don't intend to injure the civilians," said Bhishma.

"I joined the Maoists because there was nothing but poverty in my village. The government promised to bring us relief by building a road, installing electricity, opening a school and constructing a medical clinic.

"The money for these projects was given to the Panchayat, our local government, but the corrupt officials fled with the funds," said Bharat.

"Our goal is not to kill innocent people like the Chinese Communists did in Tibet. When the soldiers arrived in Lhasa they massacred 10,000 Tibetans in a single day, even those who took refuge in the Jokhang Monastery," informed Bhisma.

"We don't want to destroy the monasteries or temples of Nepal. We want representation in the Parliament. We were beginning to achieve our goal under King Birendra. It's unfortunate he died so violently.

"Now that King Gyanendra is in power, we will have to redefine our goals," added Bharat. "He will try to destroy us with the support of the Nepalese Congress Party and his allies from India and the United States."

"In the future we will have seats in the Parliament, and our leader Prachanda will become the Prime Minister of Nepal. We will be victorious!" predicted Bhishma.

"Yama Raj, a security guard from the royal palace is occupying the Medicine Cave. He believes that Nigel is working with you Maoists to destroy the monarchy," said Nima Lama.

"We'd like to meet Yama Raj and explain to him we are not conspiring with anyone to undermine the monarchy. The corrupt government will fall without our direct interference," asserted Bhisma.

"Then come with us to the Medicine Cave and tell Yama Raj the truth about the Maoists," requested Carl.

"Follow me," said Nima Lama. "I'll take you to the cave. It's not very far from here."

"We saw two soldiers taking prisoners to the cave yesterday," said Bhisma.

Carl explained to them that the prisoners were his daughter, Kathy, and Moksha's grandson, Om.

.

85

When Hariyo heard voices coming from the trail, he immediately left the entrance with his rifle and hid behind a boulder on the opposite side of the cave.

Carl was apprehensive about going into the cave with a flashlight, but he led the way with the others following.

As they continued down the narrow trail, Moksha uttered, "It's very dark in here. I feel like we're going into the mouth of a giant crocodile."

There was a stirring from the roof of the cave, which startled them. When Carl raised the flashlight and illuminated the ceiling, he saw hundreds of bats, flapping their wings and squealing.

Continuing down the narrow path, Carl shouted, "Is anyone there? Kathy, this is your father! Are you all right?"

They passed through the section of the cave where the herbs were drying. Upon entering the ceremonial hall they found Kathy and Om gagged and handcuffed, sitting in front of the Buddha.

"What the hell's going on?" shouted Carl, rushing toward his daughter and removing the gag from her mouth.

"Dad," she sobbed. "Thank God, you're here!"

Moksha removed the cloth from Om's mouth and asked. "*Ke gareko?* What happened?"

The Maoists shaded their eyes, momentarily blinded when the electric lights were turned on. Yama Raj stepped from behind the statue of Buddha with his rifle. "I'm pleased you could join us Dr. Brecht. I sent the helicopter to bring you and Moksha here from Terhathum to comfort your daughter and her boyfriend. I'm sure Nima Lama told you about the murder of the monks."

"The abbot showed us their corpses," said Carl.

"Nigel Porter is responsible for the brutal slaying of his friends," stated Yama Raj, raising his rifle. "I'm expecting him to come to the cave to try to kill Kathy and Om. That's why I cuffed and gagged them."

"My wrists hurt from these handcuffs," sobbed Kathy. "I was scared to death when I heard your voice, Dad. I thought Nigel was right behind you with a machete."

"Who are your companions wearing military uniforms?" asked Yama Raj. "They're obviously not from the Royal Nepalese Army."

"They are Maoist guards. We met them on the trail. They didn't extort any money from us because the older fellow, Bhishma, was once wounded and nurtured back to health by the monks from Tengboche," said Carl.

"Oh, you're the Maoist that got all that publicity a couple of years ago," said Yama Raj. "I saw your picture in the newspaper. The Tengboche Monastery has been a sanctuary for wounded Maoists for several years now."

"We've come to explain that the abbot did not give asylum to wounded Maoists after I recovered. He sent our injured soldiers with the help of his monks to Namche Bazaar to be treated by the doctors there," said Bhishma.

"We want to inform you that we never conspired to overthrow the Shah Dynasty with Nigel Porter and the three dead monks," added Bharat.

As the two Maoists came toward him to shake hands with Yama Raj, he backed away from them, shouting, "You are liars! Don't come near me! Take off your back packs and drop them to the floor along with your weapons!"

"The Maoists didn't come here to harm you. They only wanted to explain to you they had nothing to do with Nigel and the conspirators," reassured Carl.

"We aren't here to cause you any trouble," said Bharat, reaching for his cigarettes to offer Yama Raj the pack.

"What the fuck are you doing?" asked Yama Raj, his eyes wide with terror. He raised his rifle and fired numerous times at them.

Everyone gasped with horror as the Maoists collapsed onto the floor with blood gushing from their wounds.

"Maoist terrorists will never rule this country!" shouted Yama Raj, hovering over them. "Look, this Maoist was about to shoot me with his pistol. That fuckin' hypocrite intended to kill me!

"I'm telling you, Maoists are poisonous snakes. They can't be trusted. Nigel's behind this. He's been working with them. What's that noise coming from the next room?" he asked, pausing.

Yama Raj set down the rifle and removed a pistol from his belt as a soldier entered the room, carrying a corpse.

It was Hariyo carrying the corpse of a naked yogi, wearing only a loincloth. His arms and legs were dangling almost to the floor.

"I found this yogi a few feet from the entrance of the cave," he said, dropping the mutilated corpse onto the floor next to the dead Maoists.

"Oh my God," gasped Kathy. "That yogi was here for a visit yesterday. His neck has been gouged and his stomach ripped open."

"Nigel's responsible for another murder! He's a raving maniac. We must get help from the army and hunt him down the first thing in the morning," said Yama Raj.

"You just murdered those Maoists in cold blood," said Kathy, sobbing hysterically.

"Don't be a fool," said Yama Raj. "I showed you his pistol. He was going to kill me. I shot them in self defense. The Maoists have been murdering our police and getting away with it. They've been extorting money from villagers and conscripting our children into their army."

Carl approached his terrified daughter and gave her a hug. He whispered, "Kathy, please be quiet. I'm fearful that if you antagonize Yama Raj. He'll shoot us."

"But Dad, he murdered the Maoists in cold blood," sobbed Kathy. "I feel sick to my stomach."

"Do you know this yogi?" asked Yama Raj.

"It's Parahamsa Dev," said Moksha, shaking his head. "He brought Nigel to me twenty-four years ago."

"Nigel escaped from the jail with him and the monks. Now he's killed all four of them," said Hariyo.

"Don't pay any attention to Hariyo. He's brain damaged," said Yama Raj. "Hariyo, you must keep an eye on Kathy while we drag the corpses out of the cave. I need the help of all the men. We'll just throw the bodies over the cliff across from the entrance."

"Please remove these handcuffs," pleaded Om, rising from the cushion next to Kathy. "I can't carry the corpses wearing handcuffs."

"Of course," said Yama Raj, reaching for his key and removing them from both Om and Kathy.

A few minutes later the men were dragging the corpses out of the ceremonial room. As soon as they departed the servant entered with cups of tea for Kathy and Hariyo, who were sitting at the feet of the Buddha.

While everyone was gone, Hariyo informed Kathy that he didn't want to work for Yama Raj any longer. He hated being constantly beaten by his boss and insulted. Since she listened to him so attentively, he stretched out his rough hands to caress her long black hair.

"I won't hurt you," said Hariyo, running his fingers through her hair again. "It's soft and pretty."

"I'm glad you like it, but you're making me feel very uncomfortable," said Kathy. "If my boyfriend finds out you were touching me, he'd get very angry."

"Oh...I don't want to cause any trouble for you. I went out with a girl a long time ago. We went to a movie theater in Calcutta. It was dark inside there," he uttered breathing heavily. "The girl was a prostitute that I picked up."

"I'd like to go for a walk now," insisted Kathy getting up quickly from the cushion in front of the statue.

"But you haven't finished your tea," said Hairiyo. "We could go to the library and close the curtain to look at some books," he said, touching her hair once more. "Yama Raj told me he saw you in the library with Om. He said your boyfriend had taken off his shirt to make love to you.

"I'll take off my shirt for you if you like and show you my chest," he said, opening the buttons on his uniform and unzipping his fly.

"Please don't do that," she blurted.

Kathy was terrified and backed away from him several times as they walked around the statue of the Buddha. Hariyo kept telling her that she was beautiful and that he hadn't been with a woman for two years now. Kathy repeated that her boyfriend would be angry if he found out he was flirting with her.

Upon hearing footsteps coming from the cave, Hariyo stopped making advances toward Kathy. He quickly buttoned up his shirt and zipped up his fly. She sighed with relief when the men returned with their hands and clothing, bloody from carrying the corpses.

"Where can we get cleaned up?" asked Carl, starring at the blood on his hands. "It's too bad those men weren't given a proper burial."

"My grandfather prayed over their corpses before we threw them over the cliff," said Om, surprised when Kathy rushed toward him, grabbing him by the arm.

"Hariyo, show them where the bathroom's located. We've got buckets of water and soap there for them to get cleaned up," shouted Yama Raj. "Where's that stupid servant from the monastery? He needs to get more water."

"I would like to wash my face and hands too," said Kathy, her stomach feeling queasy.

After they washed themselves, everyone returned to the ceremonial room, where they were seated. Yama Raj ordered the servant to bring them rice and lentils before leaving to get water from the nearby stream.

No one spoke during the meal. They were worried about Yama Raj, who was pacing in front of the Buddha.

"Hariyo, I want you to go back and guard the entrance of the cave," insisted Yama Raj. "You've been lingering in here long enough."

"But I haven't finished eating," uttered his partner. "I just sat down."

"Get the fuck up and go to the entrance," shouted Yama Raj, stepping on his plate of rice and lentils.

Hariyo leapt up from the floor where he was sitting and seized his rifle before departing from the hall.

About twenty minutes later, Yama Raj paused to listen. "Shhh…Shhh…I hear footsteps coming from the entrance of the cave."

"It sounds like more than one person," said Carl.

"Shut up you fool," shouted Yama Raj, striking Carl on the face with the back of his hand.

"Why did you do that to my father?" screamed Kathy, rising from the floor. "You're crazy!"

Om rose and charged Yama Raj with his clenched fists. However, the angry guard struck him on the head with his rifle causing him to fall to his knees.

Kathy screamed hysterically at the sight of Om collapsing on the floor and bleeding.

Moksha rushed toward him, removing his shirt to use as a bandage on his wounded grandson.

"Don't move a muscle or I'll shoot," said Yama Raj pointing the rifle at Kathy.

He threw her a pairs of handcuffs, ordering her to put them on Om, her father, and Moksha.

"Kathy, you're coming with me to investigate the noise at the entrance of the cave," said Yama Raj, unaware that she fastened the cuffs on their hands stretched out in front of them, rather than behind their backs.

As he was speaking, the servant arrived carrying a pole across his shoulders, balancing wooden buckets of water.

"What's going on at the entrance of the cave?" asked Yama Raj, pausing to listen to the thunder.

The servant told them that a herder wanted to bring his yaks into the cave for shelter from the storm, but Hariyo wouldn't allow it. After quarreling, the herder departed for the Sherpa settlement while Hariyo went to investigate the noise in the bushes.

"What are you so scared about?" asked Yama Raj. "You're as pale as a ghost."

The servant said, "When I arrived at the entrance of the cave, I saw an insane monk with a machete come out from behind the bushes. I ran into the cave to escape from him because he wanted to kill me!"

"That insane monk was Nigel! Come along, Kathy," ordered Yama Raj. "You're coming with me to meet him."

Turning toward the servant who was about to leave for the kitchen. He said, "Here take my pistol and guard the prisoners. Don't let them get away."

"Oh no," gasped Kathy, trembling.

"I hear more footsteps coming from the entrance of the cave," said Yama Raj. "Kathy, you walk ahead of me. Don't worry if Nigel tries to attack you, I'll be right behind you to shoot him before he can hurt you."

"Thanks a lot," cried Kathy, her voice quivering.

They passed through the herbal room, following the path to the entrance. Yama Raj slung his rifle over his shoulder and turned on his flashlight to illuminate the path between the stalactites and stalagmites.

Near the entrance they found the slumped body of a soldier, wearing a new army uniform. He was lying face down as if he had been struck from behind.

"Be extra careful," uttered Yama Raj, handing Kathy the flashlight and removing his pistol. "Let me have a look at this man wearing Dipendra's army uniform."

Kathy was paralyzed with fear, holding the flashlight while Yama Raj approached the body, lying face down.

Yama Raj turned over the body exposing the face.

"It's Nigel Porter!" screamed Kathy.

"He's still breathing. Someone knocked him out and dragged him here. You must help me carry him back to the ceremonial room."

"I can't do it," screamed Kathy, alarmed by the shadow of someone at the entrance.

"Don't be a coward. You've got to help me. I can't do it alone," said Yama Raj, kneeling in front of Nigel.

A stranger entered the cave with a rifle and fired at the ceiling hitting the stalactites, which crashed to the ground. The vibration from the shots stirred up the sleeping bats, which swooped down squealing as they departed from the entrance of the cave.

Yama Raj covered his head with his army coat for protection against the bats diving, flapping their wings, and crawling on him. Kathy screamed fleeing down the path carrying the flashlight while bats squealed as she stepped on them.

She hurried into the herbal section of the cave, tormented by bats crawling on her and clinging to her hair, Kathy entered the ceremonial hall screaming. "Help me! Someone help me!"

Carl leapt up from the cushion in front of the statue and hurried toward his daughter. He began pulling bats from her hair in spite of his handcuffed hands.

Om tried to stand but staggered, stumbling from dizziness due to the blow to his head.

Moksha stood up and bowed to the Buddha as hundreds of bats swooped around the statue like a living tornado.

"*Bhut aiyo! Bhut aiyo!*" he shouted, informing everyone that the evil spirits had returned. He recited the mantra, *Om Mane Padme Hum*.

A few moments later Moksha seized the ritual bell near the statue. He rang the bell attempting to drive the evil spirits and the bats from the cave.

In the distance there was an enormous clap of thunder. Everyone paused as a voice boomed from the entrance of the cave.

"*Sunnos. Pahara ahile nas pareko cha.* Listen to me. The mountain is collapsing. *Sabai jana bahira ahile aunu parcha.* Everyone must come outside now!"

For a few moments there was silence in the cave. In the distance there was a steady rumbling of an avalanche. Instinctively, the bats began their exodus from the ceremonial hall, flying toward the entrance.

"I've never seen anything like this in my entire life," gasped Kathy while her father removed the last bat clinging to her back. Upon releasing the bat, it soared to the ceiling, joining the flight for survival.

86

As they were about to flee from the ceremonical room, the hostages noticed more bats flying out from behind the Buddha's statue and colliding into each other.

Several bats clung to Carl's back, and chest while others crawled up his pant legs. Moksha was also covered with them.

Kathy, who was momentarily free from bats, helped Om get up from the floor and led him toward the entrance.

"We must get out of here!" shouted Moksha, trying to yank a bat from his grey hair with his cuffed hands. He seized the trident left behind by the dead yogi and twisted his shirt on the floor around the three prongs before igniting it from a butter lamp.

When the shirt burst into flames, Moksha swiped at the bats with his torch. After scorching them, their penetrating squeals warned the other bats to take flight.

Once they were gone, everyone paused to listen to the rumbling of the avalanche in the distance. They saw the servant and cook leaving the ceremonial room, their arms loaded with sacred texts from the library.

While they hurried down the winding path, they were horrifed by the tremors of the avalance. Upon reaching the entrance, they found Yama Raj covered with bats, waving his arms wildly. Panic stricken, he seized his pistol and shot several rounds into the ceiling.

Large stalactites crashed to the floor along with loose rocks, emitting a cloud of dust, which caused everyone to cough and choke as they scrambled over the debris on the trail. Yama Raj fled from the cave, leaving Nigel unconscious on the floor, covered with bats.

"We've got to help him," insisted Carl, struggling to lift Nigel's shoulder while Kathy carried his feet.

"He's not worth it. Leave him there to die," shouted Yama Raj, stepping from the entrance into the rain.

Moksha swept the blazing trident across Nigel's uniform scorching several bats while others took flight.

Carl and Kathy dragged Nigel over the debris. Upon reaching the entrance of the cave, everyone froze as the thunder roared and lightning streaked the dark sky. The rain fell in sheets, turning the trail into a torrential stream of uprooted bushes, vines, and plants.

Yama Raj returned shouting, "Didn't I tell you to leave that murderer at the entrance of the cave?"

"We can't leave him there," shouted Kathy.

While Moksha chanted mantras, he unbuttoned Nigel's uniform so that he could breathe more easily.

Kathy knelt down to wipe the dust from Nigel's forehead with her handkerchief. Upon touching his face, she screamed, "Oh my God!"

"What is it, Kathy?" shouted Carl.

"It's a mask, a rubber mask of Nigel!" she shouted, yanking it from his face. "Why it's Hariyo!"

"What the hell's going on here?" asked Carl.

Kathy held the mask in her hand, showing it to everyone. She cried, "I can't believe it!

"The tag says the mask's made in China!" said Carl.

"Hariyo's finally waking up!" cried Kathy, wiping his bruised forehead with her handkerchief.

Carl and Om dragged Hariyo by the arms and legs to the side of the cave, propping him against the crumbling wall at the entrance.

Glancing outside they gasped at the sight of uprooted trees tumbling down the trail, with roots, trunks and branches grasping like fingers at boulders and rocks. In the distance the rumbling of the avalanche was deafening.

"Somebody hit me on the head from behind," moaned Hariyo. "I don't know who did it."

Everyone groaned at the fierce clap of thunder that shook the foundation of the cave. It was followed by a lightning bolt that struck a nearby evergreen tree.

"We must go now or we'll die on the mountain," said Moksha, leaving the entrance.

"You're not going anywhere," shouted Yama Raj, raising his pistol. "You all know too much for your own good." He said, aiming the gun at Carl. "You'll be the first to die since you brought the Maoists here to kill me."

Kathy covered her face with her hands. When she glanced through her fingers, she saw a monk wearing a maroon robe standing behind Yama Raj.

The monk's face was partially covered by a hood. He stepped from behind the boulder and rushed toward Yama Raj, knocking him to the ground.

While they were struggling, Moksha raised the trident and struck Yama Raja on the head, stunning him.

Everyone sighed with relief, pausing as the storm subsided and the flash flood receded on the trail.

A few minutes later, they heard voices. "Hello! Hello. Are you there? Om, this is your father, Muktuba. We've come to help you!"

"Dad, Dad!" shouted Om, still handcuffed. "We're here at the entrance of the Medicine Cave."

Muktuba hurried toward them wearing heavy boots, covered with mud. Behind him were half a dozen soldiers from the UN and the Chief of Police from Kathmandu.

"What a trek! We almost got killed by those trees and the force of the water on the trail. We hid behind huge boulders for at least a half hour," asserted Muktuba, embracing his son, Om. "Thank God you're safe! What are you doing handcuffed?" he asked.

"Yama Raj has the key to the handcuffs in his pants pocket," insisted Kathy.

"They're in his inner pocket," said the unknown monk with the hood covering his face. He knelt down to remove Yama Raj's keys from his pocket and handed them to Kathy. She immediately removed the handcuffs from her father, Om, and Moksha.

"Look what I have found in Yama Raj's coat pockets," said the hooded monk, pulling out three rubber masks and holding them up for everyone to see.

"He's got two masks of Crown Prince Dipendra and another mask of Nigel," gasped Kathy. "I don't get it."

"I'm sure Hariyo can tell us all about those masks," said Carl, scratching his head.

"If you tell the truth, maybe the police won't be so severe when you're brought to trial," said Mr. Shresthra.

"I'll tell you everything," blurted Hariyo. "Yama Raj and I wore the rubber masks of the crown prince on the night of the assassination. I stood outside the Billiards Room and handed him the weapons," said Hariyo. "We were also wearing Dipendraji's military uniforms. In fact, I'm wearing his uniform right now."

"He's lying," insisted Yama Raj, rising from the ground. "Hariyo's mentally retarded. I'll tell you what happened."

"Yama Raj, you are to keep your mouth shut. We've been investigating you for a long time now," asserted Mr. Shrestha, ordering the guards to handcuff him.

"Here's the second mask of Nigel," said Kathy holding it up for everyone to see. "Hariyo was wearing it when we found him unconscious in the cave"

"That's right. I was wearing that mask," said Hariyo, informing them that Yama Raj clubbed the security guard to death for allowing the prisoners to escape from jail. It was also Yama Raj, who wore a rubber mask of Nigel while attacking the abbot at Bodhnath and killing him with a machete and then wounding the priest.

"Everybody thought Nigel committed the crimes since it made the headlines in all the newspaper, but it was Yama Raj," blurted Hariyo.

"What about the yaks that were mutilated in the Solu Khumbu?" asked Carl.

"Yama Raj and I each wore masks of Nigel. We hacked up the yaks at night and blamed it on Nigel."

"What happened to the three monks and the yogi who escaped from the jail with Nigel?" asked Carl.

Hariyo told them that Yama Raj tracked them down with hunting dogs while they were escaping in the mountains. He flew them to Tyengboche by helicopter and brought them to the Sherpa village near the cave.

"Yama Raj put on a mask of Nigel and shot the monks. After killing them, he mutilated their corpses. I didn't want to help him, but he threatened to kill me if I didn't," sobbed Haryio. "I've been his slave for years."

"Why were you wearing the mask of Nigel when we found you on the floor of the cave?" asked Carl.

"I've never killed anyone, but this time Yama Raj told me to kill the yogi and then guard the entrance of the cave. If Nigel appreared I should shoot him. He ordered me to kill Muktuba and anyone else who came here. He said he'd take care of you, Kathy, and the shamans later."

"Were you working with the Maoist terrorists?" asked the Chief of Police.

"We never worked with Maoists," said Hairyo, wiping the tears on the sleeve of his uniform.

Mr. Shrestha said, "Yama Raj, you are under arrest for the massacre of the royal family."

"You're mistaken. I tell you Hariyo is lying. He's a retarded idiot!" shouted Yama Raj.

"What about Nigel Porter? Doesn't anyone know anything about him?" asked Mr. Shrestha.

"I am Nigel Porter," said the stranger, pushing back the hood of his maoon robe.

"Oh my God! Nigel! I finally get to meet you. You saved our lives," shouted Kathy.

"Tell us what happened," ordered Mr. Shrestra.

Nigel said, "Yama Raj was wearing the mask of Crown Prince Dipendra and his army uniform on the evening of the assassination. During the dinner party he went into the Billiards Room murdered the royal family and guests, using the stolen weapons of the crown prince.

"When Dipendra came from his apartments, Hariyo was also wearing a mask of him. It was Hariyo who knocked out the prince and dragged him into the bushes.

"After the massacre at the palace, l saw Yama Raj shoot Dipendra in the head with his pistol. He then placed the gun into the crown prince's hand."

Nigel told them about being arrested and escaping from the jail. Later at the monastery he was attacked in the restroom, beaten, and taken to the basement room. Yama Raj had removed his maroon robe and made him put on the saffron robe that he wore on the night of the assassination.

"Yama Raj then drugged me. When I woke up in the clothes closet, I found a machete tied to my wrist. In spite of all the negative publicity when the drugs wore off, I made my way back to the Tengboche Monastery," said Nigel, clinging to his raksha beeds.

"But how did you manage to get back here so quickly?" asked Mr. Shrestha.

"I was brought here by a helicopter. After I left Pashupati Nath on the night of the cremation of the royal family, I went to the airport, hoping to get a flight to Lukla. I prayed to Buddha to help me. Moments later I recognized the pilot, who brought Dipendra and me to Kathamandu in April. He flew me back to Tyangeboche, where I hid in the hills some distance from the Medicine Cave," said Nigel, sighing with relief.

"We must go now before the mountain collapses." said Moksha, leading the way down the muddy trail

He was followed by Yama Raj, the soldiers of the UN, and Mr. Shrestha. Next came Muktuba, Nima Lama, Hariyo, Carl Brecht, Kathy and Om.

87

Upon reaching the Sherpa village, everyone was surprised that the houses and sheds were vacant. The terrified inhabitants, fearing the collapse of the mountains, had fled with their sheep, yaks, and goats.

Yama Raj was restless with his hands cuffed. He approached the Chief of Police. "Nigel's the murderer of the royal family and is trying to blame me. Hariyo lied to you. He made up stories so that you would pardon him."

Mr. Shrestha said, "Hariyo told us everything at the entrance of the cave when you were dazed from that blow to your head," said Mr. Shrestha.

"I forgot to tell you, Yama Raj killed Ranjit Kumar when we were in the Hanuman's Army," blurted Hariyo.

"Ranjit deserved to die," asserted Yama Raj. "He humiliated me in front of my comrades.

"He was spying on us through the window. Ranjit told everyone that he saw us naked, committing immoral acts in our room. We were supposed to be celebate, but Yama Raj threatened to kill me if I didn't have sex with him," confessed Hariyo.

"Didn't I tell you to shut the fuck up," yelled Yama Raj. "You're an ignorant fool."

"I'm not stupid!" yelled Hariyo, his fists clenched.

"Hariyo was brain-injured during a karate match. You can't believe his foolish stories. They're nothing but lies," asserted Yama Raj.

"Yama Raj, we know that you were expelled from the Hanuman Army. We have evidence that you and Hairyo have been selling weapons to the Maoists in western Nepal," stated the Chief of Police.

"Yama Raj sells guns and bullets to anyone who'll pay the right price, even children," said Hariyo. "He always expects sexual favors from the boys."

"I warned you to shut up!" shouted Yama Raj, charging Hariyo and striking him on the head with his handcuffs. "That will teach to keep your fuckin' mouth shut!"

Hariyo fell to his knees from the blow. As he got up from the ground, he picked up a rock and hurled it at Yama Raj, hitting him on side of the face.

"Get away from me!" shouted Yama Raj, the blood gushing from his cheek. He backed away and fled down the path with Hariyo chasing him.

Yama Raj yelled from the harsh pain as a second rock struck him in the back. Arriving at empty yak pen, he pushed open the gate and ran toward the abandoned shed. Once inside the dark shed, he felt claustrophobic since there were no windows or exit doors. He panicked fleeing from the entrance only to be attacked by Hariyo, who threw another rock at him, hitting his face.

"Help me! Someone help me! I can't see! Hariyo's trying to kill me," shouted Yama Raj, the blood dripping down his face. He limped toward the fence behind the shed.

Blinded by his own blood, he climbed over the fence of the yak pen His heart was throbbing as he glanced at the sheer cliff below with sharp rocks protruding from the turbulent stream.

"Someone help me!" he yelled again, realizing he was trapped. He was terrified at the sight of his partner, filled with rage and carrying handfuls of stones to throw at him.

"Stop or I'll shoot!" shouted Mr. Shrestha entering the yak pen and firing into the air.

Yama Raj released his grip on the fence as Hariyo hurled the stones, which struck him on the face and chest. The blows caused him to lose his balance. He staggered backwards, screaming as he fell over the cliff onto the sharp rocks rising from the turbulent stream.

"Stop or we'll shoot," yelled the UN soldiers at Hariyo, who surrendered by raising his hands.

While the police were handcuffing him, Hariyo sobbed with tears flowing down his cheeks. "Yama Raj always called me stupid. He tortured me every day of my life. I was his slave, but now I'm free."

"We could hear screams from the trail," said Carl, entering the yak pen with Kathy, Om, and the shamans.

"The vultures are swooping down to devour his corpse," said Mr. Shrestha, looking over the cliff.

"Just look at those crows waiting for the vultures to leave, so they can get what's left of him!" gasped Kathy, clinging to Om.

88

They continued down the trail eager to arrive at the monastery. Everyone paused to listen to the sound of axes chopping in a wooded area near the convent.

"What's that noise?" asked Kathy, noticing several monks among the trees.

"They're chopping up the corpses of our monks, Vaircana, Dorjee and Ratna," said Nigel, wiping the tears on the sleave of his robe.

"We don't have enough wood to cremate them at this altitude. After the vultures and crows devour their flesh, we'll bury their bones," said Nima Lama. "This will be followed by forty-five days of chanting before they are reborn in their next life."

"The chanting may have to be delayed because of the avalanche," insisted Nigel.

"Don't look at those monks chopping the bodies. It will bring us bad luck," advised Moksha.

"There's that blue bird from the Underworld at Fewa Lake," said Kathy, exhausted from the stress.

"Ravana's demons are causing a lot of trouble here in the mountains," said Muktuba, following the others.

"We must pray to Mahakala to spare our life," said Nima Lama. "I'm fearful the whole monastery will be destroyed by the avalanche."

"Here we are at the convent," said Carl, glancing around. "It's deserted."

"I've been waiting for you to return," said the abbotess, coming out of the prayer hall. "All the nuns have fled with our sacred texts. Here comes the pilot. He's been also waiting for you to arrive."

"I've been sent here by the American Embassy to transport you to Kathmandu. We must leave before this entire region is destroyed by the avalanche," said the pilot.

Everyone paused again to listen to the thundering of the boulders tumbling down the mountains. This time the noise was louder and more intense.

"Here comes the abbot carrying a suitcase and a bundle of sacred texts," said Carl. "Do you have room for all of us in your helicopter?"

"I have room for fifteen people. I agreed to take the abbot and some monks to Namche Bazaar before we go to Kathmandu," said the pilot.

"How about the abbotess?" asked Nima Lama.

"My community is gone. I'm the only one left. I'll stay in the prayer hall and chant to Lord Buddha to spare your lives and protect the monastery."

"No, you're coming with us," said the abbot. "Here come the monks from chopping up the corpses. They will be coming with me to Namche Bazaar."

After everyone boarded, the helicopter rose into the sky with the passengers anxiously looking out of the windows.

"Oh my God, the mountain above us is collapsing. It's splitting into two sections. Just look at that fissure!" screamed Kathy clinging to Om.

"The mouth of Mahakala is swallowing the Medicine Cave," shouted Moksha.

Everyone paused as the gap in the mountains widened. They heard the deafening roar of the boulders and watched the destruction of the entire Sherpa village.

"It's Mahakala again!" uttered Moksha. "He's the Creator, Preserver, and Destroyer."

"Don't blame everything on God," asserted Kathy. "Overgrazing and deforestation are also responsible for the collapse of these mountains."

"The Earth Mother is rebelling from years of abuse by human beings," concluded Muktuba "She can only suffer from cruelty for so long before she reacts with violence. It is the law of karma."

Within a few minutes the helicopter was heading south of the monastery with the passengers gazing at the avalanche consuming everything in sight.

"Most of the monks evacuated before you came from the Medicine Cave. They departed for Namche Bazaar several hours ago," said abbot. "A helicopter came earlier to take the wounded villagers from our clinic to safety."

"It's more than an avalanche. It's an earthquake! If that fissure continues to open, your whole monastery will be destroyed," said Carl. "It's as wide as the Grand Canyon."

"Look down there. Our nuns are trekking on the trail behind the yaks, carrying our sacred manuscripts," said the abbotess. "Let us pray for their safety."

Moksha, the abbot, and the abbotess began the reciting mantras, invoking Mahakala to spare their lives, and Avalokitesvara to gaze down with compassion on the refugees fleeing from the disaster.

In the distance on both sides of the fissure, the earthquake gained momentum with a deafening rumble that shook the earth and even the helicopter. Enormous rocks crashed down, uprooting acres of trees and destroying the vegetation, creating a barren wasteland in the distance.

Nigel invoked Tara, the Merciful Goddess, to spare the lives of every creature in the avalanche's path. He also prayed to the Buddha to protect all beings.

Carl glanced out the window at the trail leading to Namche Bazaar. It was filled with refugees from the villages carrying bundles. Their yaks were weighted down with grain, cooking utensils, and children.

"Look," said the abbot. "The fissure has closed. Our monastery has been spared!"

All heads turned to survey the damage as the pilot slowed down and circled back to get a better view.

"Enormous rocks are heaped to the right and left, but your monastery is still standing," said Carl.

"The mountain directly above Tengboche has collapsed, reminding us that life is impermanent," uttered Moksha.

"Our small convent has been buried," sighed the abbotess. "The avalanche circled like a huge snake and destroyed the greenhouse and the herbal garden."

"We will rebuild the convent, but it will take us a long time to clear the debris around the monastery," said the abbot, wiping his forehead with a handkerchief.

The helicopter turned away from the monastery. Within a half hour it was soaring over Namche Bazaar where it landed in an open field.

The abbot, the abbotess, monks, Nima Lama, and UN soldiers departed for the town to stay the night, with plans to return to the monastery in the near future.

After many bows and handshakes, those departing for Kathmandu, boarded the helicopter once again. Within a few minutes they were flying south.

Carl glanced out the window, "Just get a glimpse at the sun setting on the Himalayas."

"They certainly are beautiful," said Kathy, her head resting on Om's shoulder.

89

After a turbulent flight due to a sudden storm, everyone sighed with relief as they approached the airport in Kathmandu. Glancing out the window, they got a glimpse of Bodhnath with the All Seeing Eyes, gazing in the four directions. Monks were circling the domed stupa spinning the prayer wheels while multicolored prayer flags fluttered in the breeze.

"That shrine has been around for a long time," said Kathy. "I'm grateful that we survived the avalanche."

"We could have all been killed by Yama Raj," sighed Om, holding her hand tightly during the entire flight.

Upon leaving the helicopter, the Chief of Police escorted them to his office, where Hariyo was taken into custody, but not charged for murdering Yama Raj.

Mr. Shrestha spoke to the newspaper reporters while holding up the rubber masks of the Crown Prince and Nigel. He told them how Yama Raj, wearing the mask of the prince, murdered the royal family, the abbot at Bodhnath, the three monks, two Maoist terrorists, the yogi, and guard at the jail.

He then announced that Nigel Porter was innocent of any involvement in the massacre at the palace. While the Chief of Police was being interviewed by reporters, photographers were taking pictures of Nigel in his maroon robe and smiling.

"What about Hairyo? He was Yama Raj's assistant," said the reporter, working for Rising Nepal.

"Yama Raj alone is responsible for the assassination of the royal family," insisted Mr. Shrestha. "He forced Hariyo against his will to participate in the crimes, threatening to murder him if he didn't cooperate.

"I will escort Hairyo to Shanta Bhawan Hospital, where he will be treated for intimidation by our prominent psychiatrist, Doctor Manandhar. When he has recovered his mental health, Hariyo will testify in court about the brutal slayings that he witnessed."

"Where is Yama Raj?" asked a reporter.

"Unfortunately, Yama died a violent death by falling from a cliff north of the Tengboche Monastery," asserted Mr. Shrestha. "His remains were buried by the avalanche. I doubt if they will ever be found."

Reporters interviewed Carl, Kathy, Om, and Moksha about being held hostage in the Medicine Cave. They also questioned Muktuba about helping injured villagers.

Nigel got more attention than anyone else. He was surrounded by reporters once they found out he was innocent. He told them how much he enjoyed being Crown Prince Dipendra's guest at the royal palace prior to the massacre at the palace.

"How did you survive the negative publicity when you were accused of murdering the abbot at Bodhnath?" asked a reporter from the *Times of India*.

"I am grateful to the monks and my teachers at the Tengboche Monastery for my training," said Nigel. "They taught me how to overcome adversity through prayer and meditation."

He told the press that the monastery was never a shelter for wounded Maoist terrorists and that the monks had nothing to do with the assassination of the royal family.

"What about the wounded Maoist, whom you treated some years ago?" asked a reporter from *Rising Nepal*.

"Yes, we treated an injured Maoist some years ago," said Nigel, reminding them that anyone injured or dying would be treated with respect and not turned away from the clinic in Tengboche.

When the reporters finally left, Mr. Shrestha escorted them back to the Kathmandu Guest House in a limousine with a police car leading the way.

Once inside the hotel the manager passed out the room keys. He informed the guests that after they showered and changed clothing he had a surprise for them in the garden.

Twenty minutes later Kathy and Om were the first to pass through the double doors into the garden. As they hurried down the gravel path lined with red roses and chrysanthemums, they noticed an elaborate buffet arranged on rectangular tables in front of the pomelo tree.

Smiling Nepalese waiters were eager to serve them, compliments of the owner of the hotel, whose ancestors were related to Gautama Buddha, born in Lumbini, Nepal.

"I'm starving," said Kathy, hurrying across the lawn toward the buffet. "Look at those dishes of rice, curry and platters of barbecued chicken."

"There's a mountain of bananas, papayas, mangoes, and even pomegranates," said Om, reaching for a plate.

"They have brownies, frosted cakes, and julebis," said Kathy, hearing footsteps on the gravel path. "Oh here comes my father with Moksha and Muktuba."

Om released Kathy's hand, saying. "They don't like any public display of affection. I'm really going to miss you when you go back to the United States."

"I'll miss you too, Om," said Kathy, feeling uneasy. "I never told you about Hariyo trying to hit on me. I was scared to death when I was alone with him in the cave."

"I didn't like leaving you there with him. I was shocked when he attacked Yama Raj and killed him," said Om.

"Wow," said Carl, interrupting them. "Just look at the buffet. We didn't eat very much in the Medicine Cave."

"How could anyone think about eating with bats flying around, people being murdered, and mountains collapsing," said Kathy. "Oh my God, guess who's here for dinner?"

"It's Margaret Porter. She's gorgeous in that pink silk dress and those high heels," said Carl.

"Dad, she's being escorted by Doctor Manandhar. He's right behind her," said Kathy, filling her plate with fresh fruit and desserts.

"Good evening, Carl, I've been so worried about you and Kathy, especially when I heard about the avalanche at Tengboche. I'm so thrilled that you're all safe," she said. "You remember Krishna, my psychiatrist," said Margaret.

"Of course," said Carl, shaking hands with the doctor. "Margaret, you look stunning in that dress."

"I'm so nervous," said Margaret, glancing around the garden. "I can't wait to see Nigel. I'm worried that he'll disappear again. Carl, I want you to be the first to know that Krishna and I are engaged to be married."

"We're planning to have the wedding at St. Paul's Cathedral," said Krishna. "I have relatives living in London, who are making the arrangements."

"Congratulations," said Carl, noticing that Margaret was wearing a diamond ring.

"I...I never thought I'd marry again," said Margaret, holding Krishna's hand and kissing him on the cheek.

"Mother! Mother!" shouted Nigel, hurrying down the gravel path. He was wearing a new maroon robe and sandals, given to him by the monks at Bodhnath.

"Oh my darling, Nigel," gasped Margaret, sobbing and clinging to him. "Mr. Shrestha telephoned me from

Namche Bazaar, saying that you were safe. He told me you were innocent of those crimes."

"You have no idea how worried your mother was about you," said Dr. Manandhar, introducing himself to Nigel.

"We want to take you back to London for a couple of weeks and show you the sights," said Margaret. "Krishna wants you to be the best man in our wedding."

"Congratulations, Mother, I got permission from our abbot to go with you to London for two weeks. After that I must return to my routine at the monastery. We need to rebuild the convent and the herbal garden. It's a miracle the monastery wasn't destroyed by the avalanche."

"I was horrified when I saw those mountains collapsing on TV," said Margaret. "I was afraid you and the monks would be buried alive."

"Let's get something to eat," interrupted Krishna, leading them to the buffet. "Perhaps we could sit with Carl and Kathy over there."

They don't have any vacant chairs at their table under the pomelo tree," said Nigel. "Let's sit with Moksha and Muktuba. They're eating at the table in front of the statue of the Buddha near the prickly pear cacti."

"Nigel, tell us all about how the yogi rescued you from Dr. Bhinna Atma's collapsed cottage," insisted Margaret, placing a scoop of steaming rice on her plate.

"Not now mother. I was there when Moksha performed the exorcisms to free Christopher's souls from the demons," said Nigel. "His effigy is buried over there."

"I missed the ceremony because my flight was delayed. I was so worried about you," said Margaret, taking her place at the table with the shamans. "I was fearful that the demons from Fewa Lake were attacking you."

"I was attacked by evil spirits that tried to possess me again, but I remembered my training at the monastery. I recited the mantra, Om Mane Padme Hum, until I was liberated from the demonic forces," said Nigel, bowing to Moksha and Muktuba.

Margaret and Krishna were amazed as they listened to Nigel tell them about the training he had at the monastery. They were also impressed when Muktuba told them about his five years of apprenticeship with his father to become a shaman at Terhathum.

While everyone was seated in the garden, all heads turned toward the double doors. They saw a bewildered woman wearing a safari hat, hiking boots, and khaki shorts hurrying down the gravel path.

Carl rose from his chair rushing toward the woman, who resembled Audrey Hepburn after removing her sunglasses.

"Barbara! Barbara! You're here in Kathmandu!" shouted Carl, hugging his wife and kissing her on the lips.

"I had to come to Nepal," she sobbed, returning his kiss. "Thank God you're safe, Carl! I was tormented when I received the message that Kathy had hepatitis. I couldn't leave Chicago fast enough!"

"Mom! Mom!" shouted Kathy, rushing toward her. "I want you to meet my boyfriend, Om."

"Kathy, you're safe," cried Barbara, giving her daughter a hug and shaking hands with Om. She chatted with them all the way to the table while Carl got her a plate of food.

A few minutes later all eyes shifted to a handsome young man wearing a white shirt, Levis, and cowboy boots. He hurried down the gravel path to join them.

"Dad, Kathy! You're safe! I thought you'd be trapped in the avalanche at Tengboche," he said.

"Mark, what are you doing here?" asked Carl, rising from the table to greet his son.

"You're supposed to be working at Outward Bound," cried Kathy, hugging her brother.

"Mom and I flew here together from Chicago when we found out you were sick with hepatitis," said Mark.

"I never had hepatitis. I'll tell you all about it," said Kathy, chatting incessantly about being kidnapped.

"Hello Barbara," shouted Margaret, rising from the table and hurrying toward her. "I finally get a chance to meet you and Mark. I want you to meet my son, Nigel."

"Oh," said Barbara, shaking hands with Margaret. "Nigel made the front page of the Chicago Tribune. I'm really surprised to see you here with him. I thought...I thought that you..."

"You thought I'd be in jail for conspiring to assassinate the royal family and murdering the abbot," said Nigel.

"He's innocent," said Carl, explaining to Barbara about the masks being used by Yama Raj, who was responsible for the assassination and murders.

Everyone lingered in the garden talking for hours, returning to the buffet for dessert, coffee, and tea.

As the sun set over Kathmandu, the shamans and Nigel excused themselves to join the monks for their evening prayer service at Bodhnath.

Om and Kathy invited Mark to accompany them to a club to dance. After they departed, Margaret and Krishna took an evening stroll to visit the temples and shops on New Road.

Carl and Barbara remained in the garden watching the waiters and bearers clear the tables. They sat on the stone bench under the pomelo tree.

"I...I remember this bench," said Barbara. "Oh Carl...I missed you so much. I was scared to death when I read about the assassination. It was on the evening news every day. I was frantic when I saw Nigel's picture on TV. You have no idea how worried I was about Kathy.

"Sam wanted to come to Kathmandu with me, but I put my foot down so he returned to Philadelphia. Mark flew in from Denver. We left after I found out Kathy was sick."

"Barbara, I don't know where to begin. After the assassination, Nigel was arrested and put in jail."

"Carl, you told me about it at dinner," said Barbara. "Just hold me for a few minutes."

"I missed you so much," he said, kissing her as she trembled in his arms beneath the tree. "You wore that same safari outfit when you came here twenty-four years ago."

"I wanted to surprise you," she said. "You promised to take me to the Royal Hotel for dinner and dancing for our anniversary. I'm too exhausted from the flight to even think about going there tonight."

"I'll take you to that hotel tomorrow night," he said. "It's starting to rain. Let's go to my room on the second floor, overlooking the garden."

"Let me tell you about Sam. He stayed with me for two weeks driving me crazy over painting the house and putting on a new roof. He just got out of treatment and was constantly on edge," she said, following him down the gravel path through the double doors to the lobby.

They strolled up the stairs leading to the second floor, with Barbara talking the entire time. Upon entering the bedroom, Carl stood at the patio window for a few moments to get a glimpse of the vacant garden below. He turned around and kissed Barbara on the lips.

"My luggage is still in the lobby," she whispered.

"I'll call the bellboy to bring it later," said Carl, holding her tightly against his chest. He kissed her on the back of the neck. "I love you, Barbara."

"I love you too, Carl," she whispered, trembling.

They paused, listening to a clap of thunder followed by a bolt of lightning illuminating the statue of Buddha, the prickly pear cacti, and the pomelo tree in the garden.

The Blessing

I Am the heat. I Am the rain.

I withhold. I send forth.

I Am immortality. I Am death.

I Am the manifested.

I Am the unmanifested.

The Bhagavad Gita 9:19

Srimath Swami Chidbhavananda

Biographical Information

Dominic J. Cibrario was born in Wisconsin, where he was raised on a farm in Kenosha County. He was named after his grandfather, who immigrated to the United States with his grandmother, Magdalene, from northern Italy. Dominic's parents, John and Adeline called their son, Nick. He also has three brothers and a sister.

Cibrario attended Whittier School, Lincoln Junior High and Saint Joseph High School. Afterwards he went to Racine Kenosha Teachers College for two years completing his bachelor's degree at the University of Wisconsin, La Crosse. Nick joined the Peace Corps when John F. Kennedy was in the White House and spent two years in Nepal from 1962-1964.

He did graduate work in South Asian studies at the University of Pennsylvania and studied American Literature at Marquette University, completing a master's degree at the College of Racine. Cibrario also was in the Jesuit novitiate for two years with the Chicago Province. He taught English and Latin at William Horlick High School in Racine, Wisconsin from 1970-2000. Nick took a sabbatical leave in 1976 and returned to Nepal, where he wrote his first novel, *The Pomelo Tree*, which led him to write the rest of the trilogy. After returning to Wisconsin, he married Geraldine James and raised three children.

When Cibrario retired from teaching in 2000, he published *The Garden of Kathmandu Trilogy* and *Secrets of the Family Farm.* In addition to writing, he studies Sanskrit, oil painting and sculpture, exhibiting his work at local museums and galleries.

Nick Cibrario is available to speak to groups about his novels and adventures in Nepal.

e-mail: **nickcibrarioracine@sbcglobal.net**

websites: www.pomelotree.com
www.amazon.com

Bibliography of Sources

Health Through Balance: An Introduction to Tibetan Medicine, Dr. Yeshi Donden, edited and translated by Jeffrey Hopkins, Snow Lion Publications, 1986, 27-55.

Lonely Planet Nepal by Mayhew, Bindloss & Armington, 7th Edition, September 2006, Around the Kathmandu Valley p.159-183, Kathmandu to Pokhara 236-245, Pokhara 246-249, Trekking 323-354.

Lonely Planet Tibet by Mayhew, Bellezza, Wheeler & Taylor, 4th Edition.

Massacre at the Palace: The Doomed Royal Dynasty of Nepal, Jonathan Gregson, Talk Miramak Books, Hyperion, 2002, Chapters 1, 9, 10, 11,12, 13, 14.

The Nepal Cookbook: Association of Nepalis in the Americas, Gundruk Soup p.32, Snow Lion Publications 1996.

Sprit Possession in the Nepal Himalayas, edited by John T. Hitchcock & Rex L. Jones Vikas Publishing House, 1976.

"Mahakala the Neo Shaman: Master of the Ritual," William Stabelein, "Limbu Spirit Possession and Shamanism," Rex Jones, and "Becoming a Limbu Priest: Etnographic Notes," Phillippe Sagant.

The following websites were consulted or used for information about the assassination, culture, history, politics, religion and mythology of Nepal.

en.wikipedia.org/wiki/Red_Fort pp.1-5.
en.wikipedia.org/wiki/ Jama_Masjid _ Delh. pp.1-5.

mapsofindia.com/maps/delhi/delhi.htm   pp.5-9.

en.wikipedia.org/wiki/Transport_in_Delhi. pp. 1-9.

en.wikpedia.org/wiki/Ayodhya_debate pp.1-5.

shubhyatra.com/delhi/walkingaround-olddelhi.html p.1-3.

nepalhompage.com/news/royalmassacre/ pp.1-3.

shamanism.org/ The Foundation for Shamanic Studies… Workshops & Training in Shamanism and Shamanic Healing.

news.bbc.com.uk/2/hi/south_asia/1372004.stm Nepal's uncertain future, Michael Hutt 6/4/01 pp.1-4.

news.bbc.co.uk/2/hi/south_asia/country_profiles/1166502. Stm Country profile: Nepal pp.1-4.

clinmed.netprints.org/cgi/contents/full 2002050007vil, Clinical Medical & Health. Research: A study on the use of complimentary and alternative medicine therapies in and around Pokhara sub-metropolitan city, western Nepal.

JAAIM-Outline The online journal for the American Association of Integrative Medicine…Healing traditions in Nepal, ShankarPR, Paudel R, Giri Br.

boloji.com/health/articles/01059. htm Complementary and Modern Medicine Strange Bedfellows? Satis Shroff 6/17/07.

tribuneindia.com/2002/20010603/main1.html The Tribune online edition, Nepal Prince Massacres Royal Family, Gopal Sharma and Sujit Chataterjee.
edition.cnn.com/2001/World/asiapcf/south/06/02/nepal.times/ CNN.com./World Report paints picture of prince's drunken rampage, 6/4/01.

globalpolitician.com/24658-nepal Crude revenge of history of Nepal by Salah Uddin Shoaib Choudhury – 52/08.

uninet.edu/cin2003/conf/Sharma/Sharma.html CIN 2003.Sarma. Snakes and Snake Bite in Nepal pp.1-8.

nepalnews.com.np/contents/englishdaily/ktmpost/2001/jun/jun04/index.html The Kathmandu Post, King Dipendra in 'very critical' condition pp.1-9.

nepalnews.com.nlp/archive/2001june/ar225.htm Some form of normalcy returns, Prince Regent Gyanendra is de facto King, Royal funeral pp1-6.

en.wikipedia.org/wiki/Boudhanath pp.1-4.

hinduismtaday.com /archives/2001/9-10/18-25_nepal.shtml Tragedy in Nepal Royal Family Massacred pp.1-11 with emphasis upon The King's Farewell and Rana Rulers.

tengboche.org/introduction. Htm Tengboche Monastery Development Project   2/7/09.

samratnepal.com/Nepal/trekking/classic_everest_trekking.html Trekking in Nepal, classic Everest treks, tengboche monastery, Buddhist monastery, pp.1-2.

news.bbc.co.uk/2/hi/south_asia/1368933.stm   Beauty at heart of killings mystery, 6/4/01.

edition.cnn.com/2001/World/asiapcf/south/06/02/nepal.times/
nepalhomepage.com/news/royalmassacre/ June 2, 2001
boloji.com/health/articles/01059.htm.

Made in the USA
Charleston, SC
25 July 2011